BANDOLERO
LAND OF PROMISE

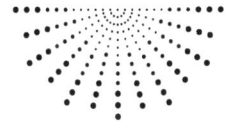

NANCY J. FARRIER

Copyright © 2017 by Nancy J. Farrier

All rights reserved.

Cover art by Ardra Farrier.

River Ink logo by Ardra Farrier.

No part of this book may be reproduced in any form or by any electronic or mechanical means, including information storage and retrieval systems, without written permission from the author, except for the use of brief quotations in a book review.

Published by River Ink Press, Apple Valley, CA 92307

Scripture quotations from the King James Version of the Bible.

Publisher's Note: This is a work of fiction. Names, characters, places, and incidents are a product of the author's imagination. Locales and public names are sometimes used for atmospheric purposes. Any resemblance to actual people, living or dead, or to businesses, companies, events, institutions, or locales is completely coincidental.

Library of Congress Control Number: 2017946997

ISBN- 10: 0-9990547-1-6 (Print)

ISBN- 13: 978-09990547-1-0 (Print)

ISBN- 10: 0-9990547-0-8 (E-book)

ISBN- 13: 978-0-9990547-0-3 (E-book)

❦ Created with Vellum

~

For my best friend Linda Tribbett, and her husband, Gary. Your exceptional love of Jesus Christ encourages me to be better in everything I do. Your faith bubbles over on everyone around you. Thank you.

~

"...Yea, I have loved thee with an everlasting love: therefore with lovingkindness have I drawn thee."
Jeremiah 31:3

~

CHAPTER ONE

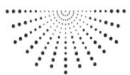

Alta California--1830's

BILLOWING sheets of gray congregated overhead. A few rays of sun stabbed through the mass to brush pale fingers across Yoana's face. Fingers too weak to warm her chilled heart.

"Your father didn't mean it." Leya clicked her tongue, and her horse trotted up alongside Yoana's.

Yoana bent over her mare's neck and pressed her face against the horse's warmth. A breeze whipped the blonde mane back, stinging her cheek. If Leya, her aunt and señorita, saw her face, she would know the chilly gusts weren't responsible for the tears. The scent of the horse and the feel of the muscles bunching beneath her usually brought comfort. Not today. Not after this morning's news.

And the confrontation with her father.

"He meant every word." Yoana straightened, but kept her face averted. "He's hated me for years. That's why he made the arrangements he did. My father wanted me out of his sight as soon as I married Gabrio. Now, with the engagement broken, I'll never be free. I'll live in isolation for the rest of my life."

"That is not true. He does love you, Yoana. Don Armenta, your father, loved my sister with his whole heart. He still mourns her loss, but he loves you too."

"He blames me for her death." Yoana watched the clouds blur through the haze of her tears. The seething mass overhead stretched shadowy fingers across the hills.

"Yoana." Leya's voice caught. "Let go of this hurt with your father. God loves you, no matter what. He loves you more than you can ever imagine."

"Maybe He does, Leya." Yoana swallowed hard to ease the ache in her throat. "But I need more."

"You think I don't understand?" Leya's question pricked Yoana with guilt reminding her of all Leya had lost years ago. "I, of all people, understand that you long for someone to hold you. You need someone made of flesh, a man who will love you. Offer you strength and comfort." Leya paused and Yoana heard her draw in a shaky breath.

"God will be enough, if you let Him."

Leya's quiet statement pierced deep. Could she be right? Had Yoana asked more of God than He wanted to give her? Maybe He wanted her to live the rest of her life in this loveless house so she could learn to appreciate Him.

Yoana dashed the back of her hand across her eyes and turned to face her señorita. "I need to run. I don't care what I told Jorge. He'll keep up with us."

Leya gasped. "You can't do that. You know there have been reports of bandoleros." Leya grabbed Yoana's reins. "Think of what those men might do to you if they caught you. Think of what your father would do if something happened to you."

A bitter laugh escaped Yoana. "You heard him. He wouldn't care at all, and you know why. You were there that day."

"But, Yoana--"

"Don't worry, that's why we have the vaqueros along. They will protect us." She tugged her reins free. Her mare danced to the side, ready for a run. "Leya, I have to. Please."

The other woman's eyes softened. She glanced over her shoulder at the two men following them. "Keep within the boundaries. You know where they are. I'll be right behind you."

A sob caught in Yoana's throat, and she kneed her mare. The horse broke into a quick trot, then stretched out to run. Yoana leaned forward, pressing into the saddle.

Perhaps she should pray instead of trying to outrun her troubles. Yet all her prayers this morning hadn't helped. Her one chance at freedom had vanished in a wink of time. Even the anticipation of having her father speak to her after years of silence proved false. Oh, he'd spoken to her, but not the words she needed to hear.

Overhead, the shrill cry of a hawk pierced the air. Yoana pressed her fingers to her mouth and breathed deep. She would not let emotion overwhelm her.

Wind whipped past, fresh with a chill from the mountains towering over their ranch. Tears dried on her cheeks.

Gabrio. Gone. After all his letters full of promises. He'd deserted her when she needed him most.

Men were not to be trusted. Ever. They only took what they wanted and discarded a woman when they were done. Hadn't that happened to Leya? Now, to her?

A shout—was that Jorge?--dragged at her attention, but she didn't look back. Leya's horse thundered close behind. Need for escape consumed Yoana. She lifted her head and took a deep breath of the crisp air. She wasn't afraid. Jorge and Juan would insure she and Leya stayed safe. Besides, her father's and brother's warnings were meant to control her, nothing more.

Strands of her hair whipped against her face like stinging flies.

Her long braid thumped against her back. Pounding hooves matched the thunder of her heart. She wanted to race along this track forever. To disappear. To have life go away. To outrun the pain.

Her mare's labored breathing warned Yoana she should slow down. The rise ahead marked a boundary she wasn't supposed to cross even when they *weren't* having trouble with horse thieves. Of course, she'd never been very good at following her father's mandates. She knew the path dipped down on the far side, but the slope wasn't too steep, was it? She hadn't been this way in a long time.

Her sorrel surged over the edge of the rise and thundered down the far side. In only a second Yoana registered that they weren't alone--and that the decline was steeper than she recalled, making a quick reversal almost impossible.

In the valley below, where a herd of her father's prized horses grazed, a small group of men moved in to surround the animals. Men she didn't know.

They were a rough, unshaved lot, most likely the bandits she'd been warned about. Yoana tugged on the reins, trepidation fisting her heart. Her mount skidded down the path, fighting the bit. The sight of the other horses proved too exciting and distracting for her feisty mare to obey. Yoana fought to get her sorrel under control before the scoundrels noticed her.

Too late.

A man on the far side of the herd glanced up. He gestured up the hill with a lift of his chin. The other men swiveled in their saddles. Yoana could feel their hungry gazes slither over her. She shuddered. The closest man nudged his horse in her direction, his face tilted up. She could see the fierceness of his demeanor.

Panic stole her breath. She couldn't think. She reined her mare hard to the side, then glanced over her shoulder to see Leya top the rise.

"Leya, go back!"

Yoana's warning must have been be lost in the rush of wind. As Leya's horse raced down the slope toward Yoana, chaos erupted. Shouts from below. Yells from Jorge as he topped the rise and fumbled for his gun. Shots cracked from the valley. Leya screamed. Jorge pitched from his saddle.

Yoana's horse reared, then lost her balance. Yoana kicked free of the stirrups. She slammed into the ground as her mount went down and rolled.

More gunshots. A cry cut off.

Yoana tried to stop her momentum, but she tumbled down the grassy slope toward the bandoleros. She gasped for air. Dread grabbed her with spiky fingers.

Leya. This couldn't happen again. She had to protect her tía.

Ground and sky became a blur. Rocks jabbed into her ribs, and her cheek stung as if she'd been slapped. She clawed at the brush until she slid to a stop--then lay still.

Silence.

Through slitted eyes she saw a pair of scuffed boots a few inches from her face. Gold and scarlet thread wove an intricate embroidered pattern along the hem of the man's pant leg. Bits of the thread had unraveled, a picture of her life spiraling out of control.

"Stop!"

Gunfire drowned out Amado Castro's shout. Not that he had any real authority over these men. He wheeled his horse toward the path to intersect with the young woman and stop her headlong race. What was she thinking? No one rode a horse down a path that steep at such a breakneck speed.

His heart began to thud as he thought of one woman who

might do this. But, no, she would not be this far from home. Her father would never allow that. Mesmerized, he watched her fight for control. The horse refused to obey. Instead, the mare flung her head high, eyes white-rimmed, nostrils distended as she plunged stiff-legged toward danger.

A gunshot. One of the men on the rise cried out as he flew backward off his horse. The second man to come over the ridge managed to pull out his pistol, but before he could aim another shot rang out. The vaquero threw his hands in the air. His pistol flew to the side. His head snapped back, and he tumbled to the ground. Blood blossomed across his shirtfront.

The fourth rider, a woman whose black *mantilla* had slipped forward to obscure most of her features, hesitated as if unsure of which way to go. She started to turn her horse back up the slope when the first young woman's mount lost its footing and fell over backward.

Amado jerked his buckskin to a halt as the woman kicked free from her horse and began to tumble down the hill. He leaped from the saddle, and she slid to a stop almost at his feet.

Another shot cracked. A horse squealed.

"Tomás, stop!" Amado yelled over his shoulder at his compadre, the youngest member of the group. The skinny youth's gun shook so hard it might have fired on its own. The boy's dark eyes were wild as his horse crow-hopped underneath him.

The woman at his feet groaned. He knelt beside her where she lay facedown in the grass beside the trail. His gloved hand trembled as he reached for her. *Please, let this be another woman, not my amoré.* He had no right to think of his former betrothed that way. Hadn't he sacrificed his love for the better good? He shook off the sadness and memories of deathbed promises.

Amado's hand hovered above her shoulder. Should he turn her over? What if she was been too injured to mov--?

She surged up in a blur of motion, shoving at him, her small fists pounding at his chest. Her fierce defiance caught him off guard, and he lost his balance, stumbled backward, and landed on his backside. His stallion snorted and danced away. Amado leaped to his feet, hauling the woman up with him. Her small, gloved hands flailed at him.

"Hey, Amado. Is the little filly too much for you?" His compadres laughed, more relaxed now that the immediate danger had passed. Since no one else had come over the hill after the women, the bandoleros assumed only two men accompanied the señoritas on their ride. They may be right.

The tenacious beauty tried to break his hold. Her fist caught him under the jaw, hard enough to snap his teeth together. Amado grabbed her arms and twisted her around until her back snugged tight against his chest. She couldn't move her hands, but her boot connected with his shin and made him glad for the deerskin boots he wore.

"Calm down." He tightened his grip until she gasped for air. He eased up. She began to struggle.

"Looks like you met your match, *amigo*." Lorenzo laughed as the caballeros gathered around. Amado glanced up to see Miguel, Lorenzo's brother, had returned with the other woman, whose horse stood hipshot, blood trailing down its hind leg. On an order from Cisto, Tomás climbed the hill, pistol ready to check on the two vaqueros. Cisto eyed the girl in Amado's arms with cold hunger. Amado whirled the *chica* around so she wouldn't see.

Why had their leader put a man like Cisto in charge of this raid?

Amado looked down at the woman—and froze. He stared into the face of an angel! Brown eyes so light they were almost golden sparked fire. Honey rich skin glowed in the light, and her heart-shaped face held more beauty than he'd ever seen. The only time he'd met her, she'd been a sassy four-year-old, but he'd know her anywhere. Yoana had grown from defiant child into a fiery beauty. If she hadn't been so angry, that full mouth with the pouty lower lip would drive him crazy. No wonder Cisto almost drooled when he looked at her.

The angel kicked him again. Hard. She jerked her arms. The little spitfire leaned forward, small teeth gleaming as she attempted to bite him. Well, at least she hadn't recognized him.

Amado caught her silken braid in his hand and yanked. She twisted one hand free to clout him on the ear. He grinned. To think he'd broken his betrothal to this beauty. If these men knew, they'd all think him loco.

"Whoa, Amado. She's fiercer than a grizzly." Lorenzo laughed. "Need a little help? I can tame her real fast."

"*Release* me." Yoana fought like a cougar.

"Stop." Amado hauled her tight against his chest again. She paused and met his gaze. The world whirled out of focus. Her eyes had small specks of gold in the brown. Long, sooty lashes made a startling contrast with her golden skin. She smelled like a flower, although he couldn't place the scent. He held his breath fearing--hoping--recognition would come.

"Let. Me. Go. *Now.*"

What he thought had been a spark of recognition faded. She struggled to pull away, but he held her tight. The desire to protect her threatened to undermine his vow. The memory of the awkward childish kiss he'd given her years ago surfaced--along with his promise to return for her. She had stopped fighting then and sobbed on his shoulder. Would she surrender now if his lips met hers? Or fight harder? The possibilities intrigued him.

"If you calm down, I might let you go." Amado glanced up as Miguel brought the second woman close.

"Who are you?" Cisto directed his question at the woman on the horse without taking his hungry gaze from Yoana.

The other woman started to speak. Yoana cut her off. "I am Yoana Ignacia Esperanza de Armenta, and you will tell this imbecile to take his hands off me."

Amado fought to retain his composure. He couldn't reveal what he knew of this woman and her family. Taking the daughter of one of the most important dons captive would be a major accomplishment. He could see from Cisto Vaca's puckered brow, the outlaw, who hailed from the north, didn't know the name.

Amado glanced at Yoana's companion. This must be her Tía Leya, although he couldn't be sure.

Leya lifted the veil as she raised her head. Her dark eyes bored into Amado. Without a doubt, Leya knew him. She'd been older when he'd visited their rancho. Her mouth opened. Amado gave a short shake of his head. *Please, don't say anything.* She must have understood, for she dropped her gaze and let the *mantilla* fall back over her cheek.

"Well, Señorita Esperanza de Armenta, who is your friend?" Vaca's eyes glittered like black ice as he leaned forward in the saddle.

Yoana's eyes narrowed. Her mouth thinned, but that lower lip still held Amado's attention. "Make him release me, and I'll tell you."

"Go ahead. Release her, Amado. I'll catch her." Lorenzo leaned over with his arms outstretched. Miguel whooped.

Tomás rode up, his wild curls poking out from under his broad-brimmed hat, his face pale against the bright red of his chin strap. His skinny legs showed between his short pants and the top of his rolled down boots. An extra revolver stuck out from under his embroidered jacket. "Th-th-the older one is hurt b-b-bad, but still alive. Th-th-the young one is d-d-dead." His face flamed as he spoke. Tomás didn't like to talk because of his speech impediment, but he'd had enough beatings from Cisto for not reporting correctly and knew to comply.

"We have to get out of here." Amado met Cisto's gaze. "The sound of gunfire may travel as far as the rancho where these women came from. If there are other vaqueros anywhere close, they'll be on their way."

Cisto nodded. "Set the little filly in front of me. We'll take them both back to camp."

"No." Amado and Yoana spoke at the same time.

"Be quiet if you want to live." Amado hissed the words in the girl's ear. He lifted his voice. "If you take these women, Cisto, you'll have every don in Alta California after you in full force. Stealing horses is one thing, but not women." He knew exactly what Cisto had in mind for Yoana.

"Let them come." Cisto laughed as he nudged his mount a step closer. "You know our camp is secure."

"This is foolish, Cisto. Why take them?" Amado had to find a way to get Yoana back home.

"If you can't think of a reason to take them, I can." Cisto's eyes raked over Yoana. She flushed, but met his gaze when it returned to her face. The chica had spunk. "When we arrive with the horses and the women, Victoro will be more than pleased."

"He won't be when her father's men follow us and wage a war." From the corner of his eye, Amado saw Yoana's gaze swing up to his face. Had he said something that triggered her memory? She'd been so young the last time he saw her. He prayed she wouldn't remember him.

"Then we'll just have to make sure they don't follow us, won't we?" Cisto's square face split in a rictus smile. His inky gaze chilled Amado.

"How do you plan to do that when you have a herd of horses to drive?"

"There aren't so many." Cisto glanced over at the small herd. The animals grazed on the thick grass, green due to the spring rains. Their hides glistened in the sun. All the dons, gentlemen of the ranchos, knew these were some of the finest horses in Alta California, maybe in all of Mexico. Don Armenta's stock had an excellent reputation, with a price to match.

Cisto turned back to Amado. "We'll divide up. Confuse the

trail. I'll take the women. You and Tomás take one group of horses. Lorenzo and Miguel take the other."

"I say we put the women on one horse. We can tie the wounded vaquero to another, and they can take him home before he dies. We can still divide up the horses to confuse the trail." Amado refused to look away from Cisto.

"You do that, and these señoritas will have their men after us before we get higher than the foothills. They're coming with us. As for you, Amado, I don't care if you return to camp or not." Cisto's revolver appeared in his hand. The barrel pointed down to the ground, but Amado knew how fast Cisto could flick his wrist to bring the gun up and kill a man. Yoana trembled against him. Leya gasped. Her panicked breathing wrenched at his heart.

"Leya. Slow. Breathe slow." Yoana's low hiss might not have reached the other men, but Amado caught the warning. He'd been right. The señorita was Yoana's tía, Leya Esperanza. That would explain the veil tied forward to conceal part of her face. Amado had to get these women away from Cisto and his cohorts, but how to accomplish this feat without jeopardizing his own mission? He'd given his word. To his dying brother. To his grieving father. A vow he didn't intend to break for any reason.

Not even one so alluring as Yoana.

"Lorenzo." Cisto's gaze didn't waver from Amado.

The bandolero sidled his mount next to Cisto's, not coming between Cisto and Amado.

"Take the horses and head toward the pass. I'll bring the ladies and catch up to you. We'll confuse the trail and divide up when we're deeper into the foothills."

Lorenzo nodded and wheeled his horse away. His quick glance at Amado said without words he thought this would be the last time they would see one another. Miguel and Tomás followed. Amado tensed as the men whistled to urge the herd over the rise on the far side of the valley. He didn't take his eyes off Cisto as the bandolero edged his horse closer to where Leya sat astride her mare.

Cisto reached out with the barrel of his pistol to catch the edge of Leya's *mantilla*. She started to pull back. Cisto's grin held no warmth or humor. The barrel of his revolver now pointed at Leya with the message that if she pulled away again, it would be the last thing she did. She froze. Her ragged gasps filled the quiet.

CHAPTER TWO

Yoana tensed. Amado tightened his hold. He didn't know how to make this spitfire understand that if she so much as said a word, her tiá would be dead, and she might be as well.

Leya's silky *mantilla* caught on the tip of the barrel and came free of the pins that held it in place. Slowly Cisto exposed Leya's slender neck. Amado could see the jagged scar that ran from the side of her chin and disappeared under the collar of her dress. Leya shivered. Her hand started to come up, but the look on Cisto's face must have stopped her. Cisto wasn't in a position to see the scar. His grin widened as he continued the slow torment. Yoana fought Amado's hold.

"Stop!" Yoana tried to jerk free.

Cisto froze. His leer faded. Shock at the thought of Cisto listening to Yoana almost made Amado lose his grip on her.

Thundering hoof beats shook the ground. Amado followed Cisto's gaze to the rim where Lorenzo had disappeared with the horses. Nothing. Amado swiveled back to see several vaqueros pull their mounts to a stop at the top of the path where Yoana had plunged toward him minutes earlier. Two of the riders were men he knew well. Men who worked for his father.

He vaulted onto his mount and scooped Yoana up in front of him before she could protest. He knew these men wouldn't put her in danger, and he couldn't afford for anyone to recognize him. "Quiet." He ground out the word in the hope she would listen.

In one smooth move, Cisto tossed his pistol from one hand to the other. With his free hand he yanked Leya from her horse to his, putting her in front of him. He faced the mounted riders with Leya as a shield. Instead of pointing his revolver at the newcomers, Cisto put the barrel against Leya's temple.

"Yoana!"

"Lucio!" Yoana's cry cut off when Amado clamped his hand over her mouth.

"Didn't you hear me? You're going to get both of you killed if you don't listen." Amado tried to calm his dancing mount and still keep his face hidden behind Yoana. Lucio, Yoana's brother, would know Amado. Unlike Yoana, whom he hadn't seen since that fateful day, Amado had dealt with Lucio several times. Could this get any worse?

"Let the women go." Lucio stood in his stirrups. His men drew their guns.

"But the señoritas want to come with us." Cisto's mockery sent a shudder through Yoana. Amado squeezed her arm, hoping to give reassurance. The prospect of returning the women to their home faded.

"I want you to turn around and ride back." Cisto moved Leya so her body blocked more of his. "If you don't leave right now, this little filly will get hurt. I'm sure you don't want that to happen." Cisto's laugh said he would love to be the cause of Leya's pain.

"You will not take them with you. Release them now." Lucio's anger rang down the hill. "If you don't let them go, you will hang. I'll see to that."

"I think you need to take your vaqueros and go." Cisto's

revolver dug into Leya's cheek. She let out a high-pitched cry. Yoana surged forward. Amado hauled her back.

"If you try anything, he will kill both of you without a thought." At his whispered warning, Amado felt Yoana relax a fraction. He had to keep her from interfering. Amado began to back his horse toward the far rim where Lorenzo and the others had driven the herd. Cisto backed alongside him.

"We are leaving, amigos. These sweet ladies will enjoy their stay with us."

One of the vaqueros fired a shot. Cisto swore. They were out of range of the revolvers, and the bullet pinged off a rock several yards below. Lucio swung around and said something sharp to the vaquero.

"That was the wrong thing to do, amigo." With a flick of his wrist, Cisto sent a bullet into the injured man who lay on the ground closer to them. The vaquero's body jerked, then lay still. An ominous silence settled in the small valley. Cisto slipped his revolver back into the holster and pulled a long-bladed knife from a sheath strapped to his leg. He stuck the tip close to where Leya's eye would be. "Now, if you try that again, this one will lose her pretty face one piece at a time."

"No." Yoana's horrified whisper echoed Amado's own revulsion. He'd known the cruel streak in Cisto, but hadn't thought the man would stoop so low.

They continued to back toward the far rise. Amado glanced behind him. What if Lucio had more men, and they were being surrounded? Cisto must have had the same thought.

"If you have other vaqueros coming around to stop us, you'd better call them off. I'm faster with my knife than I am with my gun. These little pretties will wish to be dead before you can stop me."

Lucio's horse pranced a few steps down the hill before he could stop it. "Yoana, I'll come for you."

"Their hideout is protected. Be careful."

Amado clamped his hand over Yoana's mouth. Wouldn't she ever listen? Leya cried out as Cisto's knife pricked her cheek. Blood seeped through the veil and down the exposed part of her chin.

"The same goes for you, chica." Cisto's hard tone left no doubt of his intent. "If you don't behave, this one will pay. *Entiende?*"

Yoana swallowed hard. "I understand."

Lucio and his men didn't move as Amado and Cisto disappeared from the valley. Cisto whirled his mount and raced away. Amado followed. They had a small head start. They had to make every moment count.

Cisto led them away from the tracks left by the herd. Amado knew the bandit wanted to get to the cover of the hills as fast as possible. They'd both seen rifles attached to a couple of the saddles. They might be out of pistol range, but a rifle bullet could still halt them in their tracks. The only thing that would stop the vaqueros from shooting would be the fear that they might hit one of the women. Amado didn't know what would be worse--to kill one's sister or have her carried away by bandits.

As they rounded the first curve of a steep hill, Amado heard a horse galloping behind them. He glanced back, expecting to feel the burn of a bullet at any moment. Instead, he saw a lone horseman on their trail, far enough to be out of range. He must have been ordered to follow them while Lucio went home for reinforcements.

Amado settled in for a hard ride. Yoana had quieted. Her whole attention seemed to be riveted on Leya. Amado had no idea how he would keep these two safe or how he would fulfill his promise without them all dying in the process. He'd expected to sacrifice himself, but the thought of Yoana and Leya dying tore at his resolve.

Even as worries choked his thoughts, he still reveled in the feel of Yoana in his arms. How many times had he dreamed of this? Prayed for this? He glanced over his shoulder again. Would they survive long enough for God to see fit to answer his prayer? He knew the answer.

God didn't care.

~

THE BUCKSKIN'S sides heaved as they climbed in elevation. Sweat darkened the animal's hide despite the dip in temperature as heavy clouds moved in from the west. They'd been riding for hours. Yoana's fingers ached from gripping the saddle in front of her. She kept her focus on Leya, wishing she could assure her all would well. But as the distance grew between them and the rancho, she knew she couldn't guarantee anything. What a rash fool she'd been! If she could change the outcome, she would. Jorge and Juan died because of her recklessness.

Cisto, the man who rode with Leya, scared Yoana senseless. His inky eyes reminded her of a bottomless cavern where a person couldn't begin to see the hidden dangers. Yoana wanted to leap from the horse and escape, but she would never leave Leya at the mercy of these bandoleros.

For some reason, Amado, whose broad chest supported her back, didn't frighten her at all, even though he held her captive. Despite his fierce attitude toward Cisto, he couldn't hide his empathy. Something about him, the way he looked at her with eyes the color of milk-lightened melted chocolate, told her that he wouldn't hurt her. She fought him because she needed to get away. To get Leya to safety. Not because she feared him.

Rocks rattled below them. Yoana started to turn and look. The strong arm around her waist tightened. She stiffened, resisting the urge to struggle. Maybe tonight, when Amado and Cisto were asleep, she and Leya could slip away. As long as they weren't too deep into the mountains, Yoana could find her way home.

With a plan in mind, she began to watch for landmarks. Low bushes and grass gave way to hills dotted with trees. Above them the forested mountain offered shelter for these men, and despair for the women. Before she could note much, Cisto pulled his horse to a halt. The animal's nostrils flared wide from the hard race up steep trails.

"We'll stop for a short break." Cisto nodded at the trail behind them. "I'll go on with the women. You stay here with your rifle and get rid of the one following us."

"You want him dead, you kill him." Amado's muscles tensed. Yoana watched his fingers grip the reins with utter ferocity as his free hand strayed toward his weapon. "I say we let the women go now, and no one will bother us. If you take these two, their family will hunt us down and wipe out every man in the camp. Even if you kill that vaquero, they will find you. Victoro will be furious with you for doing this."

Yoana almost laughed at the absurdity of Amado's statement. At the absurdity of her father risking men's lives for her. Maybe for Leya. Never for her.

"Victoro will enjoy the challenge." Cisto's eyes narrowed. "If things get too hot here, we can go back up north. There's more cover there. More places to hide." Cisto's oily gaze slithered over her. Yoana suppressed a shudder and saw Leya's shoulders slump. "Besides, I think this pair will be worth the price."

"We can cut over the next hill, swing back around, and meet up with Lorenzo." Amado's tone didn't carry a hint of the tension Yoana could feel in his arms. "If we mix our tracks with those of the herd, we can head for hard ground and split away from them. We can camp in that small canyon west of here. There's an outcrop of rocks that would be perfect for a lookout. No one could sneak up on us. There's an escape route out the back."

"That one is steep for riders." Cisto frowned. "We wouldn't be able to ride double."

"We could lead the horses while the women ride." Amado glanced back down the hill. "Unless you'll reconsider and leave them here for the vaquero to find. Then we don't have to worry."

Cisto's lip curled in a snarl. He leaned toward Amado. "Don't push it. They're going with us. Mention it again, and you'll be left behind as vulture food." Cisto reined his horse around, dug in his spurs, and led the way up the through the thickening trees. Pine scented the air. Squirrels skittered up tree trunks, pausing to glare down with beady eyes.

Through a break in the trees, Yoana could see the mountains stretch into the distance with canyon after canyon to confuse the way. Panic tightened her throat. If they didn't get away soon, she would never get Leya back home to safety. A chilling breeze whipped strands of hair across her eyes. She did her best to sweep the waves behind her ears.

The crunch of pine needles under the horse's hooves crackled in the silence as they rode deeper into the woods. A couple of times, when Cisto's horse turned to the side, Yoana saw Leya jerk away from him only to be yanked back. Cisto's cruel laugh crawled along her skin like itchy ants.

"You have to help us get away." Yoana pitched her voice low. Their only hope would be to enlist Amado's aid in their escape. He appeared sympathetic to their plight. "You know what will happen if we're taken to the camp. My father will see that all of you hang." That probably wasn't true, but this bandolero wouldn't know that.

"I can't help you. You'll have to appeal to Victoro when we get to camp." Amado's breath hissed past her ear.

"Who is Victoro?"

"The head bandolero."

Yoana couldn't stop a derisive laugh. "And you think this bandolero will let us leave after we see where his camp is? I'm not stupid enough to believe that."

"There is nothing I can do. I tried all I knew. If I push further, I will be dead, and you will have no one to watch out for you."

"You could help us tonight. When Cisto is asleep, you could help us escape." Curse the desperation that crept into her tone! "If you take me back to my father, he might pay you a reward. I am certain he would be grateful to you for rescuing us."

"He might be grateful, but he would hang me all the same." Amado shifted behind her. His broad chest and solid strength made her want to rest against him.

"Why do you think that? Heroes aren't lynched."

"Since I can be identified as one of the bandits who abducted you, he would think I only wanted money. Your father would have me hanged. He is a hard man." He stiffened as soon as he spoke, but why?

"You know my father?" Yoana tried to turn and look at Amado, but he held her in place.

"Don Armenta is well known in many circles. His horses are famous for their beauty and stamina, as is the don for his implacable demeanor."

"Is that why you were stealing the horses? To get back at my father for something?"

"Victoro has a buyer for fine horses. I told him your father has many herds and won't miss a few head."

Yoana opened her mouth to tell Amado what she thought of men who stole from others when Leya screamed. A wisp of dark cloth floated toward them in the breeze. Yoana gasped. "Hurry!" She leaned forward as Amado urged his buckskin up the slope. Hand outstretched, Yoana lunged out to the side and grabbed Leya's *mantilla* before the fabric drifted to earth.

Amado leaned forward and sent his mount surging up the hill to close the distance that had grown between them and Cisto. Yoana saw Cisto turn Leya to face him, even as she fought him. The outlaw was trying to ravish her. Yoana's muscles tensed as if she could will the horse to move faster. Amado kicked the buckskin again as he yelled at Cisto to stop.

As they came up behind Cisto's bay, Cisto cursed and shoved Leya from the saddle. She tumbled to the ground. Amado reined his horse to the side to keep from trampling Leya, who had curled into a ball, her face pressed against her skirt.

"Let me go!" Yoana tried to jerk away from Amado. His tight grip held her fast. "Let go. I need to help her."

"Wait until I have Cisto blocked." Amado swung his horse around to put the animal between Cisto and Leya. Yoana slid down to land hard. Her feet slipped on the pine needles, and she almost fell. Amado's grasp on her upper arm kept her from landing on her face. He released her, and she dropped down beside Leya.

"Here." Yoana lifted Leya's head so her señorita could see the veil. "Let me help you." Tears streaked Leya's cheeks. Her lower lip had puffed out, and she had teeth marks on her skin. Anger seared through Yoana. What right did this man have to treat Leya like a *puta*? Her sweet *tía* who never hurt anyone? She waited until Leya had the *mantilla* in place before she lunged to her feet and whirled to face the monster.

She turned in time to see Cisto and Amado dismount and face each other. Amado's fist connected with Cisto's jaw. The bandit staggered backward. She realized the men were too focused on one another to think of anything else. She wheeled back to Leya.

"Hurry." Yoana grabbed her *tía*. "Get on the horse." She nodded toward Amado's buckskin. Cisto's horse still shied away from the enraged men, and was too far for Yoana to reach. "Hurry, Leya. Before they see us."

Leya stumbled to her feet, her *mantilla* secure, but askew. Her hands shook as she reached for the stirrup. Her ragged gasps sounded too loud. Yoana held the reins. They only had moments until one of the bandits noticed them. She wanted to yell at Leya, to make her move faster. As soon as Leya swung up, Yoana threw her the reins and leaped up behind her.

One of the men shouted. Yoana didn't look back. She grabbed the reins and kicked the buckskin's sides. *Please, God, help us get away.* Once more she found herself plunging downhill on a runaway horse. This time was even more awkward with Leya in front of her, but Yoana didn't try to slow their descent. They had to hurry. Every twist of the path counted. Every turn gave them a bit more hope. Every step took them closer to safety.

The trees blurred. Leya cried out when the horse skidded through a thick patch of needles and slid down the hillside. Yoana pulled Leya until they were leaning so far back Yoana's head almost rested on the buckskin's rear. The animal snorted. With a few hops, he slowed his pace, his breath huffing in and out like a bellows.

When Yoana finally pulled him to a halt at the bottom of the slope, only the sound of their heavy panting disturbed the silence. Leya trembled against Yoana, her body shaking with silent sobs. Yoana put her arms around Leya as she listened for the crashing of pursuit. In their mad rush, they'd gotten off the trail. She didn't recognize any of the trees. The foliage kept her from seeing up the slope. She hoped that meant no one could see them either.

"Shhh. Leya. Breathe slowly. Keep as quiet as you can. Maybe they won't find us, and we can get back home."

"How..." A shudder ran through Leya. "How will we do that? Do you know the way?"

"I think I can figure it out." Yoana looked up hoping to glimpse a shaft of sunlight through the clouds, but the thick branches blocked much of the sky. She waited for a long time as she listened for sounds of a search. The horse dozed, probably glad for the rest after carrying two riders in difficult conditions. Yoana began to relax.

The forest came alive. Leya's soft prayers comforted Yoana. She closed her eyes, knowing she should pray too. Shadows lengthened. Yoana hoped enough time had passed so they could try to find their way out of the mountains. She didn't want to encounter any grizzly bears or big cats in the dark. Or any two-legged predators either.

"Ready?" Her whisper must have startled Leya, who sucked in a quick breath before nodding.

"We'll follow this hill around to the left and see if we can strike the trail we took up the mountain. If we do, then we head downhill be home before dark. Maybe we'll meet Lucio on the way."

"Let's go." Leya's tremulous voice caught. "Please, God, don't let those men capture us again." A shudder wracked her body as she spoke.

Finding the path proved easier than Yoana thought. She could even see the marks made earlier by their horses' hooves. Relief left her heavy with exhaustion. They could do this. By nightfall, they would be safe. At home she would go to the chapel and make a vow never to be impulsive again.

The late afternoon air held more than a hint of chill. Gray clouds scudded across the sky. The scent of rain danced in the air. Yoana shivered and longed with all her heart to be home, even if she would have to face her father's wrath.

"We're almost there, Leya. We'll be safe soon." They leaned back as the horse began another steep descent. The slow plod of his hooves echoed in the quiet. Unease trickled down Yoana's spine. Where were the birds? The squirrels?

"Did you hear something?" Leya's voice sounded loud in the silence. Yoana's heart pounded as she tugged on the reins to stop the horse.

Her ears pulsed as she listened. "I don't hear anything. Do you?" She spoke next to Leya's ear, keeping her voice low.

Leya shook her head. "I'm sorry. I thought I heard the sound of a horse."

"That might be good." Hope fluttered to life. "Maybe it's the man Lucio sent from the rancho." Yoana urged the buckskin on down the hill. The path wound around and passed through an outcropping of rocks that she remembered from their ascent.

As they rounded the curve, she caught a glimpse of the foothills far below. Several riders were heading their way. Even from this distance she could tell the horse in the lead belonged to Lucio. The distinctive dun with the white and black socks stood out. If Lucio were that far away, then whose horse had Leya heard? The vaquero's?

Yoana leaned forward to quicken the pace when Cisto stepped out from behind a tree. His left eye had swollen almost shut. Blood trickled down his cheek from a cut on his temple. Pistol in hand, he faced them without a smile...or any of his earlier arrogance.

CHAPTER THREE

Lucio Armenta tossed the dun's reins to one of the stable boys.

"Wait here." He shot the terse command at the Santiago men and the vaqueros who'd accompanied him to search for his sister and tía. He strode toward the house, anger churning a hole in his gut. He wanted to rip his father up one side and down the other. The arrogant don had justified his disdain and hatred for his daughter for too long with no one willing to face him. This time he'd gone too far.

The hacienda door hit the wall with a thud that reverberated throughout the adobe and wood structure. Windows rattled as he slammed it shut after him, too conditioned to keeping the heat out to leave the door open. Don Armenta didn't even look up when Lucio stalked into the den. His padre continued to peruse the papers on his desk, even though the flick of his gaze noted Lucio's presence.

Lucio flipped the hat from his head and beat it against his leg. A cloud of dust floated to the floor. His father hated dirt in his home, which made the small act of defiance much more satisfying. He should wait, hat in hand, like a good son. Instead, he flopped in one of his father's favorite chairs, propped one ankle on his other knee, and twirled the hat in his hands as he waited. He resisted the urge to continue to make his father notice him. The urgency of helping Yoana and Leya ate at him. He drummed his fingers on the arm of the chair.

Don Armenta placed his pencil on the desktop with deliberate care and precision, a sure sign of his irritation. Lucio almost grinned. His father's impenetrable gaze held enough fury to burn a whole mountain. Apparently this day hadn't been going right for the don. Well, it was about to get worse.

"I'm assuming since you're here there must be some catastrophic event." The don's even tone rumbled like thunder in the silent house. "Did something happen with the horses?"

"You could say that." Lucio flipped the hat up and brushed some more of the dust onto the floor. His father's nostrils flared.

"I rode out with the Santiago men and some of the vaqueros to bring the herd close to the house so they would be ready in the morning. Bandoleros got there first. They've taken the horses."

"You didn't go after them?" The don's brow knit with anger.

"That isn't all they took." Lucio straightened. He knew the rest of the conversation would be painful. "Yoana and Leya were captured. The bandits took them."

"What?" Surprise flickered through the don's eyes before he shuttered his reaction. His fingers whitened on the edge of the desk. "What were they doing there?"

"After your incredible performance with Yoana this morning, I guess she wanted to go for a ride. She convinced Leya. She also had Jorge and Juan with her."

"I want to speak to Jorge." Don Armenta rolled his pencil between his fingers. "Send him in now."

"I can do that, but you might have a bit of trouble questioning him." Lucio waited a beat. "Both Jorge and Juan were killed by the bandoleros. The man who took Leya threatened to kill her if we tried anything. We had to let them go"

"You just let them ride off with some of our best horses?"

"Well, that's telling." Lucio let the sarcasm drip. "You're more concerned with a herd of animals than you are with your daughter and your sister-in-law. I didn't think even you would be this cold-hearted."

"Those horses are some of my best. Tito Santiago is expecting them. I gave him my word. You may not value your word, but I value mine." The don's voice took on a threatening tone.

"I value the stock, but I value my sister and my tía more. I would like to be able to take some of the men and go after them. Manuel is following them, but staying back so he isn't in danger. If we leave now, we have a chance of getting them home before nightfall."

Don Armenta frowned. The pencil rolled back and forth between his thumb and forefinger. "If they headed for the mountains, you won't have a chance of finding them."

"A couple of our men are good at tracking. I'll take them. Santiago's men are willing to help too. They have to have the horses before they can head home."

"Take Ramón. He's the best tracker we have. He can follow the herd."

"What about Yoana and Leya? What if they are taken in a different direction?"

"Then I'm sorry about Leya, but she knew what she risked when she followed Yoana out of here. As for your sister, this isn't the first time she's gotten someone killed. What happens to her is her fault. I won't put any of my men in danger for a disobedient girl."

Lucio surged to his feet. He snatched his hat before the sombrero could tumble to the ground. "You're unbelievable. You'll risk the men for some dumb animals, but not for your own daughter."

"What I do is none of your business." Don Armenta's palm slapped the desktop, a sure sign his control had slipped. "What I choose to do or not do with your sister isn't up to you. Now go! Do what I told you."

"All these years, I've kept quiet. We all have, except Mateo. My brothers aren't here now, but I'm choosing to say this to you." He should shut his mouth and walk out the door, but he couldn't seem to stop the torrent now that he'd started. "All this time you've acted like you blame Yoana for my mother's death."

"Get out!" Don Armenta surged to his feet. His chair tumbled backwards with a crash.

"But the one you really can't forgive is yourself." He pointed at his father with his hat. *"You* are the one to blame for Mama's death. Not Yoana."

"Get. Out! *Now*." The don's voice dropped to a dangerous whisper.

Lucio followed suit, grinding out his words. "Remember, I wasn't a young child like Yoana that day. I was fourteen. My brothers and I know the truth of what happened. We all know why you're hiding behind your hatred of our sister." With that, he spun on his heel and strode from the room, leaving his father with the weight of the truth hanging in the air.

MEN AND HORSES milled about in front of the stables. More than usual. His father's vaqueros waited with their mounts, their anger at the news evident. They would fight for Leya and Yoana, not to mention making the bandoleros pay for Jorge's and Juan's deaths.

The Santiago vaqueros, down here to pick up the horses Don Santiago purchased, would also be willing to help. They all knew, or knew of, his sister and tía.

Everyone would want to help find the women. Don Armenta might hate his daughter, but the rest of the people on the ranch loved her. From an early age, she'd stolen the hearts of these men. They'd watched her grow from an impulsive chatterbox to a reclusive--by her father's mandate--but often impetuous woman. They all knew how much she longed for Gabrio to come for her. They would all understand the hurt she'd suffered today at the news dispatched by the don. Any of these men would have succumbed to her pleading to take her riding, just as Jorge and Juan had.

The men quieted as Lucio approached. Even their mounts calmed as if waiting to hear what to do next. Ramón, Don Armenta's head vaquero and Lucio's friend, stepped forward, his hat brim twisted in his hand. "Do you want me to track the outlaws, Lucio? I can find them quick, and we can rescue the señoritas."

Lucio drew in a deep breath. He'd been raised to respect the don, as had all the men here. They would think less of him if he criticized his father in front of them. Yet they had to know the stakes if they chose to follow Lucio. They would be disobeying a direct order of the don's.

He met their gazes. "The don would like us to find the herd. So, yes, Ramón, I'd like you to go with me and track them." A murmur ran through the group. Clearly they were wondering at his lack of mentioning the women. "I'm hoping the two who took Yoana and Leya will meet up with those who took the horses. Tracking a couple of men in that terrain is hard, but hiding the tracks of a herd of horses is almost impossible."

Ramón nodded. The other vaqueros tilted their heads, showing they understood his purpose. A few glanced skyward at the darkening clouds. They needed to move fast. Only Julio, a vaquero from the Armenta rancho, didn't move. He held his gaze steady on Lucio, as if he knew more was coming.

Lucio straightened and kept his expression free of the turmoil raging inside. "I'll take the Santiago men, since these horses are their concern. Antonio, Berto, and Paulo can go along with Ramón. The rest of you need to stay here and watch the ranch. Bring the livestock as close to the buildings as possible." The men murmured with an undertone of righteous anger. Lucio allowed himself a small sigh of relief. These were good men. They would do their best to bring the señoritas home.

"What happened to Jorge and Juan shows us how dangerous these bandoleros are. If we don't recover the women and the horses by tonight, I'll come back here or I'll send one of the men to let you know. If that happens, we'll need to let the other ranchos in the area know what's happened. Someone will need to start for Los Angeles tomorrow and alert the authorities. I doubt they'll be able to do anything, but they should know anyway. Julio, you will take care of everything here while Ramón is gone? See to the livestock?"

When the vaquero nodded, Lucio turned away. The stable boy led Lucio's horse to him. The dun had been cooled and rubbed down before being saddled again. Lucio ruffled the boy's hair to thank him. Later he would give him something more to show how much he appreciated the niño's thoughtfulness.

"Mount up. We have to beat this storm." Lucio swung onto his horse. The men going with him followed suit. The rumble of hooves reverberated off the outbuildings as they headed toward the mountains. Lucio's hand tightened on the reins as he recalled his conversation with his father. Why couldn't the man get over the past? Why could he forgive his *viejos,* his old friends, any differences, but his daughter he treated as dead to him?

He needed to call a halt and tell these men the don's instructions, but he would wait until they were clear of the ranch. Hopefully, none of them would turn back. The fact he intended to disobey the don's orders might give a couple of them pause even if they owed their allegiance to Santiago, not Don Armenta. While on this rancho, they were to follow his father's mandates. They would be guilty of disobedience if they went with him. *Por favor, Padre nuestro, let finding Yoana and Leya mean more to these men than following orders.*

He pulled to a halt at the lip of the valley where the bandoleros had taken his sister, tía, and the horses. Lucio turned to face the men. The horses quieted, their breathing evening out. Lucio cleared his throat and met the men's eyes as he related part of his conversation with his father, and then shared the don's orders to recapture the horses and forget about the women.

An angry murmur ran through the group.

"I'm not telling you this so you will be upset with my father." Lucio waited for the men to calm down. "I'm giving you a choice. I intend to go after Yoana and Leya. My father is right that the men who took them might have met up with those who stole the horses, and we'll find both at the same time. However, if that isn't the case, then I will leave the livestock and find my family."

He paused to let his statement sink in. "If you choose to go with me, you may forfeit your job. Don Armenta won't take kindly to his orders being ignored. Don Santiago might not either."

The men muttered among themselves. Lucio waited for them to quiet. "If I split off from the herd to track the women, I won't fault you for not going with me. In fact, if you want to track the livestock, that might be a good thing. I'm hoping they're going in the same direction."

"Which one will you want me to track?" Ramón asked.

"If you're willing, I'll take you with me." Lucio glanced up at the sky. "Unless we get rain in the next day or so, the herd will be easy to follow. Even if they go over rock, it's hard to hide the tracks of that many horses. Following the women and a couple of the bandoleros will be much harder. They can even use the herd's trail to cover their own tracks." Lucio met Ramón's intent gaze. "It's your choice, *mi amigo*, but I would appreciate your help."

Ramón nodded, his mouth a thin line. "I would gladly lose my job to get Señorita Yoana and your tía back home. Their safety is what matters."

Lucio knew all the men understood what it would mean if Yoana and his tía stayed in the clutches of the bandits overnight. Even with Leya there, Yoana's reputation would be lost, regardless of what actually happened. Another wave of anger swept through him at the thought of his father's callousness.

"Let's ride. We need to find Manuel and see if he can tell us what direction the bandoleros have gone. Ramón, you take the lead with me."

The dun snorted as Lucio reined him around the valley instead of going down through it. This way would be faster. He set a steady pace that wouldn't tire the horses before they reached the mountains. The sun had already passed its zenith. Clouds hung heavy on the horizon. Lucio hoped the rain would skirt them to fall on the far side of the range. He didn't want anything to interfere with their search. They had to catch these desperadoes.

As the afternoon waned, the signs showed he'd been right. The men who'd taken Yoana and Leya weren't following the horses. Not only that, but the men who took the herd had split up to make it harder to track them. Now he would have to decide whether he wanted to divide his small group and follow all the tracks or stick to one group and hope they met up at a later point.

He pulled to a halt not far into the foothills to give the horses a short breather.

There was only one choice to make. "We're going to split up here. Antonio, you and Berto follow the trail of the herd with the rest of the men. They split into two groups just down there. You can split up and follow them or choose one group to track. I'm thinking they will meet up before nightfall.

"Paulo, you go with Ramón and me. We'll pursue the women. Keep a sharp lookout. These men know they'll hang if we capture them. They'll shoot to kill."

He started to turn his horse uphill, then halted. "Thank you." His throat tightened. He didn't know some of these men well, only Ramón, but he respected their choice.

"Right, boss." Antonio nodded. "We'll get them." The vaqueros trotted off.

Lucio watched them reach the split tracks and turn uphill.

"Ramón, can you pick out Manuel's horse from the rest of these? Did he go this way?"

"No, Señor Lucio. The grass is too heavy right here. If we find a patch of bare ground, I can tell. Manuel's horse has a hoof that turns in on the right front. I can read that like a book." He grinned at Lucio, a glint of teeth showing through his thick mustache.

"Then you take the lead. Paulo and I will be right behind you. I don't want to destroy any of the tracks."

They rode in silence. Lucio thought he caught a flicker of movement in the trees up on the mountain, but it could have been anything. A deer. A bear. Even a bird stretching its wings. His heart sank. Would they be able to rescue Yoana and Leya in time? Both his sister and his Tía had suffered so much. How would they ever recover if they were ravished by bandoleros? These men had no scruples. They wouldn't care about the reputation of a don's daughter. In fact, they would brag about their conquest.

"God, please, help me find them in time."

Ramón leaned low over his horse's withers, his gaze riveted on the ground. Lucio chafed, wanting, no, *needing*, to go faster. However, he knew if they moved fast, they ran a greater chance of losing the trail and having to backtrack. That would waste more time than going slowly now to ensure they didn't get off the path.

The first of the pines loomed ahead. Ramón picked up the pace. "Once we're under the trees, we should be able to go faster. There won't be so much grass to blur the tracks." He glanced over at Lucio. "I still can't tell for sure if Manuel came this way, but I can see that two of the horses carried more weight. That would be the bandoleros riding double with the señoritas."

Lucio glanced at the western sky before they disappeared into the forest. Ponderous clouds with bellies full of rain inched closer. A sense of urgency tightened his muscles. The dun danced beneath him.

"Here." Ramón halted and gestured at the ground. "These are the two carrying double. This set of tracks is from Manuel's horse. We're going the right way." He urged his horse to a fast walk as they ascended the steep mountain trail. Lucio watched ahead. Paulo would be doing the same. Ramón's gaze would be riveted on the ground. He and Paulo had to look for any traps or to see if they could spot Manuel.

Trees closed in around them as the path leveled out. They rounded a bend. Up ahead, Lucio spotted something on the ground. "Ramón. Stop." The tracker glanced at Lucio, then followed his gaze up the hill. The quiet weighed on them as all three searched the surrounding woods for any sign of the bandits. Nothing moved.

"Paulo, wait here and keep watch. Ramón, come with me." Lucio eased his horse in front of Ramón's. Perhaps Manuel had been knocked unconscious… The vaquero rested in a heap on the ground. His vacant eyes stared up at the trees overhead. The blood pooled around Manuel's head showed he'd been shot.

The stakes had just gone up.

CHAPTER FOUR

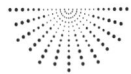

A scream echoed through the trees, then the sound cut off. Amado halted his mad dash down the mountain. He'd been following the trail left by Yoana and Leya, praying he could get to them before Cisto did. Too late. That scream meant Cisto had gotten the women. One, or both, of them might be hurt or dead.

He stilled, forcing his breathing to slow. Over the pounding of his pulse, he could detect sounds of a struggle downhill, possibly to the east of where he stood. Amado crept through the trees. He didn't want Cisto to hear his approach and take the women elsewhere. On foot, Amado wouldn't have a hope of catching up to them in time to help Yoana and Leya.

Color flashed below. He crouched and eased over until he could see between the trees to the trail. Cisto had Yoana in his arms. She fought with the defensiveness of a bear protecting her young. Amado almost grinned, but his humor died.

Cisto wouldn't tolerate her rejection. He would resort to violence. He always did.

As Amado watched, Leya rose from where she'd been sprawled on the ground and flung herself at the struggling pair. She sank her teeth into Cisto's arm. He howled. Yoana stumbled backward as his hold weakened. Cisto cursed and backhanded Leya so hard her *mantilla* flew off as she tumbled to the ground.

Amado abandoned caution as he half-slid, half-ran down the hill. No one heard his descent. Yoana screamed something and launched herself at Cisto. She hit him hard enough to send him stumbling backward. He came up against a pine tree with a heavy thud. Yoana fell to her knees, but was up in a flash. She raced to Leya and jerked her up. They started for the horse when one of Cisto's knives whirled past Yoana's cheek and thunked into a tree trunk. Both women froze.

Cisto pushed up from the ground, his pistol in one hand, the other hand reaching down to snatch up his hat. He cocked the gun, his face a snarl of hatred. Amado had no doubt what was coming. Cisto would kill Leya, then, after he'd finished with her, Yoana.

Still hidden by the brush, Amado ripped his revolver from the holster and drew down on Cisto. This could be his chance to fulfill his promise.

Before he could snap off a shot, rapid hoof beats sounded on the trail. Miguel rounded the curve and slid his horse to a stop. "Cisto, Lorenzo has the horses hidden away. We wiped the tracks since the men were following you. I doubled back to tell you, but I saw the men from the rancho." He gasped for breath. "They're close. You have to hurry. Where's Amado?"

"We got split up." Cisto's pistol barrel wavered. "You'll have to help me with the chicas."

One corner of Miguel's mouth lifted in a derisive smile. "You need help with a couple of women?" He gave a short bark of laughter.

"I don't need help." Cisto strode toward Yoana. "But they won't want to move fast."

Yoana pushed Leya behind her. Her pulse hammered. She would die before she let this dog do anything to her tía.

Stones and leaves tumbled down the hillside. Cisto whirled, bringing his pistol to bear. Miguel did the same, then relaxed. "Hey, Amado. Get down here and help Cisto. He doesn't think he can handle these feisty chicas."

Cisto glowered at Amado, who slipped his gun back in the holster. His gaze touched on Yoana for a brief moment. Relief weakened her knees, almost as if she'd been rescued from certain death.

Maybe she had.

As Amado jumped the last few feet and landed on the trail, Yoana urged Leya closer to his horse. Maybe if the three men were distracted, she could get them away. If Miguel had spoken true, then Lucio must be nearby.

Amado let out a low whistle. The buckskin snorted, moved around Yoana, and trotted over to him. She hissed as she glared at the man she'd been so relieved to see just a moment ago. Didn't he understand they needed to escape now, while there was still time?

Amado patted the horse's neck before he faced Cisto. She saw the bandit's fury burn in his eyes as he stared at Amado.

"I don't need your help. We don't need you at camp either, so you can take your horse and leave."

"Victoro sent me on this trip. Last I checked, he's in charge. Until he tells me different, I'm going back with you. Yoana will ride with me."

Yoana heard Leya's small gasp. Amado glanced their way. Was that compassion on his face?

He turned back to Cisto. "Leya can ride with Miguel."

"No." Cisto's lip curled in a snarl.

"Yes." Amado placed his hand on his pistol grip as he squared off with Cisto. Cisto's hand hovered over his own revolver. Tension hummed in the air as Cisto widened his stance in preparation for a shoot out.

"This is good." Miguel's lazy tone belied the tension. "You two can kill each other, and I get two women. I like those odds."

Amado didn't take his gaze off of Cisto, but Yoana could see him watching from the corner of his eye as Miguel leaned forward over his horse's withers. "I do wish you would hurry though. The vaqueros are getting pretty close. I want to have time to lose them before I have fun with these lovely señoritas."

Cisto's shoulders relaxed. He flexed his hands. Amado's fingers loosened, but he didn't take his eyes off Cisto.

"Yoana, come here." Amado gestured to her. Both women came to him. "Leya, ride with Miguel." Amado kept his gaze riveted on Cisto. Yoana gave Leya a quick push to hurry her along. She hadn't given up on escape, but she didn't want Leya at Cisto's mercy.

"*Vamanos, amigos.*" Miguel swung Leya up in front of him. "If we hurry, we can get out of here ahead of them" He swung his horse around and trotted back down the trail.

Cisto glared at Yoana and Amado. As Amado slipped his arm around her, Yoana fought the urge to melt into the safety of his strength. Instead, she stiffened, her chin lifted, her gaze steady on Cisto. She refused to show weakness to the tyrant.

Cisto disappeared into the undergrowth and returned with his mount. Amado vaulted onto his buckskin, reached down for Yoana, and lifted her into the saddle in front of him. As he fell in behind Cisto, tension drained from Yoana. Why did Amado seem in favor of leaving her behind one moment and taking her the next? She wanted to berate him, but her fear for Leya kept her silent.

"Where did he take Leya?" Yoana tried to keep the panic from her voice.

"Don't worry. She's with Miguel. He's not like Cisto. He has more heart, and he won't hurt your tía."

Yoana leaned forward. If only she could urge the horse to go faster. She didn't like having Leya out of her sight. She refused to allow her mind to consider the horror of their plight. Being kidnapped by bandoleros was something parents threatened their young girls with to keep them from getting in trouble. Yoana's reputation would be ruined, which for a girl of her status meant her life would no longer be a good one. The gossip would last for years, maybe her lifetime. She would not marry well. Her peers would shun her. She would live like Leya.

"Please, can we hurry and catch up to her? She'll be so afraid." Yoana looked at Amado over her shoulder. His eyes seemed to beg her understanding. Bits of light reflected in them like stars. She wanted to touch the slight cleft in his chin. The corners of his full mouth turned up. Yoana felt the heat in her face and swung back around, embarrassed she'd been caught staring.

"Please?" Yoana ducked her head as she repeated her request. Amado's breath huffed warm against her neck. He didn't say anything. She could almost hear the battle waging inside him. Would he help her?

He lifted the reins. His buckskin moved into an easy trot, not the bone-jarring gait of some horses. They quickly caught up to Cisto and Miguel. Yoana glanced down the mountain and her heart lifted.

Lucio and his men were much closer.

"We'd better get moving. We have to reach the other trail before they cut us off." Amado must have seen the men too. For once, Cisto nodded without arguing.

Cool wind gusts carried the scent of rain. Yoana shivered. Miguel rounded a curve in the path and his horse reared up as Miguel jerked back on the reins. He fumbled for his gun.

"Manuel!" Leya's quiet cry drifted back on the wind. She jerked back, and Miguel released his pistol to fight for control of the horse and the woman.

Cisto kicked his mount, letting out a wild yell. His revolver appeared in his hand as if he willed it there. Amado leaned forward, almost pushing Yoana into the horse's neck. Too late. Cisto's gun cracked. The sharp report echoed in the moisture-laden air.

"*No.*" Yoana's cry echoed Leya's sound of distress. The vaquero tumbled from the horse to lie still, a pool of blood spreading under his shoulders. Amado pulled Yoana back against him, wishing he could keep her from seeing this violence.

"Let's go before the others come." Miguel had control of his mount again and skirted the body to continue on the trail.

Cisto followed, with Amado and Yoana taking up the rear. Yoana looked once over her shoulder at the fallen man they left behind. She didn't say a word, but let her eyes convey her accusation. Amado's mouth thinned. She wanted to see regret in his expression, but instead only saw determination as he hurried to catch his compadres. Maybe she'd misjudged him. His heart must be as black as the other bandoleros'.

The increased pace made conversation impossible. They caught up to Miguel just as he turned his horse onto a narrow path that would have been difficult to find without direction. Yoana looked back after they all passed through. The manzanita snapped back into place, hiding any sign of their passage. Lucio would never know where they had gone. The path had grown so rocky she didn't think there would be hoofprints.

Darkness drifted down through the trees by the time they reached the canyon where Lorenzo had the horses penned. Fat raindrops splattered around them, forerunners to an impending downpour. They had taken so many twists and turns, Yoana didn't know how anyone could find them. Or how she would find her way home. Now the rain would aid the bandoleros.

Perhaps she could use it to her advantage too.

Exhaustion stole the last of her strength. She could see Leya asleep against Miguel. Earlier, Yoana had succumbed and leaned back against Amado as darkness fell. Her tension drained as fatigue took over. Amado hadn't seemed to mind. His strong arms held her secure against his chest. Tears pricked her eyes as she daydreamed. If only Amado were Gabrio, her betrothed, and they would be married. How many times had she pictured them together like this?

A small fire crackled in a sheltered area under an overhang of rock. The flames wouldn't be visible from outside the canyon, nor would they be affected by inclement weather. Yoana's stomach clenched as she caught the scent of roasted meat.

"Food's ready." Lorenzo stepped out from behind a tree and holstered his gun. "We put up a temporary corral." He waved his hand toward the back of the canyon. "You can put your horses there or tether them closer."

Cisto clicked his tongue and moved off toward the back of the canyon. Miguel leaped off his mount before he reached up for Leya and set her on the ground. She stumbled, probably stiff from sitting on a horse all day. Yoana tensed. She and Leya rode often, but never for this many hours. Miguel steadied Leya until she caught her balance.

AMADO SWUNG his leg over the sorrel's rump and dropped to the ground. The impact jarred every bone in his tired body. If he hurt this much, how bad must these women feel? Mountain trails always took a toll. He reached up to lift Yoana down, but she pushed his hands aside. She jumped and landed lightly on the ground next to him. She faltered, but put a hand on the horse's side to catch her balance. Yoana glared at his outstretched hand until he changed tactics to rub his face and try to hide the small grin he couldn't stop. Her impudence showed fire. He preferred spunk to the simpering women who tried to catch his eye at his father's hacienda.

"What do you find so funny?" Yoana's chin came up. Her shoulders squared. "You think this kidnapping is amusing? We'll see how amused you are when my father's men put a rope around your neck."

Amado grabbed her arm and yanked her close before she could object. "Your father's men are not going to hang me, and you had better keep quiet about who you are." She pushed against his chest, but he held her firm.

"Let go!" Her eyes sparked. "I don't care who knows I'm the daughter of--"

He clapped his hand over her mouth as her voice escalated. Miguel had walked off to care for his horse, but Lorenzo and Tomás were close enough to hear. He could see their feigned disinterest and knew they were listening.

Amado pulled her closer, despite her struggle to get away. He put his mouth next to her ear. "If these men figure out how important you are, they will threaten your death if your father doesn't comply with ransom demands. Leya will die first, and her body will be delivered to your father. Now, do you really think Don Armenta will pay a large sum to these bandoleros?"

She stilled as he spoke, then gazed up at him, eyes wide. Her full lips parted, then closed as if she wanted to speak, but didn't know what to say. His anger faded as he stared into her golden-brown eyes. The temptation to kiss her pulled at him.

"If you're afraid to kiss her, I will." Cisto's raspy voice startled Amado.

He'd been so enraptured with Yoana he hadn't heard the other man approach. He looked up to see that Miguel had returned. All the men watched. Once again, tension wound a tight coil through the group.

"I can show her how a real man treats a woman." Cisto reached out to lift Yoana's braid. He rubbed the strands of hair with his fingers.

Yoana jerked away. She shoved at Amado and wiggled around to face Cisto. "Get your hands *off* of me." Fists clenched, she met the bandit's cold gaze without flinching. "You will not touch me again."

If Amado hadn't been holding onto Yoana, Cisto would have knocked her to the ground before he dragged her off into the trees to show her what he could do. Yoana might be fearless, but he prayed she would learn a healthy respect soon. Otherwise, life would get very difficult when they arrived at camp.

Cisto's eyes narrowed. His lip lifted in a sneer. "I will touch you if I want to, chica. When I choose to do so, you will learn what it is to know a man." Cisto crossed his arms over his chest. "You will beg to stay with me."

Before Yoana could further anger Cisto, Amado said, "What will Rosalinda say to that? I don't think she will be so happy."

Lorenzo laughed. "Then we will have a fight between women. That is always entertaining."

Miguel and Tomás joined in the laughter.

After a minute Cisto grinned and turned away. "I'm hungry. Tomás, bring me some of that meat." He swaggered closer to the fire and sat on a large rock.

Yoana sagged against Amado. Had her bravado just been a cover up for her terror? He brushed his fingers across her cheek. "Come, let me get you something to eat, and then I'll put my horse up."

They walked toward the small fire. Lorenzo had just seated Leya on a log at the side of the shelter, so Amado motioned for Yoana to join her.

Tomás walked over, his head tilted to one side, eyes downcast. He moved close to Amado and spoke in a low voice. "I-I-I c-can put him up. Your b-b-buckskin." When he looked at Amado, his eyes carried as much message as his words. Tomás knew only too well what Cisto was capable of doing. He didn't want Amado to leave Yoana alone with the volatile bandit.

"Thanks, Tomás." Amado handed the reins to the young boy and went to fetch some meat for Yoana, Leya, and himself. He could see Cisto ready to demand that the women serve them. Cisto liked to be pampered. After the day they'd had, Amado wouldn't ask Yoana or Leya to wait on a man they feared. For once Cisto kept quiet when he saw the look in Amado's eyes.

As Amado cut off some meat, the sky opened up and poured like a flooded river. The noise kept them from talking. Amado focused on his food, glad a few minutes later when the rain began to slack off.

After they had eaten and washed in a small stream that ran through the canyon, Amado chose a protected place for the women to sleep--a place as far from Cisto as he could get without seeming too obvious. He brought a blanket for them to share but didn't have any other comforts.

He settled with his back to a tree, close enough to keep an eye on Yoana. He could see her in the moonlight filtering into the canyon. Her eyes gleamed as she watched the men turn in for the night. Tomás went down the canyon with Miguel. They would take turns watching for any activity. The slim possibility that Lucio and his men had been able to track them this far had been wiped out by the storm, but the bandoleros wouldn't take chances.

Quiet settled over the camp. Amado pulled his hat down lower on his forehead to give the appearance that he slept. Yoana shifted under the blanket and turned to face him. He could see her narrowed gaze as she studied him, probably trying to figure out whether he slept or not.

A soft sound came to him. Yoana turned back over. He saw her take Leya in her arms and knew the sound he heard must be Leya's sobs. Amado leaned his head back against the rock and gazed up at the dripping trees.

Was there any way he could have changed this day? He hadn't planned for it to end this way or for these women to be kidnapped. Too bad he didn't still trust God. He might have been willing to ask Him for help. But God hadn't cared in a long time.

It was up to him to work this all out.

Something startled Amado awake. He must have drifted off. A quick glance told him the blanket where Yoana and Leya had slept was gone.

And so were the women.

CHAPTER FIVE

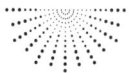

The rain dripped in intermittent patters from the branches above them. Yoana crept through the damp forest with Leya close at her back. She could hear her tía's breath hitch as she struggled to remain calm. Yoana prayed the soft ground would hide the sound of their footfalls as they escaped. So far everyone in the camp still slept.

When they approached the makeshift corral, one of the horses snorted and shied away from the rope and brush that fenced them in. Yoana inched closer, bridle in hand. Leya followed with a second bridle. Dim starlight lit the way. A second horse stomped, its ears perked, stance wary.

"Yoana, how will we get away?" Leya's whisper sounded loud in the still of the night.

"Quiet." Yoana concentrated on getting part of the fence open. She hoped she could find the buckskin Amado had been riding and one of the other tamer horses. The horses in her father's herd wouldn't be broken, and any of those horses would be a challenge. Still, she would make do with what she could catch. She wanted to get away from here. She needed to get Leya to safety.

"How will we get past the men?" Leya's voice caught in a half sob. "Even if we get past the camp, there are still two men watching the mouth of the canyon."

"Leya, if you keep this up, they'll all be here joining in the conversation. Be quiet. Please. We'll go out the back way." Yoana reached over to give Leya's shoulder a light squeeze. "Let me catch the horses. We'll release the others as we go. Maybe by morning these bandoleros will be on foot so they won't be able to come after us."

Yoana slipped inside the enclosure. Horses milled around, most of them moving away from her. Those would be her father's horses. They weren't used to people, although they weren't totally wild. A nose bumped her arm. Yoana reached up to scratch the horse's jaw and run her hand up to its ears. This one was tame. It had to be one of the horses they'd ridden today. The starlight wasn't bright enough here under the trees for her to tell if this was the buckskin or one of the others.

With deft movements, Yoana had the bridle on the animal. She led it out of the pen and gave the reins to Leya. Taking the other bridle, she went back through the opening. In a few moments, she had a second horse bridled and ready to saddle. She left the gate open as she led the horse out. This way some of the horses might begin to find their way to freedom as well. She didn't want them to stampede down the canyon and wake the men before she and Leya had a chance to disappear.

Saddling a horse in the dark was easy for Yoana, but Leya fumbled so much Yoana had to put the tack on her tía's horse too. She tried to contain her impatience. She understood Leya's fear. That her tía had been captured and tortured by bandoleros when she was a young woman only made this situation that much horrendous. It was those bandoleros who had given Leya the scar that crossed most of her face and neck.

No one would ever hurt her like that again. Not if Yoana could prevent it.

Finally, Leya swung up on the gentler of the two animals.

Yoana hesitated before mounting. She looked over at the enclosure. Only a couple of the herd were snuffling at the grass outside the pen. She led her horse over to the opening. The two other loose animals snorted and trotted away. She tugged on the brush, startling her horse. The beast spooked and scrabbled backward. Yoana almost lost her hold on the reins.

"Easy. Easy." She crooned the words as she edged closer to stroke the horse's neck. Nostrils distended, head high, muscles tight, the horse trembled beneath her touch. Within moments, the animal calmed.

The opening had to be wide enough. She couldn't take the time to do more.

She swung up on her mount's back, then motioned to Leya to follow. A few more of the herd poked theirs heads out of the opening in the fence. Satisfaction lifted Yoana's spirits. This might work. The horses from the pen would obliterate their trail, and leave the bandits on foot. She could get Leya to safety, if she could find her way out of the mountains before they starved. Or died of thirst. Or were killed by some wild beast.

She shivered as she pushed away the fearful thoughts.

Water dripped from the trees, adding to the wintry feel. Thick pine needles muffled the hoofbeats with a slight squelching sound. Anemic light filtered through the overhead branches in a few places, illuminating just enough to show the way. Yoana strained to see a path—oh, for a lamp or torch to light the way! She gave the horse more rein and bent low over its withers to avoid a limb.

Branches left a trail of moisture on their clothing as they squeezed through thick brush onto a thin trail, probably a path for the forest animals. As the horse followed the winding trace, Yoana twisted in the saddle to look back at Leya. Her señorita swayed for a moment, then straightened. Leya had to be exhausted. Her health had been frail ever since the incident that scarred her both inside and out.

The horse danced as Yoana tugged on the reins to get him to slow. She waited for Leya to catch up. When her señorita came alongside, Yoana grasped the woman's hand and gave a slight squeeze before the horses pranced a step away.

She leaned close to be heard. "We'll be home before long. You can rest then. Sí?"

Leya nodded and pushed her *mantilla* back over her head, something she only did when she and Yoana were alone. "Do you think you can find the way home? I lost track of where we were going hours before we arrived here. Yoana, we must stop and pray about this. God knows what He wants us to do."

"Leya." Yoana tugged a little too hard on the reins. The horse snorted and shook its head. "I have prayed for years and look what that brought me. My father despises me. My betrothed turned his back on me."

She clamped her lips together to stem the anger that tinged her words. She didn't want to hurt Leya, but the anger and pain had built to the point where she couldn't stop the flow. "I even tried to pray after my father's declaration about Gabrio this morning, which was followed by this debacle. We were captured not once, but twice, by bandoleros. Men died. My reputation is ruined." Yoana bit her lip to halt the venomous thoughts pouring out. She could almost see the hurt in Leya's eyes. Her señorita knew all about ruined reputations.

She drew in a calming breath. "There is a time for prayer and a time to act. Now, let's go before those desperadoes wake up. When we are out of this canyon, we'll stop to pray." Before Yoana could turn her horse, Leya's fingers dug into her arm.

"Yoana, remember the disciples in the boat when the storm came up? They needed to pray right then. We have to do that too."

"They were frightened." Yoana shook back her braid. "I am strong and not afraid of these men. We are free and will thank God when we are safe." She pulled her arm free and nudged her horse on down the trail. As she moved off, she glanced back to see Leya tug her *mantilla* over her cheek and follow.

They crested a small rise and started down a short slope. How steep were the canyon walls? Dusk had been setting in when they arrived, so she didn't have a feel for the terrain. The trees and undergrowth, combined with the darkness, kept her from knowing if they were even going the right direction. She thought about turning around, but she knew that way led to the temporary corral and capture.

Her horse flicked his ears, his nose lifted to catch a scent. She could feel tension thrum through him. What did he sense? A wild animal? She didn't hear or smell anything unusual. Bears were common in the mountains, but they made some noise as they passed, didn't they? The horse slowed.

She tilted her head back to sniff the air. Was that smoke? Had the campfire smoke drifted this far through the trees? She glanced back to see Leya's horse acting skittish. Her mount shied and snorted. He turned his head, and she could see the whites of its eyes. Her heart pounded. Her hands shook on the reins. Silence pressed on her ears. She strained to hear anything amiss.

Leya screamed. Yoana's horse leaped to the side. Her leg scraped hard against a tree branch. Leya cried out again, this time more muffled. Yoana fought to control her animal. He reared and shook his head, ears laid flat against his head. Leya's mount thundered past her. Yoana's horse lunged after the other one, but she pulled his head around to keep him from bolting.

He finally calmed enough for her to look for Leya. Yoana's breath scraped in and out as fear clutched at her chest. A few yards away, in the shadows of a giant pine, she could see the outline of a man. He held Leya's limp body against his. In his right hand he had a long-bladed knife held to Leya's throat.

Yoana froze.

Leya roused. Her head lifted a fraction. "Run, Yoana! Go!" The knife poked into her throat. Leya gasped and stiffened.

"Leya." Yoana leaped from the horse's back. She couldn't ride off and leave the only friend she'd had since her mother's death. "Stop." If only she had a gun, a knife of her own. Some way to stop this man from hurting Leya.

Brush rustled beside her. Before Yoana could turn, Amado stood beside her, his hand on her arm. She didn't even wonder how she knew him in the dark. For some reason, she wanted to melt with relief that he'd come.

"Cisto, let her go." Amado's authoritative tone gave Yoana strength. "Killing her won't help anything."

"They were trying to escape." Cisto's growl sent a shiver down Yoana's spine. She could almost see the shudder of fear that went through Leya. "They deserve to die."

"So you're telling me if someone captured you, you would be compliant and just go with them?"

Yoana almost smiled at the mockery in Amado's words.

"That has nothing to do with this. Women are different." Cisto moved his knife a fraction away from Leya's neck. Yoana stiffened her resolve. She wouldn't let this bandolero know how much he terrified her.

"Don't kill her." Amado released Yoana's arm. His hand hovered over the butt of his pistol. His fingers flexed. His whole concentration seemed focused on Cisto and Leya. Yoana held her breath, afraid even to move.

Cisto dragged Leya into a shaft of moonlight. She trembled so that he seemed to have trouble holding her up. Yoana remembered Leya's insistence on them praying before they continued. Would that have helped? Yoana didn't think so. Like her father, God would expect Yoana to prove her worth every step of the way. And, like her father, God wouldn't want to see her or be reminded of her presence. She knew Leya didn't agree with that, but she'd seen no proof otherwise.

"Muy bien. They'll go back to camp with us." Cisto lowered the knife. Amado relaxed a fraction, but his gaze stayed steady on the other man. "But they'll be tied up at night time. They can't be allowed to ride on their own either. Understood?"

"Agreed." Amado nodded. He grasped Yoana's arm. "Yoana will ride with me. Leya can go with Miguel."

"This little one can go with me. I don't care about her ugly face."

Yoana gasped. She opened her mouth to berate Cisto, but Amado's grip on her pinched. She glared at him and saw the slight shake of his head. Yoana gritted her teeth against the harsh words that threatened to suffocate her.

Lorenzo stepped out of the shadows onto the path. "What is happening?" He looked from Cisto to Amado.

"We had a little problem with the women going for a midnight ride." Amado's light tone belied the tension in the air. "Maybe you could whistle for Tomás to help you with the horses. I'm guessing the pen might be open, and the herd will need to be rounded up again."

"I'll get on that." Lorenzo went over to the horse Yoana had been riding and gathered up the reins. Leya's horse had returned, and Lorenzo left, leading both animals. A moment later, Yoana heard a piercing bird call that sounded like a hawk on the hunt. That must be Lorenzo sending a signal to Tomás.

"We need to get these women back to camp." Amado gestured for Cisto to lead the way with Leya. Cisto curled his lip into a snarl, as if he wanted to object to Amado's forwardness. Instead, he turned and jerked Leya with him into the trees.

"Let's go." Amado's grip had eased, but he didn't release her. Yoana walked beside him, the scent of the campfire smoke growing stronger as they went.

"Why didn't you just kill him?" Yoana glanced up at Amado's darkened face, wishing she could see better. "You could have shot him and let us go."

"If he hadn't stopped you, I would have." Amado slowed their pace.

"Why? I thought you would help us escape."

"Not from here. You have no idea where you are, do you?" Amado asked. "These mountains are dangerous. There are grizzlies and other animals that can kill you. If you went the wrong way, you would end up on the other side of the mountains. There isn't much there. Especially water. You could both die of thirst. I wouldn't let that happen."

"You could have killed him and taken us home." Tears burned Yoana's eyes. She didn't really want Amado to kill another man, but she couldn't figure another way out of this.

"Have you forgotten that there are three other men out there? Lorenzo, Miguel, and Tomás may not seem as bad as Cisto, but they are bandoleros. They've chosen this life for one reason or another. They are as loyal to Victoro, the leader, as a bandit can get. They would have killed us all and not thought anything of it. Is that what you want?"

Yoana bit her lip. She didn't know what to say. What to do. The hope she'd felt while on that horse was gone. Now she was as empty as a dry well. "I just want to be home." She spoke through a throat tight with pain.

"I know."

Amado's thumb traced a path up and down the inside of her arm. Yoana caught her breath at the unexpected sensation. "Then, please. Help us." She looked up again as they came to a patch of moonlight. Amado's face hardened as she watched. His grip tightened a fraction.

"I can't do that." As he spoke, they stepped into the small clearing where the campfire burned low. Cisto and Leya were there. He'd forced Leya down next to the tree near the overhang where she and Yoana had slept earlier. Cisto had a rope, and was in the process of tying Leya to the tree.

"You can't tie her that tight." Anger tinged Amado's voice as he strode over to Leya. Yoana trotted to keep up with him. "You'll cut off the blood flow, and she won't be able to sleep."

"I don't care if she sleeps." Cisto straightened, his hands on his hips. "They interrupted *my* sleep. Why should I care about theirs?"

"We're bringing them to Victoro in as good a condition as we found them." Amado knelt down to loosen the ropes.

Cisto's laugh grated. "Just like the horses. Eh?"

Amado motioned for Yoana to sit down beside Leya. He tied them both so they could lean against one another. The mountain temperature continued to dip, and the warmth would be good. Yoana tried to keep her arms apart so she could slip from the bonds, but Amado must have anticipated her trick. He pulled her wrists together and tied them tight enough that she couldn't get free, but not so tight that she and Leya would be in pain.

As Amado covered them with a blanket, his eyes met Yoana's. She could see conflict in his gaze. Did he want to let them go? She hoped so, but wasn't sure any more.

He almost looked like he wanted to say something, but shook his head and rose. He crossed to a nearby tree and sat down, his gaze on them. Rain-washed air brushed Yoana's cheek as she settled closer to Leya.

She'd missed this chance to get home, but another would come.

And she would be ready.

The next few days passed in a continuous haze of tension and fear. They wound through the mountains, going through so many canyons, switching from one trail to another, that Yoana knew she would never find her way back out. Once, when they crossed over the crest of a hill, Yoana caught a glimpse of plains far away. She didn't recognize anything. She didn't know if the foothills below were part of her father's rancho or if home was the other side of the mountains.

Leya rarely spoke. After Cisto's harsh remark about her scars, she withdrew. Even Yoana couldn't get her to talk. A few times at night, Yoana could hear Leya mumbling, most likely praying to God. Why, she didn't know. He didn't seem to care at all about what had happened to them.

On the fifth morning, Lorenzo woke them while the shadows were still so deep Yoana had to lean close to lace her shoes. He fixed coffee and brought out some dried beef for their breakfast. Excitement ran high. Yoana could feel it thrumming in the air. All she wanted was to escape, but there had been no other chances. All day she rode in front of Amado, who had become wary of talking with her after Cisto accused him of trying to return the women in the hope of gaining money. Every night she and Leya were tied to a tree to sleep. The bandoleros made sure they had no opportunity to escape.

Being trussed up at night allowed them fitful bits of sleep, but no real rest. Often during the day, Yoana would drift off. When she came awake nestled in Amado's arms, for a moment, the desire to snuggle closer overcame her determination to be home. She hated to admit how much she enjoyed the smell and feel of him.

Then comprehension would return.

"*Vamanos*. Let's go." Lorenzo and Miguel had the horses saddled before Yoana had eaten her meal.

"Give the women time to finish." Amado threw the dregs of his coffee into the fire, sending up a cloud of smoke that made Leya cough.

"Then we'll go on ahead." Lorenzo motioned to Tomás. "Miguel can come with you. Tomás and Cisto will help me with the herd. We'll see you there." Lorenzo swung onto his horse and headed up canyon to the small pen that held the rest of the animals.

"Why is he in such a hurry?" Yoana stood and stretched. Her muscles ached from the constant riding and the uncomfortable positions she slept in. She wanted to take a long walk and ease the stiffness before climbing on the sorrel for another day. Maybe soak in a hot bath until her skin wrinkled like a prune.

"We'll be in camp by midafternoon." Amado kicked dirt over the fire to smother the flames.

"Camp?" Yoana couldn't breathe. She'd known this time would come, but now that it was here, fear held her immobile. What would happen to her once they arrived? To Leya? How could they ever escape? The dried beef soured in a lump in her stomach.

"Hey." Amado stepped over to her and lifted her chin with one finger. "You'll be fine." Yoana watched his eyes. He didn't look like he meant what he said. Did he, too, wonder what would happen to her? In a camp full of bandits, how would she and Leya survive?

CHAPTER SIX

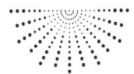

Anger churned like boiling stew in the pit of Lucio's stomach. He tugged his hat low over his eyes as the first fat raindrops fell from the sky. He wanted to curse, to hit something. First these men killed Manuel. Now the storm had moved in too fast, and they would lose the trail when the tracks washed away. Night would be here soon. This day had gone from bad to worse.

Ramón leaned low over his mount's withers. Lucio knew his friend wanted to be fast. The problem had to do with the confusion of the trail. More than once they'd had to backtrack. The two men who'd taken Yoana and Leya had joined with the herd, or part of it, at one point. They'd picked up speed only to discover later that the two bandoleros left the others at some point. They'd lost time going back to pick up the trail, thankful one of the men rode a horse with a distinctive track.

They rode in silence. Lucio didn't want to distract Ramón, so he kept quiet. The need to talk clawed at him. He had to do something to shut out the sight of Manuel's dead body. Manuel might have been hired help, but he'd been at the rancho for years and Lucio counted him a friend. Sending his amigo's body back with

Paulo had been hard. Finding Manuel's killer had become almost as critical to him as finding his sister and his tía.

A rumble of thunder shivered through the air. The clouds opened up and rain poured down on them. Lucio watched the ground turn slick as dirt became mud and lost all definition. Lucio led the way to a copse of trees and took shelter under the branches. Beside him Ramón wiped the moisture from his face with his sleeve.

"Any idea where they're headed?" Lucio hoped Ramón knew these mountains better than he did and might have an idea where to look.

"Not with the way they keep changing course." Ramón smoothed his droopy mustache. "They're smart. They've worked hard to confuse the trail. I'm not sure what direction they'll go next."

"Is there any way to keep following them?" Lucio stared up at the heavy sky. A bolt of lightning illuminated the edge of a cloud.

"I have a couple of ideas." Ramón twisted the tip of his mustache. Droplets of water dripped onto his fingers. "There are canyons not far from here that might provide shelter for the herd and for the people. We can head that direction."

"And the other idea?"

"We can continue as we are. As long as they travel under the trees on occasion we can still find their tracks. The problem is I think they're making for a couple of rockier areas. They're in the open and any trace of their passing will be wiped away within a few minutes. This rain is too hard." Ramón twisted in the saddle to look at Lucio. His eyes questioned what his boss wanted him to do.

"Let's try to follow the tracks as long as we can. If we lose them, then we'll look in the canyons you're thinking about." Lucio took his hat off and hit it on his leg to knock the rest of the raindrops off. His dun snorted, jangling the bit as he shook his head.

"I have to do what I can. We can't just turn back until we've given it our all." Lucio wouldn't let himself consider any scenario in which they went home without the women.

"Agreed." Ramón clicked his tongue. His big bay moved out into the deluge. "Let's head for those trees." Ramón indicated a stand of pines that would have been in a direct line of the trail they'd been following.

Lucio's horse followed Ramón's. He shuddered as a stream of water soaked the back of his shirt. This early in the spring, the air still held a hint of winter. When the storm moved in, the temperature had dropped. He'd been chilled even before the rain started. He couldn't imagine how hard this must be for Yoana and Leya. They weren't used to such conditions.

The rain continued. Lucio could see Ramón shivered too. Neither one of them had been prepared for this deluge. What he wouldn't give for a nice heavy poncho right now.

They slogged on through the mud. The ground turned treacherous. Even the drier areas under the pine needles turned slippery, more so as the afternoon progressed. As the shadows under the trees deepened, Ramón climbed from his horse to kneel down and search for sign.

"Lucio." Ramón straightened from studying a patch of protected ground.

Lucio could see the rivulets of water running through the moisture-laden grass.

"I've lost them. I believe they're headed up there." The vaquero pointed to a rocky escarpment uphill from their current location.

"We can try to skirt around that area. See if we can pick up the trail." Ramón shook his head. His dark eyes spoke his regret. "But I don't see that happening with all this rain."

Lucio nodded. He didn't know what else to do. They couldn't go back and pick up the trail of his familía. Maybe Antonio or Berto had discovered something while following the horses. "Let's head back. We'll try to find the others and see what they know."

Ramón reined his bay around and headed back into the steady

rain. At least the downpour had slowed. Not that it mattered. They were still soaked and cold. That wouldn't end until they returned home.

"Tomorrow we can scour the hills." Ramón tilted his head to look at Lucio from under the wide brim of his hat. "We know the general direction they were traveling. We can section off the mountains and try to cross their path."

"You're right." Lucio peered up at the gloomy slopes. They both knew the futility of the actions. These mountains went on for miles. There were more canyons than they could count. Who knew how far the bandoleros were traveling? Perhaps they weren't even staying close to here. Maybe they only wanted the horses to take them up north to sell. If so, there would be no hope of finding the women. Lucio shut off that fear before it could take root.

By the time they reached the corrals at the rancho, night had fallen. The rain had stopped, but the air still hung heavy with moisture and the threat of more rain. His heart hurt as the thought of his sister and tía at the hands of those men.

In silence, Lucio worked alongside Ramón as they took the tack from their tired mounts. Two of the stable boys appeared to lead the horses away and tend to them. Even they were quiet, unlike their usual chattering. The oldest boy nodded to Lucio's inquiry about Antonio and Berto's return. They had come in, but he didn't say how long ago.

The warmth of the bunkhouse hit Lucio when he stepped in the door. He hadn't realized how cold he'd become until now. He'd been so focused on Yoana and Leya's plight that he'd pushed his own discomfort to the back of his mind. From the corner of his eye, he saw Ramón shiver.

"Go change clothes and get something to eat." Lucio slapped Ramón on the shoulder. "You've earned a good hot meal. I'll meet you in the kitchen as soon as I talk with Berto and Antonio."

A few minutes later, Lucio strode into the dining room. The

scent of spices and roasted meat made his stomach protest. Berto, Antonio, and the three Santiago men were all seated at a long table, platters of food in front of them. Their clothes were dry, so they'd had time to change. Lucio could tell from the dampness of their hair, they hadn't been here long. One of the Santiago men had his arm in a sling.

Berto dropped his fork and stood. The hopeful look on his face faded when Lucio shook his head. A heavy silence fell over the men.

"Sit back down, Berto. Eat." Lucio grabbed a plate, rounded the table and sat across from him. "Tell me what happened."

"They split the herd into two groups." Berto sat back down, but didn't eat. "We split up to follow both of them. When the rain came, we tracked them until they joined back up. We thought we'd have them even though the prints were washing away."

Berto glanced down the table at the other men. Lucio followed his gaze to the man with the injured arm.

"They must have left one of the men behind. He shot at us." Berto nodded his head toward the Santiago vaquero. "We all dove for cover, but he winged Genaro with the first shot."

"How bad is it?" Lucio turned to face Genaro. Lines of pain radiated from the man's eyes. However, he seemed to have a hearty appetite.

"I'm fine." Genaro nodded. "It's just a scratch. Maybe the outlaw couldn't shoot straight, or he just wanted to warn us off. Either way it worked."

"So you didn't get him?" Lucio asked Berto.

"No." Berto stirred the meat on his plate with his tortilla. "We returned fire, but he had a good position, and we didn't. Every time we tried to move, he'd shoot. He stayed for quite a while. By the time we figured out he'd gone, the tracks of the herd had disappeared. We had to turn back."

"Where were you when you lost them?"

Antonio helped Berto describe where they'd quit the chase.

None of them were thoroughly familiar with the mountains, but their description gave Lucio a good idea where to look. He glanced over at Ramón, who had come in and joined the group. Ramón nodded in his direction. Clearly, he agreed with Lucio's thoughts, that the horses were going in the same general direction as the kidnapped women. Maybe tomorrow they would have an idea where to start.

The men quieted as Lucio and Ramón piled food on their plate. Lucio wished he'd taken the time to change into dry clothes, but finding out information had been crucial. Much more important than getting comfortable. He shivered while he ate, then stood to go.

"What about the horses we're to take back to Don Santiago?" Genaro asked.

Lucio paused. "I'll speak to Don Armenta. He may want to wait a few days to see if we recover the herd. If not, we have other stock. I'll see what he wants to do and let you know in the morning."

"Thank you." Genaro and the other men nodded.

Ramón sent Lucio a sympathetic look. None of the men who worked here would envy him this confrontation with the don.

And that's just what it would be--a confrontation.

Shivers tracked through Lucio a few minutes later as he scrubbed at his skin with a dry towel. Would he ever get warm again? The chill had settled in his bones, and he would do good to keep from getting sick after today. His thoughts drifted to Yoana and Leya. They had to be even more miserable, considering they were still outdoors and probably soaking wet.

He stood in front the fire he'd built in his room as he dressed. After he tugged on a dry pair of boots, he put his head in his hands. He loved Yoana. He did love her. Yet for years he hadn't had the courage to show her or to admit to himself that he cared for her. Like his brothers--except Mateo--Lucio had bent to the demands of their father, which meant ostracizing Yoana.

How could he have done that?

"God, I know I've done wrong by her. Help me to make it right. Please protect Yoana and Leya. Help me find them."

Anger welled inside him at the injustice. He pressed his fingertips to his eyelids for a moment before he surged to his feet. Regretting his past inaction wouldn't help anyone. He swept his fingers through his hair to comb the wet mass into a semblance of order. His boots echoed as he strode through the house to his father's study.

The door stood open. Don Armenta sat at his desk bent over his ledgers. Who would the don find to help with the figures now? Yoana had done it for years when no one else in the household quite understood the math. Yet his father wouldn't admit Yoana had been good for anything. Anger burned deep in Lucio's gut.

He came to a stop in front of his father's desk. Don Armenta didn't look up. Lucio couldn't recall a time when his father showed favor toward anyone. He always made the person wait until he was ready to talk with them. Don Armenta lived for power.

Lucio watched as his father scratched some figures in a ledger. He'd never noticed how gnarled his father's hands had become. He seemed to have trouble holding the pen because his fingers were twisted at an odd angle. Lucio blew out a soft breath. He didn't want to feel anything for his father, least of all sympathy. He didn't want to consider that the don might be suffering.

"Did you get the horses?" His father set the pen down on the desk and leaned back in his chair. His black eyes bored into Lucio without blinking, something that always set Lucio on edge. The don had been apprised of today's events. Why had he only mentioned the livestock?

"No. The bandoleros split up. We followed, but the rain came, and we lost them."

"I didn't ask for excuses." Don Armenta's chair squeaked as he sat forward and put his clasped hands on the top of the ledger.

"I'm not giving you excuses. I'm telling you what happened." Anger fought a war with discomfort inside Lucio.

"I heard Manuel was killed. Any other losses?"

"They shot one of the Santiago vaqueros. He'll survive though."

Don Armenta nodded. "How soon will you be able to recover the horses? I'm sure Don Santiago will want them, and the men, back as soon as possible."

"We plan to go after them first thing in the morning. If we can't recover the horses, should we cut some from our other stock?"

The don's thick eyebrows drew together. "You will find them. It shouldn't be that hard to follow fifty horses."

"That depends on the weather." Lucio glanced toward the window. "We have a general idea of where they might be heading, but they could ride all night and change course. We don't know their destination." He took a deep breath. "Another thing. I don't really care about the livestock. What I care about is getting Yoana and Leya back home before harm comes to them. Why is it you haven't even asked about them?"

"Your sister did a foolish thing today. But then, she does this often. Finally, she's paying the price for her insistence on charging off on her own. I'm sorry Leya got caught up in this, but they will have to live with the consequences."

Don Armenta waved his hand. "Your sister is worth nothing now. There isn't a man who will want her other than those bandoleros. They can have her."

Lucio stood speechless for a breathless moment. "How can you say that? She is your daughter." He snorted a derisive laugh. "Not that you even call her by name or treat her as your own."

"Enough!" The don's lips thinned to a tight line. "It is not your place to judge me. Tomorrow morning take a few men and track down those horses. If you can't find them in the next three days, we'll cut another fifty from the herd down by Mattias's hacienda." He pushed back his chair and stood. "It's late. I'm going to bed."

"This is a mistake." Lucio stood his ground and hoped his father couldn't detect his fear.

"A mistake?" Don Armenta moved around the end of the desk with slow deliberate steps. His father had been this quiet and this angry many times.

And it never ended well.

"Yes. You can't simply write off Yoana."

"After what she did to your mother, I can do anything I want." Don Armenta glowered at Lucio, his extra two inches of height to his advantage. "My wife *and* my daughter died that day."

"Your wife, my mother, died." Lucio locked his knees to keep them from shaking. "Your daughter has been alive and well all these years. I let you treat her like she died, much to my regret. No longer. I will continue to search for her until I find her and bring her back home."

"No one will want her when those men finish with her." The don's face darkened like a thundercloud.

"I will." Lucio spoke softly, but he knew his father heard. "I'll want her. She's my sister. She's precious in God's eyes, and in mine."

"Then you can have her. Take her somewhere other than this rancho. I won't have her back after being soiled by those bandoleros." Don Armenta strode past Lucio to the doorway.

"You know." Lucio turned to face his father's back. The don halted but didn't turn around. "I didn't realize until now what a coward you are."

Don Armenta whirled, fists clenched at his sides.

"You're afraid of my sister. Most of all, you're afraid of admitting your own guilt." Lucio knew the truth as he watched his father's anger burn hot.

"Find those horses. Then get out of here. I don't need you on this rancho." Don Armenta stalked from the room.

CHAPTER SEVEN

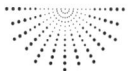

Smoke from a duo of campfires below layered through the trees. Shards of the late-afternoon sun pierced through. The buckskin stamped and snorted, tugging at the reins. Amado could feel the taut muscles in Yoana's arms. Her tight jaw must ache. She hadn't relaxed since Lorenzo went ahead of them, even though Amado dallied on the way to camp. He'd tried a few times to strike up a conversation, but she wouldn't speak to him.

Below, Victoro, Lorenzo, and Cisto huddled together deep in conversation. Women scurried around the cooking area, paying little attention to the children galloping through camp like crazed mustangs. The new horse herd must have been examined and the animals moved to the corrals at the back of the canyon. Amado hoped Victoro would follow his suggestions for selling the horses. Before they left on this mission, the bandolero leader hinted he already had a buyer and they would get more money for these fine beasts than they received from the other herds they'd raided. Amado wanted to know the name of the buyer but wasn't privy to that information.

Yoana shifted in front of him. Amado relaxed his hold.

"There are children." Yoana shot him a narrow-eyed glance

before she leaned forward over the buckskin's withers. Wisps of hair had worked free of her braid. The silken bits sparkled in a shaft of sunlight. "And women."

When she turned this time, her lips were pursed and very kissable. Amado jerked his thoughts back from the edge of impropriety as she continued. "Why are there women and children? Were they all like Leya and me? Kidnapped?"

"The children belong to the women." Amado chose his words with care. "Some of them belong to the men in camp, but not all of them."

Miguel, with Leya in front of him, kept a tight rein as his horse danced in place, eager to go down to the familiar camp. "Victoro must be happy." He angled his chin toward the women scurrying between several cooking pots and a makeshift table. "Looks like they're getting a feast ready."

"A hot meal sounds good." Amado's stomach rumbled. With only a slight twinge of regret, he gestured toward the trees at the back of the camp. "Is that Feliciana with Tomás?"

The dimple in Miguel's cheek disappeared as he followed Amado's gaze. His mouth thinned, and he jerked the reins to send his mount lunging down the path. Leya's soft squeal made Amado regret his ploy to have a few last minutes alone with Yoana.

Yoana tensed as she watched Miguel's breakneck pace. "What's wrong with him?"

Amado kept his buckskin in check as he watched the bandolero's descent. "Feliciana is with Miguel, but she is very young. So is Tomás. The two have struck up a friendship that annoys Miguel."

Amado clicked his tongue, but kept his horse's pace slow. He didn't want this trip to end. He didn't know if he could keep Yoana and Leya from harm in the camp. He wanted to do what he could, but his promise to his father came first.

"Before we get down there, Yoana, I need to say again that I'm sorry you were taken. If I could have prevented it, I would have.

Victoro is a bandit leader, but he's not a bad sort, even if he does have a mean temper. Cisto is the one you have to watch. Rosalinda is the woman to watch out for. She is Cisto's woman, although she is much more loyal to Cisto than Cisto is to her. I don't think he cares one way or the other if they stay together."

"If you want to help, tell me how Leya and I can escape."

"Do you think you could find your way home from here?" Amado tugged on the reins as his horse lifted his head to nicker at the other horses. "Don't try to leave on your own, Yoana. Even if you could find your way, there are many dangers in these hills. Dangers that even your father's men would hesitate to face. I will do what I can to help you, but I'm new here. I've won some favors today, but we'll have to see how this plays out."

"Favors?" Yoana glanced back at him.

"I was the one who told them about Don Armenta's horses."

"You *what?*" This time Yoana did more than turn her head. Her eyes widened with disbelief, then narrowed in anger. "How could you do that?"

"I had a purpose." Amado shrugged. He couldn't tell her the truth. Only one other person knew his motivation. If Yoana knew the basis for his actions, she might compromise his ability to fulfill of his promise. He couldn't let that happen.

At the bottom of the slope, they were met with excited chatter. A line of children raced toward them, Teo in the lead. "Amado."

Maria and her siblings took up his name like a chant. Amado's heart warmed. Here were the reasons he hadn't brought destruction on this camp, as he'd first intended. At a gruff command from Victoro, the children veered off back into the pines.

Leya sagged atop Miguel's horse, looking more like an abandoned waif than a grown woman. On the far side of the camp, Miguel stood chest to chest with Tomás. Feliciana huddled against a cluster of rocks. Even from this distance, Amado could see her fear.

Amado couldn't hear Miguel, but he watched Tomás turn pale

and hunch his shoulders. Tomás tried to speak, but only stuttered. Tongue-tied, he turned away. Miguel turned to Feliciana, said something, then jerked her to her feet and into a rough kiss that she didn't seem to want. Even so, she knew better than to push him away.

"Hola, Amado." Victoro raised his hand as he turned from talking with Lorenzo. "These are beautiful horses you brought us."

The older bandit, his dark hair streaked with gray, leaned forward to peer at Yoana. His face lit in a huge grin. "I see you also brought a couple of young fillies to liven our camp." His guffaw caught everyone's attention. Even Miguel broke off his kiss with Feliciana to watch.

"But what is this one who is covered up like furniture saved for the guests." Victoro motioned to Miguel. "Bring this one to me."

Miguel moved to comply, and Yoana gasped as he jerked her companion from the mount so quickly the horse shied away.

"Easy." Amado tightened his arm around Yoana's waist to hold her still. "You can't do anything. I know you want to, but she's strong." He swung down and reached up to pluck Yoana from the saddle and set her on the ground beside him.

"You don't understand. This will be too hard for her." Yoana pushed against his restraining hand.

"You'll only make it worse." Amado encircled her waist with his arm, trying to make the gesture look loving rather than restrictive. He had the glimmer of a plan and needed to set the stage.

Everyone, even the children who were still wild horses neighing and stamping, crowded close to watch as Leya stood before Victoro. Amado knew each of the women must be thinking of what it had been like when they were first taken, yet none of them showed any fear. To do that in this atmosphere could be deadly.

"The one filly is very beautiful." Victoro gave Yoana an

admiring perusal. He turned back to Leya. "Now let's see what beauty has been hidden away." Leya started to move as Victoro reached for her *mantilla*. Miguel caught her hands and held her tight. Victoro ripped the veil off and tossed it to the ground. His expression froze. Gasps rippled through the onlookers. Isabel stumbled backward on her chubby toddler legs and began to cry.

From this angle, Amado could only see Leya's right cheek. Her flawless complexion, dusky cream with a bit of rose bloom from embarrassment, made the horror he'd heard of the other side of her face even harder to bear. He recalled the description of the long scar that ran from the edge of her right eye to the corner of her mouth. The scar puckered her mouth, drawing the right side of her face up in a perpetual grimace. Another scar ran from the edge of her jaw down her throat and disappeared into the neck of her dress. Pink and knotted, the welt resembled a twisted braid. How could she have been injured this way—and how had she survived?

Leya stood, eyes downcast, gloved fists clenched in the folds of her split skirt. Her obvious shame made Amado yearn to do something to intercede, but he kept his silence.

"Put the veil back on. You're scaring the children." Lorenzo stood in the crowd, his arm around Dolores, his woman. Laughter born of relief from discomfort wove through the group.

Victoro's wife, Pabladora, trod forward to inspect Leya. Pabladora, the mother figure of the camp, put two fingers under Leya's chin and lifted her face. The whole group seemed to hold their breath as they waited for an indication of what she would do. Pabladora set the tone of the camp, even though her husband held the title of leader.

"She will not wear the veil." Pabladora cupped Leya's scarred cheek in her work-roughened hand. "She is beautiful and strong inside. She will be fine without hiding." Her double chin quivered as she surveyed the quiet group. "If I hear anyone give this woman a bad time about something she can't help, I will be very displeased."

Amado almost chuckled. He couldn't have hoped for anything better. Pabladora's commendation and protection were as good as an army regiment following Leya around. No one would dare to hurt her. Or to make a disparaging remark about her.

Now, if only the same could happen with Yoana.

"Bring the beauty here, Amado." Victoro gestured at him to move Yoana forward. Pabladora narrowed her gaze. Yoana's beauty might be more of a disability than Leya's scars. Leya garnered sympathy, while Yoana inspired jealousy. At least among the women. Among the men...

She inspired a different emotion.

Cisto stood to the side with his woman, Rosalinda. He leered at Yoana as he nuzzled Rosalinda's neck and touched her in ways a man should only do to his wife in private. His black gaze met Amado's. Cisto caught Rosalinda's ear lobe between his teeth and bit until she squealed. Her cry and his low laugh took the attention away from Yoana for a moment.

"So, señorita, what is your name?" Victoro circled Yoana, as if inspecting a horse for purchase, before coming around to face her again. He stood, arms crossed over his massive chest and waited for her reply.

Yoana lifted her chin and didn't answer. Victoro glared at her. Pabladora's mouth thinned. "Your *name*." Victoro's voice thundered, and one of the children began to cry again. Isabel joined the wailing.

Amado squeezed Yoana's arm. Her head barely moved, but he knew she caught his look. Her slender shoulders straightened. Her full lips parted. "I am Yoana Ignacia Esperanza de Armenta." Pride undergirded her words. Clearly, she expected the bandit leader to recognize the name, and she probably thought he would respect her or, at least, her father.

She would be wrong.

"My, my, aren't we the fancy one." Rosalinda sauntered forward. Her full hips swayed in a seductive walk that caught the attention of every man. If Pabladora represented the mother figure in the camp, Rosalinda represented a far baser occupation. She did her best to keep all the men drooling after her, although none of them would dare touch her out of fear of facing Cisto's wrath.

She stopped close to Yoana. There they stood. Similar age. Similar height. Similar hair color. To Amado, Yoana's wholesome splendor outshone Rosalinda's sultry beauty. Rosalinda's dusky olive skin and hazel eyes were a striking contrast, but couldn't compare with Yoana's honey complexion and milk-chocolate eyes.

As Yoana's gaze sought his, Amado's knees wobbled, and he swore the connection moved the mountain.

"So, you're a fancy girl. Too good for the likes of us." Rosalinda's chin jutted out in her usual defiant stance. Legs apart, fists on hips, her eyes snapped an unmistakable challenge.

Yoana didn't back down. In fact, she moved half a step closer to Rosalinda until the two were almost nose to nose. "I am not too good for anyone. I don't belong here. They forced me to come. My señorita and I would like to go home."

"Oooh! A señorita!" Rosalinda's curved eyebrows shot upwards as she glanced around the gathering. "Dolores, do you have a señorita? Feliciana, do you?"

Dolores lifted her skirts and made a mocking curtsy. "I seem to have grown up, Rosalinda, and I can't find my señorita." She lifted her palms as Lorenzo tugged her against his chest and the pair shared a laugh.

Feliciana ducked her head against Miguel's shoulder and didn't reply. Feliciana rarely spoke and looked like a wraith next to Miguel's darker visage. An emaciated wraith. What kept her from blowing away on the lightest breeze?

"You see?" Rosalinda rolled her shoulders back. Amado knew

she understood what that did to all the men in camp. She often flaunted her full figure, even more when she thought she could inspire jealousy in Cisto. A glance in the bandolero's direction confirmed Rosalinda's ploy had the desired effect.

"You see," Rosalinda repeated, ignoring Cisto's glare. She swished the sides of her skirt and tilted her head to the side. "Dolores and I are grown up. We don't need a señorita to dress us and comb our hair." She lifted a hank of her brown hair and let the silken strands drift through her fingers.

Yoana's cheeks flushed, but her gaze didn't waver from Rosalinda's. This whole situation had to be difficult for a girl raised in a pampered home, yet she didn't act like she was out of her element. Admiration had Amado fighting his possessiveness. He'd forfeited any right he had to her, much to his dismay. If he'd known her other than through a few formal letters, would he have chosen a different path?

"Maybe your señorita is happy to be here." Rosalinda glanced over at Leya, who stood, eyes downcast, looking as if she wished she could sink into the ground. "She can be free to live her own life without catering to your every whim." Rosalinda smirked at Yoana.

"Leya is free." The color in Yoana's cheeks deepened. Her small fists clenched at her sides. "She is my tía and my companion. She chooses to be my señorita."

"My, my, feisty aren't we?" Rosalinda tossed her head. Her dark hair swirled around her shoulders. "What job shall we give the little princess, Pabladora?" Rosalinda lifted one of Yoana's hands and pried open her fingers. "Her hands are soft as butter. Maybe she is too valuable to make her work. Maybe she's only good for one thing."

Cisto's laugh held no humor. "Now you're speaking truth. I can help her with that work."

Rosalinda scowled.

"Around here, everyone works." Victoro's thunderous roar made Yoana jump.

Pabladora patted her husband on the arm. "I will find the right job for her." She spoke in a soothing tone, but her frown stayed in place as she studied Yoana. "I'm thinking Leya is very experienced in many tasks, but Yoana will start off with mending some of our clothing. That should be an easy enough for her. Lorenzo brought needles and thread from the last trip. We have a mountain of sewing to do. Yoana will be in charge of that."

Amado noted the panic that flashed across Yoana's face. Everyone else seemed focused on Pabladora. Before they could look back at her, Yoana had taken on a mask of feigned indifference. Only Leya had any reaction. She stiffened and opened her mouth as if to say something. A quick frown from Yoana made her duck her head again.

"Good, she can start with mine." Victoro nodded at Pabladora. "If I don't get some clothes soon, all these young women will swoon when I walk through the camp naked." He grinned at his wife.

Pabladora gave him a playful swat on the arm. "They would faint from shock, and that had better not happen." Victoro grinned and hugged her ample figure to him. He planted a noisy kiss on her cheek as she struggled in his arms. Pabladora giggled like a young girl and stretched up to kiss Victoro on the chin. "Let go of me, old bear."

Victoro released her and frowned again at Yoana, who still stood rigid as if she hadn't noticed the interplay between the two. "Right now, we need to determine who will watch Señorita Esperanza de Armenta. I don't expect she will stay here on her own. I'd like to keep her long enough to decide what to do with this lucrative little sweet that has dropped in our midst."

"She's mine." Cisto spurs jangled as he sauntered forward. His malevolent gaze raked Yoana from head to toe.

Amado wanted to step between them. He could detect the

slight shudder that ran through Yoana. "I believe I'm the one who caught her when she fell at my feet."

"Fell at your feet! I detect a good story here." Victoro chuckled as he studied Yoana.

"I'm the one who insisted we bring her back to camp." Cisto stopped next to Rosalinda, who had lost much of her bravado in the face of sharing her man's affections with another woman. "Amado wanted to let her go back home, even when she knew we were bringing the horses with us."

"She doesn't belong in a camp like this." Amado reined in his temper. He had to keep a cool head in this or Yoana would pay the price. "Besides, you have Rosalinda. You don't need another woman. I think Rosalinda is enough for any man."

At his comment, Rosalinda preened and snuggled against Cisto. He pushed her away. She stumbled back, tripped over a branch and almost landed on her backside. Her embarrassment turned to anger. This wouldn't be good.

"She is mine." Cisto dropped his hand to flex above his pistol. His eyes narrowed as he stared at Amado.

"Now, now, compadres." Victoro stepped between them. Cisto hunched forward, his fingers wrapped around the butt of his gun. Did the man intend to step around their leader and draw down on him?

Victoro's bushy eyebrows drew together as he studied Amado and Cisto. "If we are to take advantage of the money our little sweet is worth, Cisto, she will have to remain as pristine as she is now. With that in mind, I believe you will have to be content with Rosalinda."

The older outlaw chucked the saucy girl in question under the chin. Rosalinda winked at him. Victoro guffawed, probably at her audacity. "Since the *dulcita* has a señorita, we will make sure she can vouch for her good name. They will both stay in Amado's shelter."

Victoro's intense scrutiny settled on Amado. "You will not

touch this one. And you will be in charge of making sure she is still here when we decide how best to get money from Don Armenta for his lovely daughter. If she escapes. If she is eaten by a bear. If she is taken by Indians, or anything else happens to her, you will pay the price."

He grinned. "I should mention that no matter how many horses you have brought us, if the little filly escapes, your life will be forfeit."

Satisfaction gleamed in Cisto's eyes. Dread knotted Amado's gut. One thing he knew. No matter how many warnings he'd given Yoana about the dangers of trying to escape, she wouldn't stay put.

Even if her departure meant his life.

CHAPTER EIGHT

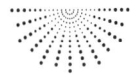

Yoana stalked after Amado, the gauntlet of stares making her skin crawl. A baby wailed. Feliciana hurried to lift the child from the blanket where the infant must have been sleeping. Anger fueled Yoana's resolve. Feliciana was little more than a child herself. How could these bandits call themselves men when they stole young girls and forced them to live in this manner? Maybe blurting out her parentage had been foolish, but at least it saved her from being forced into the bed of a man who would never be her husband. Who would never love her. Who would never protect her from her father's animosity.

Gabrio, why did you abandon me? Did your vow to me mean nothing?

At her side, Leya stared holes in the ground. Leya had been hiding behind her *mantilla* for as long as Yoana could remember. Without the familiar protection, she must feel very exposed.

The small shack Amado led them to appeared sturdy enough, thought the shoddiest buildings at the rancho were better built than this. Inside, shards of light sliced between the logs to pierce the dusty shadows. Leya stumbled on what appeared to be uncleared growth from the bare earth of the hillside. A rickety cot rested in one corner. At odds with everything else was a single blanket, neatly folded in the center of the bed.

"It isn't much." Amado swept his hand out. "I'll get another cot and blanket for you. I'll sleep outside the door."

He turned to Yoana. In the dim light, she could feel his gaze more than see it. "I can't stress enough the need for you to stay here. If you try to escape, there are untold dangers in these mountains. If you are recaptured, which you would be, you will belong to Cisto. He will not treat you well. He will enjoy inflicting pain. He always does."

His words chilled Yoana. They held the ring of truth. She shuddered at the memory of Cisto biting Rosalinda, who hadn't been able to hide the pain. Yoana had known from his smug expression that he'd done it on purpose to demonstrate his power over the woman.

She kept her expression blank, refusing to give Amado the satisfaction of seeing how his warning scared her. Beside her, Leya's fingers dug into Yoana's arm so hard Yoana thought the bone might break.

"If you attempt to leave, I'll have to tie you again at night. I don't want to, but I will." Amado took a step closer.

She could feel his warmth, so well remembered from their days on horseback. The woodsy scent that surrounded him, pine mixed with earthiness, drifted to her nose. Part of her wanted to reach out to him. To feel his arms around her again. To drift off to sleep with her head nestled against his shoulder—

What was she *thinking*? She could never be attracted to a bandolero, no matter how much of a gentleman he appeared to be.

"Can I trust you to stay?" Amado's low voice wrapped around her with a seductive pull. What *was* it about this man? She'd never experienced anything like him before. On the way here, she'd been so angry with him, yet when he talked to her, she'd been compelled to listen.

"I will do what is best for Leya and me." Yoana refused to back away from his magnetic pull that screamed danger. "That is the best I can promise."

"Then your best isn't good enough." Amado's features settled into a grim mask. "Do you realize you could get Leya killed if you try anything? Your life is of great value if they can get your father to pay a ransom. Leya is not valuable in that respect. If you don't comply, she will be the one to pay the price. With her life...or worse."

Yoana felt the blood drain from her face. Amado's words hit her hard. He kept his voice low, probably so those outside wouldn't overhear the exchange, but she could feel the force of his anger. She knew what he meant by *worse*. Leya had already suffered such indignity. Yet Amado's attempt at manipulation by using this example didn't have the effect he probably intended.

Fury burned away fear. She leaned forward, not caring that his presence tugged harder at her. "I will do what seems right. Leya will support me. I will not endanger her. I'll save her. And you will not tell me what to do." She tried to slow her ragged breathing, but the combination of rage and attraction were wreaking havoc.

Amado lowered his head until his nose almost brushed hers. "Get this, *Princesa*. I will tell you what to do as long as you are here under my protection. If you don't listen to me and do as I say, I will tie you up every night."

"And what about during the day?" *Why* was she taunting him?

"During the day, you will be doing chores with the others. There will be no time for you to slip away." Amado straightened and turned to Leya. Yoana swayed toward him before she caught herself. She wanted to cling to him. To tell him to stay with her. To chase away the nightmare that always crouched outside the door. The nightmare that hadn't left her alone since that fateful day years ago.

"Leya, do you need anything?"

His soft tone surprised Yoana. He spoke so forcefully with her. Why did he treat Leya with such respect?

"I will be fine, señor." Leya's response surprised Yoana even more than Amado's attitude toward her tía. Leya rarely spoke to anyone except Yoana, Don Armenta, and sometimes Lucio.

"I'll find out what your job is." Amado opened the door to the shack. The scent of roasting meat drifted through the opening. Yoana tightened her stomach to keep it from growling. She hadn't realized how hungry she was for something other than the dried meat that had been their fare for most of the trip. She didn't want to let bodily needs, such as hunger, overwhelm her desperation to get them back home. She must retain a clear head and make plans.

The door closed behind Amado. Yoana wanted to collapse on the floor and cry. Instead, she took Leya in her arms as the other woman began to sob. Leya had been quiet, strong as they travelled. Now her courage exacted a price. Yoana knew only bits and pieces of what had happened to Leya years ago, but this situation had to bring that horror alive again.

"It will be all right, Tía. I'll get us home somehow. I'll figure it out." Yoana rubbed Leya's back as shudders racked the slender woman.

"You can't, Yoana. There is no way we could find our way out of these mountains. We've traveled for days, twisting around through canyons and changing trails. How could you find the way home?" Leya leaned back and grasped Yoana's arms as she spoke. "Besides, you heard what their leader said. If we escape, Amado dies."

"Every time we crested a rise, I could see the plains beyond. All we have to do is watch for that."

"No." Leya's fingers tightened. "One side of the mountains is home, the other side is sure death. I overheard some of the vaqueros talk about a group of men who died trying to find their way across that desert. There is nothing but death out there. What if we get twisted around and go the wrong way?"

"I won't do that." Yoana tried to soothe Leya. "We would not be finding our way across the desert but around the mountains. There is a pass west of our rancho that we didn't go through. I kept track. When we leave, we will go west, find the pass so we don't get too high and run into any remnants of snow. Then I'll be able to find our way home."

"We can wait for Lucio to find us." The corner of Leya's mouth twisted up, puckering the scar on her cheek even more than usual.

"Lucio may not be able to do so. With all the rain, we can't count on him." She would not waste hope that after all these years one of her brothers would care about her. Lucio's words didn't always mean he would act. Not in the face of their father's ire.

"Then we will wait for your father to pay the ransom, and we'll be delivered." Hope sparked in Leya's eyes.

"You know my father won't pay anything to have me back. He's probably celebrating that I'm gone." Sadness at the truth of the statement threatened to choke her. Her father hated her so much. Forgiveness didn't exist in his vocabulary. Not for the offense Yoana had committed.

The door creaked as it swung open. Amado filled the opening, blocking out most of the fading daylight. "Victoro has changed his mind for tonight."

Yoana gasped. Horror thrust a fist into her stomach. Did the bandit leader want to send her to stay with Cisto? She swallowed hard against the bitterness and fear. The memory of Cisto's vile gaze shivered through her. Leya stiffened too, her face a pale oval in the dim light.

"Leya, Pabladora argued that you are to rest because you are more fragile. She is concerned about your health." Amado motioned to the narrow cot. "You can lie down there until supper. I'll wait to bring in more bedding until then so you won't be disturbed."

His gaze caught Yoana. She could feel the blood drain from her face. "Yoana, Victoro decided that since the men have been separated from their women for so many days, the women have the night off. You are to come and finish the supper."

"Cook? Me?" Yoana wanted to laugh at the absurdity. Her father had refused to allow her to be involved with anything around the house where he might run into her. He couldn't tolerate the sight of her. Leya had always been the one overseeing the house, giving orders through their cook.

Yoana schooled her nieces and nephews in her rooms. Her few stolen moments in the kitchen when her father left on business had taught her nothing. She knew nothing about cooking.

"Yes, you." Amado reached her in one stride and grasped her arm, his touch gentle, but firm. "The meat is roasting. There is pozole cooking that will need to be watched. Dolores has the dough for the tortillas made, so you only need to finish them in time to eat."

Yoana tugged against his hold to no avail. "I can't."

"You have no choice." Amado's hold tightened. "This is what Victoro says for you to do. No one goes against Victoro."

"But you don't understand." Yoana could hear the note of panic threaded in her words. She clamped her lips against the protests. How could she make him understand without appearing to be the pampered and privileged girl? "At least, let Leya help me." She shot an imploring glance at her señorita.

"Yoana, Pabladora is second only to Victoro in this camp. When she gives an order, it is to be followed. She insisted Leya should rest, and that is what she will do. Cooking at a camp isn't so different from cooking in your father's kitchen."

"But…" Yoana's teeth clicked together. She could see from the set of Amado's face he wouldn't be swayed. Girls always trained in the kitchen, even those from well-to-do homes. The flash of his eyes in Leya's direction reminded her that her tía's life and health depended on her cooperation. She gave a sharp nod, trying to quell the fear that threatened to overwhelm her. What would these men do to her if she ruined their meal? What would they do to Leya?

As Amado stepped toward the door, Leya caught Yoana's arm. "Wait, I need to speak to Yoana."

Amado looked back.

Leya met his gaze without flinching. "Alone. She'll be right out."

Amado nodded, stepped outside, and closed the door.

"What is it?" Dread threatened to steal Yoana's breath.

"Don't be afraid." Leya touch became gentle, and tears burned in Yoana's eyes. "Remember the verse from the Bible I made you memorize?"

"Which one?" Yoana gave a half laugh that carried a note of hysteria.

"God will never leave you nor forsake you." Leya's hand squeezed Yoana's fingers. "Don't be afraid. Ask for His help."

"Do you think God knows how to cook tortillas?"

"He knows everything." Leya's smile warmed some of the ice surrounding Yoana's heart. "You've watched as tortillas were being made. You can do this. You are very capable, and God is with you."

Yoana sniffed, and blinked away the excess moisture in her eyes. A few times she'd sneaked into the kitchen when her father was gone and watched the cook from the corner. Seeing should be enough, right? The cook made the process look easy. She nodded and hugged Leya. "Thank you, Tía."

"I will pray for you." Leya hugged her back. "You will see. God will work this out."

Outside the scent of pine vied with campfire smoke and roasted meat. Squirrels chattered overhead. The children, who had quieted earlier, raced through the trees, yipping like a pack of coyotes at play. The baby slept on a blanket near the kitchen area in the shade of a large pine. Yoana counted five children involved in the game of chase. The youngest toddled on the unsteady legs of one who hasn't been walking long. Their screeches scraped like horsehair bows down the strings of her nerves.

She followed Amado down the path to the cook fires. He showed her how to turn the meat so it wouldn't burn. Someone must have shot a deer earlier in the day, probably Victoro, since he'd been the only male here. The spitted animal dripped juice in the fire. The fat sizzled and sent up a mouth-watering aroma.

A large pot simmered over another bed of coals. Yoana could see the beans through the bubbling broth.

"You'll need to stir these, but Pabladora said they should be almost done." Amado indicated a long-handled spoon on a tree stump. Yoana picked it up and stirred around in the pot as she'd seen the women do in her father's kitchen.

"Here is the dough Dolores left for the tortillas." Amado lifted a damp cloth from a bowl. The yellow dough was as familiar to Yoana as water. She'd eaten tortillas made this way every day of her life. She used to love to watch the women in the kitchen pat the dough into shape and cook it on a hot stove, but watching and doing were different. Her father didn't even want her to observe or mingle with the women in the house, but maintained a need to keep her separate so she wouldn't endanger anyone else. She knew that had been an excuse at first to keep her out of his sight. His only concession had been to allow her to learn from the teachers who schooled her brothers and later to teach the young ones.

"It's getting late. I have to see to the horses." Amado let the cloth fall back into place. "The griddle is already in place over the coals." He pointed at the third small fire where a flat piece of metal rested on some rocks over the embers. "The others will be ready for the evening meal soon, so get started. I'll be back as fast as I can." He strode off along a trail that led toward the back of the canyon.

Quiet closed around her. Even the children had disappeared, their shouts of laughter faint in the sough of the wind through the trees. A thud like that of a blacksmith's hammer beat in her chest. Her palms slick, she wiped them against her skirt. She could go fetch Leya. Who would know? She and her tía could be gone before anyone missed them. Hope soared. Crashed. A futile thought. They had no horses. No chance of getting one since Amado would be at the corral.

Twilight crept through the forest on shadowed feet. Soon the trail out of here would be eradicated by darkness. Despite her bravado, she and Leya would never find their way in the unfamiliar territory. She swiped at her eyes with the back of her hand. That wasn't true. Soon. Soon she would find the way home.

Yoana looked around for a bucket of water so she could wash her hands. Her father's cook always insisted her staff wash before handling any food. When she found the bucket, Yoana cleaned her hands and shook them until they were dry. She didn't trust the crusty towel that hung on a tree branch nearby. She pulled a piece of dough from the mass in the bowl and began to try to shape it the way she remembered her father's cook doing.

No matter how hard she worked, the tortilla resembled an ill-formed blob with random spikes sticking out at the edges. Her father's cook always made perfect round ones, and the memory of how those tasted brought a lump that closed off Yoana's throat. Would she ever taste those tortillas again?

She flipped the misshapen piece of dough onto the griddle and began to shape another. A scorched odor caught her attention and she tried to flip the tortilla over with her fingers.

"Ouch!" She stuck her burned fingertips in her mouth. Black spots showed through the thin dough on the griddle. Yoana didn't even bother to wash her hand. Instead, she plucked the burning bit of food from the hot iron and flung it to the side. No one would be able to eat that thing anyway. Maybe the squirrels would take the evidence before anyone knew what had happened.

Yoana focused on forming the next tortilla. This one ended up looking like a road rut filled with water–long and lean. She tossed it onto the griddle and grabbed the next handful. Her mouthed thinned to a grim line. She could do this. She could.

Before she finished with the mound of dough in her hand, the one on the griddle began to scorch. She flicked that one into the forest too. This wasn't fair. Cook always did it this way, making one while the other cooked. The process never looked difficult when Cook did it. In fact, she did it so smoothly Yoana figured making tortillas should be something anyone could do.

She continued, but each small bit had to be tossed into the trees. The mass in the bowl depleted. Panic clutched at Yoana. She had to get this right. What would happen if the bandoleros arrived for their evening meal and found she'd ruined the tortillas? She flicked another tortilla on the griddle but didn't begin to form one. This time she counted to five and began to try to pluck the bread from the hot iron without burning her throbbing fingertips. She managed the feat before it burned so bad it couldn't be served. Triumph flowed through her. She could do this.

As she removed the tortilla from the heat and put it in a flat basket as the side, Yoana noticed the quiet. She couldn't hear anything. No squirrel chatter. They probably had a stomachache from the burned food. No children laughing. She glanced up to find a row of small faces, eyes wide as saucers, staring at her. Yoana paused. She tried to smile. Their solemnity, and her stress, stole any triumph she'd felt a moment ago.

The oldest boy, maybe five or six, held the toddler's hand, probably to keep the young one from ending up in the fire. The oldest girl, a little younger than the boy, held onto the other two children. Two of the girls had to belong to Rosalinda, one green-eyed, the other hazel, were mirror images of the woman.

The boy, with the round face and squashed nose, lifted one hand and pointed past Yoana. As she turned, she wrinkled her nose at the heavy scorched scent. The first thing she saw was the deer, the part closest to the flames blackened and on fire. As she hastened toward the meat, she caught the unmistakable smell of scorched beans.

"What is *this?*" Victoro roared as light flared. Yoana blinked. The bandit leader held up a lantern and stared at the ruined supper. Pabladora stood beside him, her mouth hanging open, as if frozen in disbelief.

Yoana moaned. Oh, if only a bear would rush from the forest and eat her! That would probably be more pleasant than her fate at the hands of angry—and hungry--bandoleros.

CHAPTER NINE

The stench of scorched food choked the forest air. Amado broke into a run before he rounded the last bend in the trail. The uproar of voices couldn't be good.

Yoana stood stiff as a statue at the edge of the cooking area. Her fingers twisted in her skirt were the only outward indication of her stress. Victoro towered over her, his face red and terrible in the firelight. She didn't waver or cringe at his onslaught. The other women scurried around the cooking fires like worker bees hoping to placate the queen.

Amado looked at Lorenzo, who stood with Miguel and Cisto, their faces dark. "What happened?"

"The princess just ruined our supper." Lorenzo spat the words as he made a rude gesture toward Yoana. "That woman is worthless. She burned everything. Probably destroyed the cooking pot too."

Pabladora and Feliciana were scooping beans from the smoking pot. Rosalinda had the deer off the fire and worked at slicing away the blackened portion of meat. Dolores's hands flew as she patted out tortillas and cooked them on the hot griddle.

Amado frowned at the small pile of tortillas and the almost empty bowl. What happened to the rest of the dough?

He strode toward Yoana. She hadn't seen him. Her whole focus stayed riveted on Victoro. The woman had a spine stronger than iron, but she needed to learn when to back down.

"What is wrong?" Amado addressed Victoro, but his attention stayed on Yoana. He didn't miss the flicker of relief at seeing him that flashed through her eyes before they shuttered once more. So she did feel fear. Good.

"This woman will cost us our meal for the night." Victoro almost backhanded Yoana with his wild gesture encompassing the cook area. She didn't flinch.

"We give her one simple task, and she ruins it all. How is it her father raised such a worthless señorita?" Victoro's roar echoed off the canyon sides.

Yoana's mouth pinched in a tight line. Amado knew enough of her background to know she'd heard complaints similar to this before.

From her own father..

"Victoro, there are enough beans for our supper." Pabladora moved up beside her distraught husband and took his arm. "Rosalinda will have the meat off in a few minutes. This isn't the first time most of us have eaten scorched food. We will share what tortillas Dolores can make. They may be smaller than usual, but we will not go hungry." She smiled and patted his rounded middle. "Not even my old bear."

Victoro's features softened as he gazed down at his woman. "You are a miracle worker, *mi dulcita*. What would I do without you?"

"You would be lost, of course." Pabladora pressed her cheek to Victoro's large arm. "Now go tell your men they won't faint from hunger. We will serve you in few minutes."

"Everyone will eat except this one." Victoro pointed to Yoana.

"She probably tried to kill us off on purpose. For this she will go without tonight. Amado, take her to your shelter and leave her. I don't want to see her again until morning." He glared at Yoana. "As for you, tomorrow you will make up for this by mending clothes all day."

Yoana opened her mouth as if to say something, but one glance at Amado and she pressed her lips together again in a tight line.

Good. She read the warning on his face.

Shoulders straight, she preceded Amado to the shack, where he collected Leya for supper. Inside the small hut, he lifted the lantern he'd grabbed on the way up. Leya's eyes asked questions, but Yoana shook her head.

Leya stepped outside. Amado stopped in the doorway, then set the lantern down and pulled Yoana close. She stiffened, but he didn't want anyone to overhear what he needed to say. "I will bring you some food when I bring the second cot. I'm sure you did not mean for this to happen." She relaxed a fraction against him. If he hadn't been holding her so close, he wouldn't have noticed.

In the flicker of light, he could barely make out her features. But her wounded tone of voice was clear.

"Maybe Victoro is right. If I could poison the lot of you, I would. Then Leya and I would go home and never think of you again." She whirled away from him to stalk back inside. Her foot hit against something in the dark, and she half fell onto the small bed. Amado held his breath to keep from laughing, grateful the whole contraption hadn't collapsed beneath her.

"Yoana." Leya took a step toward the hut.

Amado put out his hand and stopped her. He picked up the lantern. "Come with me." He motioned down the path. Leya complied, and they left Yoana in the dark.

A combination of strained tension and forced gaiety made the evening meal interminable. Leya sat apart from the rest of the group, the disfigured side of her face hidden. Amado watched as

Pabladora attempted to talk to Leya. When she had no success, she finally moved over to sit close to Victoro.

Amado chewed the tough meat, ignoring the bits of burned venison. The women had been able to get the beans off the top without stirring them, which minimalized the scorch flavor. His mother had done that a few times when his sisters were learning to cook. Even the small tortilla tasted good. He saved half of it and took a second portion of meat before it all disappeared. He folded the meat inside the bread and closed it in a cloth.

"Where are you going?" Victoro frowned at Amado as he made to leave the firelight.

"I need to take another cot to the cabin. Tomás said there is one in his cabin that we can use." He paused, waiting for Victoro's comment.

Pabladora spoke up. "I will send an extra blanket up with Leya. Do you need more than one?"

"One will be fine. I already had two and didn't need them both. Thank you." With that, he grabbed a lantern and strode off into the dark. The subdued gaiety of the normally rowdy group faded as he walked. Within a few minutes, he was at his own shack, opening the squeaky door.

"Yoana, I'm bringing in the cot." He came through sideways to fit the awkward bits of wood through the opening. He set the lantern on the floor. Yoana sat against the wall, a blanket tight around her. The chill from the evening mountain air slipped through the large cracks in the sides of the building. Had she fallen asleep while she waited?

Before he set up the second bed, Amado dug in his pocket and pulled out the cloth-wrapped food. "Here." He held it out to Yoana. "Something to eat."

He tried not to stare as she opened his offering and took a small bite. He knew she must be half-starved, but she ate with dainty bites, wiping her lips before she chewed. The need to sit down beside her and take her in his arms was so powerful he almost gave in. Her courage, her beauty, the knowledge she should be his, made him long to rescind his vow.

Amado watched her eat as he finished with the cot. He wanted to tell her what he knew of her. How he knew. His memory of their first meeting. But he couldn't compromise his brother's last request. He couldn't abandon the work God gave him to do. The job his father depended on him to complete. Even if it meant the sacrifice of his own life and happiness. And hers.

"I'll see if Leya is done with supper and bring her up."

Yoana started at his gruff tone. He steeled himself against the turmoil of emotions tearing him apart so they wouldn't bleed through again. His hand on the latch, he heard her say something. He turned back. "What?"

She held the cloth in her lap. Her braid wove over her shoulder, replaited while he ate. Her face needed to be washed. Her dress looked like a bear hibernated on it for a whole winter. Her cheek had a smear of soot. Still, her allure stole his breath.

"Thank you." She lifted the cloth. "For the food."

Amado nodded and left before he did something stupid. Like drag her from where she sat and kiss her breathless. Like steal her away in the night. Like forget his promise, marry her, and strike out on their own. Like take her home where she belonged.

Except she wouldn't belong there any more. She might be the daughter of a nobleman, but now she'd been soiled by association with outlaws. No one would believe her purity remained. Not even with Leya's protection.

Down the hill, in the shadow of a tall pine, something moved. Amado halted. Cisto stepped into the light. He grinned, stared at the shelter for an endless moment, then turned and sauntered back to the others.

EARLY-MORNING SOUNDS of women starting breakfast woke

Amado. He lay on his back and rubbed his eyes. Sleeping on the ground hadn't been a problem. He'd done that often enough. But he'd had trouble getting to sleep as he listened to Yoana and Leya whisper inside the small shack. Soft sobs wrenched him in the dark, but he couldn't tell which of them cried.

Maybe both.

The soft susurration of the wind through the trees threatened to have him dozing off again. He roused and stretched. The horses had to be tended before breakfast. After the fiasco of the past week, he would have to rethink his plan. Nothing had gone the way he intended. If he hadn't foreseen the possibility of Leya and Yoana being taken, how could he expect the rest of his plan to work?

By the time he returned, the camp buzzed with activity. Dolores's baby, Carlitos, had begun to cry, which happened most days. Amado couldn't recall an infant crying this much. Dolores, Rosalinda, and Pabladora all tried to soothe him. Only Feliciana had any success, and even that proved minimal.

"Morning." Amado knocked on the door before he entered. The girls had pulled the two cots together. They both sat on the bed that hugged the wall, leaning back against the rough logs. Leya ducked her head as he entered. Who had scarred her so terribly? The knife wounds were very old--at least he assumed they were knife wounds. The horror of that story would have to wait for another day.

"Time to go help with breakfast." Amado saw the dismay on Yoana's face and smiled. "There are many jobs besides cooking. You can help with serving or clean the dishes at the stream."

Yoana sat up. "There's a stream?"

"Just outside of camp. It isn't big, but it serves well for dishes and drinking water. Why?"

"Is there a place to bathe?" Her cheeks darkened. "I feel gritty from the trail."

Amado nodded. "I'll see that you get to the bathing hole today.

It's downstream, but not a long hike. We can ask Pabladora if there are any extra dresses that might fit you. That way you can have clean clothes."

Yoana pushed the extra cot out of the way and stood. She offered her hand to Leya. "That would be nice. We can wash these out at the same time. When they are dry, the other clothes can go back to whoever loans them to us. Then you can take us home."

Amado grinned. "You don't give up, do you?"

"No. I will not stay here, even if I put my life, Leya's, and yours at risk. It is something I decided last night. Leya understands." Yoana's defiant stance told Amado she wouldn't quit until she'd escaped. His amusement faded.

"I'm telling you again. Victoro isn't someone to test. He will have you whipped or tied up without food and water. He can come up with a number of punishments, which is a nicer way of saying torture. He will kill you, or Leya, without a second thought."

Amado grasped her hands, praying she would realize the seriousness of the situation. "And, as nasty as Victoro can be, he's a gentle lamb compared to Cisto. That man will hurt you and laugh. He'll listen to you scream and beg and cry, but that will only fuel his pleasure."

Yoana stared him straight in the eye and didn't flinch at his descriptions. "Then help us get away."

He sighed, released her, and stepped back. "I do not know how I can help you, but if there comes a time that I can, I will."

She studied him for a long moment before giving a brusque nod. Amado shoved the door and gestured for the women to precede him. Yoana marched past like a queen on parade. Leya started to follow, hesitated, and closed her eyes.

"Courage."

At Amado's quiet word, she opened her eyes. Instead of the fear he expected, Amado could see peace. Leya almost glowed with it. What happened to her during the night that brought on this change?

Throughout the day, Amado made excuses to stay close to camp. He worked on repairing some of the tack, a job that most of the men put off. They all seemed glad to have him working at it and left him alone. None of them seemed to suspect him of staying in camp to watch the newcomers.

Feliciana took Yoana and Leya to the stream to wash dishes after breakfast. When they finished, Pabladora brought out a couple of dresses large enough for both Yoana and Leya to fit in one garment.

"Dolores." Pabladora's sharp tone brought all the women to attention. "Take Yoana and Leya to the pool to bathe and wash out their clothing." The older woman frowned. "No argument. Keep a close eye. If they get away, Victoro will have your hide first and then Lorenzo's."

Dolores's expression lost her defiance. She motioned for the two captives to precede her and headed downstream.

Amado's heart tripped when Yoana came back to camp, her damp hair hanging to her waist in a loose mass. He hadn't realized her hair so would be long or wavy as it dried. The heavy mass glistened as she passed through thin beams of sunlight filtering through the trees. His fingers curled as he imagined the feel of winding those tresses through his hands. He noted Rosalinda's raised eyebrow as she watched him and dragged his thoughts back to his work.

Pabladora settled Yoana down with a needle and thread. She brought out a mountain of mending. Amado noted the look of panic Yoana sent Leya after as she surveyed the pile. Her hands clenched and opened. She sank to the stump beside the clothing and picked up the first piece.

Yoana's brow furrowed, she clamped her full lower lip between her white teeth and seemed to ignore everyone as she struggled to do the job right. Amado could sit here all day pretending to work while he watched her. Pure enjoyment.

Carlitos began to cry. Again.

If only he could take the infant to a doctor, but that wasn't an option. Today the baby couldn't be consoled. He screamed, drew his legs up, and kicked. His face turned scarlet with the effort.

Amado wandered over to the bucket of water and dipped out a cup. Rosalinda stalked over to Carlitos. She picked him up and screamed right in his face. The baby's arms waved in shock. Dolores came running to her son's rescue.

"What are you doing?" Dolores snatched the infant from Rosalinda.

"Can't you shut this thing up?" Rosalinda turned her wrath on Dolores. "He screams all day long. If you don't get him to be quiet, I will stuff a rag in his mouth."

"He can't help it. He is in pain." Dolores clutched the baby to her breast and backed away from Rosalinda. "He doesn't know better."

"Maybe you should take him to another canyon and stay. It's bad enough that we have all these other children running around yelling all day long. I can't listen to a baby crying nonstop." Rosalinda fisted her hands on her hips. "Cisto isn't happy with all the noise. He told me to do something about it."

"Lorenzo doesn't complain." Dolores glanced around, probably looking for Pabladora, who had gone downstream for a bath.

"Well, Cisto does, and he counts more than Lorenzo." Rosalinda's eyes flashed.

"Only because he beats you whether he is happy or angry."

Rosalinda flinched. She opened her mouth to retort just as Pabladora and Victoro came back to camp. Both women knew better than to argue in front of them, so they drifted apart. The baby hiccupped and quieted for the moment.

The afternoon waned. The men returned to camp. Tomás brought a brace of rabbits. Pabladora and Feliciana cleaned the meat and started a stew for supper. Dolores began a new batch of dough for tortillas, although she cast a few disparaging looks at Yoana as she worked. Amado noticed none of the women had spoken to Yoana, yet they all tried to talk with Leya. His heart ached for both of the women.

As they finished eating, Victoro's voice boomed across the camp. "Let me see how the sewing went." He handed his plate to Pabladora and clapped his hands on his knees.

Yoana's face paled. She had been picking at her own plate of food, but hadn't eaten more than a couple of bites. As Amado watched, a transformation took place. She seemed to realize they were all looking at her. She straightened, lifted her chin, and walked as regally as a queen to the pile of mending she had completed. She scooped up the folded clothes, carried them to Victoro, and dumped them on the ground next to him.

Amado winced.

Victoro picked up the first shirt, a small one that probably belonged to Teodoro, the oldest boy. Even from across the fire, Amado could see the large, uneven stitches that repaired a rip in the sleeve. Victoro didn't say a word. He put the shirt down and picked up a small dress. This time the tear had been on the skirt. The uneven mending left one side of the garment drawn up higher than the other.

Pabladora, seated beside Victoro, leaned over and muttered something to him. Yoana's posture became even more rigid and her cheeks reddened. She stared off into the trees, not looking at Victoro as he lifted another piece of clothing.

The last item, which would have been the first to be sewn, was a shirt of Victoro's. Amado remembered when Victoro caught the material on a protruding branch and tore a large area across the shoulder and down the back. The bandit leader held up the shirt. Black thread crisscrossed up the back of the shirt. Victoro frowned. Pabladora leaned forward to look at the front of the shirt. She said something else to Victoro, and he turned the garment around to look.

The look Victoro gave Yoana should have melted her in her tracks. Amado tensed. Victoro stood so he towered over Yoana. "Do you see what you did to my shirt?" He held up the offending garment. Yoana had sewn the back to the front. Victoro would not be able to put it on.

"First you burn our supper. Now you've wasted a day doing mending that will all have to be ripped out. You are as worthless as they come. I don't know why your father didn't take you out in the desert and let the coyotes eat you. He's probably celebrating his good fortune now that you're gone." The leader's roar trained everyone's focus on Yoana.

He bent down until they were nose to nose. "The next task I give you had better be done right. Otherwise, we might just leave you in the desert like your father should have done. Maybe he'll even give us a reward for that."

All of the camp burst into laughter except Amado and Leya. Yoana had paled during Victoro's verbal attack, but she stood her ground. Amado hoped she could find a way to please the bandit leader, because he knew Victoro wasn't above carrying out his threat.

CHAPTER TEN

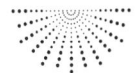

"Tomás!" Victoro roared.

Yoana bit her tongue to stifle a squeak. The needle she'd been using to coax a misplaced seam from one of Amado's shirts pierced her finger. A drop of bright red welled up and dripped onto the torn sleeve. She refused to quail in front of any of the bandoleros, but maintaining her aloofness used every bit of resolve she possessed.

Tomás trotted across the clearing, his spurs jangling, one hanging askew. He stumbled to a halt in front of Victoro and opened his mouth to speak, but nothing came out.

"Quiet." Victoro's hand sliced the air. "I'm sending you to Don Armenta's hacienda. You will deliver a note from me."

Color washed from Tomás' face, leaving his hollow cheeks the hue of chalk. Patches of stubble stood out in stark relief on his upper lip and chin. "M-m-me?"

Miguel snorted.

"Yes, you." Victoro glared down at the boy. "Pabladora has helped me with the note. You don't have to say anything, just give the note to Don Armenta and wait for his response."

Yoana shot a look at Amado. He understood why Victoro was

sending his least valuable man to do this job. No one expected Tomás to return alive.

"B-b-but, I..." Tomás clutched his middle as if he might lose his breakfast right there at his leader's feet. Chalk-white took on a tinge of green.

"No argument." Victoro clutched a handful of Tomás' shirt and jerked the boy until they were nose to nose. "You will do as you're told. *Entiende?* Understand?"

Tomás nodded. He shook so badly he resembled tree leaves in a strong windstorm. Yoana's heart ached for him. Her father would be relentless in his questioning. He wouldn't take the note at face value but would expect Tomás to tell him all he wanted to know. Tomás *should* be afraid.

"Good." Victoro released him. Tomás stumbled back but didn't fall. "Lorenzo, you will go with Tomás as far as the low hills and wait for him to return. Make sure no one follows you back to camp. Bring the horses."

Lorenzo strode from the camp toward the corrals while Victoro handed Tomás the note. "It will take you three days to reach the rancho. Maybe four or five to return, depending on how persistent they are in their pursuit."

He squeezed the boy's shoulder, his bushy eyebrows pulled together to form a line across his forehead. Tomás winced, but didn't pull away. "I'll expect you back in a little over a week. Maybe you will have some money to pay for the young señorita." Victoro shot a grin at Yoana.

Yoana's finger still smarted as she watched the pair of bandoleros top the rise out of the canyon. She wondered if she would ever see Tomás again. Her father would show no compassion just because the boy was young or a minion with no choice but to be the bearer of a ransom demand.

The days dragged by. Each one brought a new trial. So far, Yoana hadn't been able to do any of the tasks assigned to her without making a mess of them. When she washed the dishes, she dented them on the rocks or lost them in the stream. When she helped with laundry, she dropped the clean, wet garments in the dirt or wore holes in the cloth with her overzealous scrubbing. Even a simple task such as grinding corn in the metate proved too much. She'd scraped her fingers so many times, the ground corn turned red and had to be thrown away.

"Yoana, you need to tell Pabladora what you can do." Leya's soft words didn't carry far as she rubbed a salve into the scrapes on Yoana's hands. "Talk to her."

"They don't care about me, Leya. They only see me as a source of money when Tomás comes back from the Rancho." Yoana spoke up a bit to be heard over the children's whoops as they raced through camp. "Besides, the jobs I did at the rancho have no place here."

"You don't know that." Leya squeezed her hand before releasing her and screwing the lid back on the container. "God has you here for a reason, Yoana. Give Him a chance to show you what it is."

More likely her duties at home would be construed as those of a lady, and she would be mocked more than ever. Besides, what would a bandit leader need with someone who kept accounts and wrote correspondence? What did Victoro care that she had neat penmanship and a way with words. Did it matter to anyone here that she'd outshined her brothers in book learning? Or that she excelled at teaching her nieces and nephews?

"Yoana, help Feliciana dice some chilies. Rain will be here before lunch time, and the men will be cold and hungry." Pabladora added directions for Dolores, Rosalinda, and Leya. Yoana tried to ignore the relief that showed in Dolores's expression at not being assigned to work with Yoana. Feliciana didn't say much to anyone and didn't complain about working with her like the others did.

Feliciana grabbed some small green peppers from a bag and passed Yoana a knife. Yoana pitched her voice low so the others wouldn't hear. "You should have gotten some of the red ones. That way my blood won't show up so much." So far, Yoana had cut herself every time she'd tried to use a knife. Feliciana snickered, a sound so unlike her that Yoana paused to stare at the young girl. Feliciana ducked her head, hiding her pretty face behind a fall of hair.

"So how did you get so proficient at doing everything?" Yoana kept her back to the rest of the women and spoke under her breath. Maybe Feliciana didn't want to talk to everyone but would be more willing one on one.

The thin dusting of freckles across the young girl's nose stood out in stark relief to her pale complexion as she glanced up at Yoana. Large doe eyes caught Yoana's for a second before Feliciana looked back down. "My father owned a rancho, but my mother was not his wife. My mother worked for him, and I did too."

Yoana tried to hide her surprise. "Didn't your father treat you as his daughter?"

"No. He had many children. Everyone pretended my mother had been with some vaquero, but they all knew he was my father." Sadness laced Feliciana's words.

"I'm sorry. That must have been hard." Such cruelty Feliciana must have experienced in her home. Yoana had heard the taunts of other children toward those in such circumstances.

"God prepared me." Feliciana's quick birdlike glance over her shoulder told Yoana she didn't want this conversation overheard.

"What do you mean God prepared you?" Yoana asked.

"I am hurt many times by my father's children. The boys, they..." Feliciana attacked a pepper with such vigor the pieces were almost too tiny to use. "When I was taken by Miguel, the life in the camp was not as hard for me as it is for you. That is what I mean."

They worked in silence for a while. Yoana pondered what Feliciana said. Leya talked the same way, saying God had a purpose for bringing her here and a work she needed to do. So far, everything she'd tried ended in disaster. Was that God's plan? Hadn't she suffered enough in her father's home?

"I don't understand how you can see God in this. I was taught women were to behave in a certain manner or they would not be fit for God." Yoana clamped her mouth shut. She hadn't intended to say something so harsh to Feliciana. "I'm sorry, I..."

"No, don't apologize." Feliciana's eyes glittered with tears. "I know a woman should be pure until marriage. I will never have that in my body, but inside is a different thing. I have had no choice up until now. I told my father what his sons did to me."

"Were they punished?"

"No. I was beaten. Then my father found Miguel and gave me to him as long as he promised to take me far from the rancho so they would never see me again. He accused me of trying to ruin his sons by blaming them for despicable acts they hadn't done." A tear dripped from Feliciana's chin. She dashed the back of her wrist under her eyes and continued to chop the peppers.

Yoana's knife slipped. She missed slicing her finger by a hair. Her hands shook, so she set the knife down. Her heart ached for Feliciana. Life hadn't been fair to her, but life could often be cruel. People could be cruel.

"I may be with Miguel, but what choice do I have?" Feliciana stared up at her, pale features lighter than usual. "I don't know the way out of here. I don't ride well. There are many dangers, and I am not brave like you." Admiration tinged her gaze as she stared up at Yoana.

She couldn't speak. Her throat had restricted so tight she couldn't swallow. She wanted to cry at the injustice done to this sweet young girl. "How old are you?"

"I am sixteen last week. I did not tell anyone." A flush crept up Feliciana's cheeks as she went back to chopping peppers. "I did tell one person."

"One? Someone here?" Yoana picked up her knife again. She

worked slowly to keep the pepper juice from her injured fingers. The heat would burn for hours if she wasn't careful.

"Yes." Feliciana grasped Yoana's hand with her cool fingers. "If I tell you more, you must promise not to tell anyone else. Please?"

Yoana nodded.

Feliciana glanced at the other women who were all busy at their tasks. "Miguel has my body because he thinks I belong to him. I can't fight that. He is much stronger than me. But he does not have my heart. That belongs to another."

"Your heart?" Yoana paused to stare at Feliciana.

"My heart belongs to Tomás. He loves me too. We will escape here as soon as we can, and he will take me somewhere to marry me." A shy smile lit Feliciana's face. "That is why I know God loves me. He brought me here to find a very wonderful man."

"But he's an *outlaw!*" Yoana saw the fear in Feliciana's eyes at her raised voice. She darted a look at the other women. Thankfully, they didn't seem to have noticed.

"He does not choose to live like this." Before Feliciana could elaborate, the men returned to camp. Raindrops began to patter on the covering that had been erected above the kitchen area. The children screeched and raced back and forth--out into the rain and back to the fire, their shrill cries reverberating through the trees.

Yoana worked in silence alongside Feliciana. The men sat on logs around a separate campfire from where the women worked. Lorenzo and Cisto argued about something, but Yoana couldn't hear what. She could feel Amado watching her. He usually stayed close to camp, but this morning he'd gone with the others to help break the new horses. She overheard something about the buyer wanting them soon.

A screaming line of children raced past the women. Pabladora shouted at them, but they continued on without hesitating. Even the youngest, Isabel, with her short toddler strides, didn't slow down. Yoana tensed as they followed Teo, the leader, closer to the men. This past week she'd caught several examples of Cisto's temper when he backhanded Teo or Carmen for no apparent reason.

This time Teodoro was too quick. He dodged as Cisto's hand lashed out. Maria, right behind Teo, caught the slap. She flew backward through the air to land with a thud in the dirt. She spun around and knocked three-year-old Luis to the ground. Both children began to cry while the others huddled together under a tree, their eyes round with fear.

Rosalinda dropped the spoon she'd been using and raced to her children. Maria had a cut on her forehead. Yoana could see blood dripping down the girl's temple. Rosalinda turned to Cisto and began to berate him in language that made Yoana's ears burn. She'd never heard a woman talk that way, although a couple of times she'd heard the vaqueros use such coarse words when they hadn't realized she could hear them.

Cisto's hand flashed again. The crack of the back of his hand against Rosalinda's cheek sent her stumbling back. Her foot caught on something, and she sprawled on her back. Cisto, his face dark, strode over to her and jerked her up from the ground. He backhanded her again. Yoana could hear the crack from where she stood. She gasped, clutched the knife in her fist, and took a step toward the fighting pair. Feliciana's nails dug into her arm.

Feliciana's light freckles looked dark against her colorless face. "You can't. He will kill you."

Yoana shuddered. She looked back at the horrific scene. Maria and Luis huddled together a few feet from where their mother and Cisto fought. Rosalinda's lip and nose were swollen and bleeding. Cisto had scratches on his cheek deep enough to well red drops. He raised his fist again—

Amado caught his hand before he could strike.

Cisto released Rosalinda. She crumpled to the ground. He whirled to face Amado, his shoulders set, hand wavering above his pistol. "I will kill you for this."

"No, you won't." Victoro stepped between the two men, his back to Amado. He already had his revolver in his hand. "You'll go cool off and let your woman help with the meal."

Cisto struggled to get his temper under control. His hand flexed. Yoana could almost feel how much he wanted to draw down on Amado, but he would never be fast enough to get past Victoro. By degrees he relaxed, while everyone in camp held their breath.

"I'll go." Cisto turned and jerked Rosalinda up from the ground. "I'll go, but she goes with me. We need to have a little talk." He faced Amado as if challenging him to just try and deny Cisto this right.

Victoro nodded. "I'll hear nothing, though. You hurt her more, we'll come in there after you."

Cisto nodded and dragged Rosalinda to their shelter up canyon. The rain dripped down. Maria and Luis huddled together. The other children were under one of the tall pines where they stood to watch the scene. They all looked so scared, poor little ones. She slammed the knife down on the table where she and Feliciana had been working. Snatching up a rag, she bent down to get it wet in the wash water.

"What are you doing?" Feliciana asked.

"I'm helping those children."

"You can't." Horror cracked Feliciana's voice. "Cisto will be furious."

"That's just too bad." Yoana straightened and met Feliciana's gaze. "I won't allow him to frighten me so much that I can't reach out and help a hurt child."

Yoana stalked off, her head held high. At her approach, the men turned. Victoro's visage darkened. Amado said something low to the bandit leader, and he kept silence. Yoana knelt down beside Maria. Luis shook like a rabbit in a snare as he hid his face against his sister's dress.

"Let me look at that cut." Yoana smiled at the young girl and kept her movements slow, but steady. Maria flinched when Yoana raised the rag, as if she thought Yoana might hit her. From the scene that had just played out, it was not an unreasonable reaction.

As she began to wipe the blood from Maria's temple, Yoana glanced at the women. They were frozen in the act of cooking as they watched to see what would happen. Maria whimpered. Leya smiled at Yoana and nodded. Yoana turned back to the frightened children, sinking to the ground beside them, ignoring the few raindrops that made their way through the branches overhead.

"Come, sit on my lap." Yoana lifted the pair, stood, and carried them to a nearby log. Shivers shook Maria. Yoana smoothed the tangled brown waves back from the little girl's face. She hadn't seen any of the children up close this week, but when Maria looked up at her, Yoana caught her breath. A pair of forest green eyes gazed up at her, the color almost a reflection of the dark pine needles. She smiled as she cleaned off the last of the blood from Maria's forehead. "There. Better?"

Maria nodded, though she still trembled. Luis hadn't even lifted his head from Maria's shirt front. From the corner of her eye, Yoana saw the other children still huddled together, as if waiting to see what cruelty she would inflict on Maria and Luis.

"Would you like to hear a song?" Back home, Yoana's nieces and nephews loved her word games, songs, and stories. Maybe she could distract these children the same way. Maria stared, frozen, giving no indication of interest.

In a soft voice, Yoana began to sing one of her niece's favorites. By the second verse, Maria's shivers had eased. Luis turned his head to peek between his fingers at Yoana. The other children crept closer, intent on Yoana's song.

Las Iglesias son de azúcar, de caramelo dos frailes,
De melocha los monaguillos y de miel lost colaterales.

Maria giggled. "The church is sugar? I like sugar." Her bright eyes sparkled. Luis hid his face again, but at least he wasn't shaking like a rabbit facing a coyote.

"Want to hear more? Maybe Luis will like the song too." Yoana ran her hand over Luis's shaggy, dark hair.

"Luis doesn't like to sing." Maria patted her brother on the back. "He would like to play games, but Mama doesn't play games." Maria leaned closer and said in a loud whisper, "Not when Cisto is here."

"I know just the game to play with Luis." Yoana hadn't felt this carefree in days. "Luis, do you want to ride the pony?"

Huge dark eyes peeked at her.

"Mama doesn't let Luis ride the horses. She says he's just a baby, not big like me." Maria straightened.

"Well, this is a pony your mother would let Luis ride." Yoana couldn't resist giving the girl a hug. "Maria, you sit on the log beside me. Come here, Luis." Yoana lifted the small boy from his sister's lap. Panic tightened his features. She thought he might cry, but he didn't. She crossed one of her legs over the other and settled Luis on top of her foot. Clasping his hands with a firm grip, she began to bounce him up and down as she chanted the rhyme her tía had taught her.

"*Caballito, caballito...*"

Luis began to relax his tight hold on her hands as she continued they rhyme. Fear faded from his eyes and the his rounded cheeks dimpled.

"*Muy rápido*, Luis." As she spoke his name, Yoana lifted her foot higher. The small boy's hair bounced as he came down. Mouth open, eyes sparkling, his head tilted back, he began to giggle.

"He likes it!" Maria clapped her hands. The other children came forward.

"Would you like to do that again?" Yoana asked. Luis nodded, his tiny fingers clutching hers. She began the rhyme again as she bounced Luis up and down. He began to giggle, his small white teeth shining against his dark skin.

"Muy rápido, Luis!"

Yoana lifted the laughing boy higher in the air and lowered him until his feet touched the ground. Small fingers touched her leg. Yoana looked down. Isabel, Luis, and Maria's fifteen-month-old sister, grasped Yoana's skirt. Yoana caught a glimpse of hazel eyes before Isabel ducked her head.

"Luis, I think your sister would like a turn." Yoana lifted the young boy off her foot and picked up Isabel. She held the toddler with a firm grip and began the rhyme as she bounced her foot. Shy Isabel, who never talked to anyone, began to smile. On the final line, she too let her head fall back. Her melodious laughter filled the small clearing.

The other children began to clamor for a turn. Yoana laughed with them until her sides ached. A few times she noticed the women watching. Amado moved closer. He watched as she played with the children. For once the men weren't yelling about the children's screaming.

Warmth filled her. These children needed someone to care about them. Their mothers loved them, but they had no education, no way to teach them anything from books. Yoana could do that. She could teach them to read, to write, to do math, just like she did for her nieces and nephews when they were at the hacienda.

Could it be…?

Was this God's purpose for her here?

CHAPTER ELEVEN

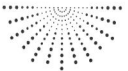

Flies buzzed in an annoying cloud around the dun as Lucio loosened the cinch to remove the saddle. The days had grown warmer, which meant the insects were increasing every day. Near the barns, no matter how clean they kept the stalls, flies congregated in clouds thick enough to choke a person.

Lucio lifted the saddle from the dun's back and tugged off the wet blanket underneath. His horse had lost weight from the daily trips to the mountains. Several days ago, he had quit asking Ramón to go with him. The Santiago vaqueros were long gone with a different set of horses. Everyone else had given up hope for Yoana and Leya, but Lucio refused to give in to despair. Maybe if he'd had some backbone earlier, Yoana wouldn't be a captive enduring…

He shook his head. He could not think of such things happening to his little sister.

As if by magic, one of the stable boys appeared at his side, eager face creased in a guileless grin. Lucio patted the boy's shoulder and handed over the reins. "Give him an extra measure of grain tonight. Rub him down good."

"Sí, señor." The boy led the complacent animal down the aisle to an empty stall.

Lucio watched until the stall door closed. He waved away a persistent fly that wanted to go up his nose, and turned toward the house. Right now, he wanted a bath more than anything. He smelled like an animal that died and lay in the heat for three days. His clothes stuck to his body and chafed his skin. He'd bathe and then go see if Ramón could come up with any other ideas of where to look for the women.

Thirty minutes later, Lucio felt almost human. He smelled more human too. He strode to the bunkhouse. The cloudless blue sky stretched in an endless blanket overhead. The sun leaned toward the west, ready to drop onto the horizon in a couple of hours. The evening meal would be served before long, so the men should have returned for the night.

The silent bunkhouse held no answers. Lucio crossed to the stable. Berto and Antonio were unsaddling their mounts. The horses weren't sweaty, as his dun had been, so the men hadn't been riding hard. They glanced up at him as he entered and nodded.

"Have you seen Ramón?"

"He is in the hacienda." Berto and Antonio gave him a funny look before glancing at one another.

"What?" Unease twisted through Lucio. He could feel that something had happened while he'd been gone today. Had there been word about Yoana and Leya?

"The bandoleros." Berto frowned at Lucio. "They sent demands."

"They did what?" Lucio shot a look at the house. For the first time he noticed the strange horse tied up at the hitching post. "Who?"

Antonio shrugged. "Some boy. He can't even get his words out right. Your father called for Ramón to help calm the bandit down so they can get some information from him. We don't know any more than that." For the last part Antonio raised his voice.

Lucio still heard him as he strode toward the house. What would the don do with the bandoleros demands?

Without a doubt, Don Armenta would never give in. He would instead issue demands of his own.

A curly-haired youth faced Don Armenta, his hat held in trembling hands. The boy didn't look old enough to be away from his mama's care, let alone to be running with a group of desperadoes. His slight frame and immaturity wouldn't instill fear in anyone.

Least of all the don.

Don Armenta sat behind his desk, back stiff, hands curled around a piece of paper. He glared at the boy as if he wanted to turn him into a pillar of flame right there in the study. His gaze didn't shift when Lucio came in, but Lucio knew his father was aware of him.

"I'm giving you one more chance to tell us where your camp is located." Don Armenta crumpled the paper in his fist. "We hang bandits, and you're no exception. Before you die, you can at least perform one act of good by letting us know where to find the others. I want my livestock back."

Fury flared. His father would kill this boy, the only link to finding Yoana and Leya, and figure the only loss to be a herd of horses. Before Lucio could say anything, Ramón shot him a glance from the far side of the youth. Lucio held his peace to see how this would play out.

"Well, what do you have to say?" Even with his now quiet tone, Don Armenta's authority carried enough threat to get his message across.

This boy had better say something soon.

"I-I-I." The youth closed his mouth and swallowed hard. "Th-th-the n-n-note." He breathed a shaky sigh.

"This note makes demands. Your leader wants money in

exchange for the women. He doesn't say anything about the horses. What about them?"

The curls on the boy's head trembled with the force of his shaking. Why had this untried youth been sent to make such negotiations? Was he expendable? Surely the leader would know the danger involved in delivering such a missive to a man like the don.

Ramón touched the boy's arm. Lucio had moved close enough to see the boy's wide, frightened eyes as he looked at Ramón. His face held almost no color at all. Maybe he would faint like a girl before they had any answers from him.

"Son, what's your name?" Ramón cajoled the boy as he would a difficult horse. His tone carried sympathy and compassion. His steady gaze seemed to hold the boy in an unrelenting grip.

"T-T-T-Tomás." The tiny bells on his short pants jingled.

"Bueno, Tomás." Ramón patted his arm. "We need you to help us out here. Don Armenta must have those horses back. He also wants the women returned. You know the punishment for horse stealing, right?"

Tomás nodded, his eyes filling with liquid. "P-p-please." He couldn't seem to get more out, although his mouth worked like a fish out of water.

"Take him out and hang him." Don Armenta waved a dismissive hand. "We won't get any more from him."

Lucio opened his mouth to protest, but Ramón gave a slight shake of his head. He must have a plan. Once again, Lucio closed his mouth and waited.

"Let's go, son." Ramón gripped Tomás's arm and turned him toward the door. The boy's knees started to buckle. Ramón leaned close and said something Lucio couldn't hear. Tomás straightened, although he still looked like a frightened deer.

Lucio followed them out the door. Ramón marched Tomás to the bunkhouse. A few of the men had returned, and Ramón nodded for them to leave. Lucio shut the door on the last of them and turned to see what Ramón had in mind.

"Have a seat." Ramón led Tomás to one of the benches along the wall and waited until the boy sat down. Ramón swung a couple of chairs around to face him. Lucio sat down beside Ramón and lifted an eyebrow.

Ramón leaned forward until his elbows rested on his knees. This brought him down to the boy's level and made him appear friendlier. "*Escúchame*, Tomás. You heard what the don ordered, right?"

Tomás nodded. He didn't try to speak. Probably because he had so much trouble getting the words out. Was that part of the reason he joined the bandolero gang?

"Now, this is Lucio Armenta, the don's son. He's prepared to make you an offer that will keep you from hanging. Are you willing to listen, or do you want to die right now?" Ramón sat back and crossed his arms over his chest. Lucio waited, his gaze not wavering as he watched Tomás grow pale once again.

What could he say to get this boy to give up information on the hideout? Tomás had to know he would die no matter what. If the bandits found out he'd betrayed them, they would kill him. If he didn't turn them in, the don would hang him.

Tomás turned his frightened gaze on Lucio. His lips quivered as if he wanted to speak, but he stayed quiet. Lucio waited, taking his cue from Ramón. He'd have to speak to the boy frankly but with some sort of compassion too. Hard to do when he wanted to grab the kid and shake him until he told him where the women were being held and if they were all right.

"Tomás." Lucio leaned forward as Ramón had done. "I need your help to get my sister and my tía home safe. First of all, I need to know--are Yoana and Leya all right?"

The boy opened his mouth. No sound came out. He clamped his lips together in a tight line and gave one short nod. Lucio tried not to show his relief. Beside him, he could feel Ramón relax too.

"Thank you." Lucio held the boy's eyes with his own. "If I promise you safety, will you help us bring Yoana and Leya back home?"

Surprise widened Tomás's eyes. He glanced from Lucio to Ramón and back. He nodded again without speaking.

"Here's what we're going to do." Lucio said a quick prayer that this would work. "I'm going to send you back to the camp with a note for your leader. That's all you have to do, just take him the note. *Sí?*"

Tomás tilted his head to one side as he studied Lucio.

"I know that doesn't make much sense to you. I don't want you to be in trouble with the men in the camp. I'm sure they would kill you if they thought you brought trouble to them. Is that correct?"

Tomás nodded.

"We're going to follow you. We'll stay well back so none of them will know. I've been scouring the mountains since you took the women. The bandoleros are probably aware of that. This will seem like I'm just doing that again." He paused to give Tomás a chance to comprehend what he'd said so far.

"What I want you to do is leave an easy trail. You don't have to make it too obvious. Ramón here is an excellent tracker. We'll trail you back to your camp. When we know where you are, we'll figure a way to get Yoana and Leya out of there." He paused, considering the plan from various angles to see whether it would work. "Will there be a way to get them out?"

Tomás shrugged. He chewed his lower lip. "M-m-maybe."

"If there is, we'll find it. You don't have to worry about that. Just act like you always do. Go about your duties and don't think about us. If you do, you'll get nervous, and they'll know something is wrong.

"When we come, I want you to get away from there. In the confusion that we cause, you'll have your chance. Take your horse and light out. I'll give the order that the men are to let you go as long as you don't fight alongside the others. Understand?"

Tomás nodded again. He'd started to calm down and wasn't shaking as much as he had been. His hat had been twisted so much he probably wouldn't be able to use it. Lucio almost smiled. This plan might work if only his father would agree.

"Go with Ramón. He'll see that you get some supper, and you have a place to sleep tonight. I'll talk with the don. You can leave early tomorrow morning to head back." Lucio shot a look at Ramón. He could see approval in the vaquero's eyes.

Now he just had to face his father.

∽

Yoana laughed at the children's delight. To see them so happy...

Her throat tightened, and she fought back tears.

Heavy footsteps and the clank of spurs interrupted the fun. The children fell silent. Isabel whimpered, and Maria let out a mewl as she clung to Yoana, trembling. Yoana knew before she looked up who had scared the children. She raised her face to see Cisto towering over her. He'd assumed the same stance when he faced off with Amado. Did he intend to shoot her? Was it so wrong to entertain children? Sudden anger surged through her. She had done nothing wrong, while he had hurt Maria and Rosalinda.

Maria jumped from the bench as if to run away. Cisto's hand shot out, and the frail girl landed in the dirt.

Yoana jumped to her feet and met his angry gaze. "Where's Rosalinda?" She hadn't meant the demand to slip out. Maria whimpered as she curled into a ball on the ground.

Cisto grabbed Yoana's tunic and yanked her close. Yoana's feet dangled above the ground. A raindrop splattered on her forehead.

"You will not question what I do, or I'll kill you." Cisto plastered her to him, his anger turning to a leer. "And that would be a shame, because I have other plans for you." His sour breath turned her stomach as his mouth descended towards hers.

WHAT HAD LUCIO BEEN *THINKING?*

His father's face darkened in anger. The don hadn't taken the idea well since it hadn't been his. Not only that, but Lucio had countermanded the don's orders by allowing the boy to live.

There had to be a way to make his father see the viability of the plan.

"You will take that boy out and hang him now. Do it close to the mountains so those bandoleros know they can't run another raid here."

"Father, think about this. If you have me hang Tomás, Yoana and Leya will die." Lucio sucked in a breath as inspiration struck him. What did his father truly care about? "If we do what I'm suggesting, we have a chance at recovering the livestock too. Those bandits have been thinking about the women and getting a ransom. They won't have had time to sell off the horses. They'll probably have to take them up north or to the coast to get rid of them. Anyone around here would know whose horses they are."

For the moment, he had the don's attention. "Let me do this. I'll bring Yoana and Leya home, and I'll recover your herd."

"The boy says they haven't been harmed. How can you trust him?" Don Armenta's chair creaked as he leaned back, his hawkish gaze on Lucio.

"We can't really." Lucio shrugged. "But he's scared. I think he told the truth. Ramón agrees that we have to try." Lucio stopped before he began to plead. Yes, he could go behind his father's back on this, but he didn't want to. Their tenuous relationship didn't need any more problems. The don wouldn't admit he needed Lucio here to help run things. His other brothers hadn't stuck around. They chose to live as far from the main hacienda as they could.

"What if your sister has been compromised? What then?" Don Armenta slapped the desk top. "Even if she hasn't been ruined, everyone will think she has. She'll end up being a miserable old maid here on the rancho."

"You don't know that." Lucio spoke quietly. "You don't know the plans God has for her. With or without your permission, I'll go after her. I'd prefer if you were behind me on this."

The don studied him for a long moment. Lucio held still under the scrutiny even though he wanted to squirm as he had when he'd been a young boy.

The don nodded. "Go. Let him leave in the morning, but don't lose the trail. I want them brought home." He rubbed his jaw as he stared down at his desk, then wrote a note and took a pouch of coins from a drawer. He handed them to Lucio. "Send these with the boy." Lucio didn't dare read the note or count the money.

"The horses. Bring the horses and the—bring the horses home." Don Armenta's near admission of his concern for Yoana and Leya told Lucio his father felt more toward his daughter than he would admit to anyone. Maybe even himself.

THE LONG NIGHT stretched into one nightmare after another. Why had he read his father's missive to the bandit leader? Lucio tossed and turned until he finally got up before dawn to spend time in prayer. He'd thought of so many ways this could go wrong, but he hadn't come up with any better plan. He would just pray for God's protection on everyone.

"Tomás, we're trusting you. Understand?" Ramón had one hand on the bridle of the boy's horse as he stood looking up at the boy.

Tomás nodded.

"Lucio talked with the don." Ramón gestured to where Lucio

stood. "This is your chance to make things right and start a new life for yourself. *Comprende?*"

Tomás straightened in the saddle. He nodded again.

"Take off then. We'll give you an hour head start. Then we're coming after you. But you head home and forget we're back there. Here's the note from the don." Ramón handed a folded paper to Tomás. The boy tucked it inside his shirt. They stepped back and watched Tomás ride past the corrals. Lucio wanted to grab his horse now and ride out with him.

"Don't worry." Ramón clapped Lucio on the shoulder. "He'll leave a trail Yoana could follow. We'll have the señoritas back home soon."

"I hope so." Lucio watched Tomás urge his horse to a canter. "I sure hope so, but I have a feeling it won't be that easy."

Late afternoon found Lucio and Ramón riding up a steep hillside. They'd been following Tomás for several hours. So far, he'd led them straight toward some of the areas they'd already covered. They should have asked him how far the camp would be.

They'd agreed he and Ramón would find the outlaw's camp. They would determine whether Yoana and Leya were still there and find a way to get them out. Then they would return to the rancho and bring enough vaqueros to get the job done. The whole thing should only take a few days...

He hoped. Lucio pulled up to give his dun a breather. "Do you think he's leading us a merry chase?" He glanced at Ramón before perusing the woods above them.

"No. I think he's sticking to the trail he was told to take. I'm sure the bandoleros knew he'd be followed. They'll have some plan to throw off pursuit."

"Well, it won't be rain this time." Lucio glanced up at the clear blue sky. "Maybe they're having him go through some rough terrain in the hope that a bunch of vaqueros won't know how to track."

Ramón chuckled. "If that's the case, they are in for disappointment. I could follow this trail blindfolded. They sent the wrong bandit if they wanted him to hide his tracks." Ramón urged his mount up the slope. "We'll go a little farther and stop for the night. We don't want to crowd him and make him panic."

The sun glinted off something uphill. Lucio opened his mouth to shout a warning—

A shot cracked.

Ramón toppled from his horse, blood blossoming across his shirtfront.

CHAPTER TWELVE

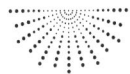

The children's sudden silence startled Amado. He'd enjoyed the excited laughter of the children far more than he'd enjoyed anything in the past few months. For the first time since he'd arrived at this camp, the children reminded him of his nieces and nephews instead of miscreants or the downtrodden.

He looked up from the bridle he'd been putting back together just in time to see Cisto hit Maria hard enough to send her sprawling. Amado tossed the bridle down. He hit the ground running, praying he'd be there in time to keep Yoana and the little ones from getting hurt. The men in camp were backing away. They would rather face a raging forest fire with a cup of water than to take on Cisto when he wanted to kill someone. But not Yoana. Never her.

He heard Yoana's defiant statement. Did she think this situation some kind of a joke? Didn't she understand the danger here? Cisto yanked her to him, but Yoana didn't even blink. Amado feared for her life, even as he admired her courage. Part of him still wanted to berate her for being so bold.

The sight of Cisto's hands on her sent a flash of rage roaring through Amado. He grabbed Cisto's shoulder and swung him around. As soon as Cisto released Yoana, Amado hit the man hard enough to send him flying backward into the trunk of a pine tree. The crack to his head didn't cool Cisto off or slow him down. He lunged upright and flew at Amado, his hands curled into fists.

"Get the children away!" Amado didn't wait to see if Yoana followed his order. He dodged Cisto's uppercut. The man stumbled past. Amado whirled to face him when he came around again. They collided with a crash that knocked the breath from Amado.

They landed hard on the ground with Amado underneath. The mad gleam in Cisto's eye told Amado the bandit thought he'd won. He hadn't. Amado grabbed the front of Cisto's shirt and twisted to the side. Cisto lost his balance. Lost his hold on Amado. Lost his advantage. They grappled. Cisto landed a couple of blows, one of which split Amado's lip. Amado hit Cisto under the chin and heard the man's teeth crack together. Blood bubbled from Cisto's mouth.

Hands grabbed Cisto and jerked him up and away from Amado. Amado scrambled to his feet, but someone else grasped his shoulders to hold him in place. His breath came in ragged gasps. Blood pounded in his temples. He wanted to hurt this man.

"Take it easy, amigo." Miguel's strong grasp kept Amado from breaking free. "Let Victoro handle this."

Amado relaxed a fraction. He shrugged off Miguel's hold, although he noted the other man didn't step away from him. Cisto fought against Victoro, his murderous gaze still fastened on Amado. Victoro slipped Cisto's gun from his holster.

"Stop." Victoro's command carried the weight of a leader speaking to his men. Cisto quieted. Victoro released him and stepped back, the pistol at the ready. Cisto swiped at his bloody mouth with the back of his hand.

"This stops now." Victoro's face turned thunderous. "I will not have you hitting the children. Not when they are only playing and do not need to be punished for anything."

"The girl belongs to Rosalinda. She's under my care." Cisto straightened his shirt.

"I am the leader here." Victoro narrowed his eyes. *"Everyone* is under *my* care, unless you choose to challenge me." With a casual movement he swiveled the revolver around to point toward Cisto.

Cisto's jaw worked. He flexed his hands. The man wanted to challenge Victoro, but odds were he'd be dead before he could take two steps. Victoro's speed and accuracy with a gun were no secret.

"As soon as we eat, Miguel is leaving to go meet Lorenzo and Tomás. Cisto, I want you to go with him." Victoro lowered the muzzle of the weapon.

"He doesn't need help." Cisto's mouth tightened to a thin line. Blood began to seep again from the cut.

"I say he does." Victoro's tone left no room to debate. "You'll go, and you'll give him no trouble."

Cisto's gazed tracked to Amado. "This isn't done. I'll go, but we'll finish this when I get back."

"You'll finish *nothing!*" Victoro's bellow startled some of the children into crying again. He looked over his shoulder at Pabladora. "Is the meal ready?"

"Yes, we'll begin serving." Pabladora made a hurried gesture to Dolores, Feliciana, and Leya. Yoana stood to one side surrounded by frightened youngsters who hid their faces in her skirt.

Victoro pinned Cisto with his sharp gaze. "Where is Rosalinda? She should be here to help."

"She's resting." Cisto tugged the collar of his shirt forward. A smug smile creased his swarthy features. "I think I wore her out."

"Is she too tired to move. Or too injured?"

Victoro verbalized the very thought that had passed through Amado's mind. Cisto may have promised not to hurt her, but trusting Cisto's word was like trusting the weather not to change.

"I will bring her out if you don't believe me." Cisto gave Amado a scathing glance and stormed off to his shack up canyon.

Miguel took the plate Feliciana handed him. He nodded at Victoro as if the leader had spoken. "I'll eat and then fetch the horses. We'll be out of here within thirty minutes."

Pale sunlight shafted through the trees. Leya brought Amado's food to him. Her eyes thanked him for interceding on Yoana's behalf. Amado smiled and winked at the older woman. Her half smile pulled at the scars on the side of her face, and she ducked her head.

Everyone in camp quieted as Rosalinda walked down the path, her hand on Cisto's arm. Posture rigid, expression taut, she walked like a woman trying to hide her pain.

The handle of the fork dug into Amado's fingers.

Pabladora rushed to take Rosalinda's hand from Cisto's arm. She handed the man a plate of food and said something to him that Amado couldn't hear. Cisto swaggered off to sit under a tall pine where he'd be sheltered from the drips.

Miguel stalked off, heading up canyon to bring the horses. Almost before Cisto had time to finish his meal, Miguel had everything ready for them to leave. The whole camp seemed to breathe a sigh of relief as the pair trotted up the path leading out of the canyon.

Amado watched until they disappeared around a turn in the trail, not caring that his food had grown cold. At the top of the rise, Cisto turned to look at Amado, staring until he rounded the curve of the hill.

As he forked cold beans into his mouth, Amado studied Yoana. She appeared to have recovered from Cisto's attack. At least, that's the front she put on for the children. But her tension showed in the swift glances she shot toward the mouth of the canyon, as if she expected Cisto to come storming back, guns blazing.

Amado wouldn't have been surprised if that happened.

Victoro finished eating and handed his plate and utensils to Pabladora, who had been whispering to him, and sauntered across the clearing to where Yoana sat surrounded by a subdued group of children. The children huddled a little closer to her as Victoro stopped in front of her. She sat with both Isabel and Luis on her lap. Carmen and Maria were snuggled on either side with Teo seated on the ground at her feet.

Yoana started to rise, but Victoro motioned for her to stay seated. A canopy of tightly woven branches kept most of the rain off of this spot.

Victoro cleared his throat. "I have a new job for you."

Trepidation flashed across Yoana's fine features. Her eyes tracked to Leya for a moment.

"No." Victoro held up a hand. "This is not the women's work that you think. I don't want any more of my shirts sewn together or my food burned to a crisp."

Yoana's complexion deepened to red.

Victoro let out a belly laugh. "I want you to work with the children." He nodded to the *niños*.

"The children?" Yoana glanced down at the little ones surrounding her.

"You are educated. From a good family." Victoro cleared his throat. "These niños need to learn. Teo and Maria are old enough. All they do is work and run around screaming like a bunch of wild bandoleros."

Yoana blinked, obviously surprised at the request. "They are still young. I can teach them some things. I can tell them stories that will help them learn later."

"Stories." Victoro beamed at her. "That would be good. I can tell stories too. About the many times we have--"

"You will not tell those stories to these children." Pabladora stalked over to Victoro and faced him, her hands on her hips, chin thrust forward. "Teo doesn't need to hear the stories you have to tell. Leya says Yoana is very good at telling about what happened in the Bible."

Victoro struggled to maintain his fearsome authority as Pabladora berated him. Amado held back a smile. What had brought this couple to this place? That Pabladora loved Victoro was evident to anyone with eyes to see. And yet it was also clear how much she disapproved of the life they lived. Amado had even heard her try to convince Victoro to give up the stealing before he was hanged, but the head bandolero refused to listen to the woman he loved.

Now, rebuffed by his woman, he stalked back to his usual seat with Pabladora at his side.

A fat raindrop hit Amado's hat and dripped off the brim. He went to where he'd been working, picked up more of the tack that needed to be repaired, and strode across camp to where Yoana sat with the children. Her eyebrows tracked upwards as he sat down on a log close to hers.

He shrugged. "I wanted to work out of the rain." Despite his best efforts, he simply couldn't stand to be away from her for another minute. If he thought he could get away with it, he would move the children out of the way and sit beside her. Better yet, he would like to be able to confide his dilemma to her. To see what she would advise him. But he couldn't.

Her gold-brown eyes reflected delight as she watched Isabel and Luis. What would it be like to have her look at him in such a way rather than with mistrust or anger? He sighed as he picked up another bridle. That would never be. Even so, for now he would listen to the lyrical sound of her voice and watch the play of emotions crossing her beautiful face as she cared for her new charges.

"Caballito." Luis pointed to Yoana's foot.

She laughed and kissed him on the forehead. "No. I think your sister needs to take a bit of a nap." Yoana shifted Isabel as the child leaned against her, eyelids closing.

"Tell me what your favorite Bible story is." Yoana waited for the children to answer, looking from Teo to Maria to the younger toddlers. The blank expressions on their faces told more than words that they knew nothing about the Bible.

She softened her voice. "Do you know about God?"

Teo brightened and sat up straight. "I do. I went to church once. I had to be very careful because God lives there. He gets very angry if you are bad in His house. He will strike you dead." The young boy pointed a finger upward and lowered his voice.

Amado shook his head. Which adult had said those words to Teo?

Yoana nodded. "God wants us to show Him respect, but He loves us very much too. Did you know that?"

"My mama loves me, but she doesn't get angry and strike me dead because I talk too loud." Teo shoved his dark curls back from his forehead.

"Why don't I tell you the story of the first man and the first woman?"

Yoana's tender smile made Amado's heart speed up, though her attention was focused on the children.

"The first ones in this camp?" Teo asked.

Maria giggled, her tiny hand covering her mouth.

Yoana's smile was warm. "No. The very first people. God made them, but let's start with what God did for them before they were even made. *Muy bien?*"

Teo nodded. Yoana shifted the sleeping Isabel to a more comfortable position.

"Before there were people or animals or plants, everything was dark." Her voice took on a hushed note. The women stopped their work, then settled down on logs to listen. Even Victoro stopped his chores.

Teo leaned his head against Yoana's leg. "Like nighttime?"

"Not like that." Yoana shook her head. "This was darkness like deep inside a cave, where you can't see even a hand in front of your face." She held up her hand and wiggled her fingers. "There weren't any stars or sun or moon. There was only God."

"All by himself?" Maria's green eyes widened. "Did he get sad and lonely?"

"Yes, in a way He did." Yoana smiled at the shy girl. "He wanted to make a man so He would have someone to love. And someone who would love Him."

"Did He cook him up in the oven?"

At Teo's question, titters of laughter sounded from near the cooking fire.

"I'll tell you how He made Adam, the first man, in a minute. First, I want to tell you all God did to get ready. You see, God knew Adam wouldn't like living in darkness, so He made the sun in the sky, the moon and the stars. That way Adam would be able to see."

"Then God made Adam?"

Amado shook his head. What a smart and curious boy Teo was. He'd never realized that before. But then, the little boy hadn't talked this much in the whole time Amado had been with the bandoleros.

"Not yet." Yoana's breath hitched. She cleared her throat. "The light and dark were there, daytime and nighttime, but God hadn't made the ground yet. So He made the earth, then the waters and the plants. You see, Adam couldn't live if he didn't have anywhere to make a home. God loved Adam so much He made this whole earth as a special home for him."

Teo leaned close. "Would God strike him dead when Adam was bad?"

Yoana winked at Teo, as if telling him to wait and find out the answer to his question. "After God made plants, He made fish in the waters and birds in the sky and animals on the land."

Amado glanced across the camp. Pabladora helped Rosalinda ease down on a stump cut as a seat.

Yoana's story continued. "God loved Adam so much that He made everything perfect for him. Then, do you know how God made Adam?" Yoana turned to each expectant face as the children waited. "He picked up some dirt." Yoana shifted Isabel and leaned over to scoop up a handful of earth. "And He made Adam from dirt."

"Dirt?" Teo's mouth fell open. He looked down at the ground and dug his fingers into the soil. "How did He do that?"

"Well, I don't really know." Yoana grinned. "But God can do anything, so He can make a man out of dirt."

"So did God make us out of dirt too?" Maria tilted her head to gaze up at Yoana.

"No, God had another plan." Yoana's face tinged pink.

Amado bit his lip to keep from chuckling.

"First, God had a job for Adam to do," Yoana said.

"He had to work?" Teo tossed his handful of dirt in the air. "Wouldn't you know?"

Yoana's lilting laughter filled the clearing and wound around Amado's heart.

She reached down to rumple Teo's dark curls. "God has work for all of us to do. What do you think Adam's first job was?"

Teo's face crinkled, then a look of horror widened his eyes. "He had to cook and do dishes since there wasn't anyone else?"

Amado covered his laughter by pretending to cough. He could see Yoana struggling with the same problem. To a young boy, cooking and doing dishes would be the worst of jobs.

"No. Adam needed to name all the animals." Yoana drew in a ragged breath and kept her focus on Teo.

"He named the animals?" Teo's forehead creased even more. "You mean like I called my dog Juan?"

"No." Yoana trickled the dirt from her palm onto the ground and wiped her hand on her skirt. "At that time the animals weren't called anything. Adam didn't give them names like Juan. The names he gave were what each animal would be, like dog, horse, cow."

"Oh, so *that's* how that happened." Teo looked as if he'd discovered the answer to life, or something just as deep.

"After that, Adam was a little sad." Yoana patted Maria's leg.

"Probably because his head hurt." Teo rolled his eyes. "My head would hurt if I had to think of all those names."

Amado did laugh at that one. He couldn't help it. Tears blurred his eyes he laughed so hard. "You're so right, Teo. My head would hurt too."

Yoana gave Amado an exasperated look that only made him grin. "No, Adam was sad because he didn't have any companion. Out of all the animals, he didn't find one that would be a suitable companion for him."

Teo clapped his hands. "Did God make him one out of dirt?"

"No. He made Adam fall asleep." Yoana bit her lip as Teo's eyes widened.

"Oh." Teo nodded. "God didn't want Adam to see how He did this."

"No. God made Adam sleep because He took one of Adam's ribs and made Adam's wife, Eve, from that rib."

Teo's mouth dropped open again. His eyes bulged as he stared at Yoana. Maria mimicked Teo, her green eyes huge.

"Adam must have been very mad when he woke up." Teo ran his fingers through the loose dirt and pine needles on the ground. "Did he have a hole in his side?"

"God healed him up. Adam was very happy with Eve. She was a very beautiful woman and just perfect for Adam." Yoana pressed her cheek to Isabel's head as the girl stirred.

"Did God make Eve so she could cook and do dishes?" Teo asked.

"God made Eve because He loved Adam and wanted him to be content. God gave Adam and Eve a perfect place to live, a very wonderful garden with all kinds of food and animals for their friends. He did that all because he loved them."

Isabel began to fuss, so Yoana stood with the small girl in her arms. "I'll tell you more of the story later. Right now, think about how much God loved Adam and Eve. Then remember that he loves us the same way."

As she walked away, Amado took in her tenderness for the children and her desire to share the story of God with them. He thought about how Adam had responded with such enthusiasm when God presented Eve to him.

He looked at Yoana again, and for the first time in his life…

He understood Adam's reaction.

CHAPTER THIRTEEN

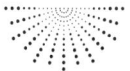

"Yoana, come sit by me." Teo patted a place on the log next to him. He sat with a plate of food on his lap having his breakfast. In the past few days, he'd become eager for more stories and games.

Yoana couldn't stop the skip in her heart. She picked up the plate of food Leya dished up for her. As she turned toward Teo, Leya placed her hand on her arm.

Leya leaned in close to Yoana. "What you've done with these children is a miracle. God has given you such a gift. I know these bandoleros won't say so, but they see the good you're doing."

Seeing the change in Teo and the children since she'd begun telling them Bible stories and teaching them songs filled her with wonder. The stories also helped strengthen her own flagging faith. As she talked about Him, she could see that God did care about her and Leya. And these children. And all of His creation. And thinking of the people of faith in the Bible helped her remember how God was with them and how He delivered them when they went through trials.

"They have calmed so much." Leya tilted her head toward the children seated on the log or the ground, all eyes on Yoana as they waited for her to join them. "There is much less tension in the camp now that they don't run though here screaming and howling like a chupacabra."

"I enjoy teaching them the games or telling stories." Yoana swallowed hard against the lump in her throat. "Maybe you're right, Leya. Maybe God brought me here for this reason. Teo is so eager to learn, especially the Bible stories." She grinned and noted the twinkle in Leya's eyes. "I still see the look of amazement on his face when I said God didn't strike them dead when they disobeyed. I thought he would never stop asking questions about God and why He loved them even though they were bad."

"The best part was when you told him God loved him just as much as He loved Adam and Eve." Leya squeezed Yoana's arm. "Your stories are truth and will help all of these people, not just the children."

Yoana carried the plate of food over to sit down beside Teo. A cool breeze lifted the branches of the tall pines. She breathed deep of the sweet scent from the trees. She loved the mountains and knew she needed to find a way to take Leya and get back home. But for now, she felt that she had more purpose and acceptance in this outlaw camp than she'd ever had at her father's hacienda. Instead of constantly looking for a way to escape, she'd almost accepted she would stay here.

Seated on the other side of Teo, Amado smiled at her. Yoana's heart fluttered. She'd noticed him watching her, his dark chocolate eyes warm with appreciation. She didn't want to be attracted to a bandolero who would end up swinging at the end of a rope if he got caught, yet her heart betrayed her--

No. She pushed the thought away. She would *not* fall in love with an outlaw.

Teo rested his head against her arm. "Can you tell me a story?"

"How can I tell you a story while I eat?" Yoana lifted her eyebrows. "I would spit food all over you."

Teo leaned close. "Victoro yells at me when his mouth is full of food."

Yoana bent her head toward the boy's. "And he spits food at you, doesn't he?" Teo nodded. Amado choked. Teo beat him on the back. Yoana bit her lip and didn't look at Amado for fear she would burst out laughing.

"Why don't I tell you a riddle? Then you can think about it while you eat." Yoana smiled at Teo's puzzled expression.

"A riddle? What's that?"

"A riddle is a description of something, but the description is tricky. You have to try to figure out what the person is talking about."

Teo pursed his lips and narrowed his eyes. "Then tell me one." He stuffed a big forkful of venison and egg into his mouth.

"Let's see." Yoana tried to remember the different riddles Lucio used to tell her. *"Blanco ha sido mi vestido,* and my heart is yellow. What am I?" Yoana took a bite as she watched Teo's brow furrow in concentration.

He opened his mouth to speak, caught her look, and swallowed first. "A white dress and a yellow heart? Is that a girl who is a coward?"

Amado choked again. Yoana smiled. "No. Guess again."

Teo glanced at Amado, who was tapping his fork on his plate. He'd finished his venison but hadn't finished his egg. He tapped the fork again near the egg. Teo shook his head, glancing from Amado to Yoana.

"I'll give you a hint," Yoana said. "You have to think of something that is white around the outside and yellow in the middle."

She watched Teo's mouth move as he silently repeated what she'd said. Amado tapped his plate again. Teo glanced over, annoyance plain on his face. Amado plinked harder with his fork. Teo looked down. She knew the minute the answer came to him.

He swung back to face her, excitement making his eyes sparkle. *"El huevo.* It's an egg."

Yoana laughed. "You're right. Very good."

"Tell me another one. I can do this." Teo stuffed the last of his breakfast into his mouth.

"One more, but then you need to do your chores. *Sí?*" Yoana waited until Teo nodded. *"Son hermanos muy unidos..."* She held back laughter at his intense expression as she finished the riddle.

"Brothers very united. They go everywhere together." Teo's concentration on the riddle kept him from noticing the look that passed between Amado and Yoana. A flush warmed her cheeks when Amado winked at her.

"It can't be Lorenzo and Miguel because sometimes they aren't together." Teo kicked at a clump of pine needles. "It isn't me and Carlito because he's just a baby, and I don't do baby stuff."

"That's true." Yoana drew in a deep breath. "You are almost a man."

"I don't know any more brothers." Teo turned to Amado. "Do you have any brothers?"

Amado's face seemed to drain of color. He opened his mouth, but didn't speak. Instead, he surged up from the log so fast Teo almost lost his balance and fell off backwards.

"I need to get work done."

What was wrong? Why was he suddenly so gruff? He'd never spoken that way to one of the children or to any of the women. He stalked off, and Teo looked up at her with a question in his eyes.

"Let me give you a hint." Yoana tried to smile and make light of Amado's strange reaction. She wanted to follow him and ask what had happened but turned her attention back to Teo. "Think of something that would work together to do jobs and would not be separated." She flexed her fingers, then got her last bite of breakfast on her fork.

"Horses on a wagon team?"

"No, because they are separated at night." Yoana stood. She held up her hand and wiggled her fingers in front of Teo's face. "What do you use when you do chores?"

He brightened and laughed. *"Los dedos.* The fingers." Teo held up his own hand and moved his fingers around. "I'm going to tell Maria." He started to run off, then came back and gave Yoana a hug before racing across to where Maria helped with the dishes.

Yoana's heart swelled. Would her father would see any good in the way she related to these children? Probably not. Her gaze tracked across the clearing to where Amado stood conversing with Victoro. What had upset him?

She carried her plate over to the cooking area. As soon as Teo and Maria finished their chores, she would give them another lesson on their letters and numbers. Teo already could count to twenty and write most of the numbers. He could say the alphabet but had trouble writing some of the letters. For only having a few lessons, he had done remarkably well. Maria caught on almost as fast, although her attention span wandered faster than a stray horse.

"There's work to do." Pabladora clapped her hands. The women gravitated to her like chicks to a mother hen. "Dolores and Feliciana, take the dishes to the stream and wash them. Rosalinda can help me get ready to wash clothes. Leya can work on the mending."

Leya picked up some shirts from the pile of clothes needing repair and sat in a spot where sun filtered down through the branches. Yoana joined her.

"How are you doing, Tía?"

"I am wondering what news will come back." Leya kept her voice low and her head down. "When Tomás returns with the answer from your father, what do you think the note will say?"

Reality crashed down on Yoana. Did Leya intend to remind her about the need to have a plan for escape? Yoana had been watching the camp routine. She knew they would need to get horses, but she hadn't figured out how to do that without alerting the whole camp to their escape.

"I know you've come to love the children, Yoana. I know, too, how your father treats you and that you are feeling more comfortable here than at home. But you have to remember when Tomás comes back with the answer from your father, both of our lives will be at risk."

"Do you think they will kill us?" Fear clutched at Yoana's throat. How could she have ignored their dilemma? Did her pride mean more than Leya's safety?

"They won't kill you." Leya tilted her head until she met Yoana's gaze. "You are too valuable. I'm the one who will either die or suffer."

"Pabladora will not let that happen. She stands up to Victoro."

"She only stands up to him in certain areas. She doesn't want him to be a bandit. She knows the danger, but you notice that he is still the leader of the bandoleros. He will not be told what to do in this "

Teo and Maria came back into camp with armloads of firewood, their chore for the day. They were almost done, which meant Yoana would have to go soon to start their lessons. "I will figure out today how to get us out of here. Tonight."

Teo and Maria raced toward her. "Yoana, we're ready."

She stood and held out her arms to them. They both hugged her and then took her hands to lead her to the spot where they drew their letters and numbers in the dirt. Carmen, Luis, and Isabel would all come over as soon as their mothers let them.

The morning passed quickly. Amado left the camp to check on the horses and work with some of them. Yoana tried to focus, not wanting to watch for his return. She would ignore how her pulse skittered like a squirrel through the tree branches every time she thought she heard him.

She enjoyed watching him work, bent over something that needed to be fixed, or talking with Victoro. His voice, his laughter, the way he moved. Everything about him appealed to her. The way he interacted with the others, especially the children, told her so much about his character. How could this man be a bandit when he seemed so morally upright? Of course, he was the one who led Victoro's men to her father's rancho to steal the horses.

Yoana leaned down to help Maria with drawing her letters as she pushed thoughts of Amado from her mind. Or tried to. Images of him crept back in without her wanting that to happen. He had the appearance of a good man but lived and worked with bandoleros. How did a woman even know a man's heart or if he would be right for her?

"Amado, come look! I wrote my name." Teo jumped up as Amado strode into camp. Amado grinned at Teo, but his gaze found Yoana. She fumbled the stick she'd been using to write in the dirt. She snatched up the branch again and bent back over Maria to hide her burning face.

"Hey, Teo, you did a good job." Amado patted the boy on the back. Teo stood tall, his eyes shining as he gazed up at Amado. Amado ruffled his hair. "You must have had a good teacher."

"Yoana is the best. She is very smart." Teo's solemn words carried respect.

Yoana lifted her gaze to find Amado still watching her. He smiled and winked. The burning in her face became a raging forest fire. She wanted to look away, but his eyes seemed to draw her in.

The sound of horse hooves coming over the rise at the entrance to the canyon broke the spell.

Tomás and Lorenzo rode around the bend, followed by Manuel. The icy touch of reality doused the flames of interest. Yoana kept her attention on the pair, hoping to discern what happened with her father. She couldn't help noting how Tomás immediately found Feliciana, and his face lit up with a smile. She glanced over at the young girl and saw her blushing. Neither of them seemed to notice Miguel's anger as he watched them. He urged his mount down the steep path, jumped to the ground beside Feliciana, and pulled her into a possessive embrace.

Too late.

Those were the words that rang through Yoana's mind. She'd put off getting Leya out of the camp because of her own selfishness. For once, she found something she was good at and someone who appreciated her, even if it was in an outlaw camp. Now Leya would pay the price for Yoana's pride.

"Where's Cisto?" Victoro met the men as they pulled their horses to a stop.

"He'll be coming, I think." Lorenzo touched a bruise on his cheek. "We had words. He chose to go off on his own."

Victoro nodded. "Put the horses up. We'll talk afterward. We all want to hear about your meeting."

Yoana hadn't even realized Amado had moved until she felt his hand on her arm. The warmth contrasted sharply with the cold fear that knotted her stomach. The only relief of the moment had been Cisto's absence. She hadn't missed the look of pity Tomás sent her. From his expression, neither had Amado.

"It will work out." Amado spoke so close to her ear that she jumped. "I promise you will be all right."

"How can you promise something like that?" Sudden anger swept through Yoana. "Victoro is the one who will determine what happens. You know Leya will be hurt if he decides that will get my father to hand over money or valuables."

"I haven't been here all that long, but Victoro seems fair minded to me."

"He's a bandolero." Yoana kept her voice low, although she wanted to shout. "He has no honor."

"Victoro is not cruel. Yes, he steals, but he doesn't get excited over doing something cruel." Amado's grip on her arm tightened. "You've seen how they treat Leya. I don't believe they will hurt her. I will do my best to see that they don't."

Yoana pulled her arm free and stalked over to where Leya sat working on the mending pile. Part of her wanted to turn back. To throw herself into Amado's strong arms and pretend that everything would be wonderful. She refused to give in to a lie. After all,

Amado had two counts against him--being a man, which meant he would turn his back on her, and being a bandolero, which meant he would hang.

Leya bent over a shirt that covered her lap. She stuck the needle into the cloth as Yoana sat down beside her. Leya grasped Yoana's hand. Her fingers were like ice. "Yoana, pray with me. We must trust God to get us through this."

"I don't know if I can."

"You *must*." Leya's intense gaze burned into Yoana. "God is our only hope. You have to believe what you've been telling the children, that God loves us so much we can't even understand the depth of His love."

"I believe it in my heart, but in my head I'm not always sure." Tears burned in her eyes. She blinked to clear her vision.

"Then you must be the one who says, `I believe, Lord. Help my unbelief.'" In a soft voice Leya began to pray. Yoana let her forehead drop onto her tía's shoulder. She loved this woman who had cared for her since childhood. Despair filled Yoana at the thought of having endangered Leya. Wasn't this what she did to her own mother?

Lorenzo and Tomás clumped back into camp, their spurs jangling with every step. Amado wandered over to join them as they squatted down near Victoro and Manuel. Yoana wanted to hear the men, but fear held her immobile. As Pabladora and the other women worked in the kitchen area, they cast glances at Yoana and Leya, their expressions grim.

"Leya. Yoana. Come here!" Victoro's shout startled Yoana. She drew in a sharp breath. Resolve stiffened her spine as she stood. Taking Leya's hand in hers, she lifted her chin and marched toward the group of men who would decide their fate.

Victoro's thick eyebrows drew together like a huge, hairy caterpillar. His eyes were darker than usual. "Yoana, your father has refused to pay anything to get you back. He says that you have been compromised, and no man of worth will want you for a wife."

He paused at the gasps from the women at the cook fires. His tone softened as he continued. "Don Armenta sent some money to pay for the return of Leya."

Yoana felt as if someone had struck her on the side of her head. She couldn't breathe. Her limbs turned numb. Darkness floated at the edges of her vision. Her father had announced to the world that he didn't want her, didn't care about her. Every bit of hope she'd ever had that he would forgive her, maybe some day love her, died in that moment. Strong arms lifted her as the world darkened.

"Take her to the hut, Amado, until we decide what to do with her." Victoro's voice sounded tinny and distant. "Miguel, you can get ready to return Leya to Don Armenta."

"No, I won't go." Leya's tone was firm.

"He paid for your return." Victoro rubbed his chin as he stared at Leya.

"I have been Yoana's señorita for over fifteen years. I will not leave her now when she needs me the most."

Yoana knew she should protest. She should to tell Leya to go, to get away from this camp and the danger while she could, but her broken heart dragged her down into a darkened abyss.

"The only way I will return to Don Armenta is if you send Yoana with me."

"He didn't pay for her. In fact, he told Tomás he doesn't want to ever see her again."

"That is his hurt speaking." Leya sounded angry. Her audacity to speak so to Victoro amazed Yoana. "He is her father. She is valuable to him."

Yoana wanted to argue with Leya. She'd only brought pain to her father. Every day when he looked at her, she reminded him of all she'd taken from him, of all she'd cost him. He would be glad to never see her again.

The silence hurt her ears. Yoana's senses returned. She could smell the mixture of horse and woods that scented Amado's clothes. Her head rested against his broad chest, and she could hear the steady thump of his heart. The sound comforted her even as she wanted to weep over the blow she'd been dealt.

A clink of coins tinkled as something dropped onto the ground.

"I'll pay for her."

Cisto's voice sent a jolt of terror through Yoana.

CHAPTER FOURTEEN

Rosalinda sprang forward, snatched up the small purse from the ground, and shoved the leather bag in Cisto's face. Her sleeve fell away from her arm to show the yellowish-green of fading bruises mixed with the darker purple of fresher ones. Amado's breath whooshed out as if he'd been punched in the stomach.

How could a man treat a woman this way?

Rosalinda's dusky olive skin flushed. "You will not buy this woman. *I* am yours. You don't need her." Her whole body shook.

"You don't tell me what to do." Cisto's mouth lifted in a sneer. He twisted the bag of coins from Rosalinda's fingers. The money clinked again as the pouch landed on the ground in front of Victoro.

"Besides--" Cisto grabbed Rosalinda and jerked her against him. "--I'm man enough for both of you." His low laugh snaked through the camp.

Tremors shivered through Yoana. Amado glanced down to find her eyelids squeezed tight. A tear leaked from the corner of one eye. Her chalky skin highlighted the smattering of freckles that dusted her nose. Amado couldn't help dropping a soft kiss on her forehead while everyone's attention focused on Cisto and

Rosalinda. Well, almost everyone. From the corner of his eye, he caught Leya watching him.

"I will not let him have you." Amado breathed the words in Yoana's ear. She shivered. Her slender fingers caught the front of his shirt, clung to the fabric. Her breath shuddered almost in a sob.

"Enough." Victoro's roar drew everyone's attention back to Cisto and Rosalinda. Cisto had Rosalinda's dress collar twisted so tight her mouth opened wide as she struggled for air. Victoro dug his meaty fingers into Cisto's arm so hard Amado knew there would be bruises similar to those on Rosalinda.

"Let her go." Victoro left no room for argument.

Cisto shook Rosalinda once more and released her. She fell to the ground. Her hands pulled the cloth from her throat. She gasped and began to cough. Pabladora stepped forward and bent down to help Rosalinda. The older woman glared up at Cisto as she helped Rosalinda to her feet, but he ignored the two of them. His focus riveted on Amado and Yoana.

"I will buy her." Cisto turned to Victoro. "You were willing to sell her to her father. He doesn't want her. I do. What does it matter who you sell her to as long as you get the money you want?"

Victoro bristled. "I asked ransom for her. I wasn't *selling* her."

"Her father would have had to pay money for her return. Isn't that the same as buying her from you?" Cisto grinned, his dark features shadowed by the evil inside him. "You said her father doesn't want her."

"I am sure her father wants her. He just doesn't want to pay as much as I asked."

"Yet he's willing to pay for the scarred one." Cisto gestured at Leya.

"Yoana is not for sale." Amado would have hit the man if he hadn't been holding Yoana. "She is not a horse to be traded to the highest bidder."

"Maybe she is like a mare who chooses the best stallion." Cisto grinned. "I'm sure she would not choose you."

Amado felt Yoana's sharp intake of air. He tightened his hold, hoping to tell her without words that she needed to keep up the pretense of unconsciousness. Her breath scattered on the breeze. Her fingers still melded to his shirt. She must be terrified.

"I think this has gone far enough." Amado spoke to Victoro. "If Don Armenta is willing to pay to get Leya back, then let that be enough for both women. I will escort them back to the rancho. We can leave today."

"You think my money is not good enough?" Cisto took a step forward. "Maybe that's because you want her for yourself. I've seen the way you look at the chica."

"Maybe I admire a woman who has the courage to come into a foreign situation like this and make the best of it." Amado tried to calm his temper. He wanted to free his arms, but didn't want to let go of Yoana.

"The best of it?" Cisto laughed. "The woman can't do anything right. All she can do is play a few games with children. What value is that? I know a much better use for a beautiful woman."

"That's your loss if you think so little of women," Amado said. "Maybe if you treated Rosalinda better and didn't hit her so often, she would be worth more to you. Or, is that what makes you feel like a man? Taking out your anger on a woman."

Rosalinda put her hand on Cisto's arm, her expression a mix of fear and longing. Cisto shoved her away and strode forward, his fists curled. Victoro grabbed him before he could reach Amado, who turned to put himself between Yoana and Cisto. Lorenzo stepped up to help Victoro restrain the man.

"I am not taking anyone's money for this woman," Victoro said. "She is not going back to her father or being sold to you, Cisto. She has been teaching Teo and Maria to write and do numbers. That is more valuable than any amount of money right now."

Cisto spat on the ground. "Book learning doesn't help anyone. Especially not girls. I don't want Maria to get any more of that nonsense."

"Maria is not yours." Rosalinda, still pale from Cisto's attack and rejection, faced him. "I say she will continue with the schooling. Maybe then she won't have to depend on some monster like you to take care of her." Rosalinda's hazel eyes flashed fire, even though she trembled. Amado knew she would face repercussions for her defiance.

Once more Victoro and Lorenzo restrained Cisto. The man's cursing jarred a gasp from Yoana. Everyone turned toward Amado. He looked down to see Yoana gazing up at him, eyes huge, lips compressed in a tight line. Her fear faded, and she pushed at Amado's chest. He eased her down so that she stood beside him but didn't release his hold. She didn't pull away.

Cisto's gaze raked over her. Yoana's chin tilted upward in a defiant gesture that Amado had come to enjoy. He liked this woman's spunk.

"I heard what you said about buying me." Yoana's gaze didn't waver from Cisto's. "You will never own me. Even if Victoro chooses to sell me to you, you will not own me."

"You will be mine. No matter what you think." Cisto jerked to try to free his arms from Victoro and Lorenzo's grasp, to no avail.

"You may possess me some day, but you will never own me."

"There's a difference?" Cisto asked in a snarl.

The look she gave him dismissed him as a fool. "An educated man would know there is."

The triumph in Yoana's tone ignited Cisto's wrath even further. He roared, yanked free, and lunged at her. Amado anticipated the move and stepped in front of her. He met Cisto with a right hook to the jaw. Cisto dropped to the ground. He shook his head and stumbled to his feet.

Victoro and Lorenzo leaped forward to flank Amado. Cisto stilled, his eyes flashing hatred.

"Don't ever try anything with Yoana again." Amado wanted to beat the man to a pulp. He wanted to kill him, as he'd been sent here to do. He'd come to this camp determined to stop the man who killed his brother. Cisto. Yet deep down, he had doubts. He had yet to find proof that Cisto was the one he sought. He couldn't just act on his dislike of the man.

Victoro faced off with Cisto. "You will leave this camp. You can take your horse and go. Rosalinda can stay here or leave with you. But you are to go. If you ever decide you can abide by my rules of decency, you can come back. Until then, you have no place here."

"I could tell the authorities where to find you." Cisto touched his jaw where Amado's fist had connected.

Victoro didn't flinch. "You could. If you do, I will hunt you down. By the time I'm done, you will beg for mercy." Every man in the camp knew Victoro spoke the truth.

The clop of a horse's hooves drew their attention up canyon. Miguel came striding into view leading Cisto's horse. He must have seen where Cisto tied his mount, figured what would happen, and fetched the animal. He handed Cisto the reins and stepped back.

Cisto turned to Rosalinda. "Get the children. We're leaving."

"No." Behind Rosalinda, Isabel clung to her mother's skirts. "Victoro said I could stay here, so I will."

"You would defy me?" Cisto's voice grew soft and full of malice. Eyes narrowed, he stepped closer.

"I will keep my children safe." Rosalinda pulled back the sleeves of her dress to reveal the multitude of bruises tracking her arms. "Some day this will not be enough, and you will kill me. And then them. I am not waiting for that."

"What do you intend to do without me?" Cisto's lip curled. "There aren't many men around here for you to latch onto and use."

"I will have Yoana teach me while she teaches the children.

Maybe if I learn, I can find work somewhere." Rosalinda cast a quick, uncertain glance in Yoana's direction.

"The only work you're fit for is--"

"Enough!" Victoro's shout must have startled Yoana, because she jumped. Amado gave her shoulder a gentle squeeze.

Victoro pointed to Cisto's horse. "Rosalinda has chosen. Take your horse and go before I decide to do the world a favor and leave your sorry carcass for the buzzards."

Cisto swung onto his mount. He cast a disparaging look in Rosalinda's direction, but didn't spare either of his children, Isabel or Luis, a hint of regard. As he reined the horse toward the trail, he turned to Yoana and Amado. His silent communication told Amado he would kill him the next time they saw one another.

He ignored Yoana as he turned his horse toward the path leading upward. Why? His avoidance seemed almost more threatening than his usual leers and threats. Amado moved behind Yoana and rested his hands on her shoulders. For a moment she leaned back against him as if drawing courage from his strength. He didn't think he could have been given a better gift.

Cisto spurred his horse and pounded out of the camp.

Amado wanted to believe that was the last they would see of him. But something deep inside knew…

Cisto was far from finished with him.

And Yoana.

THE AFTERNOON FLEW PAST. Victoro stayed in camp with Lorenzo. Amado had the sense it was in case Cisto didn't listen and returned for Rosalinda or Yoana. Amado hadn't wanted to leave, but he knew the bandit leader and Lorenzo were capable of providing protection. He went up canyon with Miguel and Tomás to work with the horses. They had most of them ready to ride, although they were a little rough.

They returned to camp to the tantalizing aroma of roasting meat. Yoana sat on the cleared space with the children clustered around her intent on learning whatever she was writing in the dirt. Yoana glanced up, and Amado winked at her. A flush crept up her cheeks. She ducked her head back down, but not before he saw the small smile tilting the corners of her full mouth.

For her sake, Amado wanted to track down Cisto and make sure he never again threatened anyone. All afternoon, Amado struggled with the decision he faced. He had more than one promise to fulfill. He'd thought the promise given to his dying brother and his father would be easy to fulfill, but he found the actual act of killing a man didn't appeal to him. Something his mother always said about God instilling certain values in a man's heart kept running through his mind. Did that mean God didn't want him to avenge his brother's death?

When he'd gone on this mission, Amado had been certain he would be doing God's work. Exacting vengeance. Getting retribution. Ridding the world of someone as terrible as Cisto, if he was the one, couldn't be wrong, could it? Not when a man did it in the Lord's name.

But now... he wasn't so sure.

After the meal, Teo, Maria, and the other children began to beg Yoana to tell them a story. Since the confrontation with Cisto, most of the children had been very subdued, especially Maria. The young girl had seen and heard firsthand the horror her mother lived through. She now stuck to Yoana like a burr to a horse's hide. Isabel, too, didn't seem to want to leave Yoana's side.

"Tell the children a story, and then we will have some music to liven the night," Victoro said. He settled down next to Pabladora and put his arm around her.

"Let's see." Yoana got a faraway look in her eye as she thought. "How about if we hear a story about being very brave? This is a story about a boy who fought a giant when a whole army was too scared to fight him."

"The army men were scared?" Teo's eyes were huge as he stared at Yoana.

"That's right. This happened many, many years ago." Yoana smiled down at the boy. "Remember we've talked about the Israelites, God's people?" At Teo's nod, she continued. "Well, the Philistine army, Israel's enemy, came against the Israelites. They wanted to fight, and they were very mean."

"Like Cisto?" Maria's whisper caught at Amado's heart.

"Maybe even meaner." Yoana hugged the girl. Maria shuddered and hid her face against Yoana's arm.

"The Philistines had a man who was a giant. He challenged anyone from the Israelite army to fight him. The Israelites were so afraid that they ran away every time the giant came out."

"A giant?" Teo looked around the camp. "Was he bigger than Victoro?"

Yoana nodded.

"Bigger than Lorenzo?" Teo's eyes widened at Yoana's nod. "Bigger than Amado?"

"He would have been about as big as you if you were standing on Amado's shoulders," Yoana said. All the children looked at Amado, their mouths open.

"The giant's name was Goliath, and he came out every day to challenge the Israelites."

"Did anyone ever fight him?" asked Teo. "Did they shoot him with their gun?

"They didn't have guns back then. They only had swords and bows and arrows. Remember, this was a long time ago."

"Did the Israelites find a strong man to fight for them?" Teo's intent expression focused on Yoana.

"Actually, there was a boy, maybe the age of Tomás or a little younger. He lived in the hills taking care of his father's sheep. He loved God, though, and trusted God to always take care of him. His name was David, and he often had to fight bears or lions to save the lambs." Yoana reached over to smooth Maria's hair.

"One day, David took some food to his brothers who were with the Israelite army. He heard the giant when Goliath roared out his challenge. All the men ran away, but David wasn't afraid."

"How could he be brave when all the grown men were afraid?" Teo asked.

"Because he knew that God would take care of him. David also knew that God didn't want this giant to threaten His people."

"What did he do?" Teo had risen up on his knees, his fingers gripping Yoana's skirt at the knee.

"David told his brothers he would fight the giant. The king tried to give David armor to wear, but David refused. He fought bears and lions without armor. Plus, he knew God would help him."

"Did he take a big sword?" Teo asked.

"No. He used the same weapon that he used with the animals who tried to hurt the sheep. He used a sling with a rock in it."

Maria and Teo's mouths fell open. They both looked over at Tomás, who blushed deep red.

"Just like Tomás uses on the rabbits." Teo breathed the words, and Maria nodded.

"That's right," Yoana said. "David took his sling. Goliath thought it was pretty funny the army would send a boy against him. David swung the rock around in the sling and let fly. The rock flew so hard, when it hit the giant's forehead, it got buried there."

"He killed him with a rock? Just like a rabbit?" Teo couldn't suppress his shock.

"No, the rock knocked him out. Goliath fell down, and David took Goliath's sword and cut off the giant's head."

Teo crawled up next to Yoana. "Did Goliath's army kill David?"

"No. They were so afraid that they ran away. The Israelites chased after them and killed many of them."

"Ay! Oh!" Teo sat back on his heels.

"Ay!" Maria repeated as she leaned her cheek against Yoana's sleeve.

"So, if someone yells at us or at someone we know, God says it's all right for us to kill them?" Teo's earnest question struck at Amado's heart.

"Oh, no." Yoana smoothed the boy's hair back from his forehead. "God wants to be our protector. God doesn't want us to be afraid, but to trust Him with our life and the lives of those we love. The Bible teaches us God will watch out for us so that we don't have to seek vengeance."

"So we just leave them alone no matter how bad they are?" Teo scrunched up his face.

"God asks us to trust Him." Yoana's gaze tracked to Rosalinda for an instant.

"That is a hard lesson to learn, Teo. Tomorrow, I'll tell you more about how much God loves you and how we know that."

"Let's have some music." Victoro slapped his leg. Miguel pulled out his guitar. He began to play and Lorenzo began to sing a lilting melody that brightened the mood of the whole camp.

Amado couldn't get the story of David and the giant out of his mind. He slipped away from the others and walked up canyon, Yoana's words echoing in his head. She had to be wrong. God would want him to avenge his brother's death. He'd given his promise before God to both his dying brother and his father. Besides, if he let Cisto and the others go, he would be breaking his promise. Didn't God also expect him to fulfill his promises? To honor his word?

The sound of restless horses jerked him out of his reverie. He'd reached the top of the trail overlooking the corral when he heard the scream of a horse in pain.

CHAPTER FIFTEEN

An animal's scream raised bumps on Yoana's arms. The music stopped. Miguel tossed his guitar to Dolores. He, Lorenzo, and Victoro leaped to their feet.

"Tomás, stay with the women." Victoro snapped out the order. The men grabbed their rifles and raced up the path.

The younger children began to cry. Maria hid her face against Yoana's arm. Even Teo scooted close enough to wrap his arms around her legs. She could feel the tremors of his small body.

Yoana searched the trees for Amado. He'd gotten up when she finished her story and stalked into the woods. She wondered at the time if she'd said something to upset him, but couldn't imagine what that would be.

She didn't see any sign of him.

A gunshot cracked. A revolver, from the sound of it. But the men who just left had carried rifles. An animal roared. Another horse screamed. Yoana couldn't stop the shudder that wracked her body.

"Quick!" Pabladora waved her hands. "Get the children over by the fire! Tomás, add some wood. Build the fires up. Hurry!"

Tomás stumbled as he rushed to the woodpile. He grabbed a few sticks and threw them at the flames. Most of them missed.

"Teo." Yoana knew the young boy usually helped with building the fire. "Remember how brave David was?" Teo nodded, and Yoana smiled at him. "Why don't you be a brave boy and help Tomás with the wood."

Teo leaped to his feet. He raced across the clearing to the pile of sticks he and Maria had gathered earlier in the day. He lifted an armful and marched to the closest fire. Tomás seemed to calm as he watched the younger boy work. He gathered an armload and went to the other fire and stoked the flames. Within a few minutes both fires were blazing high.

Another roar vibrated the very air of the forest. Yoana picked up Luis and Isabel, hugging them close. Maria clung to her skirts. Carmen cried too hard to move, and Yoana didn't know how to carry the third child.

"Let me help." Leya raced over and picked up the wailing Carmen. She and Yoana hurried to the cooking area with their charges.

The staccato cracks of more gunfire erupted. Another roar, this one closer. Yoana's heart pounded. She moved with the other women until they huddled together between the roaring fires, the children inside the protective circle they formed.

Tomás stood, legs akimbo, his rifle held in both hands. He shook like a leaf, but he didn't run. He faced up-canyon as they listened to something crashing through the brush, coming closer.

Feliciana, face pale, started toward Tomás. Pabladora grabbed the girl's shoulder and stopped her. "If he needs to shoot, you'll only be in the way. Stay here. Don't distract him."

Victoro shouted something. Amado answered. Yoana's knees wobbled. Amado was alive! Knowing that strengthened her.

Leya stood next to Yoana, holding Carmen in a tight embrace. The young girl had her face buried in Leya's neck. Leya's eyes were closed. Her lips moved in prayer.

Something shifted just outside the firelight. *Oh, God, please protect us. You protected David in the Bible. Help us now. Show these people how You are there for all of us.* Yoana's blood chilled as a huge bear skidded into the clearing.

Someone screamed. Tomás raised his rifle, but the barrel shook so badly the shot went wild. The bear stood on its hind legs and let out a roar that shattered the night. Yoana had never seen anything so magnificent--or terrifying.

All the children began to wail except for Teo. He charged toward Tomás before anyone could grab him. Teo snatched a burning limb from the fire as the bear dropped down and began to run toward them with dizzying speed. Teo turned and thrust the burning stick into the bear's face.

The bear bawled. The sound ate through Yoana like acid. The flames touched the beast's nose, and the bear reared up on his hind feet a second time. His furious growl made Yoana want to clap her hands over her ears. Her heart pounded. "Teo! Get *back!*"

Dolores clutched Carlito to her chest as she too cried out to Teo. Yoana handed Isabel and Luis to Rosalinda. She leaped toward Teo, even as she knew she'd be too late. The enraged bear came down. One huge paw swiped at Teo and knocked him into the flames. The beast turned and raced off into the night.

Yoana hurtled over a log to reach the boy, and she snatched him from the flames. *God, help! Please!* The men raced into the clearing, Amado in the lead. He bounded across the open space to grab Teo from Yoana and drag her back from the fire.

Amado dropped to the ground with Teo under him. Dolores cried out. Yoana turned and held her hand palm out to caution Dolores. To reassure her Amado had done the right thing. All the women rushed toward them.

Turning back, Yoana watched as Amado sat up. Teo lay stretched out on the ground, his clothing still smoldering, his eyes closed. Yoana's throat caught on a sob. Had Teo given his life to save them?

The young boy opened one eye. He peered up at Yoana and the others clustered around him—

And grinned.

Black soot covered his face. His white teeth gleamed amidst the dirt. He laughed and sat up. "Yoana, I was brave just like David!"

She dropped to her knees beside the boy and gathered him in her arms. She couldn't stop the tears or the thanksgiving that poured out of her as she realized the miracle God had performed.

"Did you see how I hit that bear in the nose with the fire?" Teo pushed away from her. Excitement lit his eyes as he turned to Amado. "I made him really mad."

"I guess you did." Amado's voice sounded gruff. "I didn't see it, but I sure heard him."

"Teo." Yoana wanted to grab the boy but feared he might be hurt beneath all the grime and soot. "You need to sit down so we can see if you're injured. That bear hit you pretty hard, and then you fell into the fire."

"I *flew* into the fire." Teo's chest puffed out. "I flew like a bird. Like a hawk diving." Teo made a downward motion with his hand and a keening sound through his teeth.

"That you did." Yoana nodded, trying to eject the sight from her mind. The terror of the moment still made her pulse race.

Teo sat down between Amado and Yoana. Amado unbuttoned the boy's ruined shirt. He looked up at Dolores. "Can you get him some clean clothes?"

Leya said, "There's a little warm water left in the bucket if it hasn't spilled. I'll bring it with a rag to wash him."

Yoana shot her tía a grateful look. "Teo, do you hurt anywhere." She leaned close with Amado to peer at the boy's chest, half afraid that they would find broken bones or burns.

"My back hurts a little, but not much." Teo reached behind him on the left side to touch the spot where the bear's paw must have connected with his small body.

Yoana didn't know how the boy could even move.

"Turn around." Amado eased Teo from the ground to help him. Dolores placed a pile of clean clothes on the ground beside Yoana. She took one look at Teo's back and covered her mouth with her hands, unable to stop the cry of dismay. Lorenzo moved to slip his arm around her.

Teo's back hadn't been cut by the bear, but the skin already mottled with dark bruises. Amado began to run his fingertips across the boy's ribs. Teo gave no indication that the touch hurt him. Yoana couldn't believe he wouldn't cry out or pull away. She turned to look up at Amado and saw her own amazement reflected in his face.

"Teo, does this hurt at all?" Amado pressed harder in the darkest area of bruising.

"Not really." Teo tried to look over his shoulder.

Leya brought the bucket of warm water and placed it on the ground next to Yoana, then handed Yoana a clean rag.

She got the rag wet and began to wash Teo's back and arms. The bruising looked like Teo should be on his deathbed, but he didn't seem to be affected by it. They turned him back around and began to clean his face and neck, checking for burns. There weren't any.

There was only one explanation.

God.

"This is incredible." Amado touched Teo's face and then his back. "How did this happen?"

"Leya and I were praying." Yoana glanced up at her tía. "This is a gift from God for a very brave boy who defended us." She helped Teo put on his clean shirt and then watched as Dolores enfolded him in her embrace.

Amado stood and offered his hand to Yoana. She took it, stiff from crouching down so long. He didn't release her hand when she stood, and she didn't pull away. The warmth of his touch comforted her. She longed to leap into his embrace. To relish his strength. To rest in the safety he offered.

Amado had so many honorable qualities. She'd once thought Gabrio, her betrothed, would have such qualities, but her only memories of him were from when she'd been four years old. The only real memory she had was his promise.

The promise he hadn't kept.

"We'll need to be up early so we can track the bear." Victoro's forehead creased, his mouth pressed into a thin line. "I know at least one of us got a shot in him. He's wounded and will be that much more dangerous."

Teo pushed away from his mother. "I burned his nose!"

"That you did, son." Victoro nodded. Lorenzo tugged a hank of the boy's hair.

"We should take turns watching the herd in case he comes back in the night." Victoro glanced at the women, whose faces still reflected fear. "If he does come back, he'll want the horses, not us. You don't have to worry."

"Tomás and I will take the first watch. Lorenzo and Miguel will take second watch. Amado, you're on your own with the third watch, but it's doubtful he'll be back then. You good with that?"

Amado nodded. "I'll get you all up early and have the horses ready to go. As soon as it's light enough to track, we can be on his trail."

"Sounds good." Victoro nodded. "Now, let's get these *niños* in bed. We've had enough excitement for one night." Victoro led Pabladora to their small shelter, closest to the cook fires.

Yoana hugged each of the children and kissed them good night. Maria clung to her, not wanting to go home with Rosalinda. Yoana met Rosalinda's gaze. This woman had often been antagonistic, but now she just seemed sad. "Will you be all right tonight?"

Rosalinda shrugged. Yoana didn't know why the other woman

refused to talk with her. She turned to pick up the bucket of dirty water.

"Will you teach me?"

Rosalinda's blurted question brought Yoana back around.

"Will you teach me to read and write?"

Yoana smiled. "Of course. We can start tomorrow if you'd like. Have you ever had any schooling?"

Rosalinda shook her head. "I was only a young girl when they took me." She turned away and led her children to their home.

Yoana watched her walk away. She used to feel so sorry for herself, but now she realized so many besides her lived much harsher lives.

THAT NIGHT, Yoana had trouble sleeping. Visions of the huge grizzly rampaging through camp, tossing the children every which way, tormented her dreams. Every little sound startled her awake. Her heart pounded as she strained to hear what had awakened her, only to discover some night creature or bird had been responsible.

In the morning, her eyes felt so gritty it was as though she'd washed them with sand.

By the time she made it to the cooking fires, the men were gone to hunt the bear. Yoana tried to hide her disappointment. She'd wanted to see Amado before he left. What if he didn't come back? She shuddered at the vivid images from her dreams. *Please, God...make them go away.*

The day dragged by as she taught lessons for Teo and Maria. Carmen and Luis listened, but were too young to sit still for long. They loved the songs and games though. Luis begged every day for her to play caballito with him. He would bounce on top of her foot and laugh so hard everyone in camp smiled.

Pabladora had Dolores and Rosalinda cut a chunk from a deer

in the late afternoon. Feliciana built up the fire and Leya helped her spit the roast. Yoana overheard Pabladora say when the men returned they would be as ravenous as the bear, and food needed to be ready.

Dolores mixed up some dough for fresh tortillas. She began to cook them, and the scent made Yoana's stomach rumble. Teo and Maria laughed. Teo dropped to the ground as if he'd fainted, his new favorite thing to do. Maria turned to look at Yoana. The young girl's face turned white. Her green eyes grew round with fear, and she screamed.

Yoana whirled around. On the rise just above her, the grizzly rose up on his hind legs and roared. His huge body towered over Yoana. She had no place to run!

The children.

Her heart thundered. Only Maria and Teo were with her. Carmen and Luis had gone to the stream with Leya and Feliciana. The babies were with their mothers by the cook fire.

"Teo. Maria. Don't run." Yoana reached behind her, relieved when the two children grasped her hands. Maria held so tight Yoana knew her hand would go numb within minutes.

The bear dropped down to all fours. He swung his head from side to side. His beady eyes focused on her. Saliva dripped from his open jaws. Yoana froze in place. What should she do? The fires crackled a song of refuge, but she'd never make it there. Not with the two children.

"Teo!" Dolores screamed out her son's name.

"Dolores." Yoana tried to keep her voice calm. "Dolores, can you hear me?" She didn't take her eyes off the bear.

"What, Yoana?" Pabladora answered her. "We're listening."

"Move slowly and build up the fire. Don't scream or make fast movements. Maybe he will leave and not bother us." Yoana tried to keep from shaking. She didn't want to let Teo and Maria know how terrified she was.

The grizzly took a step toward them, then stopped, lifting his massive head to snuffle the wind.

Maria whimpered, pressing her face against Yoana's leg.

The bear took another step. He raised his nose and curled his lip. Sharp teeth glistened in the fading sunlight.

"I'll get a stick." Teo's voice shook thought he tried to sound brave.

"No!" Yoana spoke firmly. "Not this time." *Please, Lord, make him listen.* "A burning stick works. A regular stick will only make him angrier."

With a low growl, the bear charged down the slope. Someone screamed, but Yoana waited. When the animal was only a couple steps away, she pushed Maria and Teo to the side. As soon as she released them, she leaped the other way, hoping to confuse the angry beast.

The bear roared its fury.

Yoana stumbled and fell as the bear swiped at her. Massive claws caught the sleeve of her dress and ripped it away. The bear shot past her, then skidded to a stop. It turned toward Yoana and roared again.

Someone shouted. A horse whinnied in terror. The bear turned to face the new threat. It rose up on its hind legs and a ferocious roar shook the ground.

Yoana threw a desperate glance at the children. Teo held Maria tight. The little girl was crying and wanted to come to Yoana, but Teo held her back. *Please, God, don't let the bear hurt the children.*

Amado thundered over the rise on his buckskin. He already had his rope in his hand when Yoana saw him catch sight of the bear. Lorenzo, right behind him, had his lariat shaken out too. As the bear dropped down to charge, Amado sent a loop sailing over the grizzly's head.

Lorenzo spurred his horse to the other side and dropped a second loop over the bear's head. They both urged their mounts backward to draw the ropes tight. If they could keep the bear still enough, one of the others could make the kill.

The bear fought with a fury Yoana had rarely seen. She'd heard Lucio talk about the bears he and the vaqueros at the rancho had roped, but she'd never seen one this close.

Victoro and Miguel raced up to add their lassos to Amado's and Lorenzo's. The bear's claws dug into the earth, sending huge clumps into the air.

Yoana scrambled toward Maria and Teo. The little girl had begun to hit Teo because she wanted to get to Yoana. The bear was too close to them. She had to get to them. She should have run with the *niños* while she had the chance.

"Tomás!" Victoro bellowed at the young man. "The rifle. *Shoot.*"

Tomás hurried down the path on his horse. He brought out his rifle. This trembling boy? How could Victoro trust him to shoot again?

Yoana reached Teo and Maria. She folded Maria into her arms and hugged the frightened girl close.

"Steady." Amado's voice sounded too calm for the situation. Tomás took a deep breath, his chest heaving. He steadied the gun and fired.

The bear reared up, jerking Miguel sideways in the saddle. The rope loosened a fraction, and the bear surged forward--straight for Yoana and the children, his slavering jaws dripping bloody saliva.

CHAPTER SIXTEEN

"Lucio."

The command in his father's voice halted him as he had his hand out to open the door. He'd been on his way to see Ramón, to find out if he would be strong enough to help him look for Yoana and Leya today. Lucio chafed at the delay. He didn't want to face his father again. They'd had more arguments in the past few weeks since Yoana had been kidnapped than they'd had for all of his thirty years before that. Don Armenta couldn't seem to understand that God had finally given Lucio the courage to stand for the right instead of bending to his father's ungodly demands.

"Sí?" Lucio stood in the doorway to his father's sanctum, his office. The place where he reigned as king. He fought to remember God called him to honor his father. How could he honor such a man?

"Lucio, I want you to take a message to Mateo for me today. He needs to send some of the horses from his herds to the main hacienda. I have a couple of buyers coming next week. Since we lost the livestock to the bandoleros and had to replace them for the Santiagos', we're running short on our best stock. Mateo should be able to get some ready within a few days."

"I'll send Berto to do that." Lucio strode toward the desk, his hand out, as his father finished scratching the pen against the paper.

"I want you to go." Don Armenta met Lucio's gaze with unwavering determination. "I know what you have planned for today. I heard the men talking about Ramón being ready to help you search, but your time is wasted there. You need to admit that you won't find your sister and tía. It's been too long."

"I will not give up." Lucio curled his fingers into a fist. "They haven't sent Leya back after you paid money for her release. I think there is still hope. They're probably considering how to get more money out of you. If that's the case, they won't have harmed Yoana or Leya."

"You are a dreamer, boy." His father's face darkened, his mouth thinned to an almost invisible line. "These men think nothing of killing someone. They won't care at all about taking a girl's innocence and discarding her when they're done."

"So, you'll just write her off? Both of them?" Lucio forced his fingers to uncurl and drummed his hand against his thigh. "You might do that, but I can't. All these years I've known the truth of what happened the day our mother died. I've kept quiet by telling myself I was respecting you. In truth, I was afraid. No more. I refuse to sacrifice Yoana any longer. I'm going after her. You can find someone else to send your letter."

Lucio whirled on his heel and stalked from the room. He expected to hear his father disown him or tell him he'd lied. Silence followed him instead. He didn't even look back as he left the house. Maybe he shouldn't have talked to his father that way. Maybe he'd been disrespectful. But didn't he have a duty to protect his sister--and to tell the truth?

As he approached the stable, he saw Berto leaning over the rail as he watched Antonio work with one of the newer horses. The young stallion, a beautiful palomino, would make someone a great horse some day, but right now the noble creature didn't want to let anyone sit on his back. Antonio eased down into the saddle as two of the other vaqueros held the stallion's head.

When they let go, the horse shot into the air as if God had a rope above and jerked him aloft. Lucio paused to watch as the horse twisted and bucked. Antonio stuck to him like a burr. Sunlight glinted off the palomino's coat until the shine dimmed as sweat darkened the gold to brown. Lucio could feel every jolt in his bones. He'd been in Antonio's place often enough.

The men cheered as Antonio brought the stallion to a halt. The horse's sides heaved with the effort to shake his rider.

Lucio headed for the bunkhouse. Since Ramón had been shot and Lucio had to let Tomás go and bring the tracker back to the ranchero, Lucio had tried to track his sister by himself, going out almost every day. But he didn't have the same skills as Ramón. He'd lost the trail and hadn't been able to find anything until yesterday.

"Hey, Amígo." Lucio grinned at Ramón, who still had his arm in a sling. The wound to his chest had almost taken his life. Lucio had managed to slow the bleeding and get him back to the rancho. One of the women had healing skills, and she'd spent several days caring for Ramón before they knew for sure that he would live.

"I'm ready to go." Ramón shoved his hat on his head. "As soon as we're out of sight, I'll take this dratted rag off my arm. Eulalia hounds me worse than a mother hen. She follows me around as if I'm going to drop dead if she doesn't watch me every second."

"You have Eulalia to thank for your life, my friend." Lucio squeezed Ramón's shoulder. He didn't want to touch him hard because the lines from the pain he'd suffered still creased his face.

"I know." Ramón stuck his head out the door and looked both ways before he stepped outside. "But I'm fine now. She doesn't need to treat me like some *bebé* who needs his bottle."

"From the look of you, I'm wondering if you missed a few of those bottles. If you get any thinner, your clothes will slide right off." Lucio laughed as Ramón stopped and perused his sagging pants.

"The way she feeds me, I'll be too fat for my horse to carry me before the month is out. That woman wants to stuff food down my throat all day long."

They stepped into the dim interior of the stable. The boys working there already had Ramón's bay and Lucio's dun ready to go. The two horses stood hip shot, heads hanging, eyes drooping. Lucio figured his horse needed all the rest he could get with all the mountain travel they'd gotten lately.

They led the horses out, but before they could mount, a woman's voice drifted across the courtyard. "Ramón. Ramón, wait."

He groaned and dropped his forehead against his horse's side.

Lucio bit the inside of his cheek to keep silent. He pretended to tighten the girth strap of the saddle. If he looked at Ramón, he'd burst out laughing.

"Ramón, you need to take this with you." Eulalia huffed up to them holding a basket that could almost carry a cow. Short and round as a butterball, Eulalia mothered all the men. Her graying hair straggled out of the braids wound around her head. Red-faced, she smiled so wide Lucio couldn't help but smile back at her. Even Ramón lost some of the scowl he'd gotten when she'd called to him.

Lucio decided to help Ramón out since the man had been kept from doing anything for so long. "Now, Eulalia, we're not taking a pack mule with us. Let me see what you've got here." He took the basket and almost groaned at the weight. He set it on the ground with a thunk.

Ramón leaned down as Lucio flipped open the lid. Spicy scents wafted up. Lucio drew in a deep breath, and saw Ramón do the same. Eulalia did most of the cooking, and all the men loved her food. Several towel-wrapped parcels filled the basket. Lucio reached down. They were still warm.

If he hadn't just eaten, he would open these right now.

Lucio looked at the tracker. "Why don't we each take a couple of these to put in our saddle bags?" He handed two of the packets to Ramón. "That way we'll have enough for today and maybe some for tomorrow." He could see the disappointment in the droop of Eulalia's mouth.

"Don't worry. I'll make sure Ramón eats his food. He's as skinny as a starved dog." Lucio shot an amused glance at Ramón, who glowered at him.

"You take good care. Watch that shoulder." Eulalia stood with her hands on her ample hips and watched as they rode from the yard. Ramón kept looking over his shoulder as if he expected her to climb on a horse and follow them.

Lucio chuckled as Ramón picked up the pace. "Relax. We'll be out of sight as soon as we hit that rise. Just make sure you don't lose that bandage. You'll need to put it back on before we get home."

They rode steadily until they came to the steeper trails up the mountains, where the horses couldn't go as fast. Lucio kept a close eye on Ramón, not convinced the man was ready for a full day in the saddle. When the sun stood overhead, he called a halt so they could eat some of Eulalia's food.

"What have you found so far?" Ramón chewed a huge bite as he spoke.

"I lost the trail. I told you that, but then two days ago, I found some signs. It looked like a horse heading away from where I thought the camp might be. I followed the horse and saw the man who took Leya. He was by himself."

"You didn't get him?" Ramón frowned.

Lucio shook his head and swallowed some tortilla. "He saw me and took off like lightning. He knew these hills better than I. I didn't want to chase him too far and end up shot and left for bear bait."

"Did you try to track where he'd come from?" Ramón caught a bit of meat that fell from his tortilla and popped it into his mouth.

"I went for a ways. I heard some shooting, but I couldn't take them all, so I returned to the rancho." Lucio swiped his arm across his mouth to wipe away some grease. "My father would never have agreed to me bringing more of the men unless I'd actually seen the camp. We'll find it by tomorrow and then go back for help. I want to make sure this is where Yoana and Leya are being held."

"That makes sense." Ramón wiped his hands on his pant leg. "You ready to go?"

They rode hard the rest of the day. Lucio showed Ramón where he'd seen the lone bandit. They looked around the site but didn't find any evidence the man had made a camp there. He must have moved on.

That night, after they made camp, Ramón fell asleep sitting up. They'd built a small fire in a sheltered group of rocks where the flames wouldn't be seen. Ramón's chin dropped against his chest, and he began to snore so loudly Lucio feared someone might hear. He shook his compadre awake and made him stretch out where he'd be more comfortable.

When the fire died down, Lucio slipped into his poncho and lay down with his head on his saddle. Through the boughs of the tall pines, he caught a glimpse of the inky night sky dotted with stars. But the beauty couldn't still his thoughts.

What Yoana must be going through?

This had run through his mind over and over since she'd been taken. He wanted to push the abhorrent thoughts away, but feared that without them pushing him, he would lose hope and not work so hard to find her.

Had she given up on him coming to save her? Most likely. Why would she think he would do so? For years, he'd been the brother who left her at their father's mercy.

"God, please give me the chance to make it right with Yoana.

Protect her. Protect Leya. Help Ramón and me to find them tomorrow. Give us wisdom as we go against these desperados."

Lucio closed his eyes. Anger at his father's complacency threatened to choke him. He drew in a shuddering breath. "God, please, help me to not be angry. Help my father see what he has done wrong to Yoana. Please, God, bring healing to our family."

In the morning, Ramón looked more rested, and his color was better. That was good. They would have had to turn back if the older man hadn't recovered from the day in the saddle. They began the laborious process of looking for the camp.

Lucio led the way to the place where he'd heard the shots.

Ramón climbed down from his horse. Lucio joined him as he knelt to look at the worn path. Even Lucio could tell most of the tracks belonged to animals that wandered through the forest. He couldn't see any hoof prints in the dirt.

"No one's come along here for a while." Ramón stared up at the surrounding trees. "That doesn't mean we aren't close. This is mainly for animals. There might be another path not far from here that the bandoleros use." He pointed up at the branch above them. "Look at that."

Lucio squinted as he looked up. "What? I don't see anything."

"That broken branch up there." Ramón indicated a thin branch that dangled above them. The needles were still green but wouldn't be for long. "Even a big bear wouldn't have done that. I'd say a man on a horse has been through here within the last week or two."

CHAPTER SEVENTEEN

The bear snapped the rope taut. Amado's buckskin stumbled to the side. Miguel's cinch broke, and he hit the ground. The saddle, lariat still attached to the pommel, scuttled after the grizzly. Amado's heart seized as the beast, jaws agape, raced straight for Yoana, Teo, and Maria.

"Lorenzo, pull!" Amado reined his horse back. The buckskin dug his hooves into the earth and sat back on his haunches, neck bowed.

Lorenzo and Victoro did likewise with their mounts. Amado's gelding's ears were back, nostrils distended, but it didn't give an inch. Miguel's horse, free of restraints, skittered sideways through the trees. Without a saddle, the horse would be useless in this fight anyway.

"Tomás, shoot!" Victoro yelled at the frozen boy.

"No, Tomás." Amado sent a frantic glance at the inexperienced youth. "He's too close to Yoana and the *niños*. Miguel, get a gun!"

At Victoro's grim nod, Amado prayed the man understood the countermanding of his order. Tomás would be too nervous to make an accurate shot. He could just as easily shoot Yoana or the children as shoot the bear.

The grizzly didn't slow as the ropes tightened. Instead, with the momentum he had going, he began to drag the horses. He'd almost reached Yoana. She stumbled to her feet, fumbling for the children. Her foot slid on the pine needles, and she fell. She threw herself on top of Teo and Maria and pressed the *niños* to the ground.

Amado grabbed his rifle from the scabbard. "Miguel!" When the man looked, Amado tossed the gun to him. Miguel snatched the weapon from the air with practiced ease. He swiveled back to get a clear shot.

"Drag him back." Lorenzo fought to control his terrified horse. The bay reared and bucked, the smell of the wild animal driving him mad.

Amado urged his gelding back. The horse grunted as it fought not to give ground to the grizzly. Victoro, too, began to drag at the bear. The beast rose up above Yoana, its roar echoing through the forest. It whirled back to face the men, but as it did so, a huge paw swiped at Yoana. The claws caught her arm where the sleeve had been torn away. Red blossomed across her golden flesh.

Amado cried out his fury. He wanted to rush to her side, but if he did, the bear would win. So he worked with the buckskin to hold the bear in place.

Miguel dropped to one knee. He snapped the rifle to his shoulder, and the report cracked. The bear jerked. Miguel snatched up the second rifle he'd been carrying. He raised the gun--and sent a bullet straight into the grizzly's brain. The bear screamed. Rushed forward. Reared up—

And fell over backwards.

The roaring ceased.

Amado's pulse thrummed in his ears. The bear didn't move, but even so, Miguel chambered a third round. Keeping the gun pointed at the beast, he walked closer. When he stood only a few feet from the grizzly, he sent another shot through the bear's ear.

Amado flipped the rope free. He dropped the reins, knowing

his buckskin would stay in place, and leaped from the saddle. He raced to where Yoana lay beside the two children. Blood soaked the pine needles at her side. The gash in her arm gaped open.

If they didn't stop the bleeding, she would die.

"Yoana." He dropped to his knees beside her. She lifted her head, eyes glazed. Teo and Maria huddled next to her, trembling, clutching her skirt.

Amado tore off his shirt. He wound the material around her arm to staunch the blood flow. He gathered her in his arms and lifted her, spinning to the women.

"Pabladora, she's hurt!"

The women were huddled in a group around the other children near the fires. Pabladora broke away and hurried toward him.

"What happened? We couldn't see her." She touched the blood-soaked shirt and pointed to a table. "Put her there. Rosalinda, go get my sewing needles and thread. Dolores, put on some water to heat. Teo, go find Leya and Feliciana. I'll need them too."

Amado tried to be gentle as he laid Yoana on the table. She moaned. Her lips were pressed in a straight line and ringed in white.

Rosalinda set the sewing items on the edge of the table, panting from her run to Pabladora's shelter. She pushed Amado out of the way and began to unwrap the soaked shirt.

"Dolores, are there some more rags." Rosalinda pushed the edges of the cut together. "Some of the muslin ones would be best. Bring a wet cloth too, so we can wash the blood away before Pabladora stitches this wound."

She looked up at Amado and frowned. "If you're not squeamish around blood, you can stay and help hold her down. It will hurt when Pabladora starts the sewing."

"I can hear you."

Amado could barely hear Yoana's strained voice over the pounding of his heart.

Leya rushed up to them. Her face pale, she grasped Yoana's hand on the other side of the table from Amado. "Yoana." Tears glittered in Leya's eyes.

"It's just a scratch, Leya." Yoana attempted to smile, but her mouth wavered in more of a grimace.

Pabladora came around beside Rosalinda. They bent together to examine the deep cut, then stepped away and conversed in low tones. Amado couldn't hear what they were saying, but from what he'd seen of the injury, he didn't need to hear them.

They weren't sure if they could save Yoana's arm.

"Watch her, Leya." He stalked over to Pabladora and Rosalinda. "I'm not a doctor, but I do know a thing or two." He kept his voice low so Yoana wouldn't overhear. The two women waited, their brows knit. "We need very hot water to clean the needle and the thread you are going to use. We will wash her arm. The blood is not spurting, so that is good. The cut is deep, but if we clean it well, then sew it up good and keep the bandages changed and clean, she will be fine."

"The bear's claw would have dirt on it." Pabladora shook her head. "That is the big danger. There could be dirt inside the arm that we don't know about. We need to find a way to clean the cut."

"I'll have Lorenzo bring that bottle of tequila he's been saving." Dolores set a bucket of steaming water on the ground beside the table. Rosalinda and Pabladora nodded. Dolores ran for the alcohol while the other women began to clean the items they needed to use. A few minutes later they were ready.

"Come, Teo, you can help us with the bear meat." Lorenzo motioned to the boy. Teo strutted along beside Lorenzo, his focus taken from Yoana. Pabladora nodded at Feliciana, who took the other children off to play.

Pabladora leaned close to Yoana. "This will hurt, but we have to clean the wound." She unwrapped Yoana's arm, started to tilt the bottle, then stopped and glanced at Amado. "You got her? I've seen grown men come up off a table like this when alcohol hits such a wound."

"I've got her." Amado leaned his weight over Yoana's midsection while Leya and Dolores held down her feet and legs. Rosalinda stood beside Pabladora to help hold Yoana's arm in place.

"Look at me, Yoana." Amado watched as she tore her gaze from what Pabladora was preparing to do. "Keep your eyes on mine. Scream if you need to but remember the children." He winked at her.

Yoana narrowed her gaze, looking at him through slitted eyes as if she'd like to send the grizzly after him. He knew when Pabladora poured on the alcohol, for her eyes widened and tears welled up. She pressed her lips tight together but didn't scream or cry out. The only sound she made was her sharp intake of breath.

Stronger than any man in camp. Including him.

"That's done." Pabladora capped the bottle and set it on the ground beneath the table. "Now, we need to do the stitching. This won't feel so good either. Amado, I don't know what you're doing, but keep it up."

He didn't blink as he stared at Yoana. She blinked away tears as the needle entered her tender flesh. Once again, she didn't cry out. Instead, her whole focus centered on Amado. He thought he could drown in her eyes. The golden-brown depths were filled with pain and anger at the moment, but he'd never seen a stronger woman. He could still see her throwing herself on top of Teo and Maria when the bear charged them.

By the time Pabladora finished stitching and cleaned and bandaged the wound, Yoana had turned as pale as one of the fluffy clouds in the sky. Amado wanted to drag her into his arms, to sit and hold her and not let go.

If these feelings kept up, his heart would be lost. Maybe it already was.

Pabladora lay her hand on Yoana's shoulder. "There. Amado

will help you over to the fire. I think you need to sit and rest for a while. We'll clean up and get started on something to eat. I believe that deer is a bit too well cooked." The older woman smiled and winked at Yoana. "The venison looks like you cooked tonight."

Pabladora began to clean up her supplies. Amado caught the stench of burned meat and glanced over to see that when the women built up the fire, they hadn't taken the time to remove the spitted roast. The charred meat wouldn't be fit for a dog to chew on right now.

He scooped Yoana up in his arms, not giving her the choice of walking. She pushed against him with her uninjured arm but didn't have the strength to stop him.

He grinned at Pabladora. "I think there might be some fresh bear meat for supper. I would love to sink my teeth into that grizzly."

The women laughed and began to chatter among themselves. Amado strode to a log near the fire. He sat down with Yoana on his lap.

She struggled to sit up. "Let me go. I can sit on my own. What will everyone think?" She pushed upright, but he kept his arms around her.

"Leya." Amado waited until Yoana's *señorita* came over. "If I carry Yoana up to the shelter, will you help her change her dress. This one seems to be ruined."

"I can help her up the path." Leya held out her hand to Yoana.

"I don't want her to fall. She'll be a little weak from blood loss. I can carry her." He had no desire to let go of Yoana. He wasn't sure he'd be ready to let her go even at the shelter, but she would need privacy to change out of her bloodied dress.

At the shelter, Amado waited outside to help Yoana back to the fire. She came out on Leya's arm, her cheeks hollowed. She started to walk, then swayed. Amado scooped her up, cuddled her close, and strode back down the canyon.

After supper, Teo sidled up to Yoana. Maria came with him, acting like she wanted to sit on Yoana's lap, but Rosalinda cautioned the children to leave Yoana alone. Amado saw what a struggle that was for them.

He understood.

Teo looked up at him. "Can we sit close to you?"

"Of course." Yoana's smile looked a bit strained but genuine. How she loved the children.

"I think you were as brave as David today." Teo's brown eyes shined as he spoke. "You were as brave as me when I poked that bear with the burning stick."

"That *was* brave." Yoana swayed a bit.

Amado moved closer to support her without appearing too intrusive. He caught the grin Miguel flashed at Lorenzo.

So. The men knew he had feelings toward Yoana.

Teo turned adoring eyes up to Yoana. "Have you ever seen anyone rope a grizzly before?"

"I did a long time ago. I've heard of it being done many times but only saw it once."

"Where?" Teo leaned forward.

"At my rancho. My brothers and some of the vaqueros roped a bear." Yoana seemed reluctant to tell this tale. Should he interrupt?

"Was their grizzly as big as this one?" Teo inched closer.

"I remember it being very huge." Yoana shivered. "But I was a small girl, about the size of Maria, so I may not remember right."

"What did they do with it?" Teo placed one hand on Yoana's knee. The boy had become enraptured with her and her stories.

Amado almost chuckled. Hadn't they all fallen under her spell?

"Well." Yoana cleared her throat and glanced over at Leya. "You know that vaqueros sometimes find grizzly bears in the mountains. Some of the bears come out of the mountains and attack the horses or cattle. When they do that, they must be destroyed. So the vaqueros have made a game of capturing the bears."

"A game?" Teo and Maria both gaped.

"That's right." Yoana nodded. "Killing a bear is dangerous, but vaqueros enjoy a bit of danger. They like to capture the bear and make the killing a challenge."

"How?" asked Teo.

"The bear that my father's vaqueros captured had been destroying some of our prized horses. We also had a very dangerous bull that my father wanted to punish and kill."

"A mean bull?" Teo's eyes were dark with excitement. "What did the bull do?"

"He..." Yoana swallowed hard. She looked over at Leya again, her expression almost one of desperation. Leya's eyes filled with tears, but she nodded at Yoana.

"The bull killed someone on our ranch." Yoana cleared her throat. At the pain in her voice, silence fell over the small group. Amado longed to comfort her but stayed still.

"Who did he kill?"

"Teo, that's enough." Dolores moved to stop her son, but Yoana held up her hand, palm out.

"It's all right, Dolores. He's just curious. That's a sign of how smart he is." She smiled down at Teo, although anyone looking at her could see the strain on her face.

"He killed my mother." Yoana spoke so softly Amado knew only the ones closest to her heard.

Tears spilled over to track down Leya's cheeks.

"Your mother?" Teo's eyes were round. *"Why?"*

Yoana cleared her throat. She opened her mouth to speak but nothing came out. She closed her eyes for a moment, as if she was praying.

"My mother was trying to rescue me, Teo." Yoana blinked. She swiped at her eyes and sniffed. "I wasn't a very good girl. I didn't obey my mother. I wandered into the pen where the dangerous bull was kept."

"You didn't see him there?"

"I wanted to show how brave I could be. I did it to show off. I thought I could cross the pen before the bull would notice me. I was wrong."

"So your mother was brave like David, but God didn't rescue her?" Teo tilted his head to one side as he studied Yoana.

"Sometimes God has another plan, Teo. There are many people in the Bible who died doing God's work." Yoana's breath hitched.

"Is that why your father and brother wanted to make the bear fight the bull?" Teo asked. "So the bear would hurt the bull very bad like they were hurt?"

"Teo, I think you are too smart for such a young boy." Yoana leaned forward to cup his cheek. "Yes, they wanted a way to hurt the bull like he had hurt them. But do you know what?"

Teo shook his head, and Yoana smiled.

"It doesn't work that way. Just because you are hurt, you can't hurt someone else and feel better. The hurt will still be there until you ask God to take it from you. Along with the anger and bitterness and all those emotions that come with being hurt."

Amado felt as if all the breath had been sucked from his lungs. He'd been struggling with the need to let go of his anger and hatred but hadn't figured out how to do so. He'd wanted vengeance, but that wouldn't ease the pain of his loss. *Oh, God, help me.* He'd been in pain for so long over his brother's death, and now...

Now he knew that the pain, the drive for vengeance, were destroying him. *God, I don't even know what to ask. I've thought you wanted me to make things right. I've made promises to others, to myself. If killing Cisto won't free me from the suffering, what am I to do? Help me, Lord.*

"Who won the fight? The bull or the bear?" Teo, in his boyish innocence, wouldn't quit.

"Neither one of them won the fight." Yoana shook her head, sadness shadowing her eyes. "They were both severely wounded. They fought for a long time, but in the end, they both died horribly."

"Did you watch it all?" Teo's eyes widened.

"Yes, I had to." Yoana glanced over to where Leya sat, her hand covering her mouth. Tears still streamed down her face.

Amado wanted to put his hands over Yoana's mouth and stop her words. Maybe if she didn't say what came next, it wouldn't be true.

"Why did you have to watch?" Silence hung heavy over the camp as Teo asked the question. No one moved. No one spoke. Dolores's cheeks reddened as if she were embarrassed at the things her son asked of Yoana, but she didn't stop him. Perhaps because Yoana given permission for him to ask. Amado thought it more likely she let Teo ask because she wanted to know the answer.

Yoana caressed Teo's wavy hair. "I had to watch because my father made me. He wouldn't let me close my eyes or turn away. I was four years old, and he believed I killed my mother as surely as if I'd shot her with a gun."

CHAPTER EIGHTEEN

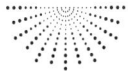

The chill of the night brushed like ice against Yoana's face. She shivered. Pain spiked up her arm and through her body. She'd been trying to get to sleep for hours, but the throbbing kept her awake. Even when the agony eased, the image of the enraged bear thundering toward her, Teo, and Maria brought the terror rushing back. Gaping jaws. Angry eyes. Massive body. Earth-shaking roars.

Every time she closed her eyes, those memories filled her with new horror.

Yes, they'd all applauded her bravery, but no one realized how terrified she'd been. She wasn't brave. She just didn't want to be responsible for anyone else's death. Her father had been right all along. Her mother died because she'd been impulsive. She wouldn't allow Teo or Maria to be torn apart because of her.

She shifted on the narrow cot. The light blanket tightened on her arm. A small moan escaped before she bit her lip to contain the sound.

"Yoana." Leya raised up on her side and reached across to touch cool fingertips to Yoana's forehead. "You feel a bit warm. Are you awake?" Leya swung her legs around and sat up.

"I'm sorry I woke you." Yoana loosened the blanket and bit back another groan at the stab of pain that shot up her arm. "I've tried to be quiet."

"You only woke me a couple of times. I think you dozed off and moaned in your sleep." Leya stroked some stray strands of hair from Yoana's forehead. "As soon as there is enough light, we'll check your bandage and clean the wound. You're sweating. Hopefully, that means if you had a fever, it's broken already."

She hoped Leya was right. Infection meant she could lose her arm, even her life. "I don't know how anything harmful could be in there after Pabladora poured the tequila in the cut. I thought my whole body caught fire."

Leya gave a soft chuckle. "I remember your father using that on me one time. I decided I would rather risk death than have that happen again. However, the alcohol does help. Maybe you shouldn't have resisted Lorenzo and Victoro when they insisted you drink some to help you sleep."

"I can't imagine drinking that foul stuff." Yoana grimaced. "When I was very young, I took a sip from my father's glass when he wasn't looking. I nearly choked to death. The same fire I felt in my arm last night burned my throat and stomach that day. I never tried it again."

Leya chuckled again. "I don't think I heard that story. Did it happen after I came to your rancho to live?"

"No, this was before my mother died." Yoana fell silent. Telling Teo the story last night had brought the painful memories to the forefront of her thoughts, and she couldn't push them back. Images of the bear and bull fighting replayed as if she stood there once again, her father holding her head to force her to watch. The bleeding animals. The roars of challenge. The bellows of pain. The cheers of the vaqueros. She hadn't thought of them in a long time until last night. Now she wished the memories could be forgotten forever.

"You know, Leya. I don't understand how the vaqueros find it entertaining to watch the bear and bull fights. I thought it was cruel, even though the bull killed my mother. He did so because of me." Yoana swallowed past the constriction in her throat.

"I don't understand either." Leya took hold of her hand and squeezed gently. "Men are very different from women. They see the world through different eyes. Sometimes the things they do are not honoring to God, but then some of the things women do aren't either."

"You're right." Yoana shifted. She bit her lip to stifle a groan. Would she ever again find a position that was pain free?

"And you were not at fault for your mother's death. You. Were. Not." Leya's tone firmed as she spoke. Yoana didn't have the strength to argue the point.

A shaft of moonlight shone through a crack in the logs that made up the shelter. Leya released Yoana's hand and bent over to press her eye to the crack. "Try to get a little sleep. Morning will be here soon."

Quiet settled over them, but the ache in her arm wouldn't let Yoana sleep. Did Amado still sleep outside the door? At first, he'd done so to keep her from escaping. Now, though, she was sure he did it to protect her in case Cisto decided to sneak into camp in the middle of the night.

"Leya, are you still awake?" She didn't think her tía slept because her breathing hadn't deepened, but she spoke softly just in case.

"Yes." Leya's mumbled words told Yoana she'd been on the verge of drifting off.

"I'm sorry to wake you again, but we need to talk." Yoana eased over on her side so she would be closer to Leya. She spoke softly so the sound wouldn't carry. If Amado slept outside, she didn't want to wake him and have him overhear this conversation.

"What?" Leya sounded more awake.

"Shhhh. Keep your voice down."

"Why?" Leya rolled over to face her.

"I don't want anyone to overhear us." Yoana took a deep breath. "I've been awake most of the night, so I had time to think. We have to escape from this place and get back home."

"Yoana, we've discussed this before. They watch us too closely. The horses are all up canyon. To get out we would have to ride through camp. Plus, Amado is right outside all night long. How would we get past him?"

"I haven't figured it all out, but I've come up with a plan of sorts." She prayed the plan made sense and would work, because it sounded pretty weak. "Amado leaves sometimes to check on the camp or to go into the trees." She could feel a warm flush creep up her cheeks. "Anyway, we can listen for him to leave and sneak out. We can hide until he goes back to sleep and then slip away to where the horses are kept."

"What about riding through camp? What if the horses make noise or Victoro has one of the men watching the trail? He's been doing that since Cisto left." Leya had a trace of fear in her voice.

"I didn't hear him send anyone to watch tonight."

"Yoana, you were in such pain, you hardly knew when Amado carried you up here. After you told the story, you just slumped against Amado and almost went to sleep."

Yoana closed her eyes as she tried to remember what had occurred after the children went to bed. She could recall the low murmur of voices. The clink of cups as the men finished their drinks. Mostly she could still feel the warmth of Amado's presence. His strength. The comfort she felt resting in his arms. The real reason she had to leave here now. That and her fear for Leya.

Her eyes had drifted shut, but they popped open as another thought hit her. "Leya, the other day I overheard Victoro talking with the men. He said they would be taking the horses to the buyer soon. When they do that, there won't be as many men in camp. We can escape then. It would be perfect."

"Victoro is not going to leave the camp unguarded after the

incident with Cisto." Leya's voice rose. They both held their breath and listened. There wasn't a sound from outside.

"Then he'll probably leave Tomás. He won't be hard to fool."

"Yoana, you still haven't said how you plan to get us through camp after we get the horses."

"There has to be another way out of here. The bear attacked the horses first, and he didn't come through camp. I'm sure we can find our way out without coming past the shelters."

"How will we know which way to go?"

"Lucio taught me how to tell direction with the stars. As long as the night is clear, I can find the way."

"In the forest? Yoana, most nights we can't see more than a few stars. You're used to being out in the open. We would have to go to the top of a mountain or find a clear area to get a good look at the sky. I just don't see how this will work. When they brought us here, we took such a roundabout way, I don't think we can find our way home."

"Leave that to me." She reached over and patted Leya's shoulder. "I've always been pretty good at directions."

"What about food? The trip here took at least a week. How will we hunt for food?"

"They took that long because they wanted to make sure Lucio hadn't followed us." Yoana drew a deep breath to keep from sounding angry. She knew her señorita was afraid, and for good reason. These bandits might seem mild in the camp, but they were unpredictable.

"We both know where Pabladora stores the dried meat. We can wrap some up to take with us before we go for the horses. If we're quiet, they'll not hear us. I think it will only take two or three days to reach the rancho."

They fell silent. Yoana listened to the night sounds. She could tell dawn approached. The air felt different, and the forest sounds changed as early morning drew near.

"Yoana, promise me we won't go until your arm is healed."

Leya reached over to touch her cold fingers to Yoana's arm. "If we do this, you have to be strong."

"It all depends on when the men leave to take the horses. I don't think they'll go for a few days at least. That should give me time to heal. As long as I'm not running a fever, I should be all right."

Yoana didn't say more. A few minutes later she could hear Leya's deep breathing. Her arm still ached as though glass shards ran through her veins. She went over and over her plan. There were so many uncertain parts. For instance, she'd never been in the area of the canyon where the horses were corralled.

What if she had trouble finding the tack? What if she couldn't find horses tame enough for them to ride? Yes, they were both accomplished horsewomen, but neither of them could handle a greenbroke mount on a mountain trail. Plus, with her injured arm, she wouldn't have the strength she usually had.

God, please, help me with this. You know my feelings for Amado can't be allowed to go further. He's a thief. He's probably a killer. I can't fall in love with a man like that. What am I to do?

Hot tears traced down her temple. She pressed the back of her hand to her mouth to stifle any sounds of crying. She didn't want to wake Leya again.

Yoana didn't know when she finally dozed off, but full sunlight streamed through the cracks in the wall when she awoke. Sounds of talking and cook pots clinking drifted to her. Her arm had settled down to a dull ache instead of the sharp pain she'd had most of the night.

She rolled over. Leya had already gotten up and left. She must be helping with the breakfast. Yoana swung her legs to the side and sat up. A wave of dizziness swept over her. Nausea rippled through her. She lowered back to the cot until the worst of it passed. It must be a result of blood loss, pain, and lack of sleep.

After a few minutes, she tried again. This time she lifted more slowly. The room whirled in a slow circle, but nothing like the dizzying pace before. Her dress lay folded on the floor beside her cot. She managed to get dressed without standing up, afraid she wouldn't be able to keep her balance if she tried the two things at once. She stood. The effort took every bit of determination she could draw on. Her body seemed to weigh more than a grizzly.

She held onto the doorframe as she stepped outside. Teo and Maria were picking up firewood very close to her shelter. Teo dropped his armload of sticks when he saw her.

"Yoana!" He raced toward her but stopped an arm length away. Yoana breathed a quiet sigh of relief. If he'd hit her full speed, they both would have toppled.

"Yoana, guess what Tomás made me?" Breathless, Teo danced in place as he waited for her to respond.

"Why don't you help me down the path? I can sit down, and then you can show me." Yoana held out her hand. Teo came beside her so her hand rested on his shoulder. Maria trotted on ahead of them. They moved down the path, with Yoana amazed at the young boy's attention to her need when he had exciting news to tell her.

Amado spotted them when they were halfway to the cooking area. He came striding over, but Yoana shook her head at him. She forced a small smile. Even though the nausea had returned, and the weakness made her want to fall down in a heap, she didn't want to disappoint Teo.

Amado seemed to understand and fell into step alongside them. "How are you this morning? Leya said you had some trouble sleeping last night."

"I'm a little better. The wound isn't hurting as bad as it did during the night." Yoana sank down onto a log with a small sigh. "Now, Teo, show me what wondrous thing Tomás made for you."

The young boy's face glowed as he turned so she could see the long stick tied to his waist. "He made me a sword." Teo pulled the stick free from its makeshift scabbard. Yoana could see the knife marks where Tomás had hacked a crude point and blade. He'd tied a cross piece on for the hilt.

"Tomás said I'm the best bear fighter he's ever seen. I reminded him of the brave men who used to fight with swords, so he made me one." Teo's chest couldn't have stuck out any further. Yoana bit her cheek to keep from laughing.

"I believe that is the finest sword I have ever seen." She leaned forward to admire the wooden blade. "If I ever need someone brave to defend me from a bear, I hope you will be the one."

"Teo, where's the wood?" Dolores stood a few feet away, her hands fisted on her hips.

Teo struggled to stick the sword back into the loop at his waist. "I'm going. I had to help Yoana." He raced off full tilt to bring wood for his mother.

Amado sat down beside her. Leya and the other women came over, concern evident on their faces.

"How are you feeling this morning?" Pabladora lifted the light shawl from Yoana's shoulder. The night before she had taken the sleeve off of a shapeless dress that would be easy for Yoana to get on and off. She explained that she didn't want the sleeve to bind on the wound, and Yoana could wear a shawl for modesty.

"It isn't hurting as much." Yoana winced as Pabladora felt the exposed skin around the bandage. "That might change soon."

The older woman shook her head at Yoana's dry tone. "After breakfast, we'll change the bandage. I don't think you bled too much. That is good. The arm isn't hot, so I don't think there is fever." Pabladora draped the shawl in place. "I think you'll live to fight another bear."

"I hope I don't have to." Yoana held herself upright by will alone. She didn't want anyone to know how awful she felt. "I have Teo, brave bear fighter, to defend me."

The women chuckled as they returned to their work. The day crawled by. The stitching in her wound looked ghastly when Pabladora changed the bandage, but that was more because of the dark, heavy thread Pabladora had used. The wound itself looked pretty good considering how deep the cut had been.

Rosalinda and Feliciana both came midmorning when the children were there for lessons. Feliciana knew some of her letters and numbers, but Rosalinda hadn't had any book learning. Why was Rosalinda in this camp? Feliciana couldn't be out of her teens yet. Rosalinda wasn't much older than that, yet she had three children. What had brought her here? Yoana wanted to ask, but she'd wait for a time when the children weren't around.

Leya insisted Yoana take a nap in the afternoon. The other women agreed. Yoana tried to protest, but she was so tired she could hardly stay upright. Amado helped her to the shelter before he left to help the other men. She slept until almost suppertime, when she awoke to a subtle scraping sound outside the door. The shadows were deep. Too deep to see much. She sat up to straighten her hair and smooth her dress. It must be Leya come to get her for the evening meal.

The door swung inward with a slight creak. A shadowed form stepped inside.

"*Muy bien*, Leya. I'm awake." Yoana finished tucking stray strands back into her braid and looked over—then stilled.

Whoever had come inside wasn't Leya. It was a man, but Yoana couldn't see who he was.

"Amado, is that you?" Yoana frowned. "What are you doing in here? Is something wrong?"

"Hush." The man crossed to the cot in two swift strides. She could smell the familiar scents of forest and horse, but this wasn't Amado. This man's stench made her eyes water. She felt she should recognize him, but she couldn't gather her thoughts enough to focus.

She opened her mouth to scream, but the man clamped a grimy paw over her face. She tried to pull away, but he jerked her up against him.

Cisto.

Her heart almost stopped, then picked up a pounding rhythm that wracked her whole body. Yoana tried to struggle, but she was so weak, and he was so strong.

"Now we're going somewhere we can play, sweet thing." Cisto's laugh chilled her all the way through. "We'll go someplace where no one will hear you, even though I'll make you scream. I used to like Rosalinda because she would scream so nicely. Now, she never does."

He bent to place a moist kiss on her mouth as he moved his hand. Yoana turned her head so he missed her lips and slobbered on her cheek. He cursed. She threw herself backward. He grabbed her arms to stop her.

The pain that radiated out from her wound stole Yoana's breath. Black spots danced before her eyes. She could feel herself falling. Cisto caught her before she hit the floor. He threw her across his shoulder and carried her from the cabin. Yoana tried to scream. To cry out for help. To fight.

She fell into darkness instead.

CHAPTER NINETEEN

Amado rubbed the palomino's nose. The horse lowered his head to nudge Amado's shoulder. This was a good horse. His spirit and intelligence formed an unbeatable combination. If the stallion hadn't been stolen from Don Armenta, he'd consider asking Victoro if he could buy him.

"Hey, Amado, you have that one tame enough to do women's work." Miguel leaned against the makeshift fence.

"I want a horse who will cook and do dishes for me." Lorenzo picked a weed and stuck it in his mouth to chew on. "Maybe I could take this one."

"You want me to teach him to hold a razor in his teeth so he can shave you?" Amado grinned at Lorenzo's mock horror. "I can let him use Miguel for practice."

"That might be going too far." Lorenzo leaned his elbows on the fence. "I am thinking of getting the palomino a nice apron to wear. He'd look so cute while he's stirring the beans."

Amado slipped the halter off the horse and opened the gate to leave. The sun had drifted low enough that the woods would soon be dark. Time to get back to camp. Back to Yoana. Had she slept?

She'd been so exhausted he almost had to carry her to her cot for the second time.

"Ready to head back?" Miguel patted the palomino, which stuck its nose over the fence to investigate the men. "I'm so hungry this horse is looking good to eat."

"I think I'll go by the stream and clean up first." Amado coiled his rope and hung it with the other tack in a small sheltered area near the corral.

Lorenzo chuckled. "Cleaning up for the sweet young filly that's off limits?"

Miguel laughed. "If I didn't already have Feliciana, I might be cleaning up too."

"You may not have Feliciana for long." Lorenzo raised an eyebrow at his brother. "She sure makes eyes at Tomás. I can tell she makes him nervous. The boy stutters so badly he can't get a word out when she's close."

"That boy's still in diapers." Miguel's look turned dark. "Feliciana needs a man, not some baby."

Lorenzo laughed and clapped Miguel on the back. "We're going back without the side trip to the stream, Amado. See you in camp."

As the brothers headed down the well-worn trail, Amado took the path leading to a bend in the stream above camp. He liked this spot because it was so pretty and private. He could bathe in the quiet and take some time to consider his next move.

The chilly water only came to his neck when he sat down. Amado shivered until he adjusted to the coolness. The day had been warm, so he'd looked forward to the refreshing pool.

He leaned back with his head against a soft spot on the bank and relaxed as he considered the question brought up by Lorenzo and Miguel. What did he want to do about Yoana? He knew the answer. He also knew he couldn't just take her and run. He needed to leave this camp--to go after Cisto--but he couldn't abandon Yoana and Leya to the mercy of the bandoleros. These men weren't the desperadoes he'd expected them to be, yet they weren't honorable men either. Without Cisto around, the others might be misguided and wrong in the way they lived, but they weren't killers. Unless provoked.

How could he take Yoana and Leya with him? If he snuck them out in the middle of the night, he wouldn't be able to return and fulfill his promise. To break his word went against everything he stood for. He would fail his father.

Yoana's story about her mother's death ran through his mind. What she'd said about vengeance rang true. He had this deep need to exact retribution on the man who killed his brother in such a cruel and vicious way. He'd made a promise before Mario died in his arms. A deathbed promise had to be kept. Didn't it? That would be what God wanted. Wouldn't He?

Amado had gone to church with his family. They said morning and evening prayers in the chapel. He knew what God expected-- that Amado care for his family, prove his worth by being a protector and provider. He'd failed to protect them, so all that was left to him was retaliation.

Cisto deserved to die.

Amado had given up everything when he agreed to do this for his father. Everything.

"God, please, I've always thought I knew what You wanted. If I'm wrong, then show me what to do. Help me keep Yoana safe. And Leya. Help me to keep my word to my family."

He climbed from the creek, shivering in the light breeze as he sluiced the water from his body and shook his head to get the excess from his hair. From down-canyon the scent of roasting meat made his stomach rumble. Amado dressed and headed back to camp. If only God would write a message in the dirt, like Yoana did when she taught the children. That would be so much easier.

Teo and Maria were huddled together drawing letters and numbers in a cleared spot on the ground when Amado reached the camp. The change in the children since Yoana had begun to work with them amazed him. She had such a gift for teaching.

"Amado, come look." Teo stood and gestured wildly. "See what we did? We both wrote our names, just like Yoana taught us."

Amado knelt on the ground beside Maria. The letters they'd scrawled were almost indistinguishable, but when he studied the scratches, he could read their names. "That's very good. You must have a good teacher." Amado hugged Maria and thumped Teo on the back. The boy beamed up at him as Amado stood.

"Is Yoana still sleeping?"

Teo rolled his eyes "She's been asleep all day." Clearly the boy thought this was strange.

"She got hurt pretty bad yesterday, Teo. She lost a lot of blood, which makes a person tired, and then her arm hurt a lot so she couldn't sleep." Amado ruffled the boy's hair. "Besides, she hasn't been asleep all day. She gave you lessons this morning."

"I know." Teo dug in the dirt with his toe. "But she hasn't told any stories or riddles today."

Amado laughed. "Maybe after supper tonight, she can tell some. I'm going to get Leya. We'll go up and fetch Yoana, since it looks like the meal is almost ready."

He strode across the hard-packed earth of the clearing to where the women chatted as they worked. Darkness had fallen fast, and he couldn't see beyond the reach of the firelight or lantern light. Leya bounced Carlito on her hip while Dolores dished up a plate of food, probably for Lorenzo or Victoro.

"Leya, is Yoana awake?"

"I haven't seen her." Leya turned so her unscarred cheek faced Amado. "If you bring a lantern, we could go check on her. I meant to do that before it got too dark, but we were busy, and I lost track of time."

Amado fetched a lantern. Leya handed the baby off to Dolores, who'd returned from taking a plate of food to Lorenzo. Amado guided Leya up the path, one hand on her elbow to steady her in the dark. They stopped at the same moment the lantern light fell on the shelter.

The door hung askew as if it had been given a vicious kick.

"Wait here." Amado released Leya's arm, switched the lantern to his left hand, and pulled his pistol. His heart hammered as he approached the hut. A stale scent hung in the air--the stench of unwashed male.

Amado kicked the broken door out of the way and raised the lantern high. One of the cots lay on its side. The blanket had been dragged in the dirt. Yoana had gone, but not of her own will. Amado knelt to look at the footprints. The hard-packed earth didn't show much, but he could see the impression of the edge of a boot, the toe pointed toward the shelter. The only boot print going the other way dug deeper into the earth. Whoever took Yoana had carried her out of here.

"Yoana." Leya's soft cry interrupted Amado's study of the ground.

"Someone's taken her." He grabbed Leya to steady her, forcing his touch to be gentle. He wanted to get his hands on the culprit who endangered Yoana. But he had to be practical. "Let me take you back to camp and get help. We'll find her."

"Victoro, Yoana's gone." Amado yelled across the camp as soon as he had Leya in enough light that she could make her own way. His chest ached. This place lacked life without Yoana's vibrant presence.

The men set their plates down and hurried over, their spurs jangling like bells. The women gathered together near the fire.

Teo rushed over, eyes wide. He pulled at Amado's pant leg. "Did another bear get her?"

"No, not this time. You stay here. We'll find her." Amado led the men up the hill.

Victoro pushed into the shelter. "What happened?"

"See for yourself." Amado held the lantern high so the other men could see. He pointed to the boot prints and told them what he thought.

Victoro went inside and sniffed the air. "Cisto. I've smelled him often enough to know he's been in here." He strode outside. "I'll go back and get another lantern. Amado, start tracking him. Lorenzo and Miguel, get the horses. Tomás, stay here and guard the women. I don't want that lowlife sneaking back around to take Rosalinda or to hurt any of the women or children. You watch carefully, *sí?*"

Tomás, pale in the feeble light, nodded. He turned back toward camp, his rifle clutched in one hand. Victoro followed him as the brothers raced up-canyon toward the corral. Amado turned back to the prints, bending over and moving slow so he didn't lose the tracks in the dark. A mixture of dirt and crushed pine needles scented the air. He wasn't even sure if a full moon would help with the tracking in this dense forest. Desperation pressed at him, but he had to take this slowly and carefully, or he would lose her.

He left broken branches as signs so Victoro, Lorenzo, and Miguel would be able to follow him as soon as they had the horses and guns. By the time they caught up to him, he'd found where Cisto had tied his horse. He and Yoana hadn't been gone for long.

Amado swung onto his buckskin. "Any of you have any idea where Cisto will take her? We could split up if you do. I could track, and two of you could go look elsewhere."

"He has a place of his own, but it is far from here." Lorenzo rubbed his jaw as he studied the ground lit up by the lantern. "I don't think he will wait that long to hurt her."

Anger wrenched at Amado. He'd focused on following the trail and hadn't allowed himself to consider what Cisto would do to Yoana. Couldn't allow himself to consider.

"He almost killed a woman in Los Angeles." Lorenzo shook his head. "I had hoped he would change. That night I heard the woman screaming and him laughing. I've never seen a man enjoy hurting a woman like that. He was better with Rosalinda, but only out of fear of Victoro."

"Let's go." Amado leaned low over his buckskin's withers as they moved through the woods. Small animals scuttled away. An owl hooted, answered by another. Cisto would have an advantage by being able to go faster, but they would have the benefit that their horses weren't riding double. As soon as they hit a trail, they would be able to pick up the pace.

Amado would make sure Cisto had no time to hurt Yoana. And if he did...

Cisto would know pain of his own before he died.

Amado's conscience twinged. Would that, too, go against what God expected? Yet how could it be right to let Cisto get off without punishment? Years ago, Amado's father told him a man might get away with a lot of wrongs here on earth, but there would come a day when he had to stand before God.

And face judgment.

Amado would rather face a posse of angry men than one angry God. God would call Cisto to account for the women he'd hurt and the other crimes he'd committed. Still, Amado couldn't stand back and do nothing if Cisto hurt Yoana. *God, help me know the right thing to do.*

They tracked Cisto until they reached a trail that wound up the mountain. Amado picked up the pace, stopping every so often to make sure the hoofprints of Cisto's mount were still there.

"Do we know this is his horse for sure?" Miguel asked.

Lorenzo's gave a grim nod. "It's his, unless he traded horses. His horse has that notch on the outside of his left hoof. That's how I always knew which way Cisto went when we were out anywhere."

In the dark a coyote howled. The rest of the pack took up the mournful cry and faded into the distance. Once Amado heard a heavy animal moving off uphill through the trees. Was this another grizzly?

The men crested a rise, and the trail dropped away into the dark. Victoro had taken the lead, and he raised his hand to signal a halt. They listened to the night for several minutes. Even the horses seemed to realize the need for quiet because they didn't stomp or snort.

Far below them, Amado detected a sound. Was that hoofbeats? He glanced at Victoro, whose heavy brows were drawn together in fierce concentration.

Victoro turned to him. "We need to douse the lanterns. If he sees us coming, he'll be able to pick us off."

"If he can find the trail in the dark, so can we." Amado put out his lantern, and Lorenzo followed suit.

The absence of the light momentarily blinded them. Amado waited for his eyes to adjust, then nudged his buckskin forward. "Let's go, Victoro. We may not be able to see much, but the horses can."

The trail took a steep downward turn. Amado leaned back in the saddle to help with balance. His horse slipped a couple of times on some loose rock. Amado hoped the sound didn't carry too far. He didn't want Cisto to know how close behind him they were--

Wait. Was that a muffled cry from far below? Amado tugged his horse's reins. The others stopped and listened. Nothing. Amado looked at the men. "Did you hear something?"

Victoro shook his head. "I'm not sure. I thought I might have, but now I'm just not sure."

"Do you know where he's going?" Amado peered into the darkness. "This isn't the way to town."

"There's a lot of rough country ahead. If he continues, he'll be in the desert by tomorrow. We'll be able to see him if we're still higher."

"I don't want to wait until morning. Who knows what he could do to Yoana if we don't find them tonight." Why didn't the moon come out? The trees on this side of the mountain weren't as thick.

If the moon came out, they might be able to see Cisto or his tracks. They could split up. Circle around. Cut him off.

As it was, they were blinded by the night and their lack of knowledge of the terrain.

"Let me take the lead." Miguel urged his mount forward. "I've ridden in this area before. I know a few of the trails and the canyons."

Amado released a quick breath. Maybe this would help. They followed Miguel at a little quicker pace until they reached the floor of the valley. They were in a long narrow draw between two towering hills. Amado could see the trail ran along the floor for a long distance. His eyes had adjusted enough to the starlight to get a good bearing of where they were going.

"Let's try to make up some time." Amado urged his gelding out in the lead.

They hit a patch of loose rock, and Amado slowed his horse. From behind him, Miguel spoke in a low voice. "Amado, stop."

He reined in his horse. The others halted right behind him. Amado's buckskin lifted his head, pricking his ears pricked forward. His nostrils distended. The animal must smell another horse because he didn't have the look of an animal who'd scented something he feared.

A scream tore through the air, then cut off. The sudden lack of sound proved almost more frightening than the terrified cry.

"Let's go!" Amado clicked his tongue as he leaned forward.

"Amado, not too fast."

He didn't want to listen to Miguel's warning. That scream had been Yoana.

At a dip in the trail, Amado's buckskin slid down on his haunches. Amado leaned back so far he rested on the horse's rump. When his mount regained his footing, Amado slowed a bit. He didn't stop to look back to see if the others had safely made the drop. Yoana needed him.

Another cry. A man cursed. The sound echoed off the

surrounding hills. Amado reined in his horse. Where *were* they? Someone scrabbled through rocks just down the trail. Amado urged his horse forward.

"Let me go!" Yoana's voice came clear through the night air.

"You're *mine*." Cisto's gruff words were vile. "Now we're going to have some fun." He laughed, and the sound chilled Amado.

He slipped from the saddle and wrapped the buckskin's reins over a tree limb. Odds were good that Cisto and Yoana were no longer on horseback. Cisto must think he'd gotten away without anyone following them.

"Let. Me. Go."

Amado almost smiled. Yoana sounded angry, not scared.

He crept toward the sound of scuffling. Behind him, he thought he heard the others halt their horses. Through the branches of a bush, he caught sight of the struggling pair. Cisto had thrown Yoana over his shoulder. She hit at his back and struggled in his grip.

"Hold still!" Cisto found a patch of grass. He slung her down on the ground and stood over her with his legs spread apart. "You may not love this, sweetheart, but you will remember me."

"You won't get away with this. Amado will come for me."

"There isn't anyone coming for you. Your father wouldn't pay to have you back. Victoro and his boys won't care one bit that you're gone. You're all mine. This is the face you'll remember, not Amado's."

Cisto started to kneel. Before Amado could step from the brush, Yoana moved.

She whipped a gun from under her skirts. Her face twisted as she pointed the pistol at her attacker. "Remember *this!*"

The shot cracked in the still night.

CHAPTER TWENTY

Agony arced up Yoana's injured arm. The gun wavered. Her shot went wild as Cisto dove to the side. She brought her left hand up to steady the pistol for a second shot. Cisto rolled toward her, his jet-black eyes colder than the night around them. If she didn't kill him, he would kill her. But first…there would be worse than death.

"Cisto!"

Yoana jerked at Amado's voice. Her second shot missed Cisto's chest, but grazed his arm. He reversed direction faster than a striking snake.

A shot dug into the earth where the bandit had been. Amado! He must have shot at Cisto.

Cisto lunged for his horse, and it snorted, rearing its head back. He'd barely touched leather when he reined his mount into the darkened brush.

In the moment before he disappeared from sight, Cisto's gaze crashed into Yoana's. Hatred burned into her. The cold smirk on his face showed none of the pain he must feel from the bullet. The only message he conveyed was that he would return for her. And the next time…

She wouldn't escape.

Amado stepped into the clearing and fired another shot. Cisto's horse crashed through the brush, emerging on the trail several feet downhill. In the pale starlight Yoana couldn't make out more than a vague outline as Cisto plunged down the dark slope at a breakneck speed.

She wanted to shoot again. She really did, but her fingers refused to work. Exhaustion stole her strength. The pistol clattered to the ground. She'd missed her chance. Now she would live with the knowledge that Cisto would not rest until he possessed her.

"Where is he?" Victoro stepped into the small clearing, followed by Lorenzo and Miguel. All three had their revolvers drawn.

"He got away." Amado indicated the trail. "Go bring the horses while I see to Yoana. Maybe we can catch him before he gets too far."

"No." Victoro shoved his gun in the holster.

"No?" Amado whirled to face the bandit leader. "What do you mean? This is our chance before he gets too big a lead."

Victoro crossed his arms over his wide chest. "We only caught him this time because he didn't expect us to come after the girl. He knew she held little value to me and thought I wouldn't care. Now he'll have the advantage."

"There are more of us." Amado's jaw muscles flexed.

Yoana fought to stay upright as she watched him. She could almost follow his thought process as he planned how they would go after Cisto. When had she come to know him so well? To realize what he thought without him saying anything? To draw comfort from his strength? From the security he offered? A trill of danger echoed through her as she realized how deep her feelings were for this bandolero and how wrong those feelings were. Wrong--and right.

"Amado." Miguel motioned toward Yoana. "She would never last if we try to chase down Cisto. Look at her."

He turned. Yoana tried to meet his gaze with some fire in her own. She failed. Gray wavered at the edge of her vision. She swayed and couldn't seem to stop. Amado shoved his pistol in his holster and strode toward her. His strong arms caught her before she hit the ground. From far away she heard him talking to the others.

"You're right." How could Amado sound so grim and angry when his touch held such tenderness? "Bring the horses. We'll get her back to camp."

"Cisto will come for her again." Victoro sounded concerned. For her? Odd that he would care.

"He doesn't like to lose, but we'll be ready this time." The bandit leader's bluster warmed her. Yet none of them would have a prayer of protecting her if Cisto determined to kidnap her again. Which he would.

Gray darkened to black, and Yoana didn't hear any more.

She woke to the gentle motion of the horse under her and Amado's strong arms around her. She breathed deep, her head resting on Amado's chest. He'd turned her sideways in the saddle to make her more comfortable. Her arm and her head ached like she'd been trampled by a herd of horses. Fatigue weighed her down, but she was glad to be awake. Yoana had a vague notion of Amado talking to her, but she'd been too deep asleep to recall anything he might have said.

"Querida." Amado's breath whispered across her brow. "Are you awake?"

Yoana thought about not answering him, about pretending to sleep. She could revel in the feel of him without any guilt. If she snuggled deeper against him, maybe he would believe she still slept. Maybe no one would know how right she felt in this man's arms. This man who would hang if Lucio or her father caught him.

This man she'd come to love.

She couldn't avoid the emotions stirring within her. This bandolero treated her better than any of the men in her own family. Amado truly cared for her even though he'd seen her at her worst. Regret pricked at Yoana's conscience. Tomorrow. Tomorrow, she would talk to Leya about escaping. The danger in staying grew greater by the day.

The horse surged upward. Rocks rattled downhill. The motion sent a jolt of pain from Yoana's arm to her whole body, and a muffled cry slipped out.

"Pobrecita, lo siento."

Amado's apology barely registered through the haze of pain. Yoana bit her lip to keep from crying out again. He reined in the horse, but the cessation of motion didn't stop the ache. Hot coals smoldered in the wound in her arm.

"What is it?" Victoro's gruff voice came out of the night.

"She's hurting." Amado's voice rumbled through his chest and against her ear. Yoana felt his cool cheek against her forehead. "I think she has a fever."

"We're only about an hour out of camp," Victoro said. "Pabladora can help her once we get there. It will be almost daylight by then."

"I'm going to rest here with her for a moment," Amado said. "Why don't you all go ahead. Let the women know we're coming. They can have the fire lit and some water heated by the time we get there."

"I'll have them make up a poultice for her." Victoro clucked to his horse as he called to Lorenzo and Miguel. Yoana heard the clatter of hooves as their horses scrabbled up the hill.

"Yoana, can you hear me?"

She didn't want to speak. She didn't want him to hear tears

and weakness in her voice. She nodded, not lifting her head from his chest.

"We'll wait here until you're well enough to go on. I'm not going to push you." Amado brushed the hair from her cheek, and she loved the sensation of his touch. She didn't want him to stop. She knew she should push away from him, but just for tonight, perhaps this would be acceptable.

"I'm going to have to move you a little, *querida*. I need to wet a cloth to try to bring down the fever. *Muy bien?*"

"No." Yoana dug her fingers into his shirt and blinked against the night. She hadn't even realized until now that she had the garment in her grasp.

"Why not?" Amado dipped his head to place a soft kiss on her brow.

"Hurts too much."

"Part of that is because of the fever." Amado tightened one of his arms around her while reaching for his canteen with the other hand. In a few deft movements, he had a cool, wet cloth pressed to her head.

His soft voice drifted around her. "When I was a young boy, I fell from a horse into an arroyo. A sharp rock cut my arm so deep I thought I would bleed to death before I got home. My mother cared for me, but I had an infection. My whole body hurt more that the original cut. For days, my mother sat by my bedside and used wet cloths to keep the fever down. It worked, and the fever broke. That's what we will need to do with you, Yoana. Don't worry. I'll see that you are well cared for."

The cool cloth felt like a bit of heaven. Her headache eased a little, and she knew she should say something to Amado, but she couldn't find the words. He caressed the rag down the side of her face to touch each cheek. She'd never had a man touch her in such an intimate way. No one since her mother had touched her with such loving care. She should protest but had neither the strength —nor the desire—to do so.

The horse stamped, and Yoana groaned, the jolt like a physical blow. The horse snorted, and she could feel the tension in the animal.

"Yoana, we have to move." Amado draped the damp cloth over her forehead, picked up the reins, and gave a soft click of his tongue. The horse snorted again, then started uphill. Yoana moaned. She tried to be quiet but couldn't help the small sound that escaped.

"Quiet, querida. I think someone is following us. Maybe Cisto. At the top of the hill, I'll move off the path. We'll try to lose him." Amado cradled her close.

The concern in his voice worried her. Amado should put her aside somewhere, at least until he could determine who tracked them. The need to make the suggestion nudged at her, but she couldn't find the resolve to do so. Even the fear of Cisto and the urgent need to get away couldn't overcome the lethargy weighing her down.

The clop of the buckskin's footfalls broke the quiet of the night. Nothing rustled in the brush. No night birds or animals disturbed the silence. All the mountain's inhabitants might be holding their breath to see what would happen.

Yoana's senses stirred as fear pushed aside her fatigue. She could feel the tension thrum through Amado. The strong arm that cradled her closely had turned to steel as his muscles tightened. She could hear the thunder of his heart as she rested against him. Her own pulse picked up speed as she listened for any telltale sound that would indicate Cisto's presence. Had he followed them?

A stumble. A huff of the horse's breath. They were off the trail. Branches brushed against her, some with a feathery caress, others with a sharper touch. The scent of pine filled the air. The darkness closed in, wiping out the light of the stars within the close-set trees.

Amado eased the buckskin to a stop. He leaned close, and his lips brushed her ear and sent a shiver through her. "Stay absolutely quiet." He didn't raise his head away from hers. The intimate connection wrought havoc with her senses.

Longing encouraged her to lift her head the slightest bit and turn. Her lips would meet his. The overwhelming urge almost made her cry out. At the same time, her mind screamed "danger" to her. She could hear Leya's warnings in the back of her mind and knew her señorita would be praying for her protection from all danger, including the danger of a bandolero's love.

The gelding's head shot up, and it tensed. Amado leaned forward to pat the horse on the neck. He slipped his revolver free, and Yoana saw the sheen of sweat beads on his brow. A chilly touch of air told her she had moisture on her forehead too. Her stomach knotted as they waited. Tension spiked the air until Yoana thought she would scream.

A shaft of moonlight filtered through the branches overhead. Two brilliant orbs gleamed in the darkness. Yoana stifled a cry. Amado must have felt her reaction. His head swiveled to the side. The horse snorted and danced away a few steps. The eyes blinked and were gone.

Amado breathed a sigh as he holstered his gun. "It's all right, querida. It was only a cat on the hunt."

Yoana shuddered, and Amado chuckled. His cheek pressed against her hair, and she heard him breathe deeply.

Now that the danger had passed, her lethargy returned. She didn't say a word as Amado clucked his tongue and the buckskin wove back through the woods to the trail. As they rode, sounds returned to the forest. Small animals skittered through the undergrowth. Yoana relaxed. Maybe Cisto would realize the futility of coming for her again. Maybe she would be safe. Maybe...

Questions burned within her. Questions that needed answers...but was she brave enough to ask them?

She'd always thought bandoleros were criminals because they weren't smart enough to do anything else. But none of the men in

Victoro's band were stupid. Amado had the intelligence to run her father's rancho. From the way he thought and reacted to situations, he'd been well educated.

"Why are you a bandolero?" Yoana cringed? How could she let herself speak the thought aloud?

Amado straightened in the saddle. He didn't speak for a long while. When he finally answered, his voice was gruff. "I had no choice."

"What do you mean?" She eased up to stare up at him. In the dark, his eyes were so shadowed she couldn't read his expression. "Everyone has a choice in what they do."

"Sometimes circumstances take away our choices." Amado looked down, and she could read a burning intensity in his gaze that made her want to squirm. "Was it your choice to be in the bandit camp?"

Yoana swallowed hard. "No, but I was kidnapped. You weren't kidnapped, were you?"

"No, I joined with Victoro because I had to."

She could sense his reluctance to talk, but she refused to sit in silence as they rode. She had to find out more about this man. "Have you been a bandolero long?"

"Not long."

"What about your family? Did you have a wife or children you left behind?"

His heart thudded in his chest as she settled back against him. Amado cleared his throat. "My family doesn't know where I am. I have no wife or children. I am dead to my family."

They were silent as she absorbed the sadness in what he'd revealed. Even though her life had been difficult, she couldn't imagine never seeing her family again.

"Didn't you have a señorita waiting for you?"

"I did." He shifted to lean her more against his chest and switched hands on the reins. He circled her waist with his arm to hold her steady even though he didn't need to. "I had a beautiful woman I was to marry. My heart still hurts when I think of her."

"Then why don't you leave this place and go to her? Take her somewhere and make a life together." Yoana kept her voice even so she wouldn't give away how much the thought of him loving another woman hurt her.

"I can't. Her family would no longer have me. They will give her to someone more deserving." She felt him rest his chin against the top of her head. "Besides, I don't recall the girl of my memories so much anymore."

"Why not?" Yoana's words came out soft as a whisper. The buckskin had slowed so much they barely moved. Her pulse sped up as his arm tightened around her waist.

"Because I never truly knew her, and now I find myself thinking of someone else." Amado bent his head until his breath touched the curve of her ear. A shiver raced through Yoana.

"But she will be very disappointed if you don't come for her, won't she?"

"Maybe." Amado's lips touched her temple. "Then again, perhaps she won't remember me at all. We were very young when we were betrothed."

The horse stopped in the shadow of a huge pine. Cool air brushed against Yoana's heated face. Amado's hand came up to cup her chin. He tilted her head back until she gazed up into his eyes. For an unfathomable moment, the world stilled as he gazed down at her. She held her breath as his mouth descended toward hers.

The brush of his lips against her mouth sent a jolt through her. Her fatigue faded as if it had never been. She lifted her hand to touch his cheek. Stubble pricked the pads of her fingertips. She reached up to touch his dark hair, amazed at the silken texture.

Amado pulled her to him. He groaned as the kiss deepened. Yoana heard Leya's voice as if from a distance. Did her señorita always have to be her conscience? Leya's voice grew louder. Calling her name.

Yoana jerked back away from Amado. He lifted his head to stare off into the trees.

"Yoana. Yoana! Where are you?"

They heard the clop of hoofbeats a few seconds before they caught the movement through the trees. Amado shifted Yoana so she faced forward.

She hoped the gray light of dawn would still be dark enough that Leya couldn't see the heat flooding her face. Her tía could always tell when Yoana had been guilty of something. This was one time she didn't want Leya to realize the lines of impropriety she and Amado had crossed.

"We're here, Leya. Right here."

Amado urged the horse forward. Yoana smiled. She could almost hear his angst at being interrupted. He leaned close as their horses closed the distance. "This isn't finished, *querida.* Not at all."

CHAPTER TWENTY-ONE

For the next two days, Amado puttered around camp like an old man. Miguel asked him to go hunting with Lorenzo and Tomàs and himself to replenish the supply of meat. Amado declined with some lame excuse about needing to chop wood for the fires. In reality, he couldn't dispel the feeling that Cisto would show up at any moment and kidnap Yoana again. Every unusual noise made his heart hammer and sent him grabbing for his pistol.

He saw little of Yoana. Worn out from her ordeals, she slept most of the time. Leya hovered over her, refusing to help with chores if it meant leaving her niece alone. Pabladora seemed to understand. Good thing, since the only way Amado could relax at all came from Leya's attentiveness to Yoana.

Fever and infection made Yoana toss and turn. When Amado peeked in on her, his heart stuttered at her pale-as-a-wisp-of-smoke countenance. She was fading away...

Pabladora nursed her as if she were one of the young children, constantly clucking over what she ate or fussing at her for trying to get up when she didn't have the strength. Amado might have been amused, but he wanted time alone with Yoana. With so many women flitting this way and that around her, he had no chance.

He swung the axe again, the jolt as the blade bit into the wood reverberating through his whole body. The physical work helped. It gave him time to contemplate his growing need to tell Yoana the truth of why he'd come to this camp. The truth of his objective.

The truth of his name.

He'd had ample opportunity to sneak away and bring the authorities, to capture and hang Cisto. Yet he'd put off his duty, his promise, all because of a growing love for the strongest, bravest woman he'd ever met. Every day strengthened his love for her. Every day made his decisions that much harder. Every day brought him closer to disappointing his father.

He leaned the axe against a tree and wiped the sweat from his brow with his arm. Wood chips clung to his damp skin. Amado looked over to where Maria and Teo waited for his signal to come and gather the wood to stack. He'd made it a rule that they wait so he didn't have to worry about one of them getting in the way of his blade.

At his nod, the two children scampered over, Teo in the lead. "This is a bigger pile of logs than yesterday, Amado. You are very strong." Teo gazed up at Amado, his eyes shining.

Amado ruffled the boy's thick, wavy hair. "I'm also stinky and dirty." He grinned as Teo nodded and pinched his nose.

"You and Maria stack this wood while I head over to the stream and wash off." He grabbed his shirt, but didn't put it back on. The garment had been clean this morning, and he didn't want to soil it. He glanced up the hill to the shelter where Yoana rested.

Late afternoon sun still bathed the clearing in a golden light. He remembered the horror of discovering she'd been taken by Cisto. He knew Leya was with her. Yoana should be safe for the few minutes he'd take to get clean.

At the stream, Amado took off his pants and shook out the wood bits. They needed more, but he didn't have clean ones to change to. It would be enough that he'd have on a fresh shirt. The water washed away the itchy sweat and dirt. He lay back against a rock and let the stream flow over him as he pondered his next move.

"God, I don't know what to do." The picture of his father's grief-stricken face as he knelt next to his murdered son caught at Amado's heart. Anguish had filled the don's eyes as he begged Amado to seek vengeance. Without hesitation, Amado agreed. How could he not? He'd given the same promise to his brother moments before he'd breathed his last.

Amado waited for some revelation from God, some guidance about what he should do. When nothing came, he ducked under the water to wash his hair. He climbed from the stream and sluiced the water from his body. The wind dried him, but left him shivering as he tugged on his clothes.

Excited voices chattered as he reached camp. Pabladora and Rosalinda were at work preparing to cook a large haunch of the deer the men brought back. Feliciana used the metate, grinding more corn for tortillas. Dolores sat near the fire, nursing Carlito as she watched a pot of pozole. Leya and Yoana were nowhere in sight.

The combined scents of sizzling meat and soup made Amado's stomach murmur.

As he climbed the path to his hut, he saw that Leya sat outside the door, her back against the wooden structure, the lowering sun lighting the area around her. She smiled at him and stood.

"She's still sleeping." Leya gestured to some rocks several yards away. "Come, we'll sit over here and talk. We can still see or hear if she needs us, but we won't disturb her."

Amado followed the small woman. He couldn't help but admire her, how she'd gone from hiding from the world to settling in here, helping out, talking, laughing. The level of acceptance for her here had to be different from that of Don Armenta's society. Maybe, in an odd way, being here gave her a chance to recover emotionally as she never could at the don's hacienda.

He sank down beside her. Leya studied the bustle of the scene below them for a moment, then looked up at him. "Why haven't you told her, Amado?"

Her words hit him like a hard fist. He fought to breathe. He'd almost forgotten Leya recognized him, though she hadn't said a word. Probably because they hadn't had time alone. Plus, Leya, of all people, would respect his secret just as she kept her own secrets.

"She needs to know." Leya studied him with her fathomless gaze. "She needs to be back home. Safe."

"Don't you think I know that? I've tried." Amado swallowed to clear the hoarseness from his throat.

"Not very hard." Leya studied his face with an intensity that made him want to squirm. "I want to know why you're here. I don't believe the rumors I've heard. At least not all of them."

"What have you heard?"

"I know about your brother." Tears glistened in her eyes.

"How?" Amado had to look away from her sympathy before emotion overcame him.

"Servants talk. Bad news always travels fast, even across great distances."

"Then you probably know why I'm here."

"For revenge?" Her eyebrows shot up. "Amado, God doesn't want us to take vengeance into our own hands. That is for Him to do"

"I made a promise." Amado held himself stiff. No matter his doubts, he still struggled with the need to fulfill his father's wishes. "God wants us to keep our word."

"Am I right to assume this also has to do with honoring your father?" Her small hand weighed heavy where she rested her palm on his arm.

He stared down at her. How did this woman know so much? "Perhaps."

"Amado, when someone is in pain, they often say or do things they regret. They ask favors they wouldn't normally ask. Consider your father. He's a good, upright man. He loves God. If he hadn't been so grieved, would he have asked you to seek vengeance?" Her question knifed through his heart. Hadn't he pondered that very thought?

Before he could say a word, she continued. "I think you already know the answer, but you don't want to admit it. If you truly believed you should be seeking retribution for your brother's death, you wouldn't be sitting around camp watching over Yoana."

Amado closed his eyes and dropped his chin to his chest. God hadn't answered him earlier. Had he waited to use Leya to speak to him? "All I know is I want to do two jobs at one time. I need to be in two places at once, but I can't. For some reason, right now, being here to protect Yoana is more important than anything else. My father may condemn me for that. Even God might if I go against my vow."

Before she could respond, the shelter door opened. Yoana stepped out, her face pale in the low light. She leaned against the doorway and looked down toward the camp. Then she turned her head and caught sight of them, and her face brightened. A smile tilted her full lips. Amado's heart lifted. All problems drifted away in the warmth of that smile.

Leya rushed to support her charge before Amado could even move. "Yoana, you should have called."

Fool! While you sit here spellbound by Yoana's beauty, her tía meets her needs. He strode to her other side.

"Don't pick me up." Yoana held up one hand. "I need to walk and gain some strength. I've been doing nothing for too long."

Leya moved ahead of them on the path, allowing Amado to walk alongside Yoana and support her. The smell of roasting meat floated on the air, and his stomach rumbled again. The corner of Yoana's mouth lifted. Amado grinned and shrugged. He wanted to say so much but didn't dare with Leya so close to them. That had probably been Leya's reason for lingering. She wanted to hear what he had to say. Frustration welled inside him. Couldn't he have a few minutes alone with this woman who had stolen his heart?

"Yoana, you're awake." Teo dropped the log he'd been placing on the stack of wood and raced toward them. Amado held out his hand to halt the boy's sprint before he crashed into her.

"I see you're working hard." Yoana held out her hand for Teo to take. "Maria, too." Yoana's smile turned to the young girl who shadowed Teo. "Did you chop all that wood, Teo? You must be very strong."

"Nah." Teo dug his toe in the pine needles. "Amado did that. He's the strong one. Maria and I helped him."

"Well, it's very nice that you and Maria are helping. Lifting all those logs will make you strong like Amado." Yoana glanced up at him and winked. Amado grinned. His heart soared in his chest.

"Will you tell us a story tonight?" Teo stood in front of Yoana as she sat down.

Yoana held out her arms. "Maybe after your chores are done and supper is over." The two children leaped forward to give Yoana a hug. Amado knew they were almost as enraptured by her as he. They'd been so worried when Cisto took her. What would they think if they knew the plan forming in his mind?

As they ate supper, Amado sat away from Yoana so Teo and the other children could have time with her. He watched the forest, although the light dimmed to the point that he couldn't see beyond the glow cast by the fire. Still, something…wasn't right. He couldn't say what. Perhaps it was the growing discord between Miguel and Tomás over Feliciana.

"Now, Yoana." Teo dropped to his knees in front of her, his face bright. "Now will you tell us a story?"

Maria dropped down beside Teo, imitating his every motion. Amado couldn't stop a smile.

"Very well, but not a long one, Teo." Yoana swiped a stray

strand of hair that escaped her braid and swung across her face as the wind picked up.

Amado could see fatigue etched in the dark circles under her eyes. "Maybe you should wait and tell a story tomorrow when you're more rested." Amado started to stand, but Yoana shook her head.

"No, Teo has been very patient. I can wait another hour before I go back to bed."

"Besides, she's been sleeping more than a bear in the winter." Teo shook his head, his expression showing he didn't understand how anyone could sleep so much.

"That's true." Yoana started to reach out to Teo and winced as she moved her injured arm. "I need to do more work and get stronger. Right, Teo?" The boy nodded. Maria watched Teo and moved her head up and down in an exaggerated motion that had her light brown braids bouncing on her shoulders. Amado chuckled.

"Now, what story would you like to hear?" Yoana leaned back against the tree behind her.

"I want to hear about all the bad people and what God did to them." Teo folded his arms across his chest. Maria's eyes grew round as her brother went on. "The last time you told about God's people being made slaves because they didn't really love God. You said He had a plan of something to do that would end their slavery. I think God is going to kill them all. That's what Victoro would do if no one listened to him."

Victoro roared with laughter and slapped his knee. Most of the camp joined in. Hearing the words must sound funny coming from such a young child. Amado could see in their faces that this fact of life held little fear for them. Sudden death was simply a part of their life.

Yoana's eyes widened for a moment, and she looked like she wanted to bolt. Instead, she dropped her gaze and focused on the children gathered around her feet. She smoothed her dress and smiled. "Remember, Teo, how the Israelites had to make sacrifices for the sins they committed? We talked about that before."

Teo nodded. "They were very bad. Like when they didn't trust God and let a giant make fun of them."

"That's right." Yoana winked at the boy. "We're all like the Israelites in a way." She held up one hand to stop Teo's protest. "Yes, I know you would fight the giant like you fought the bear."

Teo beamed.

"But you have also done things wrong. Like not listening to your mother or not doing what you were told to do. Maybe even lying? Am I right?"

Teo ducked his head for a moment before meeting Yoana's eyes. "But I'm not the only one."

"That's right, Teo." Yoana leaned forward to caress the boy's cheek.

Oh, to be the one whose cheek she touched with such tenderness. Amado shook his head, concentrating on the story.

"God's word tells us we have all sinned, just like the Israelites. Remember the Ten Commandments God gave to Moses?"

Teo nodded again.

"Well, we've all broken at least some of those. Do you know what the punishment is for that?" Yoana smoothed a hank of Teo's hair.

Teo's forehead crinkled. "My mother usually whips me."

"When we sin against God, the punishment we deserve is death." Yoana smiled as if to soften her words. "However, God has given us a great gift. Do you know what that is?"

Teo chewed on his lower lip. "A sword? You know like David used on that giant."

"Hmm. That would be fun to have." Yoana laughed. The lilting sound struck deep in Amado's heart.

"Remember when we talked about God's Son, Jesus?" Yoana looked at each of the children as they sat up. They'd loved the story of the baby born in a stable. "God's gift to us is Jesus, who died for all the things we do wrong. Jesus did this so that we don't have to die for our sin. When we believe in Him and ask Him to be our Savior, then He forgives us for what we've done wrong."

Teo's forehead creased.

As Yoana went on, Amado admired her ability to explain the need for a Savior in terms the children could understand. How would the listening adults receive her words? He glanced up to see most of them riveted on Yoana. Only Tomàs, Feliciana, and Miguel were missing.

A scream echoed through the woods. Everyone spun to peer into the darkness. The men surged to their feet and drew their guns. Tomàs stumbled into the light and fell to one knee. Miguel strode into the clearing, one hand wrapped around Feliciana's upper arm, the other holding his pistol. He dragged her in front of Victoro and halted, his face dark.

"What's this?" Victoro holstered his gun as he faced Miguel.

"I caught them--together." Miguel gestured at Tomàs with his revolver. "He knows to stay away from my woman. I've warned him. This time he leaves or he dies."

Victoro's bushy eyebrows shot up, and he stroked his mustache. "Is this right, Tomàs? You've been warned before. Were you with Feliciana?"

Tomàs stumbled to his feet. His knees shook. He'd lost his hat, and his curly hair clung to his scalp in damp rings. His mouth opened and shut as he struggled for words. Feliciana sobbed, her eyes huge in her pale face.

"P-p-please." Tomàs held out his empty hands.

Victoro whipped out his pistol. The shot rang in the air—and Tomàs dropped to the ground in a heap. Feliciana screamed, jerked free from Miguel, and threw herself on Tomàs's body.

Yoana shot to her feet. Amado leaped forward and grabbed her to keep her from doing something that might cost her life.

Victoro holstered his gun again and grinned at Yoana. "There. I punish. Just like God, huh?"

CHAPTER TWENTY-TWO

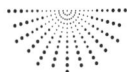

Yoana froze in place. She stared at Tomás, lifeless on the ground, and Feliciana prostrate over the man she loved. Nausea spiraled up her throat. She held her breath and willed her body not to react. Leya's life, and hers, depended on her control.

She wrenched her gaze from the pool of blood creeping from under Tomás and looked into Victoro's cold eyes. She repressed a shudder. How could she have forgotten? How could she have become so complacent that she forgot who these men were? They killed without thought or care. Tomás lived among them. Ate with them. Talked, joked with them. Yet none of them would grieve his death. No one except Feliciana.

"Let's go." Miguel dragged Feliciana up from Tomás. "You and I need to have some time together." The pale girl gave no objection as Miguel hauled her up the slope to the hut where the two of them stayed. Yoana opened her mouth to call out to Feliciana, but Amado made a low warning in his throat. Her teeth clicked as she snapped her mouth shut.

Though amusement crinkled the corners of Victoro's eyes, one wrong move, and he would turn his gun on her.

A small hand slipped into hers on the opposite side from

Amado. Something tugged on her skirt. Yoana glanced down. Teo wrapped his moist fingers around hers, while Maria hid her face in Yoana's skirt. The young girl's shoulders shook, but she made little sound. Yoana could see the tears in Teo's eyes, but he showed no other emotion.

How much had these young children lived with to make them react so little to the horror of a senseless death? Had there been others killed in front of the children? The thought sent another wave of nausea skittering through her. No one should have to endure this kind of fear.

"I think it is time we all turned in for the night." Victoro shoved his revolver in his holster and crossed his arms over his wide chest. His gaze never wavered from Yoana. "Dolores, Rosalinda, get your children."

Yoana started to turn away. Her heart pounded hard enough to make her light-headed. Victoro would never release her or Leya now that they'd witnessed him committing cold-blooded murder.

"You." Victoro pointed a finger at her. Yoana halted in midstep. "You will wait here. Leya, too."

Silence thickened until Yoana thought she wouldn't be able to draw another breath. The women herded the subdued children out of the clearing and up the slope to their sleeping quarters. Tonight none of the children complained, which in itself told a tale of how frightened they were.

Victoro glared at Pabladora until she sent Yoana a sympathetic glance and left. Only Lorenzo and Amado were left to hear what Victoro had to say. Leya stepped close, her fingers twining with Yoana's in much the same way Teo's had a few minutes earlier. Yoana could feel the tremors shivering through Leya, yet her tía showed no fear. Yoana squeezed her hand to show she understood.

"Yoana, your father refused to pay a ransom for you. By now, you are worthless to him. He will never believe you have not been compromised." Victoro paused to glare at Lorenzo, whose low laughter and lascivious look chilled Yoana. The man leaned back against a tree trunk and pulled out his knife to pick at something in his thumb.

Anguish stiffened Yoana's spine. She would not show how those words, and these men's contempt, intimidated her. Even the low pulsing ache in her arm faded as she waited to hear her fate.

"I didn't go after Cisto to bring you back out of the goodness of my heart." At Victoro's words, Lorenzo let out a loud bark of laughter. Victoro shot him a glare. "I will make some money from you a different way." He grinned.

At her side, Amado tensed. His arm slipped around her waist. Had he even realized he'd done so? She tugged, and he loosened his hold. Still, he remained tense.

"I have this amigo in Los Angeles. He is always looking for young ladies of good breeding who will enhance his establishment." Victoro grinned, his yellowed teeth showing through his thick mustache. Yoana's fought to keep from losing what she'd eaten for supper.

"*Mi amigo,* he will pay a very good price for you. Maybe not as much as a father should, but still plenty. We can all go north for the summer. Pabladora will enjoy that. She loves the mountains there."

Lorenzo's gaze had darkened as Victoro spoke. He lost his relaxed air, although he didn't change positions. Yoana could feel malevolence coming off of him in waves. Despair clutched at her. Why couldn't her father have loved her? Didn't God care enough to keep this from happening to her? To Leya?

"I-I ask one thing." Yoana lifted her chin as she spoke. Victoro didn't say anything, but cocked his head as if waiting for her to continue. She swallowed, her mouth dry as the hills in summer. "Please have someone take Leya back to my father's house. He has already paid a ransom for her."

Victoro chuckled. "She had a chance. She chose to stay here. Even with her scars, I'm sure my friend will find a use for her too.

After all, in the dark who will notice any disfigurement?" He and Lorenzo both laughed.

Yoana started to speak, but Victoro slashed at the air with his hand. "No! I don't care what you have to say. I will have enough trouble with the other women. When you are gone, maybe Cisto will come back. He may be unpredictable, but he's a good bandolero."

"Before we take her, can I have a night with her?" Lorenzo's gaze felt like an oily residue. "Maybe with both of them." He laughed.

"No, she will bring a better price if none of you have been with her." Victoro looked at Amado, who had been very quiet. "Is there something you have to say?"

"I will pay for her. For both of them." Amado's quiet words filled Yoana with both hope and fear. She wanted him to do whatever was necessary to take her away from here. And yet, what would happen to Amado? He'd been kind and protective, but if he refused to leave this life, would he become like Victoro? Would he someday kill without a thought of the consequences or the life taken? She wanted to say no, but in truth, her hope had been shaken tonight.

"You don't have the money," Victoro said.

"I have my cut from the sale of the horses. I will give you all of it." Amado took a half step, which put him in front of Yoana, cutting off her view of Lorenzo.

"That may not be enough." Victoro twisted his mustache in his fingers. "My amigo will pay well for these two." He shook his head. "I'll tell you what. I will go to my friend and make a deal. You can go with me, if you want. If you can still pay more for the women, then I will let you buy them. Agreed?"

Amado seemed reluctant. Likely he was thinking of Tomás, whose body still lay on the ground. He would need to be careful not to anger Victoro.

The leader shrugged. "Now, take the women out of here.

Watch them carefully. I don't want to lose them. I think they will be almost as valuable as the horses." She heard him slap his hand on something, probably Lorenzo's shoulder.

"Maybe we will give up stealing horses and start stealing the daughters of the dons." Victoro strode away, followed by Lorenzo.

As the bandoleros climbed the hill, Amado and Leya stayed quiet. Drained from the horror of the evening, Yoana dragged her steps as she followed them to the hut, her mind whirling.

"I have to go back down to see that Tomás gets buried properly." Amado pulled Yoana around to face him at the door of the hut. She could see the misery in his eyes and the drawn hollowness of his cheeks. He did care about Tomás. Her doubts settled. How could she have thought so little of him? Amado wasn't like the other bandoleros.

"You'll both be fine. I won't be gone long." Amado released her arm with a caress that ran down to her fingertips. A little thrill raced through her at his touch.

"I'm very tired. Leya and I will go to bed." Yoana put her hand on the doorframe for support.

"Then I'll be very quiet when I return. Sleep well." Amado's gaze strayed to Leya, and he nodded. He wanted to say more but wouldn't do so while Leya stood close enough to hear every word.

Inside, Yoana waited near the door. She listened to Amado's footsteps fade as he trod down the path. Her heart hammered in her chest. She'd been contemplating an escape, and now seemed like the best opportunity.

"Leya." Yoana kept her voice pitched low. "Get some things together quickly. We're leaving tonight. Right now."

"What? What are you talking about?" Leya stepped close enough that Yoana could reach out and touch her, but the dark kept her from seeing the expression on her tía's face.

"You heard what Victoro said. He will sell us in Los Angeles. You know what they will do to us there." Yoana grasped Leya's cold fingers and wrapped them in her hands. "We have to escape.

Tonight. They won't be expecting this. Victoro thinks Amado is watching us."

"We will be caught. We haven't prayed about this. What if Cisto finds us?" Panic tinged Leya's words.

Yoana wanted to comfort her, but they had to leave before Amado came back and caught them. "Leya, if we go right now, Amado will think we are asleep when he returns. He won't find out we're gone until tomorrow morning. Tomás usually watched over the horses at night. With all that happened tonight, there's a chance they won't think to replace him right away. This may be our only chance." She lifted Leya's trembling hand until she'd pressed it against her heart. "Please. I lost hope for a minute down there. I even questioned God. But I prayed too. I believe He has provided this opening for us."

Yoana closed her eyes and fought for calm. She could feel the waves of distress flowing off of Leya. This wouldn't work unless they both wanted the same end. "Leya, let's pray again right now. I feel sure this is what God is urging us to do, but I understand you need to know His will too."

Leya's grip on her hand eased. Yoana took a deep breath. "Father, God, please guide us. You know Your plan for us. I have to admit that I'm afraid to stay here any longer. Help us get home safely." Yoana paused and swallowed hard. "God, I know I hurt my father. Please, heal our relationship. Help me to love him, and help him to forgive me."

She stayed silent a few minutes, her emotions too strong. She couldn't catch her breath. Leya squeezed her fingers. A lone tear leaked out and trickled down Yoana's cheek. She pulled her hand free and swiped at her face with the back of her hand. "What now, Leya?"

"How will we get home?" Determination tinged Leya's tone.

Yoana almost laughed with relief. "I've watched the way they leave. If we're quiet, we can go that way tonight. I think I can get us home. Thank you for going with me."

Leya leaned close to rest her forehead against Yoana's shoulder. Her ragged breathing slowed to a calmer note. "I will trust that God can guide you, Yoana. Thank you for asking Him."

Yoana backed up a step. "Do we have any food up here?"

"There is some jerky wrapped up and hanging in a bag on the wall. I kept it here when you were sick. I tore off bits for you to swallow."

"Perfect." Yoana gave her tía a slight push. "Get the meat and another shirt or cloak in case the nights are cool. We won't be able to light a fire." As Leya fumbled her way across the floor, Yoana snatched up a cloak she had used when wounded.

"Hurry, Leya. We don't have much time." Yoana slung the cloak around her shoulders and eased the door open. Nerves clawed at her stomach as she studied the shadowed landscape. Wind soughed through the branches of the tall pines, a music she often found beautiful but which frustrated her tonight. She needed to hear what the men were doing. To discover where they were.

"I'm ready." Leya touched Yoana's shoulder.

They slipped outside into the clear, cool night. Something rustled in the brush, and they froze. Yoana held her breath as she strained to hear if Amado or one of the other men had come this way. Metal clinked against a rock, the sound drifting up the hill. Yoana drew in a deep breath. Amado must still be digging the grave for Tomás. Sadness clenched at her, but she forced the emotion away. She had to concentrate.

Yoana put her lips close to Leya's ear so she could speak quietly. "Follow me and try not to make any sound. We'll go slowly until we're away from the shacks and on the trail to the corrals. *Sí?*"

Leya nodded.

Yoana moved out through the trees. She chose her steps carefully, grateful that Leya followed her lead.

Night sounds were amplified as they worked their way past the camp. One of the children sobbed. Dolores hushed her fussy baby. Yoana paused close to the hut shared by Miguel and Feliciana. A sharp slap cracked the air, accompanied by a cry cut short. She heard Miguel's gruff voice pitched too low to make out the words. How she wished she could take Feliciana with them. The young girl might stand a chance if she could escape this life.

Voices drifted up on the wind. She could make out Amado's tone, but not his words. She thought she heard both Victoro and Lorenzo. With Miguel still in the shack with Feliciana, she and Leya should be safe. She prayed the horses would know her enough not to make a fuss when the two of them approached.

She found the path a few minutes later and stopped beside a huge pine tree, listening for any sound of pursuit. No one yelled. There were no disturbances to the peaceful night. Her pulse leveled out a bit. She tugged on Leya's hand, and they stepped out onto the path.

Yoana had only been on this path once, and then she hadn't gone all the way to the corrals. She knew Leya had never been there either. She caught the occasional scent of horses on the wind, and the animals' stamping, restless noises.

Her nerves were frazzled by the time they had two horses saddled and ready to ride. She'd chosen Amado's buckskin and the dappled gray that had belonged to Tomás. The boy wouldn't need his mount now, and they could make good use of the beast.

"We'll lead the horses back through camp." Yoana whispered into Leya's ear, even though they were well out of hearing range of the others. At least, they were if they had all gone to bed as they'd said. She refused to think that someone might have decided to come check on the horses before turning in. "Once we get on the far side, we can mount, but we'll need to keep to a walk until we get far enough away that they won't hear us. *Muy bien?*"

Leya agreed, and they started off. The muffled sound of the horses' hooves seemed to echo like gunfire, yet Yoana knew the susurration of the wind in the trees would cover up any noise they were making. As they approached the camp, she slowed her horse and then stopped.

The fire had burned down to embers. The orange glow lit the area with an eerie light. Nothing moved. None of the men were in sight, and she couldn't hear any voices. Yoana closed her eyes and sent up another prayer that God would protect them and get them away safely. She gave a light tug on the buckskin's reins and stepped into the open area.

The next hundred yards felt like miles. Yoana could feel eyes watching her, although it was just her imagination run wild. She and Leya made the other side of the clearing and wound up the path leading from the canyon. At the top of the rise, Yoana halted.

No one yelled. No gunshots shattered the quiet. A shaft of moonlight filtered through the trees and bathed Leya's face. Yoana could read the fear and tension in her tía's posture. She nodded, and they both looped the reins over the horse's necks and swung into the saddles. Yoana gave a quiet click of her tongue. The gelding flicked his ears and ambled down the path.

They rode in silence for a long time. Yoana gave her mount his head, and he took a path that wound through the hills and looked a bit familiar. She thought maybe they had come in on this trail, but everything looked different at night. Leya had to be exhausted, and Yoana's arm ached so much she wanted to cry. Yet they had to keep going. They had to be far enough by morning that they wouldn't be caught easily. She only prayed they were going in the right direction.

Yoana finally reined in her mount and turned to Leya. "Let's take a short break." Before she could say more, Leya let out a cry of pain and tumbled from her saddle to the ground.

CHAPTER TWENTY-THREE

Lucio held up his hand to halt the riders behind him. Another stop. They'd lost too much time waiting for his father to give permission to take the vaqueros and raid the bandolero camp. Every delay chafed at his nerves.

He swung down from his horse and stepped over to Ramón, who knelt beside the trail. Ramón pointed to a set of hoofprints in some soft earth at the edge of the path.

"Do you recognize them?" Lucio squinted in the early light. If only he had the eye for detail that Ramón had.

"This one belongs to one of the horses that carried off Yoana and Leya. The other is the horse Tomás rode to the ranch when he asked for the ransom. They're heading away from the canyon, and they're both carrying riders."

"In that case, I'm glad we came a different way this time. Otherwise, we might have run into them."

"True." Ramón peered into the dense forest around them. "We would have lost our surprise if that happened."

"Let's move." Lucio stood. "I wanted to be there before the camp wakes, but we won't make that. We'll try to catch them while they're still eating breakfast and thinking all is well. How much farther do you figure?"

"We're almost there." Ramón swung back on his horse. "How do you want to play this? Do we ride in and take them by surprise, or sneak up and look first?"

"We're riding with vaqueros, not bandoleros. We'll have the others hang back while we take a look. We can arrange a signal for them to come."

Twenty minutes later, Lucio and Ramón lay side by side on the rock outcropping that looked down into the bandolero camp. They'd been here once before. This very spot. But the two of them hadn't been enough to rescue his sister and tía.

Lucio expected to see the early morning cook fires surrounded by women fixing food and the men waiting to eat. Instead, the cook fires were burning and the women cooking, but something wasn't right. Four men stood to one side and seemed to be arguing. A barrel-chested man, the obvious leader, appeared to berate the others for something. The women cast uneasy glances at the men. Lucio and Ramón were too far away to hear what was being said, but they could see that the man with his back to them was unhappy about something.

"Where are Yoana and Leya?" Ramón asked. "I don't see Tomàs either."

"We warned him we would be coming. Maybe he left the camp already." Lucio eased forward to study the path leading into the canyon. The unnamed fear that had been with him ever since he and Ramón returned from witnessing the attack on Yoana bloomed to life. "Ramón, what if she didn't make it? What if...?"

They'd been helpless to do anything that day, but today would be different.

"We know the bear hurt her, but Yoana is strong. Maybe she's in one of the shelters and Leya is tending her." Ramón shifted and a pebble rattled away behind them. The two men froze.

Lucio waited for the bandoleros to swing around and see them on the rocks. Tension thrummed though him. He swiped one sweaty palm against his shirt. *God, please let Yoana and Leya be safe. Help us get them out of here.*

"The women keep looking up the hill at the shack built into the hill. The bandit with his back to us is pointing there." Ramón gestured with his chin.

Lucio followed his motion and studied the cabin with the door hanging askew. "If that's where they're keeping them, why is the door open?"

"I don't know, but I say we bring the boys up and get this going. Right now is the best time to take the camp because Yoana and Leya won't be in danger."

"If we go in from here, the path is so narrow only one of us can go through at a time. They'll hear us coming and pick us off before we have a chance to do anything." Lucio studied the hill behind the camp. "What if you take a couple of the men and circle uphill? Come in behind that hut and down that way."

Ramón frowned as he studied the terrain. "That depends on there being a path through that way. With the hill rising up like it does, I'm not sure we can get through on horses, but we will try. We could give you cover with gunfire from that direction if needed. You would have enough time to get everyone through from this end."

"Let's do it." Lucio slid backward off the rock, and Ramón followed him.

Lucio strode beside his friend. "As soon as we have the camp under control, I want you to take your men and check the cabins. See if you can find Yoana and Leya. Don't bring them down if there is any danger."

"I'll take Berto and Paulo with me." Ramón pushed aside a branch to step into the clearing where they'd left their horses and the men. "Give us a few minutes, then move into position. I'll give this signal when we're ready." He pursed his lips and gave a soft birdcall.

Lucio nodded. He turned to the men and explained the plan.

"We're not going in with the intent to kill. We only want to capture the bandoleros and free Yoana and Leya. There are women and children in the camp. I don't want any of them hurt."

Lucio watched Ramón, Berto, and Paulo head uphill through the trees. He prayed the bandits wouldn't hear anything or catch a glimpse of the men as they passed through the pines. If the desperadoes got even a hint they'd been discovered, Lucio and his men wouldn't have a prayer of getting the women out of there unharmed. Even the thought of those young children being hurt in the crossfire bothered him.

He could still see the image of Yoana protecting the boy and girl from that bear. Until that moment, he'd never realized the depth of his own sister's bravery. As he and Ramón hurried back to the ranch for reinforcements, he'd thought of all the times Yoana had taken their father's verbal lashing and stood strong. She'd been much more courageous than any of her brothers, but they hadn't seen that. He and his brothers had only seen her as a weak girl, one who caused their mother's death.

That did not describe Yoana at all.

"Let's go." Lucio led the rest of the vaqueros to the head of the path leading into the canyon. He stopped just shy of going over the top so they'd be out of sight until Ramón and the others were in position. His dun danced in place, as if he could sense Lucio's nervousness. Lucio wished he had a view of the camp so he'd know where all the men were positioned. He closed his eyes and sent up a quick prayer for the safety of his men. Ramón's birdcall drifted to them on the wind.

"Now!" Lucio lifted his revolver. He motioned to Antonio, positioned on the rocks above with his rifle. Lucio kneed the dun, and the animal surged over the hilltop with the rest of the men right behind him.

They thundered down the trail. Lucio saw the bandits whirl and look up. Shock registered on their faces, and three of them went for their guns. Antonio's rifle cracked. Dirt flew up in front of the men. If they didn't stop, the next shot would hit one of them. *Please, God, let Antonio hit his target.*

Up the hill behind the bandoleros, Ramón and his men rode their horses around the cabins. Ramón fired a shot in the air. One of the bandits swiveled to face the new charge. The leader, a stocky man with a heavy mustache, fired at Lucio. The bullet sounded like an angry bee as it whizzed past his ear. One of the horses behind him squealed in pain.

Antonio's rifle cracked again. The bandit leader stumbled back. He clutched his chest and fell forward to his knees. One of the women cried out and rushed toward the men. The rest of the women huddled together, the children protected in the middle.

More gunfire echoed in the canyon. Another of the bandits dropped to the ground. The older woman reached the fallen leader, but a bullet caught her. She dropped beside him. Lucio held up his hand to stop the shooting.

Quiet descended. The women and children sobbed. The two uninjured bandoleros dropped their guns and stood with their hands in the air. The older woman dragged herself to the leader and collapsed with her head on his chest. Their blood mingled and soaked into the ground.

"Tie them. Watch for weapons." Lucio motioned to Berto, who had come down the hill, and the vaquero moved to the two unarmed bandits to see if they had any hidden weapons. The third man on the ground had a leg wound. He tried to scoot over to his gun, but Berto kicked it away. One of the other vaqueros grabbed a loop of rope and, none too gently, tied the man.

Lucio crossed to the fallen leader, careful to keep out of the way in case the man only pretended to be hurt. Above the bushy mustache, the man's eyes were open and blank. The woman faced the man, her head resting on his chest, tears tracing down her cheeks. As Lucio leaned over to check her, she released a gasping breath and stilled. With the amount of blood she'd lost, there was nothing he could have done for her anyway.

"Lucio." Ramón hurried down the slope toward him. "I couldn't find Yoana or Leya anywhere."

Lucio surveyed the group of women and children. They were frightened, but might talk. The injured bandit had a mouth so foul Lucio didn't even want to try to talk to him. He turned to the other two, who had both been tied with their arms behind their backs. One of them looked like a slightly younger version of the injured man. Lucio had to wonder if they were brothers. The other man had his head turned away and down, not an attitude of defiance like most bandoleros.

Lucio stalked over to the two men.

The swarthy lookalike glared at Lucio with such malevolence Lucio knew they would have to watch him close. The other man finally turned to face him. Lucio halted in midstride, his mouth open in shock.

"What are you doing here?" He blurted the question before he thought.

"You know this man, Amado?" Swarthy turned his hatred toward the man.

"Amado?" Lucio cocked an eyebrow in question. Amado gave a curt nod.

"Well, *Amado,* you and I need to talk. Where is my sister, Yoana? And Leya?"

"We aren't telling you anything." Swarthy spat on the ground.

"Shut up, Miguel." Amado took a step away from Miguel as if distancing himself in case things went wrong. "This attitude won't help anything."

"And what will?" Miguel's eyes blazed. "You know they're going to hang us. There's no getting around that."

"You could at least act like a man and try to make provisions for your woman." Amado gestured with his chin toward the group near the campfires. "You could think of Feliciana's good for a change instead of your own hide."

Miguel's mouth thinned. "She can die with me."

"Well, that's noble of you." Amado snorted.

"Enough." Lucio gestured at Berto. "Tie Miguel over there with the other one. Not too close. I'm going to talk with Amado." Lucio took Amado's arm and led him far enough away so they could talk in private.

Lucio faced the man he thought he'd known. "Where are my sister and tía?"

"I don't know." Amado leaned back as Lucio took a step closer. "Listen to me. I *don't* know. We had an altercation here last night. Yoana and Leya went to bed. I thought they were asleep, but this morning when they didn't come out, I looked in the hut. They were gone."

"What do you mean they were gone?" Lucio didn't know whether to be angry or scared. "Where could they have gone?"

Amado explained about Cisto taking Yoana captive. He told the whole story, including Cisto's promise that he would return for Yoana. "I don't picture him taking Leya. Even if he thought she would alert the rest of us, I think Cisto would have killed her instead of taking her with him."

"Then what do you think has happened?"

"My guess is Yoana convinced Leya to run with her. She's probably trying to get back home."

"Why would she do that when she's hurt?" Lucio saw the question in Amado's eyes. "I was here with Ramón and saw the bear attack her. There hasn't been time for her to heal, especially if that lout kidnapped her right away."

"Desperation." Amado's mouth thinned. "Last night, Victoro, the leader, threatened to sell Yoana and Leya to a man he knows in Los Angeles."

"Sell them?" Lucio gaped. "The daughter and the sister-in-law of a don?"

"A don who would not pay to have his own flesh and blood returned." Amado's level gaze didn't flicker from Lucio. No, this man did not act like a bandolero. "And yes, sell them to a man who sells women to men who don't care. In fact, if I understand right, the man gets a better price for women like Yoana and Leya because of their status."

Lucio stared at the ground, wrestling back the rising anger. "Is that the bandit leader?" He nodded toward the dead man.

"That's him."

"Too bad he's dead. I would enjoy killing him, and not nearly so fast." Poisonous hatred welled up inside Lucio. He turned away from Amado and the others. *God, help me not to be like this. I don't want to be ruled by anger and hatred, but when I think about what this man might have done to Yoana and Leya....*

He drew a deep breath, then turned back to find Amado watching him, understanding in his expression. Lucio forced his eyes to stay on Amado and didn't look at the others. "Where is Tomàs?"

Surprise widened Amado's eyes. "Tomàs? How do you know him?"

"He brought the ransom note to the hacienda. We convinced him to help us. Ramón and I were following him when someone shot Ramón. We lost the trail. It took us weeks to find this hideout."

"Victoro killed Tomàs last night." Amado gave a full account of the previous night's events. By the time he finished, Lucio felt sick. How hard this must have been for Yoana and Leya to witness. Why couldn't he have been here for them? Gotten them out of this camp before such tragedy struck?

"I need to find my sister and tía." Lucio froze as a memory popped up. "When we were coming to the camp this morning, we saw the tracks of two horses heading away from camp. One of them had a nick in the hoof."

"That would be my buckskin." Amado frowned. "Were there only two?"

"That's all Ramón saw."

"Did either of them carry double?"

"If so, he didn't mention it." Lucio located Ramón across the clearing and motioned him to come over. "Do you think either of those horses might have been carrying two riders? The ones we saw earlier."

Ramón stared hard at Amado, questions in his gaze. "Maybe if they were children. Not adults though."

Lucio looked at Amado. "Any children missing?"

He shook his head. "They're all here. So, Yoana took Leya last night and escaped. She probably waited until I left, and then they sneaked through the woods to the corrals. We didn't post a guard, although we should have. I think Victoro thought since I'd be sleeping in front of the door, Cisto wouldn't be able to get to the women. He didn't perceive any other threat."

Lucio looked at Ramón. How could this be? "If we had come up the other path, we might have found Yoana and Leya! As it is, we missed them completely."

"Let me help you find them." Amado's intent gaze bored into Lucio. "We have to get to Yoana before Cisto does. The man is dangerous. He'll kill Leya without a thought. He'll kill Yoana, too, after he's done with her."

Amado's words sent a chill deep into Lucio. "Ramón, get a couple of the men to dig graves for the two who died. Then those vaqueros can take the other two bandoleros back to the ranch. If there are enough horses, they can take the women and children, too. Otherwise, we'll need to get horses up here. There's no way to bring a wagon here."

"There should be enough horses at the corrals. Cut me loose, and I'll help. I can show you where the horses are." Amado's gaze didn't waver as he studied Lucio.

"Why should I take you? How can I trust you?"

"Because I give you my word that I only want the best for Yoana." Amado hesitated. "I remember Ramón is good at tracking. You'll want to take him too. If Cisto has them, we'll need someone to help us find them."

The look in Amado's eyes convinced him. This man was as determined as Lucio himself to find the women. "Get the men started, Ramón. I'll go with Amado to see what the horse situation is. Have the women pack up what they need, but watch them. I don't want any of my men shot by some vindictive woman."

Lucio waited until Ramón had gotten out of earshot and turned to Amado. "Does my sister know who you are?"

"No. I couldn't tell her. It would be too dangerous."

"I'll ask again. You've become a bandolero. Why should I trust you?"

Amado's jaw tensed. His eyes narrowed. "Because I love your sister. I would never do anything to bring her harm." Amado leaned forward. "She is my heart. I will protect her with my life."

Lucio knew truth when he heard it. He nodded, and Amado started across the clearing to a path leading into the woods. As Lucio followed, he saw some of his men head off downhill carrying shovels. The children huddled together near the women. The woman who appeared oldest of the mothers, who would still be younger than Lucio, held a sobbing teenage girl. Behind them, in a shaft of morning sun, stood a woman whose brown hair glinted with red highlights. Her eyes flashed as she glared at Lucio.

This one...would cause much trouble.

"That's Rosalinda, Cisto's woman. Or she was." Amado spoke low. "She hated Yoana because Cisto wants Yoana for himself and no longer cares about her."

So. That explained the rebellious look. The woman must be afraid. And a woman afraid would bear close watching. But first they had to find Yoana and Leya...

Before the desperado killed them.

CHAPTER TWENTY-FOUR

Urgent need chafed at Amado's nerves as he helped Lucio saddle the horses and lead them back to camp. Lucio wanted to go after Yoana and Leya, but he didn't seem to understand the urgency or the danger the women were in. No matter how much Amado stressed the danger they faced from Cisto, Lucio still seemed to feel duty-bound to make sure his men were ready and able to depart with all the captives.

What had Leya said to Amado?

"*God puts us in situations so we can learn.*"

God, what do You want me to learn here? That I'm useless in protecting the woman I love, just like I couldn't protect my own brother? Am I supposed to stay silent while all those I love die off?

Amado bowed his head. God wanted him to have faith. To trust that He would be there with Yoana and Leya. He would protect them.

Trust.

Easy to say. Hard to do.

"Berto." Lucio's call caught Amado's attention. "When you get to the rancho, make sure the men are secure. The housekeeper will see to the women and children. If any of them aren't cooperative, lock them up, too. Send men for the authorities and for the other dons who are close. They'll want to be on hand for the hanging."

"What do I tell Don Armenta?" Berto asked.

Lucio's tone grew hard. "Tell him I've gone after Leya and Yoana. I should be only a day or two behind you. Yoana will try to get home, but she may have gotten lost. That's why Ramón is going with me."

"What about the other one? Do we prepare a rope for him too?"

Lucio glanced over to where Amado waited next to Ramón. "If he's a bandolero, he'll suffer the same fate as the others. Ramón and I will see that he stays with us."

If…so perhaps Lucio was as yet undecided.

As Lucio strode over to where Amado and Ramón waited by the horses, Amado forced himself to be quiet and wait when he wanted to vault onto the horse and race from the canyon in pursuit of the women.

"Vamanos." Lucio swung up on his dun. Jaw tense, he looked over at Amado. "If you give me any trouble, I'll shoot you. I won't hesitate because I know you and your family. The only reason you're going along is that you may be a valuable help."

Amado nodded. He'd expected no less. If he were in Lucio's boots, he would be the same way. Maybe even less receptive in allowing him to help.

Lucio let Ramón lead the way. Amado fell in second, with Lucio bringing up the rear, most likely to keep an eye on Amado. Miguel and Lorenzo watched him ride away, their narrowed, angry stares telling him exactly what they would do to him if they had half a chance. Amado turned away from them and urged his mount to a canter as he followed Ramón over the rise and out of the canyon.

Squirrels scrambled up tree trunks and chipmunks darted into the undergrowth as Amado and the others rode past. Occasional glimpses of blue sky filtered through the overhead branches. A cool breeze caressed Amado's cheeks, filling his nostrils with the ever-present scent of pine. He longed to have Yoana beside him to share the beauty… the peace of the forest. He prayed he would have the chance one day soon.

They kept a quick pace for the first hour, varying between a fast walk and a trot as the trail allowed. Finally, Ramón held up his hand. He swung down and studied the trail before walking over to Lucio.

"They're not traveling fast. I imagine it was too dark when they passed this way. Yoana would want to be safe but would keep going through the night to get as far away as possible."

"Do you think she knew to stay on this trail?" Lucio asked.

Ramón cocked an eyebrow at Amado. Both men watched him and waited.

He would not hide the truth from them. "She doesn't know much. We came in on this path, but that was several weeks ago. We'd been riding for days to throw off any pursuers, so I don't know how well she will be able to figure out the way home. My guess is not well at all. The only other time she's been away from camp is when Cisto took her, and they didn't come this way. Plus, that was at night, too."

A pinecone hit the dirt in front of Amado's pinto. The horse snorted and danced to the side. Amado tightened the reins. What he wouldn't give to take off on his own instead of having to wait for Lucio.

"Let's go." Lucio waited until Ramón mounted. "Be careful, Ramón. In the dark, she may have missed the trail. Still, we need to go as fast as we can. If this Cisto is after Yoana, I want to reach her before he does."

For the next couple of hours, they traveled at a brisk walk. The soft earth showed hoof prints, and at a bend in the path, they could see where Yoana and Leya got off among the trees, but when the trail wound back around, they found it again.

At a point where the path widened, Lucio trotted up beside Amado. "Why did you do this, join these men?" When Amado stayed silent, Lucio seemed to think he should answer his own question. "For the money? Your father has enough of that, and a good portion would be yours. For excitement? Maybe. I hear some men crave danger." Lucio cut him a look. "Did you even stop to think of the hurt you would cause?"

"I did this because I had to." Amado couldn't look at the man he once called friend. "I don't expect you to understand."

"And your father? What about the consequences for him?" Anger narrowed Lucio's eyes and sharpened his tone.

"My father knows enough." Amado looked away. To his right, the trees opened up on a panoramic vista, hills fading into the distance. Trees marched across, and far away he could see the valley where Don Armenta's ranch lay. Maybe Yoana and Leya were well on their way home. He hoped so.

The pinto snorted and skittered to the side again. Ramón's horse had stopped, and he swung down and knelt beside a widened area of the trail. He took off his hat and scratched his head as he studied the sign.

Lucio dismounted and joined his vaquero. "What is it?"

"Something happened here." Ramón gestured to a scuffed place in the pine needles. Amado urged the pinto forward and leaned down to get a look.

"If I were to guess, I'd say someone fell off a horse." Ramón rubbed his jaw. "You can see where the body hit the ground and the hoofprints moving away aren't as deep, so the horse wasn't carrying the same load."

Lucio frowned. "Leya and Yoana both know how to ride. Why would they fall off?"

Ramón motioned them to stay as he moved around the small area. He ended up near the scuffed place. "Come here." He waved his hand at Lucio, and Amado cursed his bound hands, which made it impossible for him to climb down and see what they were looking at.

Ramón pointed to a darkened spot in the dirt. "I would say someone fell because they were hurt. This looks like blood."

Blood!

Cisto. He'd found them.

Amado bit off a curse. *How could you let this happen, God? Why didn't you take care of them?*

"Can you tell any more?" Lucio's mouth stretched to a grim line.

"I would say this happened to Leya. Yoana would be the one in the lead, and this is the second horse." Ramón ran his hand through his hair before he slammed his hat back on his head. "Whatever happened, the one who fell got back on the horse and rode away."

Ramón stood and crossed to the far side of the clearing. He studied the ground then straightened. "The bad news is that a third rider joined them here. The hoofprints are deeper, so the rider is bigger. Heavier. A man, most likely. He rode off with Yoana and Leya."

"Mount up." Lucio swung onto his dun. "We don't stop until we find them. If this man is as bad as Amado says, we don't have much time."

This time as they rode, trepidation set the pace. Ramón hurried them along while the tracks were easy to follow. When the prints turned off and went up a slope, even Amado could have tracked them. What was Cisto doing? Huge clumps of dirt were gouged out as the horses passed. Well, they would find out soon enough. Cisto wasn't stupid. He had a reason for everything he did.

At the top of the rise, they looked out over a slope covered with rocks. The large slabs went off in all directions. So…this explained Cisto's actions. Following them across this terrain would be painstakingly slow.

"We have to split up." Amado grimaced at Lucio's and Ramón's startled expressions. "It's the only way to keep Cisto from getting too far ahead. Ramón may be a good tracker, but even he won't be able to follow now without taking his time. If we split up and each go down a different way, we can look for where their tracks start up again. It will save time—" he met Lucio's gaze "--and it may save their lives."

"We would have to do that three ways to be effective." Ramón stared down the slope before turning back to Amado. "There are only two of us because we can't trust you."

Amado ignored Ramón. He focused on Lucio, watching for some sign of softening. Lucio didn't blink. His dark eyes seemed to bore into Amado.

"Lucio, you know you can trust me."

"Two months ago, I would have agreed." Lucio continued to study Amado. "Now…I don't know."

"For Yoana's sake. For Leya, you have to." Amado pulled his hands apart as far as they would go. "If this man gets to a place where he feels safe, your tía and sister will die horrible deaths."

Pain flashed across Lucio's face. Good. He needed to understand what was at stake.

Lucio shut his eyes for a brief moment, as if to erase the vision of his sister and tía being hurt. He pulled his knife, and Amado tensed—

Lucio flicked the blade across the ropes at Amado's wrists. The ropes dropped away, and Amado rubbed his raw wrists.

Ramón stepped forward. "Lucio, are you sure?"

"Leave it, Ramón." Lucio held up his hand, palm out. "I'm not sure, but we have to try this." He turned to Amado. "If you betray me, I will hunt you down. Understand?"

Amado nodded. He pointed at the slope. "I'll take the left. Lucio, you take the right, and Ramón can go down the middle. When we reach the bottom, Lucio and I will work our way toward Ramón. If one of us finds their tracks, we can wait there or leave a sign."

Lucio's mouth quirked up. "I set you free and you start giving orders." He nodded, pulled Amado's gun from his saddle bag and handed it to him with a look that said he'd better prove worthy of trust. "It's a good plan. Let's go."

~

Amado led the pinto down the steep slope. Small stones rattled downhill as they passed. Cisto and the women were already past this point or he would be able to hear them. There was no way to traverse this hillside without making noise.

Near the bottom, the rocks petered out. Trees closed in, and Amado found a trail. He studied the ground, but couldn't find any sign other than from wild animals. A bear had passed through not long ago. At the edge, he could see the doglike prints of a coyote. He turned to his right to follow the path around the hill to meet Ramón and Lucio. As he did, he noticed a skidding mark.

A horse had slid as it crossed the trail.

Amado tied the pinto and moved into the undergrowth. He found traces of a horse's recent passing. The dirt still held moisture and hadn't dried from being turned over. His nerves hummed. Maybe Cisto hadn't been able to travel fast after all. Amado was sure Yoana did her best to slow him down. Maybe…

God had brought him here so he could rescue Yoana and Leya.

Amado hurried back to the trail. He should find Lucio and tell him, but that would take too long. He ripped a piece of cloth from his shirt and tied it to a branch beside the sliding hoofprint. If Ramón saw the rag, he would know to follow. *Please, God, let them come soon.*

He wrenched the pinto's reins from the branch and mounted the horse. Bending low, he urged the pinto into the undergrowth.

Now he had the advantage. Cisto would be slowed down with the two women.

Quiet surrounded him. Were the wild animals in hiding because Cisto had just passed through? If Leya were hurt, Yoana could be making Cisto stop so Leya could rest. A dangerous game. If Cisto tired of stopping or thought pursuit might be close, he would kill Leya.

Off to his left, Amado caught a hint of sound. He slipped from the saddle. He didn't want to tie the pinto up too far from where Cisto held Yoana, but he wanted to be ready to keep the horse from whinnying and alerting Cisto to his presence.

Behind him, Amado heard a faint shout. He winced and hoped Cisto hadn't heard the sound. From the angry tone ahead, he thought Cisto wouldn't hear much. As he drew closer, he could make out Yoana's voice, although he couldn't understand anything she said. Anger and authority rang in her tone though.

He had to smile as he crept toward them.

"You have to let us go." Yoana's voice rang through the woods.

"I don't have to do anything." Cisto's low growl chilled Amado. Even though he'd known Cisto had Yoana and Leya, in the back of his mind he'd hoped that wasn't true. Amado looped the pinto's reins over a branch and eased through the woods toward the voices.

"Leya will die if I don't get her back home soon. You'll have her death on your hands."

Cisto laughed. "You think I care? Do you know how many I've killed? One more won't matter."

"My brother will find you."

"Your brother doesn't care about you any more than your father does." Cisto's laugh contained the same cruelty as his words.

Amado slipped through the last barrier. Leya lay sprawled on the far side of a small cleared area, unmoving. Amado would have thought her dead, except, if she were, Cisto would have taken Yoana and ridden on.

Yoana stood in front of her tía, legs apart, hands fisted at her sides. Her skirt had a tear toward the bottom of one side. The sleeve of her blouse had been ripped, probably by the brush. Cisto wouldn't have stopped once he started.

A long scratch made a red welt along Yoana's cheek and down her neck. Her hair had come partially out of the braid. Fierce defiance shone from her eyes.

She'd never looked more beautiful.

Amado hadn't thought he could love her more, but seeing her like this proved him wrong.

"My father knew that even if he gave in to Victoro's demands, you would not return me alive. Victoro would have taken the money and kept me."

"So why did he offer to pay for the scarred one?" Cisto leaned back against a tree trunk as he watched Yoana with his feral gaze.

She lifted her chin. "To buy time. While you were debating what to do with me, my brother found the camp and prepared to attack."

"If that is true, then where is this brother of yours?" Cisto swept a hand around the clearing.

"He's right here."

Amado started as Lucio stepped from the trees at the end of the clearing farthest from him, gun in hand. There was no sign of Ramón.

Yoana whirled to face her brother. Cisto's pistol appeared in his hand as if by magic. Amado had his pistol out and to the side to get a clear shot. Yoana stood between him and Cisto.

"Lucio, you're here." Yoana's hand flew to her throat as she stared at her brother.

"I came for you. Just like you told this bandolero." Lucio kept his gaze—and his revolver--trained on Cisto. "If you want to live, you need to drop the gun."

"You drop yours, or I will kill you." Cisto smiled. "Then I will have some fun with the chicas before I kill them."

"Wait." Yoana held out her hands. "Lucio, don't worry about me. Let him have me. You have to take Leya home and get her help. She's hurt. Please."

"I will take good care of your sister." Cisto sounded relaxed, but his stance told Amado otherwise. "She is right. The scarred one will die if she doesn't get help soon."

Amado could see Cisto's finger tightening on the trigger. He knew he had to do something or Lucio would die. "Cisto." He stepped from behind the tree.

Yoana gasped as Cisto swung around, dropping into a crouch. Lucio fired, but his bullet flew above Cisto to hit the tree behind him. Amado shot at the same time Cisto fired at him. Amado's bullet grazed Cisto's arm. He grunted as Cisto's bullet struck his shoulder and flung him backward. He stumbled against a tree, a broken off branch cutting into his back through his shirt.

Pain exploded through him. As if from a far distance, he heard Yoana scream his name.

CHAPTER TWENTY-FIVE

"*Amado!*" Yoana dropped down to cover Leya's inert body. She watched as Amado crashed backward into a tree. Bits of wood littered the air. Another gunshot.

Cisto cursed and leaped on his horse. Blood ran down his arm. Lucio fired again, but Cisto moved too fast. He disappeared into the brush.

Yoana froze. Her pulse thundered in her ears. Lucio had come here? For her? Amado. Leya. Her tía.

Yoana's thoughts swirled as she tried to figure out what to do first. Whom to help.

She took a moment to check her señorita. Leya still breathed, but hadn't regained consciousness. She would be safe for the moment.

Yoana raced across the clearing to Amado. *Please, God, don't let him die. Please.* She dropped down beside him, almost afraid to touch him. When she saw his chest rise and fall as he took in a breath, she sobbed with relief.

"Amado." She brushed her fingertips across his unshaven cheek. "Can you hear me?"

His eyes fluttered open. He blinked up at her and smiled,

sending her pulse dancing. He lived! He had come for her! All her resolve to forget this man fled. She wanted to fling herself across him and beg him to be all right. Beg him to live for her. Beg him to love her as she loved him.

Lucio dropped to his knees beside her. "Leya is all right. We have to look at Ga...Amado's wound." He took hold of Amado's arm and eased him from his side onto his back.

Color drained from Amado's face, but he didn't make a sound.

Blood gushed from a wound high on the left side of his chest. Lucio jerked the bandana from his neck. "We have to staunch the bleeding. This is bad, but if we get the blood to stop, he might have a chance. Hold this, Yoana. I'll need to see if the bullet came out the back."

Ramón ran into the clearing. He raced over to them. "What happened? I heard the shots."

Lucio filled him in as Ramón studied Amado's wounds. "I can do this, Ramón. Go see where Cisto went. I don't want him to sneak up on us."

Ramón hesitated. "Your tía?"

"She's weak from blood loss." Yoana's teeth chattered, making speech difficult. "We have to get her home soon."

"For now, see to our safety here." Lucio sent a pointed look at Ramón. The vaquero leaped on his mount and trotted from the glen. At the place Cisto went into the trees, he slowed and bent over to study the ground.

Blood from Amado's shoulder soaked through the bandana to coat Yoana's hands. She swayed on her knees. All the stress and tension of the past days pressed down on her.

Lucio grabbed her arm. "Let me take this." He tugged the bandana from her hands. "You go check on Leya. *Sí?*"

She glanced across the clearing to see her tía still prone on the ground. She nodded. If she tried to say anything, she would shatter into a million pieces. How could she not? When the two people who mattered most to her might die because once again she had been impulsive.

Yes, she'd left camp for a good reason.

Yes, she'd prayed first.

But did she wait for God's answer, or did she just assume He wanted her to do what she thought was best? She'd pressured Leya into going with her, when, if they had remained where they were, Lucio would have rescued them.

Yoana knelt in the grass beside her tía. Her heart ached so much she didn't know if she could stay upright. Leya rested curled up like a child, as fragile as glass. Her eyes were closed, her papery lids pale against her dusky face. Even her lips had little color. If not for the steady rise and fall of her chest, she might be dead.

As gently as Yoana could, she lifted Leya's arm. A small moan came from her tía's parted lips, and a tear leaked from the corner of her eye and traced a lonely track across her cheek. Dried blood caked her side where the knife blade had entered. Yoana had bound the wound earlier, but she'd done it so fast that the bandage hadn't held. Blood still seeped from the angry cut. Dark bruising stained the skin around the wound.

Yoana lifted Leya's blouse and fought the knot to untie the cloth. She refolded the thick part and placed it on the wound, biting her lip when pressing down caused Leya to groan. "I'm sorry, Leya. I have to stop the bleeding." After a few minutes of pressure, Yoana retied the bandage.

Ramón returned. Yoana left Leya and hurried over to see if he had found Cisto.

"He's gone." Ramón swung down from his horse. "I found a place that looked out over the valley below and saw him travelling fast toward the desert. Maybe the coyotes will find him and have a meal." He knelt next to Lucio. "Will this bandolero be able to ride?"

Amado struggled to sit up. His handsome face had turned gray against the dark stubble. Gaunt lines on his cheeks gave them a sunken appearance. Pain reflected in his eyes and in the pale line around his lips. Oh, how Yoana longed to take away his hurt.

"I'm fine to ride." Amado pushed at the ground and tried to stand, but his eyes rolled back, and he dropped back to the earth unconscious.

"Well, that answers that." Ramón nudged Amado with his toe. "Think we can tie him on his horse?"

"We'll have to." Lucio stood, weary lines on his face aging him.

Why had her brother come for her when their father was against it? Had Lucio defied the don? Had her father changed his mind about her? No, after all these years, the don wouldn't capitulate. He would never change his mind. Especially now, after she'd been with the bandoleros for so long…

She backed away. She should disappear into the desert like Cisto. She'd made so many poor decisions and hurt so many people. They were better off without her. Maybe she deserved Cisto and his cruelty.

"Bring his horse." Lucio nodded at the pinto. "It may not be wise to move him, but if we stay here, he'll die for sure. If we can get him back to the ranch, we might be able to save him."

"Somehow that doesn't seem right." Ramón scratched his head. "Seems like we'll just save him for the hangman's noose."

Yoana gasped at Ramón's words. The thought of Amado at the gallows along with the other bandoleros horrified her. He didn't deserve that!

Lucio's gaze snagged Yoana's. "Where are you going?"

She halted, unable to back away from her older brother. "I am leaving." She twisted her fingers together. "I have to."

Lucio stood in one fluid movement and crossed to her. "You have to come back home." He grasped her hands in his and held tight when she tried to tug free. "We need you at the hacienda. The children will be back any day. I'm sure they've missed you."

Tears burned her eyes. The mention of children reminded her

of Teo, Maria, and the others in camp. How she missed the little ones. She didn't even know what had happened to them. Or to the others in camp. That Amado accompanied Lucio and Ramón to find her showed Lucio had raided the bandolero hideout. Were they all dead? The thought cut her deep.

"I am no good." Yoana swiped her cheek against her shoulder. "I bring misery to everyone." She grimaced at Lucio's sound of disagreement. "Besides, the don doesn't want me back. I am more worthless to him than ever."

"I can't speak for our father, Yoana. He is a hard man." Lucio eased his grip, his thumbs brushing against the backs of her fingers. "But I will speak for myself. I have done you a disservice all these years. I should have spoken up for you, but I didn't. That has changed. I will be your advocate from now on. You will not have to stand alone against the don."

She stared into her brother's dark eyes, and what she saw there stunned her. Compassion, and perhaps...love? An emotion swept through her that was so strong she trembled. Someone in her family cared. Someone besides Leya. Someone cared enough to face down the don.

She nodded, and Lucio pulled her into a hug. He held her tight for long minutes as her tears dampened his shirt.

When he pulled back, his voice was gentle. "Come. We must get Leya and Amado home. I'm sure you want to know what happened at the bandolero camp. I will tell you on the way." Lucio placed a kiss on her forehead and stepped away.

He and Ramón made quick work of getting Amado tied to his mount and Leya ready to go.

The trip home proved slow and tedious. Lucio had Leya in front of him on his dun. He rode beside Yoana long enough to relate the taking of the bandolero camp and the deaths of Victoro and Pabladora. Yoana's heart ached for them, even as she knew this might be the better end. Pabladora loved her bandit leader.

She would never have been able to watch him hanged. She prayed they were now in a better place.

They kept going through the night. Lucio didn't want to risk taking Leya and Amado on and off the horses.

"We need to get them home fast, Yoana." Lucio looked over at her as they rode abreast on a wider part of the trail. "Once we get them cleaned up and in a bed, they will heal faster. The longer we're out here in the mountains, the more danger there is from infection." Yoana knew the truth of that. She could still feel the ache in her arm from the bear attack.

"Lucio, why did you come for me?" She had to know.

He shifted Leya so that she rested against his other shoulder. He studied Yoana for a while before he turned back to watch the trail. "For years, our father has treated you unfairly. I've been too much of a coward to speak. Our brother, Mateo, spoke up, but Father banished him."

"What!" Yoana gaped at her brother. Mateo hadn't been around in years, but she'd never known why. Only that no one ever mentioned him.

"He tried to talk with the don about his treatment of you. Our father refused to listen and sent Mateo to live on the outer reaches of the rancho. He threatened to disown him completely if he defied him again." Lucio cleared his throat. "Emiliano and Diego stayed close but not at the hacienda. They, too, disapproved of your treatment. I remained at home because I feared standing up to Don Armenta."

"I thought my brothers chose to marry and move away. I barely remember Mateo." Yoana's eyes burned. All along she'd had family who cared about her. They loved her no matter what she'd done. "I thought you all hated me." Yoana almost choked on the words.

"Why would we hate you?" Lucio stared at her wide-eyed.

"Mother died because of me."

"Yoana, you were a baby. Four years old. How can such a young child be responsible for anything?"

"I was always impulsive. I didn't listen." Yoana sniffed. From the corner of her eye, she could see Lucio watching her, but she couldn't look at him.

They rode in silence for several minutes. Up ahead the path narrowed, and they wouldn't be able to ride side-by-side. Lucio pulled his horse to a stop. Yoana did likewise. They faced one another, and the compassion in his gaze brought tears to her eyes.

"I found the bandolero camp the day you were attacked by the bear," Lucio said. "I couldn't help you, but I watched you protect those two children. That bear would have killed you if the men hadn't pulled it back so fast. Remember?"

Yoana shuddered. "It all happened very fast."

"You could have gone a different way and not been hurt, Yoana. Why did you try to protect those children?"

She gaped at him. "They would have been killed. One swipe of that paw, and they both would be dead."

"But what if they were where they shouldn't be? Would you still have protected them?"

Understanding flowed over her in a wave. She nodded. "Yes. They wouldn't mean to do anything wrong. They're just children."

"Yet the boy is older than you were that day you ended up in the pasture where you didn't belong."

Lucio's gentle tone told her he held no grudge. Had she only imagined the family's disapproval all these years?

"Yoana, Mother didn't even consider her own safety when you were in danger. She would never have wanted anyone to blame you for what happened. We all know that." Lucio's tone brooked no argument.

"Father doesn't." Yoana shook her head. "He's always believed her death to be my fault."

"That's not true, Yoana."

"What?" She gave him a startled look. "How can you say that?"

"Because I know the truth. Someday maybe Father will admit it to you. That story is not mine to tell though." Lucio kneed his dun and moved ahead of Yoana.

She followed, lost in thought. What did her brothers know that she didn't?

By riding through the night and taking a shortcut, they reached the hacienda before Antonio and Berto returned with the others from the bandolero camp. Yoana wanted to cry with relief when she climbed from her mount. Stiff from disuse, her legs almost buckled under her.

The stable boys scampered out to take the horses and lead them away. She usually helped care for her horse, but right now she could barely walk to the house. Besides, she needed to oversee Leya's and Amado's care. Should she try to see her father? Would he want to see her?

∼

FOR THE NEXT TWO DAYS, Yoana spent her time going from Leya to Amado, making sure they had clean clothes and bandages. She spooned bits of broth into them, even though much of the liquid trickled out again. She tamped down the hurt from her father's refusal to see her.

Early on the morning of the second day, Lucio came to Amado's room. Yoana sat by the bed, bathing Amado's brow. One of the other women worked on some mending as she sat with Yoana.

Lucio studied Amado. "How is he?"

"He had a fever, but I think it has broken. I'm hoping he will wake up today." Yoana smiled up at her brother. "Have you seen Leya? She woke up in the night, but I think she's asleep now."

"I spoke with her." Lucio pulled up a chair on the other side of the bed. "Yoana, we need to talk."

She twisted the rag to wring excess water from it before meeting Lucio's gaze. What she saw there chilled her. "What is it?"

"I know you heard Antonio and Berto arrive last night with the others from the camp." He paused until she nodded. "We are going to hang the bandoleros tomorrow. That will give time for some of the other rancheros to arrive."

She couldn't breathe. She knew what Lucio had to say but wanted to shut her ears so she couldn't hear.

"He's trying to tell you not to waste your time with me since they are going to hang me tomorrow too."

At Amado's words, she spun around, and his gaze captured hers. Her pulse leaped—he was conscious!--and then plummeted.

Conscious…just in time to die.

CHAPTER TWENTY-SIX

An odd cacophony of sounds drifted through the window. Amado tried to see outside but couldn't. Children's laughter vied with the steady thud of hammers against wood as the vaqueros built a gallows. The breeze drifted in laden with the scent of roasting meat as the household prepared for company. From what he'd heard, many of the dons in the area were bringing their families to view the hanging and celebrate the capture of the bandoleros.

And he might be one of the men dangling at the end of a rope.

He didn't have much hope of avoiding the gruesome death. No matter what he said, there would only be his word against that of many others. To all intents and purposes, he'd fit in well with the gang of bandits. Who would believe the truth? Wouldn't they see it as just his way of weaseling out of being lynched?

He'd fought exhaustion and sleep, trying to figure a way out of this, but couldn't come up with a plan. Lucio and Don Armenta insisted the hanging take place as soon as the other familias arrived. There wouldn't be enough time to convince anyone of his innocence. He had no hope of his father arriving in time to vouch for him.

Amado closed his gritty eyes and tried to pray. Would God

listen? Amado had failed everyone. His father. His brother. Yoana. Why would God care about a worthless person like him?

The door to his room scraped across the floor. "Amado?" Teo's loud whisper pulled Amado from his morbid reverie.

He forced a smile. "Hey, amigo, what are you doing here?"

Teo and Maria tiptoed into the room. Teo glanced back out before he pushed the door shut. The pair scampered over to the bed. Maria, suddenly shy, ducked behind Teo and peeked around at Amado.

"We sneaked away." Teo stuck his thumbs in the waistband of his pants and stuck out his chest. "Yoana is supposed to watch us. She told us a story and then had to leave to check something." He grinned. "She told us to behave, but she didn't say we had to stay right there. We can behave here with you."

Amado chuckled, then winced as the movement lanced pain through his upper body. "So, what story did Yoana tell you this time?"

"She told us about Saul."

"Paul." Maria's eyes twinkled as she leaned closer to Teo and whispered the name.

Teo rolled his eyes. "Not the Saul who got to be the first king but a different Saul."

"Paul." Maria smirked.

"So, why does Maria think his name is Paul?" Amado bit the inside of his lip to keep from laughing at the two.

"Well, his name *was* Saul." Teo glared at Maria until she covered her mouth with her hands, her eyes full of mischief. "But then his name got changed to Paul."

It still amazed Amado how much of the stories this little one remembered. "What happened to him?"

"He was a very smart man and a Jewish leader." Teo pursed his lips. "But after Jesus died, Saul hated the Christians. He went around killing them."

"That's not very nice." He'd never heard about this man in the

Bible, but then his church attendance had been all about appeasing his mother.

"Paul." Maria poked Teo with a chubby finger.

"I'm getting to that part." Teo frowned at his friend, who wrinkled her nose at him. He shook his head and turned back to Amado. "One day, *Saul* wanted to go to some town and kill a bunch of Christians. So you know what God did?" Teo's eyes lit up.

"Let's see." Amado scratched at his stubbly chin. "Since God loves Christians, I'd say he killed this worthless guy to protect His people."

"That's what Victoro or the don would have done." Teo nodded. "But Yoana said God is different because He knows what we're like inside, in our hearts. God wanted to give Saul another chance. He waited until Saul was out on the road, and God spoke to him. There was a bright light, like lightning."

Teo waved his hands and made thunder sounds. Maria followed his example. Despite how cute they were, Amado wanted the rest of the story. He could almost hear Yoana's lilting tone as she told this one to the children.

"When God spoke to him, Saul fell down on the ground. He went blind and couldn't see anything! Yoana said Jesus talked to him. Afterward his name changed." Teo's hushed tone stole Amado's laughter.

"Paul!" At Maria's shout, Amado and Teo both jumped.

Teo clapped his hands. "Yep. His name changed from Saul to Paul, and he became one of the greatest Christians. He wrote a whole bunch of letters that people still like to read."

"So here you are." They all jumped as the door scraped open to admit Yoana and Lucio. "We've been looking all over for you children."

Maria ducked behind Teo, and the boy faced Yoana, straightening his shoulders in a gesture very reminiscent of the posture Yoana took when she was in trouble. A smile tugged at the corner of Amado's mouth. Yoana and Lucio seemed to be fighting their own smiles.

"Your mothers are looking for you." Yoana crossed the room to ruffle Teo's hair. "Why don't you take Maria back now. Lucio and I need to talk with Amado."

"Sí, señorita." Teo took Maria's hand. "'Bye, Amado. We'll try to come see you tomorrow if we can." He shot a quick glance at Yoana before he and Maria scurried across the room and disappeared into the hall.

Lucio closed the door as the patter of little feet faded. He crossed to the bed.

Why couldn't they just let him be alone? He'd like to take some time to consider the story Teo had told him. But determination was clear in Lucio's features.

The time had come to let Yoana in on Amado's secret.

"Lucio insists we have something to talk about." Yoana accepted the chair that her brother pulled to the bedside for her. He dragged another over and straddled the seat, his steady gaze not leaving Amado.

"It's time for you to tell Yoana who you really are." Lucio ignored the startled glance Yoana gave him and kept his eyes on Amado.

"Who he really is?" Yoana's eyebrows drew together. "He's Amado."

"Amado who?"

"I don't know." Yoana nibbled her full lower lip. "I don't think I ever heard him say his last name. But then none of the bandoleros went by anything other than one name."

"Do you want to tell her, or shall I?" Lucio's challenge was clear in his tone.

Amado opened his mouth. He did want to tell her. He had tried so many times. Yet fear stilled his tongue. Would she still care about him? Would she hate him when she knew? He didn't think he could bear that.

"Are you saying you knew Amado before you came to the camp?" Yoana gave her brother an incredulous look. "How could you?"

Lucio waited, then finally turned to his sister. "You know him too. You just haven't seen him since you were four years old."

Confusion flashed across Yoana's delicate features. She looked from Lucio to Amado, seeming unable to make sense of her brother's words. "Who are you?"

"My full name is Gabrio Amado Santiago."

Understanding--and then hurt--flickered across Yoana's face.

He grabbed her hand. "I wanted to tell you, but I couldn't."

She jerked her hand from his and stumbled to her feet. "Gabrio? My *betrothed?* Who broke our betrothal with no explanation? You became a *bandolero?*" Tears sparkled in her eyes, and she backed away from the bed and out of his reach.

"Yoana, please, you have to listen to me." He tried to sit up, but the pain through his chest made him fall back.

"You've known all along who I am, but you couldn't trust me with the truth? Why?" Her eyes were huge.

"Please, sit down." Amado gestured at her vacated chair. "Let me explain."

"Please, Yoana." Lucio patted the chair. "This is something I would like to hear too."

Yoana moved like she walked across glass shards. She eased down into the seat, but moved it back a few inches from the bed so Amado couldn't reach her. He couldn't blame her. He'd never intended to hurt her like this.

"A few months ago, my father's rancho was plagued by a group of bandoleros. They stole our horses and cattle. They killed one of our vaqueros and ravished his wife." Amado rubbed his hand down his face, wishing he could wipe away the horror of finding the man and his wife. "She didn't survive."

Yoana gasped, and her face drained of color.

Amado turned his gaze away. "The worst of the bandoleros

had the name of Cisto. Everyone feared the man. He seemed unstoppable."

"Couldn't you catch him?" Lucio asked.

They'd tried. How they'd tried. "The gang proved to be very wily. They would split up and attack at different times and areas. We tried to find them but came up empty every time. My father offered a reward, but that didn't help."

Lucio leaned forward. "What happened?"

Amado swallowed hard. "My best friend, Tito, and my younger brother, Mario, received information about this Cisto and where he might be found. I was off with some of the men searching in another area, so they decided to try to catch him on their own. One of the vaqueros overheard them but didn't realize when they were going. We didn't have the chance to stop them."

A shudder racked him. The bed creaked. "By the time I returned home, they had been missing for three days. My father and I rode out to find Mario and bring him back."

"Did you find them?" Yoana eased her chair closer to the bed. Amado turned his face toward the wall, not wanting her to see his anguish.

"It took four days of steady riding. We finally saw buzzards circling overhead…and knew. Tito died quickly. A gunshot to the head. Mario didn't fare so well. Cisto had tied him down… he used his knife and took his time with the killing. I almost didn't recognize Mario… but Cisto hadn't killed him. He left him for the birds to finish off. He was near death when we arrived. Before he died, Mario begged me to get revenge. I gave him my word I would.

"We took him back home. Tito too. We buried them, but my father blamed me for my brother's death. He told me the only way to make this right would be to find this Cisto. We devised a plan. I would join the bandoleros, pretend to become one of them, and bring them to justice. I did that up north, but by that time Cisto had left the country with another group of bandoleros. Once you become a bandolero, you are part of a brotherhood. And you learn information the dons and vaqueros don't have. When I heard Cisto had joined Victoro's band, I came down and met up with Victoro."

He turned to meet Yoana's eyes. "I had to break our betrothal to protect you. I knew I would eventually be recognized, that word would spread I'd become a bandolero. And I knew I would either die at the bandit's hands or I would be found and hanged. I couldn't sully your name along with mine."

Amado reached out and almost wept when her slim fingers twined with his. "I tried to protect you that first day. I wanted Cisto to send you back, but that didn't work. Instead, I put off doing what I'd promised Don Santiago, my father. I put off killing Cisto so I could protect you. Yoana, I didn't expect to love you so much."

"Why didn't you kill Cisto and bring my sister and tía home?"

Amado had almost forgotten Lucio was there. He looked at Yoana's brother and was met with Lucio's stone-cold gaze.

"There was no chance to do so without putting Yoana and Leya in more danger. If I died in the attempt, the women would have met a far worse fate than living in a bandolero camp."

Yoana turned to her brother, laying her hand over his. "He's right, Lucio. The women were treated horribly and had no say as to who took them. Victoro intended to sell Leya and me to some brothel in Los Angeles as soon as they could get us to town."

Lucio leaned toward Amado, his eyes hard. "How can we believe your story? Maybe you're only saying this to save your neck. The story we heard from Don Santiago's vaqueros said you left home and no one knew where you went."

"That's the story my father told after I left." How could he make Lucio believe him? "We had to make my joining them believable. Everyone had to think I disappeared and didn't care about family any more."

Lucio stood. He moved his chair back against the wall. "I

always liked you, Gabrio, or Amado, whichever you want to be called now, but I didn't know you well. I'll speak to the don about this." He took Yoana's arm to help her stand. "I'll let you know what our father says, but I don't see a way out of this for you. Yoana told us you were the one who led the bandoleros to our herd the day she and Leya were kidnapped. That alone would lead to your hanging."

Amado nodded. "I understand. I knew going into this what I faced if I was caught. My only regret is that Cisto is still running free."

Lucio escorted Yoana from the room, and Amado leaned back against the pillows. He'd spoken only part of the truth to Lucio. He couldn't bring himself to admit to the rest. To the chances he'd had to kill Cisto. Times when he probably could have gotten Yoana and Leya safely away from the camp. But that he couldn't bring himself to kill a man without giving him a fighting chance. He'd wanted to wait until he had the chance to tell Cisto why he'd come. Now…if only he'd taken the shots.

But regret served nothing. Tomorrow he would die, and Cisto would still be alive to torture and kill whomever he chose.

Teo's Bible story flitted through his mind. Had that been true? Did God love everyone, even a man who would hunt down and kill God's people? If that were true, then maybe God would love and forgive a man who hadn't protected his own brother.

Amado closed his eyes. As he talked with God, peace and forgiveness stole over him. It was so powerful he could not stop the tears from coming. He'd been wrong, so very wrong, about everything. He could see it now. His father requested he join the bandoleros because of his grief. Deep down, Amado knew all along revenge would only grieve God. But he'd wanted so much to enact his own version of justice. To hurt the man who hurt his family. He'd wanted to do it because…

He hadn't trusted God.

Forgive me…Father, forgive me.

Sleep pulled him down into restful arms. Amado knew nothing more until morning.

~

THE SUN LIT THE HORIZON. They would come for him soon.

The dread Amado had felt yesterday had washed away during the night. With God's help, he would face whatever would come. Nothing would happen to him without God allowing it.

He eased up in the bed. The shooting pain that plagued him yesterday had also abated. Today's ache was tolerable. Amado swung his legs over the side of the bed. On a table near the wall rested a basin of water, soap, and a razor. If he had to hang, he could at least look like himself, not like some ruffian no one cared about.

Dizziness swept over him when he stood. He swayed, grabbed the bedpost, and waited for his senses to settle down. By the time the door opened a half hour later, he sat in a chair, clean-shaven and dressed in clothes that had been left for him.

"It's time." Ramón stepped into the room, his palm resting on the butt of his pistol. His bushy eyebrows raised as he looked at Amado. "You going peaceably, or do I need to tie you?"

"I'll go." Amado eased upright. "I'm not moving fast, but I can go on my own."

Ramón stood to one side and gestured for Amado to precede him out of the door. Silence filled the house. At his home, everyone rose early to spend time in prayer every morning. Were the members of Don Armenta's household in the chapel praying for Amado's soul?

The morning air held a crisp freshness that made him suck in a deep breath. He loved this time of day. Flowers were opening up, their brightness adding to the beauty around him. When had he stopped noticing all the little wonders God gave every day. Why had he waited until the day he would die to be so aware?

"Ramón." Yoana hurried toward them along a path. Her beauty outshone the delicate blossoms that grew by the walkway. "I would like to speak privately with Amado. You can watch from there." She gestured toward the shade of a tree and then led Amado away.

Ramón acted as if he wanted to stop them but kept quiet. Amado glanced over his shoulder and caught the warning in the older man's gaze.

The dappled shade cast a variegated pattern across Yoana's face. Amado put his back to Ramón so the vaquero wouldn't be able to see them talking. His pulse quickened as he looked down at the woman he loved. Dying wasn't so hard, but leaving Yoana…

That was agony.

"I'm sorry I doubted you, Amado. Gabrio." Yoana's eyelashes feathered against her cheeks as she closed her eyes for a moment as if to gather her thoughts. "Lucio talked with my father. Don Armenta is adamant. You are to die along with the other bandoleros, no matter what your intent might have been. He sees you as guilty of stealing horses even though we have the animals back."

Tears glittered like tiny diamonds in her eyes. One escaped, and Amado reached up his thumb to catch the drop. He cupped her cheek with his palm. "Querida, I love you more than you'll ever know. You are the bravest, most godly woman I've ever known. You've taught me so much."

"You're the one who has taught me." Yoana placed her fingers on his. "I love you too, Amado. I don't think I can bear it if you are hanged today. You don't deserve to die."

"Don't worry, querida." Amado tugged her a step closer. His gaze fixed on her full lips, and he wanted nothing more than a last kiss. "God will take care of me. He'll watch over you too. Your stories have taught me that. You've given me a gift of knowing God, which is more than I could have asked." He lowered his head to touch his lips to hers.

What began as a gentle kiss swept a fire of longing through him. He could feel Yoana's response as she leaned toward him. The ground trembled—

Amado broke off the kiss and leaned his forehead against Yoana's. A glance beyond her told him a group of horsemen had thundered through the gates leading to the rancho's front yard.

The observers were gathering.

It was time.

CHAPTER TWENTY-SEVEN

Yoana refused to think of Gabrio as Amado any longer. That had been his name as a bandolero, a life that hadn't been his choice. She'd fallen in love with Amado at the bandolero camp, but she'd fallen in love with Gabrio years ago through letters they'd exchanged.

Now the tenderness of his kiss brought tears to her eyes. How long had she dreamed of this day? Of him, here with her? But her dreams hadn't included a gallows rope. How could she bear this if her true love died today? If only there were a way to stay here in his embrace and make the world go away.

When Lucio had confronted her father and told him Gabrio's story, he told her he thought he detected a softening in their father. But in the end, Don Armenta hadn't conceded. Since they had no way to prove Gabrio's tale, the don ordered Lucio to hang him right along with the others.

Vibration shook her limbs as hoof beats thundered in the air. She tightened her arms around Gabrio. They both knew what this meant. The audience had arrived. They would be thirsty for retribution and revenge. Yoana's eyes stung, but she refused to give in to emotion. She would stay strong for Gabrio. She would.

"God, please protect Yoana." Gabrio's low voice wove a web of comfort around her aching heart. "Be with her today, Lord. Be with her always. I've loved her for so long. You know my heart. Give us both the strength to endure this day." He fell silent. His warm hands cupped her shoulders. His thumbs caressed her in a soft pattern that any other time would have thrilled her. Now numbness crept through her. Would she ever again feel anything but pain?

"Time to go."

At Ramón's directive, Gabrio gave Yoana's shoulders a gentle squeeze. He trailed his fingers down her arms in a last caress, then released her and stepped back. His warm gaze didn't leave hers.

Across the yard near the stables, Yoana saw the hastily erected gallows. Three ropes dangled as grim reminders of the event taking place in mere minutes. Lorenzo and Miguel, their hands tied, fought their captors as they were marched to the structure. Most of the vaqueros from the Armenta rancho were in attendance, along with some from the surrounding area who had gotten word of the hanging. She leaped forward to grab Gabrio's hands with both of hers.

"Now." Ramón placed his hand on Gabrio's arm, and her beloved nodded. He brought their joined hands up and pressed his lips to her fingers. "Go inside, querida. I'm not asking you to watch, but I am asking that you show everyone how brave you are." He dropped a light kiss on her brow as she released him.

Then he turned, and strode alongside Ramón without looking back.

A feather light touch on her arm caught Yoana's attention. Through a sheen of moisture, she turned to see her tía's sympathetic gaze. Tears shone in Leya's eyes. Her lips pressed in a tight line as if to hold her emotions in check. Since they had returned, Leya wore her concealing *mantilla* only when they were outside. She still avoided being around strangers who might not understand, but she was more relaxed around the *familia*.

Her confidence had blossomed in the outlaw camp.

"Oh, Leya. I love him so much. How will I live if I lose him?" Yoana's breath caught in a half sob.

Leya stepped closer and slipped her arm around Yoana. "Somehow God will give you the strength. I have no idea how He will do that. I don't understand why this is happening to you and Gabrio."

Yoana cleared her throat to ease the tightness. "I spent much of the night in prayer. God has given me peace beyond my comprehension, but I ache for what we could have had."

She paused to watch the small knot of women from the rancho, which included Rosalinda, Feliciana, and Dolores. Only Dolores wept. Feliciana's face held a curious mixture of triumph and grief. The young girl must be glad to be rid of Miguel but saddened at the death of Tomàs. Rosalinda's fiery nature shone as she stood erect, shoulders back, defiance evident in her demeanor.

Yoana eased her grip on Leya's fingers as she realized she must be hurting her tía. "I can only hold fast to what I know…" Tears clogged her throat, and it took moments before she could speak. "I feel God's love holding me. I have begged him for Gabrio's life —" she didn't try to stop the tears from flowing "--but I will trust Him, whatever His answer."

The murmur of voices from the group of vaqueros near the stable rose in volume. Yoana glanced at the house. Several unfamiliar horses were tied to the hitching rail, but she saw no sign of Don Armenta or Lucio. Where could they be?

"Come, Yoana." Leya tightened her hold on Yoana's waist. "Let's go inside. You must not watch this terrible thing."

She held her ground. "I can't leave him, Leya. I have to do something to stop this, but I don't know what." Her gaze sought Gabrio. He stood apart from Lorenzo and Miguel, still with his hands free. Ramón stood next to him, and the two were in deep conversation. As if he felt her gaze, Gabrio looked up and met her eyes. Even from this distance, she could feel the touch of his glance like a caress.

Father God, help me. What do You want me to do?

Deep within, a stirring began. It rose and intensified, until Yoana could no longer stand still. "Leya, I have to go talk to my father." She spun toward the house.

"Lucio already talked with him. He will only hurt you."

She looked back. "What do I care about getting hurt if I have a chance to save Gabrio's life? Pray for me, Leya. Pray that God lets the don hear what I have to say."

She cast one last glance at Gabrio, whose eyes were still on her. She put all the love she could into one last look, then raced toward the house. She didn't care how unseemly it would be to barge in on the don when he had company.

Not when Gabrio's life hung in the balance.

~

THE COOL INTERIOR of the adobe home gave Yoana little comfort. Voices came from her father's study, and her insides quivered. She paused, one hand on the wall to steady her shaking limbs. She could do this. She hadn't spoken to her father directly in years. But for Gabrio, she would face the don's wrath. His hatred.

Had Esther in the Bible been shaking as she came into the king's presence, knowing he held the power of life and death for her? Yet she had prayed and done what she needed to do for her people.

Yoana leaned against the cool wall and closed her eyes. "Father God, help me to remember You are the One Who holds the power of life and death over me. Over Gabrio. I believe. Please, help my unbelief."

Hot tears stung her eyelids. "Give me courage to stand strong." She leaned over to swipe moisture from her eyes with the hem of her dress, then bit her lips to give herself some color. She smoothed any wayward strands of hair--then walked toward her father's den, her soft shoes making little noise on the hard floor.

Before entering, she paused for one deep breath. Voices--male voices--raised in discord grated against her nerves. There were so many she couldn't sort them out. Some seemed familiar, some not. Well, whoever met with her father, she couldn't wait any longer.

Yoana stepped through the open doorway. Her father stood behind his massive desk, one hand rapping on the surface with his knuckles, the other gesturing toward the door. Toward her.

She couldn't take her eyes from him. She didn't even glance at the others in the room. They were her father's cohorts, here for the show, and didn't matter. The only one she noted besides her father was Lucio, his face dark as he stood at the corner of her father's desk, fists clenched at his sides.

The don's black gaze found her. Pierced through her and held her motionless. Where, oh where, had Esther found the courage to approach the king? She had had incredible beauty and a sweet spirit to aid her. Yoana had nothing. She'd been trouble from the time she'd been born, hurting everyone who ever knew her. How would she hope to gain her father's respect enough for him to listen to her now?

"You." Don Armenta spat the word. Silence fell in the room. Clothing rustled as men swiveled to look at her.

She opened her mouth to ask his favor. One favor.

"Get out of here!" The don flung out his hand, pointing a gnarled finger at the door. "I don't want you in my presence." He turned his back.

Hope fled. Silence pressed a weight against her, and she fought to breathe. Her father's stiff back said everything. He still hated her. Still couldn't bear the sight of her. Still wished her dead. Maybe she should offer to die in place of Gabrio.

She stepped back into the hallway, turned, and ran. Her vision blurred. Her feet slipped on the floor, and she almost fell. Behind her, noise erupted, but she didn't stop to listen. Her fingers fumbled for the door latch. Outside the sunlight blinded her, and tears blocked her vision. Which way should she go?

A hand grabbed her arm. She started to jerk away, but Leya's face swam into view as she pushed the edges of the *mantilla* over her shoulders. Compassion shone in her eyes. The jagged scar on her cheek had darkened in color, something that happened when Leya got upset.

"Yoana." Leya's voice caught. She opened her arms and dragged Yoana close. How many times had Leya provided refuge for Yoana when her father's hatred wounded her?

"Come." Leya led her around the corner of the house, away from the gathering of people and into the privacy of the garden. She sank onto a bench, pulling Yoana down with her. "Tell me."

"He refused to even talk to me. Turned his back." Yoana wiped few tears from her eyes—and then she stilled. No. she would mourn this lost relationship no longer. She had a Father Who loved her. The don might hold power over her earthly life, but he'd given up the right to be called her father.

God...Father...help me, please. "There is nothing I can do to save Gabrio." Yoana grasped both of Leya's hands in hers. This would be her one regret. Gabrio, the love of her life. Her heart. Yet she couldn't help him.

Leya smiled. Yoana gaped at her. Leya's eyes shone and her smile widened.

"There is no hope that we can see, Yoana, but that is just the time when God can truly work. I can't wait to see what He will do. Let's pray." Leya bowed her head. Yoana followed suit. As she listened to Leya's heartfelt prayer, hope began to unfold within her once again. She may not be able to do anything, but God could do *all* things. Whether He chose to give Gabrio more time here on earth or not, He had a sovereign plan.

She would do as she'd told Leya earlier. She would choose to trust Him no matter what. With her life. And with Gabrio's.

She heard the creak of the hacienda door opening. The tramp of booted feet crossing the yard. Yoana reached deep within, drawing on a reserve of strength only God could give—and stood. "Time to go."

She pulled Leya up with her, and they made their way to the gallows. The sight of the milling crowd shook her. Many of those gathered she didn't know, but she glanced at the edge of the crowd—and halted.

Her brothers! They must have returned from the coast in time for the hanging. Lucio hadn't joined them. But why?

"We should go stand with Dolores, Rosalinda, and Feliciana." Leya tugged on Yoana. If we must be here, then we need to give them our support."

"No."

At Lucio's voice, Yoana turned to see her brother standing behind them.

"The don wishes you to take Yoana to her room, Leya. He is adamant. She is not to watch." He didn't wait for Leya to comply, but took Yoana's free arm and began to guide them to the back entrance of the hacienda.

Over her shoulder, Yoana caught one last glimpse of Gabrio. She wanted to fight to stay. To be there to support him. Across the yard, she saw the don, her father, watching her with his implacable gaze. Hope curled into ashes.

Father God...it is in Your hands.

She allowed Lucio and Leya to lead her to her quarters.

GABRIO IGNORED the jeers of the crowd and the growing number of people. He'd watched Yoana enter the hacienda moments ago, full of confidence. When she came stumbling out minutes later, he could see defeat in the bow of her shoulders. He longed to comfort her. Tell her all would be right. He'd made this choice on his own. Even if he'd done this for the right reasons, his choice had been wrong. He must face the consequences.

Men exited the house, striding toward the gallows. The neighboring dons. Don Armenta spoke with Julio, his head vaquero. Julio nodded and then mounted the platform. He put a hood over Lorenzo's head and then the noose around his neck. He did the same for Miguel before approaching Gabrio.

Dread laced through Gabrio. The ropes binding his wrists chaffed. *God, I know I must face the consequences of my actions, but I don't want to die. Not now. Now when I've found her again. I want to spend a lifetime with Yoana. To protect her. God, please, if it be Your will, I want life. But if not...*

Julio came up behind him. Gabrio waited for the noose to be put in place. He'd requested they not use a hood. Gabrio straightened. *If not...I trust You.*

"Gabrio." Julio spoke so low Gabrio almost didn't hear him. "You have been pardoned. The don asks that you come with me."

The ropes holding his hands dropped away. Gabrio stood, frozen in place. Don Armenta *never* showed compassion. Why had he done so now?

Gabrio looked at the group of dons gathered below the platform—and stared. Could it be...?

His father stood beside Don Armenta. His father! Gabrio's knees shook. By the time he stepped to the ground, his father came forward to embrace him.

"My son. I am sorry for the grief I caused you. Please forgive me." Don Santiago held Gabrio close, his touch a balm to Gabrio's aching heart.

"Finish it. Now."

As Julio carried out Don Armenta's order, and Miguel and Lorenzo suffered the punishment for their wrongs, sorrow tore at Gabrio. Across the way, he saw Delores crying on Rosalinda's shoulder. Thank God none of the children were present. But what would happen to them all now? He would speak with his father and see if the Santiago rancho could use them.

"Come." Don Armenta led Lucio, Don Santiago, and Gabrio toward the house. He paused in the hallway and turned to them. "I must speak to my daughter first. Then you can see her." He nodded at Gabrio.

They followed him through the house. Lucio shrugged when Gabrio sent him a questioning look. It seemed no one knew what the don was up to.

Don Armenta led them to a room with a closed door, where he knocked as he motioned them to wait. When the door opened, the don entered the room, leaving the door open. Gabrio heard the rustle of clothing. A sharp intake of breath.

"Father." Yoana's tone spoke of her shock.

"Yoana. Leya. I need to speak with you." The don paused for a long moment. Gabrio's nerves vibrated as he waited to see what the don would say. What he would do.

"I knew." Armenta paused, his voice gruff but not hateful as he spoke to his daughter. "I knew the bull was dangerous. Your mother begged me to get rid of him. Said he would kill someone." Sorrow choked his words. "I didn't know it would be her."

Gabrio didn't know if the gasp came from Yoana or Leya. Lucio's mouth had thinned, and he nodded at Gabrio. But there was no surprise in his features. So…he must have known the truth but kept quiet all these years.

"I am offering a gift to you. A gift I hope will make amends for the wrong I have done to you all these years."

Don Armenta strode from the room, and Gabrio stepped back. The man may have admitted to his wrong, but had he truly forgiven Yoana?

The don halted beside Gabrio. "Go to her. Your father explained what happened. I have much to think on." He raised his hand as if to touch Gabrio's shoulder, but instead lowered it and strode away. Don Santiago nodded at his son, then followed Don Armenta down the hallway.

Lucio grinned at Gabrio. His eyes, the same color of brown as Yoana's, shone. He motioned to the open doorway and leaned close to Gabrio. "She is yours, amigo." He winked. "If you are sure you want her. She's a troublemaker, that one."

Gabrio didn't even try to hide his grin. He'd been given the gift of life and the gift of Yoana. He couldn't thank God enough. "The she and I will be a fine pair, don't you think?"

Lucio studied him a moment, then nodded. "The very best."

CHAPTER TWENTY-EIGHT

"He knew?" Yoana whirled to face Leya, whose mouth hung open in shock. "My mother was afraid of the bull? Did you know this?"

Leya shook her head. Her hands came up, and she covered her mouth with her fingers. "I did not know, *mija*. I didn't." Leya's hadn't called Yoana *little girl* in years.

He'd known, and yet he treated her as he did? And he let Gabrio die on the end of a rope? Why had her father told her this? Had he just apologized to her? That couldn't be. He never apologized to anyone for anything.

"What did he mean he has a gift for me? Don Armenta doesn't give gifts." Yoana wanted to tear at her hair. Maybe the years of silence were better than this terse, meaningless discourse her father bestowed on her.

Leya gasped. Her eyes widened. She wasn't looking at Yoana now but staring at the doorway behind her as her fingers edges the *mantilla* forward across her cheek.

"I believe he meant me."

Yoana wheeled around. The room swirled. Gabrio stood before her as large as life. But he couldn't be here. Her thoughts scattered, and she stood frozen in the center of the room.

"I believe I am the gift Don Armenta is giving to you."

His mouth moved. He spoke. He *lived.*

He opened his arms, and she flew to him. His embrace felt like a taste of heaven on earth.

"How?" She gasped for air. Tried to calm her racing heart. *"How?"*

He grinned down at her. Lifted his hand to brush a strand of hair from her face. "God. Only God. By some miracle of His, my father arrived in time. I don't know what transpired between the two, but whatever my father told your father changed Don Armenta's mind about hanging me."

"The don changed his mind." She couldn't grasp the concept. Don Armenta had admitted wrong doing and changed his mind. All in one day. And he'd spoken to her. Without censure. Spoken.

To her.

Yoana dropped her head to Gabrio's chest. He hugged her close. His breath stirred the hair at her temple. Joy such as she'd never known swept through her and lifted on wings of praise to God.

YOANA AND GABRIO spent the afternoon walking in the garden, with Leya in attendance, of course. No one looked at her askance or acted as though her time spent with the bandoleros had branded her.

"Yoana." The deep voice drew her attention from Gabrio. Her brother, Mateo, whom she hadn't seen in years, stood a few feet from her, flanked by her brothers Emiliano and Diego. Only Lucio was missing. Mateo opened his arms. She fought tears as she threw herself into his embrace.

"Mi hermana. Lo siento." His whispered words were a balm to her heart. Her throat closed tight and she couldn't speak the

words she wanted to say. The rest of her brothers surrounded her, shaking hands with Gabrio, hugging her.

"Tía Yoana! Tía Leya!" The cries of her nieces and nephews changed her tears to laughter. The children surrounded them, hugging and chattering about their recent trip to the coast. Yoana knelt down to embrace each one, so thankful to be here with them. This afternoon she would have to check on Teo, Maria, and the others from the bandolero camp, along with their mothers.

"Gabrio. Yoana. Would you come to the don's study, please?" Lucio strode toward them, more relaxed than Yoana had seen him in years.

"You too, Tía." Lucio bowed and held out his arm to Leya. She allowed him to escort her, and they all went inside.

Her father's office had filled with people. Her brothers, Mateo, Emiliano, and Diego filed in after them. Don Santiago and some of his men were in attendance, along with some of the Armenta vaqueros.

Don Armenta stood behind his desk. He met Yoana's gaze. She faltered. After so many years of being despised and ignored by this man, she couldn't fathom the change in him. She would think this an act put on in front of acquaintances, but he'd never bothered to do such a thing before.

"Please, have a seat, Yoana. Leya." Her father gestured to chairs placed close to his desk.

Gabrio gave Yoana's hand a light squeeze as he led her to her place. He stood behind her, his hand on the back of the chair, fingertips touching her shoulder. She drew comfort from his closeness.

"Yoana, Leya, we have come to some decisions and wanted to talk with you." Don Armenta tugged at his collar and cleared his throat. "First, Lucio and some of the vaqueros have been scouring the hills looking for signs of this Cisto, who absconded with you."

He paused. Gabrio's fingers tensed. Did he feared a reversal of the decision to let him live?

"This morning, two of the vaqueros reported back. They went as far as the pass to the west of us and found a body, which they believe might be this bandolero. The remains had been ravaged by wild animals, but they recovered this." He held out a belt buckle.

"That belonged to Cisto." Gabrio strode to the desk to pick up the piece of metal. Yoana didn't want to look.

"This was under the body. We believe that means this Cisto is dead and will be no further threat to you." Don Armenta frowned. He glanced at his friend, Don Santiago, and nodded.

Gabrio's father stepped forward. "We have also discussed what to do with the women and children who were held captive, as you were. They have no families to take them in, so Don Armenta will keep one of the women here to help with the house. The others will go to the Santiago rancho, where they will be welcomed to work and live if they choose to do so."

"How will you decide who goes where?" Yoana asked. It could be hard for these women to split up, but the children...she couldn't imagine Teo and Maria being separated. They were so close. Teo might be fine, but Maria would be lost without him.

"We gave them each a choice." Don Santiago pursed his mouth. "Feliciana and Dolores chose to go north with us. Rosalinda will stay here."

Leya glanced at her and nodded. Feliciana would be better with Dolores than Rosalinda. All of the women would be under a don's protection and have a place to live and work to do. And with time, perhaps they would find peace and healing.

"I believe there is something else that needs done before we go out to our guests and share the evening meal." Don Armenta sent a pointed gaze toward Gabrio. His fingers tightened on Yoana's shoulders.

∼

THE EXPECTATIONS of the two dons weighed on Amado...Gabrio.

He'd been the bandolero for so long, he struggled to recover his true self.

Don Armenta told Yoana he'd brought her a gift, meaning Gabrio's life. In truth, Gabrio had been given a great gift. One he couldn't grasp yet. He'd come to terms with his need to die for what he'd done. This sudden grace had been his undoing. He deserved death. He'd been granted life.

When Yoana had told the children at the bandolero camp of God's grace extended to all, Gabrio hadn't understood.

Until now.

Through his fingertips, he felt the connection to Yoana. As if their hearts beat with the same rhythm. He knew what the dons were asking, and he nodded at his father. At Don Armenta.

The two patriarchs were giving their permission for him to continue as Gabrio.

He brushed his fingers across Yoana's shoulder as he rounded her chair. She smiled up at him, some confusion clouding her eyes. All of this must be as unnerving for her as it was for him. She'd also been granted the unexpected gift of forgiveness and love.

Everyone in the room stilled as he knelt beside her chair. Gabrio picked up her hand. He couldn't keep from kissing her fingertips before he met her gaze. He smiled. Her eyes rounded.

"Yoana. My beloved. I broke our betrothal out of necessity, nothing else. My heart has always been yours. I am asking if you will agree to renew our betrothal? Will you be my wife?"

Tears glittered in her eyes. Her full lips reddened. She pulled her hands free to cup his face and leaned toward him.

Don Armenta cleared his throat, and Yoana sat back. Dropped her hands to her lap. Her face flushed, and she snapped open the fan Leya passed her. Her sisters-in-law tittered, and Gabrio thought he heard a masculine chuckle or two from the group.

Yoana offered a subdued smile. "If my father is in agreement, I would be happy to accept your betrothal." Her sultry tone made Gabrio want to snatch her up and twirl her around. Oh, to be once again under the trees of the forest with no one else around!

Leya cleared her throat, and Gabrio started. He'd been swaying toward Yoana. He brushed his palms on his pants and rose, then bowed to the dons. "I am asking that our betrothal be a short one."

Lucio snorted. Don Santiago coughed and covered his mouth, and Gabrio fought to keep from grinning.

"Don Santiago and I will discuss the details of the betrothal." Don Armenta rapped his fingers on his desk as a swell of murmurs circled the room. "We will let you know our decision. Leya, will you resume your duties to Yoana?"

"I will." Leya dipped her head toward the don. As she did so, she tilted to one side, allowing the *mantilla* to part, and winked at Yoana and Gabrio.

"Yoana, will you do me the honor of walking with me in the garden?" Gabrio leaned over to offer her his arm. She didn't put pressure on him, but he felt the warmth of each finger through the cloth of his shirt.

Don Armenta nodded at them. "You will join us for a meal with our guests as soon as the food is prepared."

Leya stood to follow Gabrio and Yoana from the room at a discreet distance.

Gabrio led Yoana around the house to a bench and indicated Leya should take the seat next to her. They needed to talk, and he had too much energy thrumming through him to sit down and relax.

His gaze met Yoana's beautiful eyes. "The plan has always been for us to marry, Yoana, and for me to take you to the Santiago rancho. Is that still what you wish?"

Gabrio smiled as she gazed up at him. Even with scratches still evident on her face and the gauntness of her cheeks, her beauty amazed him.

"I will do whatever you decide." Yoana took Leya's hand. "Will you come with us? If Don Santiago agrees."

"You no longer need a señorita, Yoana." Leya smiled, and her beauty in that moment rivaled Yoana's. "I will stay here and help. Rosalinda is going to be here. I can be a señorita to her children and maybe help her with her learning." Leya patted Yoana's arm.

"I will miss you so much." Yoana hugged Leya. "You will come visit."

"I will." Leya hugged her back.

Yoana's eyes shone as she turned back to Gabrio. "When do you wish to marry? I know our fathers are deciding, but I'm sure they will listen to what you say."

He couldn't wait any longer to touch her. Gabrio caught her hand and lifted the slim fingers to his lips. "I would marry you this moment and steal you away." He pressed her palm to his cheek. "However, I think we should wait a few days until I am stronger."

Her eyes widened. "I forgot. You hide your discomfort so well."

Discomfort? With her hand in his, he could run for miles! "I am fine. I believe my father will want to stay for a few days to visit your father, his old friend. But I will talk with him. I am anxious to take you to your new home and start our life there." He drew her to her feet and slid his arms around her.

Yoana lifted her hand to cup his face. He lowered his head for a quick kiss—and the sharp rap of a fan on his leg brought him back to reality. He grinned at Leya and her mock glower, then savored Yoana's unfocused gaze as she nestled in his arms.

They had been set free. She from being a prisoner, first in her own home to her father's guilt and bitterness, then in the camp. She had also been freed from her own guilt over her actions. And he? The drive for revenge no longer held power over him. Relief and joy at the lifted burden filled him with an unexplainable sense of freedom. His bandolero days were past. What awaited him now was God's promise. A future and a hope.

And all with this woman at his side. The one he'd given up and found again. His love.

Gabrio grinned at Leya, who held her fan at the ready, and lowered his lips to Yoana's once more.

Let the punishment come.

Some prizes were worth it.

Author's Note

I had the great blessing of being moved from the Midwest to Southern Arizona and living there for years. When I moved to a small community, most of my neighbors were Hispanic, whose families lived there for generations. I fell in love with them, with their families, with their culture, and, of course, with their food. Oh, the food.

What I loved most was their sense of family. No matter how distantly related, you were still family. At Christmas time they would come together to make dozens and dozens of tamales. The children were give masa (dough) to work with and taught the love of cooking together and being together. Such wonderful traditions and a great way to pass on recipes and concepts.

My daughters often weren't hungry at suppertime and I would discover they had been at one house or the other "helping" make tortillas. And sampling. They loved those fresh tortillas with melted butter then, and they still do now.

When I discovered the 1830's in Alta California, then part of Mexico, I knew I wanted to write about this great era and the wonderful people. I know I didn't do their culture justice, and I took license with the events, but I fell in love with Yoana, Gabrio, and the other characters in the story.

During this time in Alta California, there were instances of rancheros pitting bulls against grizzlies. This is hard to fathom in

AFTERWORD

our day, but is historical fact. I tried to show a reason they would do this when the bull attacked Yoana's mother. Usually, this was an event for familias from neighboring areas to attend.

In *Bandolero*, Yoana's father took out his grief and guilt on her. Over the years his heart hardened, and he justified his actions because he harbors unforgiveness. God is ever quick to forgive when we ask. How can we not forgive others? Don Armenta learned a hard lesson, but there have been many times lessons have come hard for me too.

Thank you for taking the time to read *Bandolero*. I hope you enjoyed your journey into Alta California and will come back for more stories in the Land of Promise series.

God Bless you,

Nancy J. Farrier

ACKNOWLEDGMENTS

Writer's are a community unto their own, and I love being part of so many wonderful groups. Thank you to all who have helped me.

∽

Thank you to my daughter, Ardra, for the lovely cover art, and the many times you talked me down from my panic. Thank you to all my daughters, Anne, Abigail, Ardra and Alyssa for your constant encouragement.

∽

Thank you to Karen Ball and Louise Gouge, my editors who took the words I wrote and made the story so much better.

∽

To Jesus Christ: You are my all. I can't thank you enough for calling out to me and for helping me to hear.

ABOUT THE AUTHOR

Nancy J. Farrier is a multi-published, award winning author of historical and contemporary Christian fiction. She writes Southwest fiction with real life issues. She lives in Southern California with her husband and cats. Nancy loves reading, bicycling, and needlework.

Please connect with Nancy J. Farrier here:
www.nancyjfarrier.com
nancy@nancyjfarrier.com

ALSO BY NANCY J. FARRIER

Brides of Arizona

The Cowboy's Bride

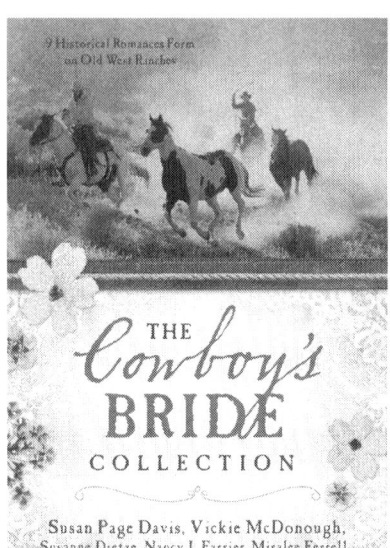

Made in the USA
Lexington, KY
17 October 2017